ARCHANGELS

BEGINNINGS

A. G. WILLIAMS

DEDICATION:

First, for the LORD my God and His glory, but then for my
family and friends.
You have loved me, prayed for me, and encouraged me through
these years of writing.
Thank you so much. I love you all.

ENDORSEMENTS:

"Archangels – Beginnings is engaging, and the story holds your interest all the way through. I particularly enjoyed the chapters during creation, when Private Charrael was stuck in the crevice, and the battle between Michael and Lucifer. I'm sure anyone would love this book as much as I did."

Justin Naylor, Mechanical Engineering Student, Akron University.

"I so enjoyed *Archangels – Beginnings,* and at times, I couldn't put it down. The Author's passion shines through. I recommend this action/adventure book for all readers."

Angela Gulley, Entrepreneur.

"Archangels – Beginnings is captivating and eye-opening. This fiction book utilizes a format where angels are soldiers. It presents a plausible explanation of how Lucifer could persuade one-third of the angels to follow him in a rebellion against God. And it shows there is a real battle going on for our souls.

As a missionary with Wycliffe Bible Translators for over twenty years, I recommend this book to help young and old alike see how Lucifer (Satan) is real and is a liar. Bible translators have seen thousands of people in hundreds of language groups set free from demonic holds on them when they hear and read God's Word in their heart language and accept Jesus Christ as their Lord and Savior."

Wycliffe Bible Translator Missionary, Deborah Milliken.

"As somebody who doesn't read that much for leisure, I thoroughly enjoyed *Archangels – Beginnings*. The writing is excellent throughout the entire book, and it is a very easy read. The story is thought-provoking, and it answers questions as to how creation could happen. I recommend this book for teens and adults, and I hope you enjoy it as much as I did."

Dr. Nick G. Koinoglou, DC, Dipl. IAMA,
Family Health Physical Medicine, LLC.

"*Archangels – Beginnings* is an interesting book of fiction dealing with conflict, supremacy, and power. It uses in its staging a military presence, and as such, it keeps the reader's interest throughout the entire book. Even though the military presentation is not descriptive of how the US military operates, and the hierarchy is somewhat different, you still see the same loyalty, leadership, and allegiance.

Besides Archangels Michael and Gabriel, Private Charrael became a hero. This brave private defected because of his allegiance to God Almighty. I recommend this fascinating fictional book for young adults and older readers."

Retired Sergeant First Class and Author, Kenneth Harper.

There had been three archangels – now only two. I could not help but wonder what would happen to the two humans when evil came to Earth. This book, *Archangels – Beginnings,* held me spellbound. Anita's description of Lucifer developing pride is intriguing. Every chapter aroused my curiosity for the next. Like me, you will not want to put this book down.

Joan Essinger, AFC Women's Bible Study leader and Author.

The description of the angels, the glory this author brings to Almighty God, and the plausibility of the story will engage the reader and leave them wanting more. I recommend *Archangels – Beginnings* for all ages. I'm so thankful to have had the chance to read it.

Patty Ruehle, former Assistant to the Dean,
Kent State University – Salem Branch.

THANK YOUS:

A special "Thank you" to Ken Ham of Answers in Genesis. In God's perfect timing, Mr. Ham, you gave advice through your assistant to write this book, which includes the days of creation from Genesis 1 and 2, but also to add a disclaimer, and I did. Your encouragement was priceless because I felt it was the LORD speaking through you. I have learned much from visiting The Creation Museum and The Ark Encounter in Kentucky, as well as reading your books, listening to your lectures, and asking questions on the AIG website https://.answersingenesis.org. Thank you sincerely.

Thank you also to Cristel Phelps, Managing Editor of Fiction, Elk Lake Publishing, Inc. Through all our correspondence, Ms. Phelps, you made *Archangels – Beginnings* better than I could have imagined. I will be forever grateful for the time, energy, and attention you gave me.

Thank you, Pastor Rick Sams, Pastor Emeritus, Alliance Friends Church, for critiquing my first three chapters in the early stages of writing, for encouraging me to continue writing, and to finish this book. Your friendship is priceless.

Thank you to Nichole Stone, my niece, for being my very first editor. Although you only edited Chapter One, which ended up being Chapters Seven and Eight, the words and phrases you suggested greatly inspired and made me a better writer. You encouraged me to keep on writing and to complete the story the LORD had given.

DISCLAIMER:

Archangels – Beginnings is a work of Biblical fiction. It is not, by any means, a commentary on the Holy Bible. Some of my characters are taken from the Bible, and I have created a scenario of events where Scripture is silent. However, when the Holy Bible does speak of creation, angels, and Almighty God, I strive to remain true to Scripture and faithful to their nature as revealed in God's Word. If you see similarities to real-life events or people, be assured, none were intended.

TABLE OF CONTENTS

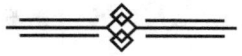

And He said to them,
"I saw Satan fall like lightning from heaven."
Luke 10:18

CHAPTER 1

PRELUDE TO THE BEGINNING

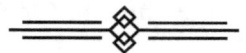

In the vastness of never-ending eternity, the infinite God had his being. Engaged in deep contemplations, he drifted through the endlessness, and a misty haze encircled. With his every move, delicate strands glittered then swirled like smoke caught by the wind.

The precise moment to begin the conversation had arrived. The Father stirred, and the fiery glory of his Shekinah flamed. At once, the haze disappeared. "Do you see it?"

"I do," the Son said. "Do you see mine?"

"Absolute perfection."

"What about my portion?"

"Ah…Spirit. It's brilliant."

Pleased by the design, the Son took the lead. "Now that we've planned, let me bring it to pass." He spoke, and the whole of Heaven burst into existence.

"Beautiful! Exactly as envisioned," the Spirit said, causing a shimmering ribbon to radiate out from the Shekinah. "But…we've not yet been contained in a dwelling."

"Not contained, Spirit. Just resting. We are still everywhere present."

As the purity of the Holy One stepped into creation and his full presence settled, Heaven glistened in the light of his glory. Sailing to the Mount of Holiness, his radiance hovered above the shelf-like plateau that jutted out from the mountain. Instantly, the elevation lit up, glowing as the flame of a candle, and bathing all in a warm, glimmering brilliance.

Here, in this splendor, the Three-in-One God paused, considered his handiwork, and what they planned as their next act. But the Spirit broke the silence. "It's all spectacular," he said, perusing southward, "The city, the palace, and the buildings, everything's perfect, especially the Scroll Room and the Forge."

"I'm drawn to the Armor Room and the contour of the Arena," the Son said, watching the iridescent ripples of their Shekinah float down to the plains.

"They are superb, Son, yet neither function without the Forge."

"I know, Spirit."

After inspecting the mountain's base and the Garden of Fiery Stones near the east perimeter trees, the Father's blazing hand pointed south. "Observe the plains between the city and mountain. They emerged precisely as conceived, ideal for our helpers to assemble, and vast enough to hold them all."

"Agreed, Father, but feast your eyes on Glory Street with the Trees of Life lining its walkway and the riverbanks. How I long to feel the texture of the leaves, pluck their fruit, and taste the goodness. I want to drag my fingers through the cool river water and splash it on my face."

"All in due time, Son. We've much work beforehand."

"Yes," the Spirit said, "like creating helpers. Our plan cannot come to fruition without them."

His glory brightened. In a voice that blasted through Heaven, raced over the plains, shook trees and buildings, and caused deep vibrations in the water, the Most High God said, "Angels!"

Heaven's plains roared to life with the force of a mighty whirlwind. A multitude of wings unfurled, and a myriad of beings swelled with the breath of Heaven. Just above the mountain's plateau, another spectacle ensued. Four unique angels materialized and surrounded the divine glow of God's Shekinah.

Overhead, a celestial ballet unfolded with more distinct angels coming into focus. Their voices created a harmonious chorus proclaiming the holiness of the Almighty seated upon his throne. The original quartet, once silent sentinels, quickly added an extra layer of adoration and seamlessly blended into this angelic choir.

Below, on the plateau floor, three tall and powerful archangels, of which I was one, stood before his glory. When my lungs filled with air, I took in the sights, and at once, the sacredness of the Holy One fell heavy upon me. My head bowed. Praise flowing from God's throne drove me to worship, yet how I knew worship escaped me.

It felt natural to extend my wings toward the two on either side, and as our wingtips united, we three illuminated with a radiant light. The archangel on my left then projected this resplendence along with an ethereal melody down to the countless under-angels on the

3

plains. Each worshipper bowed their head, and together, we adored our holy LORD and King.

When illumination waned and worship suspended, I refolded my wings, as did the others. Standing there, gazing at the scene before me, questions flooded my mind. *How did I get here? Did I just appear in this place?* Everything I observed seemed new to me but somehow familiar.

I scanned the plateau and studied my environment—the mountain, the plains, the city, and its buildings. My chest tightened. This feeling made no sense. Not having a recollection of how I got here or where I was before unnerved me. *What if there wasn't anything before?*

"Archangels," the Most High said, causing more distress. "Follow us to the Throne Room."

I looked left and right. The two on either side of me seemed to grasp this command, as did I. The three of us moved offstage and descended the stairs to the secondary level, awaiting his transfer. When the LORD settled in his Throne Room, we stepped toward the final staircase and descended.

Reaching the mountain's base, where the west perimeter trees towered above, I said, "Gabriel, Lucifer. Ready. Wings. Launch." *Wait?* How did I know to do that? And how did I know their names? Do I know mine? *Yes!* I'm Michael.

We rocketed into the limitless zone of God's glorious light, soared over the Ivory Palace City gate, and landed on the threshold of the city's most mammoth structure, the LORD's Ivory Palace, for which this city is named.

Standing before the palace door, my shoulders hunched, and my head lowered. I felt small, insignificant, and unworthy. I wanted a moment to ponder, but the door opened, and we entered. Lucifer led, I followed, and Gabriel brought up the rear. The grandeur of the Ivory Palace Great Room amazed me. My breath caught, even though I recognized everything. "This feels routine. Not at all like my first visit," I whispered.

Lucifer's head snapped in my direction. "Did you say something, Michael?"

My face felt hot, but I covered and waved him off. "Never mind, it's nothing."

"Okay," he said, shrugging.

Trekking through the Great Room with its lofty columns and rich purple tapestries, my chin dropped. But soon, the palace angels shook me out of my stare. I smiled and greeted them as the Senior Angel approached. "Chief Princes," he said, "it's an honor. Please allow me to escort you to the Throne Room."

"Thank you, Gordel." I jerked to a halt, and my hand covered my mouth. I knew his name, too!

"Everything alright, Chief Prince Michael?"

My brows furrowed, but then relaxed. "Yes, Gordel, I'm fine. Let's continue."

We ambled down the long marble hall, passing occasional alcoves with elegant decorations and benches, until we faced massive double doors overlaid with gold. Gordel nodded and took his leave. I glanced at my golden reflection and straightened my stance while the sentry guards grabbed the handles. When the doors swooshed open, my hair and linen robes swayed with the breeze. I inhaled, exhaled, and entered God's presence.

Without warning, holiness draped upon me. I lost all sense of my companions and struggled to remain upright. Falling face down, I venerated the Sovereign LORD.

A tiny flame crackled atop the golden altar positioned near the throne. Spicy-sweet incense burned, and the aroma floated upward with the smoke. It diffused and entered my worship.

When our heads lifted in praise, God's Shekinah intensified, and his flaming brilliance filled my eyes as it did the whole area of his throne. Staring into his glory, I thought I saw a hint of a body moving amidst the fire, but nothing tangible. "Welcome, Archangels," he said, prompting us to rise.

Welcome? So, this is our first visit! But it feels as though I've been here a thousand times. It's strange yet familiar. *How can that be?*

"Michael," the LORD said, causing a shockwave to shoot through me. "We know you have questions, so allow us to answer."

I jolted, and my eyes hit the floor. "Of course, Majesty."

"You three, we have just created, along with our cherubim, seraphim, and all other ranks of angels. And yes, this is your first visit to Ivory Palace."

My head jerked up. *I knew it...*

"However," the LORD continued, "it feels familiar because we have placed within all angels an innate sense of belonging, an understanding of their surroundings and duties, as well as great intellect and abilities. You will explore and discover Heaven's mysteries."

Lucifer pinched his blond eyebrows together. "Heaven has mysteries?"

God shifted, causing a dazzling glow to escape his glory. "Yes, and you will also learn about me."

"Learn about you?" Lucifer said, cocking his head. "How?"

"As you stand in my presence, see my face, and assist by performing your duties, you will learn."

"LORD," Gabriel said, extending his arm, "I understand you created us. But who created you?"

The Almighty appeared to reposition himself, and as he did, a flame sparked toward us. I flinched, yet the LORD took no notice. "I am not created," he said. "I am eternal. I have always existed with no beginning or end. And, I do not give my glory to another."

"Most High," I said. His fiery glory flickered and reflected in the Throne Room's golden furniture that seemed to stand as watchmen guarding his purity. "I know you are sacred...I...I mean, holy. I felt your holiness on the plateau, yet much stronger as we entered your presence. And, standing here, I can tell you are not only different than us, separated, because you are our Creator, but you are above all and sovereign."

"Correct, Michael. See, you're already learning."

"But how did I learn this? Was it just observation?"

Within his gleaming brilliance, I think I saw God's head nod. "Observation, Michael, together with the enhanced intelligence we provided for our archangels. You three are special. Now, step forward while we bestow upon you your assigned roles."

We hiked our shoulders and moved from the outer court. Passing the altar and laver, we entered the holy place. Lucifer positioned himself on my left, adjacent to the solid gold lampstand. Gabriel stood to my right, near the gilded table displaying bread. I held center, the spot before the golden altar where the incense smoldered and its smoke wafted into the most holy place, the throne of the Almighty. As we situated ourselves, I noticed the furniture had a curious placement. If you drew lines to connect the pieces from the outer court to the throne, it resembled something like an arrow pointing to God. *Hmm...*

Once we settled, the LORD spoke. "As your Sovereign, we created you equal in ability but entrusted to each a different station and duty."

"Michael," the Son said, "you are my archangel and our guardian. Your station is the Armor Room."

"Guardian?" I lowered my head. "I'm honored, my King."

"Gabriel," God's Spirit declared as a gentle breeze encompassed us and retreated into the fire. "You are archangel to me, and you have the joy of being our messenger. The Scroll Room is where you will work."

"Thank you, Sire."

"And Lucifer," the Father said, "you are my archangel. You have the distinct privilege of being our luminary—the angel of light—helping others to understand and worship me. You alone, walk in the midst of my Garden of Fiery Stones."

Lucifer's shoulders raised and lowered. "Your favor, LORD, is overwhelming."

We each bowed before the infinite God, accepting the role allotted. Then, as we stood in his presence, gazing toward the throne, somehow, I sensed the Almighty had concluded our conversation, even though he said nothing. I stepped back, bowed again, and moved toward the door. Lucifer and Gabriel followed.

When we returned to the Great Room, Gabriel said, "I'm leaving for the Scroll Room. What about you, Michael? Are you going to the Armor Room?"

"Yes…ah…that is my assigned station. Lucifer, where are you headed?"

Lucifer tilted his head. "Not sure yet. Maybe my chamber or possibly the stone garden."

"Okay…um…do you…" Before I could say anything else, Lucifer and Gabriel dispersed. I wanted to ask if they thought this whole thing was peculiar, but no. My lips squeezed together, then parted as I sighed and moved toward the exit.

"That went well," the Father said.

"Did Michael seem hesitant to you?"

"Yes, Son, but that's how we created him."

"Very true," the Spirit said. "This character trait is the thing that will get him through the trials ahead and make him victorious."

I strolled up Glory Street, where towering Trees of Life lined both sides of the walkway. Yonder and to my right, the crystal-blue river rippled, chattering a soothing sound. Heaven's glory filled my nostrils with the sweet scent of flowers and a freshness wafting from the river. As I tried to bask in the peace, questions returned. *Why am I the only one who feels strange about this, but settled all the same?* I shrugged.

Arriving at the Armor Room, I shuffled onto the porch, and the sentries came to attention. When I nodded my greeting, they tugged, and the double doors opened.

The mammoth Armor Room looked precisely as expected—tall, plain white marble walls with a central cubicle three-quarters of the way back. My office lay halfway up on the right wall, and just beyond it, adjacent to the cubicle, rested the inspection bay with empty tables and bins awaiting a shipment of armor. "This is so odd," I whispered. "I feel like I've stepped into the middle of a story."

I paused a moment before making my *usual* rounds. Examining the Grand Hall, I took mental notes on where I'd store the armor and how I wanted it organized. "It's all quite perplexing," I muttered and retreated to my office.

Seated behind my desk, the large window to my left gave me a sweeping view of the Grand Hall. From here, I could monitor all Armor Room activity. The window extended beyond the desk to encompass two guest chairs and abut my office door. Peering out to the cubicle, I pondered the raised platform whose floor mirrored the height of the cubicle. Somehow, I knew I would use this platform to command the angel soldiers as they dressed for battle. At once, that odd feeling returned, and I wondered if Lucifer or Gabriel felt the same.

Gabriel, I suspected, had already entered the Scroll Room. No doubt, he occupied himself with God's word and would organize each scroll to perfection. Lucifer? He must have gone to the Garden of Fiery Stones.

A rap at the door jolted me, and Randiel, my Armor Room supervisor, poked his head in. "Chief Prince, a shipment of armor has come from the Forge. Would you like to handle it, or should I?"

"Thank you, Randiel. I'll take care of it. You can observe."

"Very good, Sir."

I rounded my desk and caught the door as Randiel exited. The receiving bay rested at the far end of the Armor Room. Diligent angels worked hard to unload the carts, but stifled their activity when they noticed me. "You're doing a good job," I said, motioning for them to resume. "Carry on."

The angels sorted and stacked the armor while I checked off each item on the clipboard. They inspected and repolished the golden battle gear and hung it in the Grand Hall according to my orders.

The other pieces, our sparring equipment, would skirt the back wall. This way, angels would have easy access when they advanced to the Arena for practice.

Period after period, except for moments of worship, things continued without change. And as the LORD's fiery glory overflowed and permeated Heaven, I finally let go of my angst and just reveled in God's peace.

CHAPTER 2

IN THE INTERIM

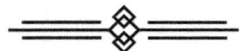

The Scroll Room stood south of the Armor Room and farther from the city gate, yet it faced the same street, the main thoroughfare of Heaven. After the palace, the Scroll Room was the most valued building in Heaven. Created to house the written word of the eternal God, a modest entrance veiled its immensity.

Gabriel sat at his desk, the hub of the mammoth wheel-shaped library. His wings draped over the back of his chair as he laid open a new length of papyrus-like material and lifted his quill. With precision, he penned the words flowing from the LORD, but soon his brows creased, and he rubbed his forehead. "Most High, may we pause for a moment?"

Even though God knew all thoughts, he asked anyway. "Gabriel, why the anxiety?"

Gabriel looked up from the words he'd just written, not sure how to voice his concern. "Majesty, I...I comprehend some of these words individually, but not all. Putting them together clouds my understanding. I sense cataclysm and dread." He laid his quill above the scroll and covered his face with his hands. After a brief delay, he said, "I know I must inscribe each flawless word, Sire. But if I can't grasp the meaning behind them, how can I be sure the scroll is correct?"

Compassion flowed from God's Spirit, enveloped the archangel, and retreated. "Aww…Gabriel, I know this is a mystery. It's meant to be. I won't let you fail in your duty, for I cherish and protect every letter. My Word is perfect and eternal, just as I AM, because it is me. I AM the Word. Penning is a great honor. So, let's continue."

Gabriel bowed his head. "Thank you, Sire. While I may not fully comprehend, I trust you, and I am honored."

Dictation resumed. Gabriel wrote steadily and only halted when the Almighty's voice paused. "The grace of the Lord Jesus be with all. Amen."

Though Gabriel had no knowledge of the words he just recorded, by the LORD's inflection, he knew to lower his quill. "Thank you for the privilege, Majesty," he said as he checked every character of his penmanship. "I'll get this fitted, rolled, and stored immediately."

"Gabriel, you are our special messenger. Now, raise your head and tell me what you see."

As Gabriel's eyes focused on the far wall, an ornate golden entryway materialized on the once plain white surface. "I see a door."

"Good. Stand and enter."

Gabriel gasped. "And leave the scroll unfinished?"

"Only, for the moment."

The archangel approached and noticed a key in the lock. When the tumbler clicked, the door inched open. The small room contained one item: a solid gold box. "Open it," God said.

Gabriel held the lid as he peered inside. "It's empty, LORD."

"Yes. And this is where you will store the new scroll. It is my crowning Word."

"Crowning? I don't understand."

"I know, but you will. For now, finish your work and lay it here in this box. Replace the lid and lock the door. Later, we will seal it."

"Seal it, Sir? …Sir?" When no response came, Gabriel obeyed orders. Hurrying to his desk, he fitted the material to the golden rods, rolled them, set the knobs and finials, and bound it. He gently lowered God's precious Word into the box, secured the lid, and locked the door.

Taking a step back, he stared at the Scroll Room's new addition and ran his fingers over the embossed gold. Its smooth, raised carvings felt cool to the touch. Up close, Gabriel couldn't quite make out the design. But moving back to his desk, the moldings came into focus. "They resemble eyes," he said, "seven of them. Fascinating."

God had provided all angels with a place to call their own. Archangels occupied separate chambers, large and spacious, with room for their attending chamber angels. Others of lower ranks were housed two, four, eight, or even sixteen to a chamber, depending upon their rank. The majority of angels lodged in barracks, yet each had their own space.

Lucifer's chamber was especially beautiful, befitting him as the angel of light. His atrium dome towered above all, and could be seen from Glory Street if you were looking for it. But the surrounding trees obscured the dome from most of the walkway and the small garden at the entrance of the angel housing.

Hastening toward his chamber, Lucifer kept his head down and ignored any under-angel greetings. He had much on his mind and was desperate for the solitude of his atrium. Reaching his stoop, he glared at his sentry guards since they were too slow in the opening.

Stepping through his chamber door, Lucifer patted his chest to ease the tightness. Far across the main room, he spied his glass-enclosed atrium and felt its pull. Bounding through its entrance, the intoxicating scent of flowers filled his senses. Coupled with the soft tinkle of crystalline water trickling from his decorative fountain, Lucifer found the peace he sought.

Reclining by the tranquility pool's far edge, a satisfied sigh escaped his lips. The ripples appeared cobalt blue from the mosaic tile lining the pool, and as they glided toward him, the glorious light of heaven danced around the room. Calmed by the beauty, Lucifer dragged his fingers through the cool liquid. When the waves smoothed out, he leaned in and glimpsed his reflection. Something familiar and pleasant bubbled up from within. He jolted, drew back, and the sensation died down. As he snuck another peek, the feeling returned, and his eyes drifted shut. He inhaled, held the experience for a moment, but then thought better of it and jumped to his feet.

Lucifer emerged from the atrium, nodded to a chamber angel, marched across the main room, and pushed open the exterior double doors. His hair and garments rustled while the sentries flinched, came to attention, and saluted.

"At ease, Soldiers. I'll be stepping out."

"Yes, Sir," they said with a slight quiver in their voices.

"Summon me if there is a need. And please, don't be concerned. You angels are doing a fine job, and I am pleased."

"Thank you, Chief Prince," the guard on the left said, nodding in relief. The other guard echoed his sentiment and added, "We appreciate your kind words."

Lucifer smiled. But as he trekked to the city gate, he thought about the stone garden and this new incident in his atrium. With breaths shallow and quick, he paused to pat his chest. "The pool was supposed to calm me, not cause more anxiety," he whispered. "What should I do?"

In the Garden of Fiery Stones, every occurrence like this had consumed him. Peering at his beauty there, Lucifer felt such bliss that he couldn't think of anything else. But when it surfaced in his atrium, he knew he was hooked. As hard as he fought it, the lure reeled him in. So, right or wrong, Lucifer launched.

The Garden seemed to welcome him with its soothing cadence. Strolling the ornamental paths, he lost himself in the mellow rhythm, and his apprehension dissolved. Rounding the bend, he found the rock fast becoming his favorite, and in its sleek veneer, Lucifer's reflection reappeared.

He smiled, stepped closer to the boulder, and stroked the smooth surface. His finger outlined the contours of his face, his steely-blue eyes, the graceful lines of his neck, and his powerful limbs. Before long, delight turned to bliss, and bliss exploded into ecstasy. Mesmerized by his beauty, Lucifer wrapped his arms around himself and squeezed. *I never want this to end.*

Soon, ecstasy intensified but quickly converted to a dread that tried to seize him. "What is this?" he said, tearing his stare from the rock. Lucifer's senses returned. "That's never happened before. I need to leave."

Yet something internal didn't want him to leave. His feet felt weighted and glued to the path. Panicking, he gasped for breath and started to shake. By sheer willpower, Lucifer stuffed down the dread and dragged himself back to the garden's gate. But as dread resurfaced, a chill sliced through. "No!" Lucifer screamed. He launched to escape the snare and streaked toward Ivory Palace City.

While I loved everything about Heaven, I did have my choice spots like the Armor Room and the Forge, but especially Glory Street. Strolling in either direction made me smile, and I seemed to bounce instead of walk. This moment was no different. Harvester angels high above gathered luscious fruit from the trees. The River of Life, clear like crystal, trickled a cheerful tune. A giggle escaped my lips as I approached the contemplation bench, and in that instant, contentment wrapped me in a warm blanket.

I moseyed past the bench to the river's edge, and Ivory Palace, shimmering in the LORD's light, came into view. Breaking from its majesty, I turned to gaze at the Mount of Holiness. There in the distance, an undetermined object hurtled toward me. I stiffened. "What is this? Couldn't be an angel, it's coming in too fast. Does it mean harm? Do I need to defend the palace?" *Maybe*. I'd never seen anything like it. "I better meet this intruder head-on. It cannot enter the city until I know what it is."

Moving back to the bench and preparing to launch, I again eyed the suspicious entity. It had shifted, and its faint outline flashed against the lighted horizon. It was an angel! I exhaled, ran my fingers through my hair, and grabbed the back of the bench to steady myself.

Easing onto the seat, I was still wheezing as Lucifer zoomed in from the plains and landed in front of me. Attempting to recover and hide my alarm, I said, "Wow, that was fast. Why the rush?"

He scrunched his face. "Oh, no reason."

I tipped my head to the side. "You look out of breath—almost like you were fleeing something. What happened?"

"Nothing," his gaze slid from mine. "Just needed some speed."

"Well, you sure accomplished that."

"Yeah, it felt good," he said with a faraway look.

"So, are you headed to the Dining Hall? Lucifer? Lucifer." He stared at me, but his eyes didn't see me. I stood, grabbed his shoulders, and yelled, "Lucifer!"

"What?" he said in a huff.

"I asked if you were going to the Dining Hall."

"Oh, sorry. Deep in thought." He cocked his head. "Yes, I was on my way to the Dining Hall. Are you?"

"I am, but I'm waiting for Gabriel." I sat back down. "He'll be along soon."

Lucifer plopped onto the bench beside me. "Okay, I'll wait with you."

"Great," I said, reaching over and patting his shoulder. "Listen, I was thinking about exploring Heaven. There are still a few places I haven't checked out. You want to come?"

He tapped his lips and shrugged. "I don't have anything special on my agenda for after our meal, so yes, it sounds like fun. Is Gabriel coming?"

"Haven't asked him yet."

"Asked me what? Gabriel said, walking up from behind."

I twisted around in my seat. "Gabriel, you're here. Why didn't you say something?"

"Seemed you two were having a serious conversation. I didn't want to interrupt until I heard my name. So, what were you going to ask?"

"Do you want to come exploring with Lucifer and me?"

"Yes!" Gabriel leaned forward with a glint in his eyes. "What are we exploring?

"We haven't decided yet," I said, rising. "Let's talk about it while we eat."

"Sounds good to me."

"And me." Lucifer motioned for us to follow.

Grins and luscious scents greeted us as we entered the Ivory Palace Dining Hall and meandered to our table. The succulent fruit and moist cakes hit the spot, and our conversation made it a joyous mealtime. We decided to investigate the Mount of Holiness even though Lucifer had already explored it on several occasions. "I'll show you my finds," he said.

"That's terrific. Are you ready, Gabriel?"

"I am. Let's go."

We walked to the city gate and launched from there. Soaring over the plains, I couldn't contain my smile. Being with my two friends and exploring the Mount of Holiness, it just didn't get any better. God is so good. He provides work for a sense of accomplishment, worship to remember our place, and this beautiful gift of friendship.

The mountain appeared tiny from the gate, but now it loomed before us. Alighting on the plateau housing the Shekinah Glory Base, we each found something of interest to explore. The boulders intrigued me. Gabriel inspected the base area. And...Lucifer? "Lucifer, where are you?"

"I'm here," he said, peeking up from under the plateau.

"Did you find something?"

"Not really. Just an indentation...ah...I guess that's what you'd call it."

"I'd like to see it," Gabriel said, starting toward the edge.

Lucifer waved his hand. "Nah...it's nothing special."

Gabriel stopped and returned to the base area to continue his investigation. I had just begun inspecting another boulder when Lucifer called out, "Let's head to the top, and I can show you some really cool sights."

"Sounds great." Looking toward Gabriel, I yelled, "We're going to the peak."

He halted and pivoted. "Okay, I'm right behind you."

"Find anything extraordinary?" I said as he drew near.

Gabriel shook his head. "Just a rock foundation and a few small boulders to the side."

CHAPTER 3

THE CAVERNS

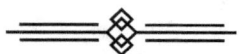

We gazed upward and eyed dense, lush greenery with splashes of colorful wildflowers dotting the mountain. Trees and boulders jutted up here and there, so we flew a little, climbed a little, and finally reached the summit of the Mount of Holiness.

As I rotated back to front, my mouth dropped open. "I don't believe I've been this high before. The perimeter trees look like miniatures."

"They do," Gabriel said as he peeked over the tip to the rear. "Hey, Lucifer, the backside of the mountain seems treacherous."

"It is, but how about this view?" Lucifer extended his arms to show the panoramic scene of Heaven.

Gabriel gulped. "I'm speechless."

"Me too!" I said, pausing to take it all in. I tramped over to inspect the rear portion of the mountain. "Lucifer, Gabriel's right about the backside. It's rough, and unless you know a way, I don't think we can climb down."

He snickered. "We can't. But that's why God gave us wings."

Shaking my head, I chuckled back, "Right."

"You both just needed to see all of Heaven from the peak to really appreciate it." Lucifer inhaled, and his shoulders rose. "Still," he said, exhaling, "the backside's nothing like the front."

I took one more look at Heaven from this height. "Wow, that's an understatement, but we are going down, right? I so want to explore the bottom."

"And you shall." Lucifer waved us closer. "Just wait 'til you see what I found."

The three of us dove off the pinnacle, and our wings shot open. Weaving in and out of trees and foliage, around rocks and cliffs, we finally landed on a narrow path. "This is strange," I said, "but I don't know what I expected."

Gabriel grabbed the side of the mountain to steady himself. "Me either. Lucifer, what did you want to show us?"

"It's around the west side. Follow me, but be careful—the trail tapers in places, and there are hidden crevices."

The trail did narrow in a few sites, yet it wasn't too difficult to maneuver. And I didn't see any crevices. Instead, the terrain appeared smooth with rolling mounds and tall grasses.

Lucifer led us around a bend, and we entered an opening under an overhanging crag camouflaged by nearby greenery. The trail emptied into a strange rock formation resembling a doorway. Lucifer shoved the large rock, and it creaked open. He jumped in and waved. "Come on."

I hesitated, unsure we should enter, but Gabriel pushed past me and sprang inside. "Michael. You have to see this. It's remarkable."

I took a deep breath and exhaled with my first step toward the door. Shifting through the opening, I gasped at the mountain's hollow innards. *Was the Mount of Holiness only a shell?* "Lucifer, what is this place?"

He leaned back and folded his arms across his chest. "I call it The Caverns."

"That's a good name for it," I said, pointing straight across the massive rotunda. "Look, that almost resembles a stage with steps leading to it."

Lucifer held out his arms. "I know. I haven't examined it yet, but I agree."

"Seems as though these caverns are endless," Gabriel said. "It's like they run the whole length, width, and height of the mountain and maybe beyond. But I'm wondering what purpose it serves. You know everything the LORD creates has a function."

"True." My fingers drummed my chin. "Maybe we can ask if we get the chance."

Gabriel pointed at me. "Good idea."

We explored as much of the caverns as we could, even the far recesses, the nooks and alcoves that seemed to stretch on forever. "Lucifer," I said. "I don't think I would have discovered this on my own."

"I know I wouldn't have found it," Gabriel said. "But I'm glad you did."

"Aww, thanks. I'm thrilled I could show it to you."

"This has been such fun—more than expected." I gazed again at the remarkable rotunda. "We've been gone for a while, though. I need to get back."

Gabriel nodded. "I think we all do. So, lead us home, Lucifer."

Our trio launched from the nearby clearing. We zoomed around to the mountain's front, past the plateau, and out to the plains. Nearing the Garden of Fiery Stones, Lucifer slowed his flight. "I'm going to check on things in the garden," he said, veering off. We nodded and continued to Ivory Palace City.

As Gabriel and I strolled up the Glory Street walkway, we reflected on the mountain, the caverns, and Heaven's perfection and harmony. Reaching the Armor Room, we said our goodbyes, and Gabriel continued on.

Entering, I remembered my first day. Then, it felt strange, but now, familiar and serene. The Grand Hall was almost full of battle gear, and soldier training was ongoing. As I walked to my office, nagging questions returned…not the ones of where I was before. I had new questions. Why were we forging armor and training for battle when things were so peaceful? And what or whom would we fight?

Lucifer alighted before the garden's gate and paused to contemplate its intertwining scrollwork. He alone walked among the fiery stones and often wondered why no one else came there. Recalling Michael had visited once, Lucifer remembered he didn't stay long. Although awed by the garden's grandeur, Michael felt unsettling jostles caused by the rumble of the boulders, and he left quickly.

Since the intense cadence soothed him, the way the Armor Room seemed to calm Michael, Lucifer struggled to understand. But having no answer, he shrugged, brushed it off, and took a step closer.

The gate reacted to Lucifer's presence and opened on its own. He stepped through, and the stones pulsed with fire in their belly. Strolling the paths to their beat, he found his favorite mirrored rock. The light from its flames and those of the surrounding boulders enveloped him. Lucifer stood motionless, gazing at his reflection. As he stared, his beauty lured him in and once again seized his being. It was here he fled on his last visit.

But this moment was different. The dread had vanished. Lucifer inhaled deeply as a gentle warmth mushroomed from within and melted any foreboding. He smiled, lifted his chin, and allowed himself to admire his face. His breaths quickened, and his chest tightened, but Lucifer ignored the inner warnings and continued to stare. Each exquisite feature entangled his thoughts until he felt light-headed and giddy.

Eyes riveted on his beauty, Lucifer's bliss soon changed and gnawed at his insides. When he attempted to pull away, the strange grinding increased, yet now it mixed with ecstasy—back and forth—gnawing to pleasure to gnawing. Lucifer fought as best he could, but he knew he was losing. "Let go!" he shouted and shot upward.

Reaching the city gate, he was still panting. *This is getting worse. I need to stay away.*

"Chief Prince Michael," Randiel said, stepping into the inspection area. "Generals Bradiel and Justel brought their platoons for training. I have them in the back choosing sparring equipment."

"I'll be right there, but first I need to finish inspecting these last three shin guards."

Randiel nodded. "Alright, Sir. I'll let them know."

"Thank you," I said, "and Randiel, I do appreciate your efficiency." He delivered a timid smile and exited the area. I picked up one shin guard for the rank of private, checked the specs, examined the straps and buckles, ensured the edges were smooth, and gave it my stamp of approval. I did the same for the other two and hurried to meet the soldiers.

Down the long hall, out the back entrance, through the gates, and we entered the Arena. I paired up the platoons and demonstrated each maneuver. "This is the lunge," I said, grabbing the sword grip from behind my head. Stepping forward, back leg straight, front knee bent, I jabbed my blade in the direction of my invisible foe. "It's an offensive action of thrusting one's saber. You'll launch yourself by pushing off from your back leg, and this will keep your opponent on defense." I paused while the angels practiced.

"Now, the parry," I said, twisting and rocking my sword as though repelling another's. "The parry is blade work intended to deflect or block an incoming attack. A smaller parry is better since a larger one will open you up to your opponent's thrust." Seeing their understanding nods, I continued, "And finally, the riposte. It's a counterattack to answer a challenger's strike and the immediate action to use after a successful parry. This keeps your adversary moving backward. Any questions?"

They all stood silent or perhaps overwhelmed. "Okay then," I said. "Head to your assigned rings and commence sparring on my command. Generals, please tend to your platoons, and I'll observe."

"Yes, Sir," they both replied.

I held up my arm and pointed with each command. "Angels, en garde! Prêts? Allez!"

Ready…set…go, and swords clashed. The deafening sound reverberated through the Arena, and the platoons performed with great skill. I corrected a few maneuvers, but overall, their moves were crisp and clean, and I was pleased. Platoon 10 impressed me. I sounded the gong, shouted, "Arrêt," and sparring ceased. "Thank you, angels, excellent work. Return your gear to the Armor Room, and you are free to go. Bradiel, Justel, walk with me."

The soldiers sped to the Grand Hall while the generals and I talked. "You both have warriors with excellent ability. They will serve the Most High well in battle."

"Good to know, Sir. Thank you for your kind words and leadership," Bradiel said.

"And training," Justel added. "Our angels are only this good because of your superb instruction."

I nodded. "My pleasure." When we arrived back in the Grand Hall, I said, "I'll be here if you need anything more."

"Thank you again, Chief Prince Michael," they said in unison. And as I watched them exit, I wondered anew why we trained for battle. It didn't make much sense to me. Still, the Almighty knows, and I've elected to trust him.

CHAPTER 4

FIGHTING CHANGE

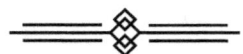

Slinking through the city gate, sure anyone who saw him would know what he had just experienced, Lucifer hustled down Glory Street toward his chamber. In the distance, he thought he saw Bradiel and Justel conversing, so he ducked into the nearby garden. The comfy bench located around to the right seemed perfect.

Masked by the tall flowers and shrubbery, Lucifer sat trying to quiet himself, but when a group of under-angels passed by, he jumped up and listened until their voices faded. "Good, they didn't see me," he whispered, peeking out and taking a step toward home. "I'd better get to my chambers. Hopefully, the generals are gone—I'm not up to talking."

Back on Glory Street, Lucifer saw the walkway was clear. As he dashed to his chamber, he heard footsteps coming up fast behind him. "Chief Prince Lucifer," Wyael yelled. "Please wait."

Lucifer halted midstream and pivoted. He took a deep breath and smiled, relieved that First Lieutenant Wyael and Second Lieutenant Maysel were running to meet him and not the Generals. These two

Lieutenants greatly admired him, and knowing this eased his distress. "Wyael, Maysel, what can I do for you?"

Maysel gasped for air. "We heard you explored the backside of the Mount of Holiness and found some intriguing sights."

"I did! I also showed them to Chief Princes Michael and Gabriel. They were impressed."

Wyael's eyes grew big. "Could you take us there?"

Lucifer crossed his arms. "No, absolutely not! You know that side of the Mount of Holiness is off-limits to under-angels."

"I've never understood that," Wyael said, scrunching his face.

"It's because of the rough terrain." Lucifer cocked his head and stroked his chin. "But I'd like to tell you about it."

Maysel jerked to attention. "Great. May we come to your chambers now, Sir?"

Wyael sighed. "Maysel, don't you remember our task?" Turning to Chief Prince Lucifer, he said, "Sir, General Reedael ordered us to gather soldiers for training and escort them to the Armor Room."

"I remember now." Maysel moaned, and his shoulders drooped.

Feeling their disappointment, Lucifer raised his eyebrows. "Lieutenants, how about we get together later for a nice discussion?"

"That would be wonderful, Sir," Wyael said. "I also have questions about the LORD, if that's alright."

"It's more than alright. I'm positive Archangel Michael and Archangel Gabriel would like to be included. I'll arrange it and get back to you."

"Oh, thank you, Sir." The Lieutenants saluted and hastened down the walkway toward the under-angel barracks.

Lucifer stood there to watch and listen as long as he could, determined to know whether or not they had detected his anxiety. Satisfied they hadn't, he continued on his way.

Entering his dwelling, Lucifer nearly ran into his lead chamber angel. Andiel jolted. "How may I serve you, Chief Prince?"

"I don't need anything right now, Andiel, but thank you for asking."

"You're welcome, Sir," he said, stepping to the left so Lucifer could pass. "Please call if you need me."

"I will." Lucifer nodded and continued across the room. He entered the atrium, peered through the glass-domed rooftop access, and shook his hands as the anxious feelings returned. He paced around the tranquility pool, but the tinkling fountain didn't help, even though Heaven's light streamed through and bathed the foliage in a shimmering glow.

Lucifer rubbed the back of his neck, struggling to avoid the glistening water, yet the pull was too great. He drew close, leaned in, and there it was—his image. Lucifer's breath caught, and his body felt like a rising thermometer. *What a rush!* "This feeling isn't only in the Garden of Fiery Stones," he whispered. "It's here too and getting stronger. But there's just something about that garden...."

Lucifer shivered as pleasure surged. "Stop this obsession! You are not going to the garden!" he shouted and jumped back from the pool. In the process, he knocked over a gigantic planter. It crashed to the floor and shattered. Pieces scattered and covered the mosaic tile.

Hearing the commotion, Andiel rushed from the other room. "Did you call me, Sir?"

"No," Lucifer snapped, irritated at the intrusion. "But since you're here, you should know I'm leaving. And I don't want to see this mess when I return."

Andiel's shoulders dropped, and his head lowered. "Yes, Sir," he mumbled as Lucifer shot up through the circular Atrium access.

Hearing sounds uncommon to Lucifer's chamber and Heaven, Gloriel rushed in. Seeing the clutter and Andiel's vacant stare, he asked, "What happened?" When Andiel didn't answer, the chamber assistant laid a hand on his shoulder. "Sir, are you alright? What happened?"

Andiel slid his hand over his face and pushed back his light-brown hair while he and Gloriel just stared at the disorder. "Chief Prince Lucifer broke this planter and wants it cleaned immediately."

Gloriel's head whipped in Andiel's direction. "That's a new one."

"For sure," Andiel said, sighing. "And Prince Lucifer's tone of voice shocked me. It was sharp, and he's never talked to me that way."

"I'm sorry, Sir," Gloriel said, ogling the chaos.

"Thanks. Let's just get this cleaned up."

Lucifer soared over the city, longing for the Garden of Fiery Stones, but he fought his desire. Swooping onto the Glory Street walkway, he hoped this would settle him. He rubbed his neck, wrung his hands, and sucked in shallow breaths. Pacing up and down the street, he whispered, "Michael and Gabriel...such good friends could help. But if I tell them my struggle, will they understand? Maybe. Oh...

maybe not. I have to try, though." Lucifer scanned his surroundings. "Aha, the Scroll Room."

He bounded up to the door. When Gabriel opened, Lucifer's knees buckled, and he grabbed the casing for support. "Are you okay?" Gabriel said.

"Yes, I'm fine." Lucifer straightened his stance. "Not sure what that was. How are you?"

"Good…busy, but that's not unusual. Come in. Hey, I have something to show you."

"Oh yeah?" Lucifer said as he stepped through the doorway. Instantly, the holiness of God's Word enveloped him, and every anxious thought fled. He closed the door and leaned against it, enjoying the freedom. Lucifer drew in a deep breath—something he hadn't been able to do since his last visit to the garden. He held it and exhaled. Calm infused him, and, for the moment, he felt like his old self.

"Lucifer. Gabriel. Come to the Throne Room," the Almighty said.

"Yes, Majesty," they both replied.

Zipping out of the Scroll Room, Gabriel said, "I didn't get to show you my new item."

"I know, but I'll visit again soon. You can count on that!"

"Good because you'll love it."

—————⌄—————

Arriving at the palace door, they noticed me bounding up the walkway. "Michael, so good to see you," Lucifer said, wrapping his arms around my shoulders and Gabriel's. "Ah…the three of us together again. Such fun."

We entered the Throne Room and bowed before the all-powerful God, and his Shekinah brightened. "What satisfaction we gain from observing our archangels. Watching you go about your duties and interact with our under-angels is a joy. You all are precious to me."

I lowered my head. "Thank you, my King."

"Sovereign," Lucifer said. "Is there some way we may further assist you with the under-angels?"

"You may, and it is for this reason I called you here." As the LORD shifted on his throne, iridescent waves of his glory escaped and hopped around the room. "We are preparing to do something new. All heaven's inhabitants must be made ready."

Gabriel's eyes glimmered. "How can we be of service?"

"Since you three have been given greater intellect and wisdom, you will now focus more on teaching, instructing, and guiding my under-angels in their knowledge of me."

"LORD," I said, bowing, "what honor you have placed upon us. Thank you. May we also help in other ways?"

"Additional information will be provided as needed."

And with that, the conversation and our meeting ended. We exited Ivory Palace and dispersed to follow the Almighty's orders—teaching as many as we encountered.

CHAPTER 5

ALTERED

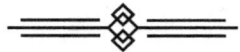

"Michael, buddy," Lucifer called from the Armor Room entrance.

I stuck my head out of my office door. "Here I am. What's up?"

"I have a group of under-angels who want to learn more about Heaven and our LORD. You in?"

"Yes, of course," I said, jogging toward him. "Where's the meeting?"

"In the small garden near our chambers."

"The one with the comfy bench and the tall flowers?"

Lucifer nodded. "Yep."

Finally reaching the entrance, I said, "Is Gabriel coming?"

Lucifer tilted his head. "Maybe. Right now, he's busy reorganizing the scrolls of God's Word. But if he finishes early, he'll join us."

"So, this is happening now." I started out the door but halted. "Let me speak with Randiel, and I'll follow after you."

"Great. See you there."

I sprinted to Randiel's cubicle and strode through the door. "I'm stepping out, Randiel. Summon me if you need me."

His head bobbed. "I will, Sir."

Hustling out the Armor Room doors, I paused for a moment. My heart raced with anticipation of this new opportunity to obey God's orders. I felt like skipping down the walkway toward the angel dwellings, but I restrained myself and just walked swiftly. Rounding the corner, I heard laughter wafting from the garden.

The under-angels stood and greeted me as I slid through the entrance. "Wyael, Maysel," I said. "Good to see you. Juael, Willel, Ennel, and Gragael, good to see you too. Lucifer, this is a terrific group."

"I know, right?"

I sat on the bench next to Lucifer while the under-angels picked their spots on the floor around us. We analyzed the Mount of Holiness, the view from the plateau and the peak, the mountain's rough backside terrain, and the caverns—especially the caverns. Lucifer and I explained how the Mount of Holiness seemed like a shell, similar to a bowl placed upside down on a table, kind of like the structure of the Forge. But just as Gabriel tiptoed in behind them, Wyael said, "So, God created us, but who created him?'

"Ah…Gabriel, glad you came," I said, raising my arm to welcome him. "Here's a good question for you." Patting the cushion between me and Lucifer, I hoped Gabriel would be willing to answer.

"Oh, sure," he said, taking a seat. Gabriel seemed to study the under-angels as he got situated, maybe pondering his response. He inhaled, and his chest swelled, then emptied as he answered. "Angels, when I asked about this, the Almighty informed us he was not created. He is eternal. He always was and always will be."

"So, he's not created like us?" Wyael's face puckered. "Does that mean there's no one higher?"

"Correct." Gabriel smiled. "That's exactly what it means, but there is more."

"And," I said, chiming in, "he's sacred and holy. In fact, you can feel his holiness in the Throne Room. It's like heavy purity."

Gragael groaned. "How can purity be heavy?"

I sat a little straighter as I attempted to answer. "It's hard to explain. All I can say is the weight of God's holiness forced me to the floor, face down in worship, when I encountered it. Yet the feeling was almost indescribable, and sort of blissful."

Willel flinched. "If that's the case, then I guess heavy purity is a good description."

Gabriel seemed pleased as he stretched his arms wide toward the under-angels. "You got it. And God's holiness did the same to me. But you also must understand the Almighty is completely different and separate from us."

Wyael jerked. "How so?"

"Before him," Gabriel paused and looked up, "nothing else existed but him."

"Really?" Maysel's voice cracked.

"Yes." Gabriel peeked at me and then turned back to the under-angels. "All we see and all we are is because of the Most High. He is Creator. We are the created." Gabriel patted his chest and continued. "In other words, he made us, but no one made him."

I jumped up and air-drew a triangle. "It's like this. God the Father at the apex. God the Son at the right angle, and God the Holy Spirit at the left angle. Get it?" Blank stares peered back at me. "Here," I said, "let me explain it another way. Not only is God different than us and distinct, he is sovereign—the supreme, three-in-one, ruler." My arms created a high, semi-circle-like arc as I attempted to encompass and cover all of us in the garden. "You see, God is above us, knowing all and keeping all. He is all-powerful and everywhere present."

Maysel's arms crossed his chest. "How are we supposed to comprehend that?"

Gabriel and I looked at each other. I had said everything I knew. And, if Gabriel had any other knowledge, I figured he would have shared it.

"We won't fully comprehend," Lucifer said, causing our heads to jerk in his direction.

"Why?" Wyael and Maysel said in unison, verbalizing my exact thought, and probably the thoughts of every angel listening.

Lucifer sighed a woeful sigh. "Because angels," he said, "we are not God."

The under-angels gasped. My mouth fell open, and I grabbed the bench and eased myself down. It was the most profound statement I'd ever heard Lucifer speak—and—nothing less than pure truth.

"Angels," Lucifer said after a long pause. "I think you have enough to ponder. We'll have other meetings."

The garden emptied, and the three of us sat together as though transfixed. "That was deep," I said, breaking the silence. "I can't wait for the next discussion."

Gabriel shook his head. "I agree. I wish I hadn't missed so much of this one. I'll be sure to be here for the follow-up. Lucifer, are you looking forward to another meeting? Lucifer?"

I peeked around Gabriel. Lucifer's eyes appeared distant—like he was somewhere far away. "Lucifer, are you okay?"

"Lucifer!" Gabriel said, elbowing him.

"What? What was that for?"

Gabriel threw his hands in the air. "We asked you a question, and you didn't answer."

"Yeah," I said. "You had that funny look again. Where do you go when you tune us out?"

"Sorry." Lucifer shrugged. "What was the question, Gabriel?"

"We wondered if you were excited about our next discussion. That's all."

"I am. But I'll see you two later." Lucifer launched from the small garden without explanation. He flew over the city gate and out to the plains.

"That was strange, don't you think?" I said as Gabriel and I departed.

"No, Michael. Lucifer's just being Lucifer."

I cocked my head and smirked. "If you say so."

Lucifer flew to his haven, the Garden of Fiery Stones, wrestling with the answer he gave the under-angels. He hadn't been to the garden since the gnawing incident, but now, with this meeting, the lure was more potent than anything he had experienced. Suppressing it felt impossible.

As he landed, something stirred within him, and when the gate opened, he hesitated, one step in, then jumping back. "Go home, Lucifer," he said to himself. "You were going to stay away, remember?" *I remember. But perhaps I was mistaken.* "The Garden soothes my anxiety." *So did the Scroll Room and the Word of God. Why not go there?* "I don't know," he mumbled. "I only know I'm drawn here. Seeing my image in this place relieves me, and it's easier than explaining my torment to Gabriel or Michael." *Besides, what's the use of going home? The feeling's there, too.* "I need the garden's serenity to resolve whatever this is, so I can go home."

He hiked his shoulders and stepped through the entrance. At once, the iridescent rocks awakened and again triggered a crushing ecstasy. Lucifer doubled over. "What's happening?"

The huge stones appeared to answer. They rumbled as the fire deep within their core kindled and then spouted. Like pipes of a calliope releasing steam into the air, the boulders expelled their flames in rhythmic sequences and reflected on the adjacent rocks.

The cadence calmed Lucifer for the moment, and he continued wandering the ornate paths. Reaching the center and his particular boulder, he whispered to his reflection, "I shouldn't have come."

Amid the warm blaze of fluctuating firelight, Lucifer lingered, staring at his beauty. It sucked him in and gripped tightly with a blissful feeling that twisted his thoughts. "But look at me," he whispered. "I am exquisite…magnificent…and as the angel of light, my fiery glow is just as brilliant as God's Shekinah." Lucifer took a deep breath, held it, and when he blew it out, he said, "So, the question is, do I believe the answer I gave the under-angels?"

Eyes fixated on his stunning reflection, he stroked his chin and pondered his reply. More thoughts bombarded, swirled, and then brought demented clarity. "For them, I do," he said, "they aren't like God...but...but...I am."

"Lucifer, stop!" he cried, trying to regain control, shake the obsession, and keep his eyes off the mirrored rock. "Ah," he screamed, covering his face with his hands. "I can't fight this anymore!" When he lowered his arms, the draw of his image pried open his eyelids and once more dragged him back. Gazing at his alluring face, Lucifer conceded. *Why do I want to fight anyway?*

With that, the inward spark ignited, and some unknown yet blissful sentiment slithered up from the nucleus of his being. Intoxicated by euphoria, Lucifer inhaled deeply. His chest swelled, and his eyes drifted shut until tentacles from within uncoiled and constricted his throat. His eyes bulged, and he clawed at his neck to free himself, but it was too late.

Pride had spawned. It sunk deep, saturated his essence, and altered his very nature.

CHAPTER 6

INWARD, OUTWARD, OR BOTH?

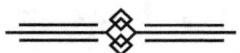

Lucifer grinned, flipped back his hair, and sauntered through the Ivory Palace City gate like he owned it. "Things look different," he said, "and I feel so free. My struggle is gone. I know who I am now, and more importantly, I know what I need to do."

In the distance, Lucifer saw Wyael and Maysel coming up the walkway. "Hmm…these two might make good assistants." *They could do for me what we archangels have always done for the Most High.* "Ha…I'll bet they'd jump at the chance to serve me." *Slow down. You have to be careful. Can't reveal too much yet.*

The Lieutenants noticed Lucifer and came running. "Wyael. Maysel," he said. "Good to see you again. Are you on duty?"

"We're on our way to report for duty, Sir," Wyael said.

"Alright, I won't keep you." They saluted, and Lucifer returned their salute. As each moved toward their intended destinations, Lucifer swung around. "Hey," he said, motioning for them to return. When they got near, Lucifer stepped even closer, creating a huddle.

"I wondered if you two are still interested in seeing the backside of the Mount of Holiness and the caverns?"

"Still interested?" Maysel shouted.

"Shhh," Lucifer said.

"Well, I am. Are you Wyael?"

"Yes, but I thought the back side was off-limits to under-angels."

"It is," Lucifer said. "I've been thinking, though. You both are exceptional, and I value your loyalty. I want to reward you with a visit to the mountain."

Straightening his stance, Wyael said, "Should we obtain permission from the Most High first?"

Lucifer scowled. "Listen, this is my call, something He doesn't need to know. Are you having second thoughts?"

Wyael gasped. "No, Sir. I'd love to see everything Heaven has to offer."

"Good. After our next worship period, you two meet me in the west perimeter trees. When the angel armies disperse, I'll show you what I've found."

"Thank you, Chief Prince Lucifer," Maysel said, saluting. "We'll be there. Right, Wyael?"

"Yes. Where exactly should we meet?"

"Enter the trees by the west staircase," Lucifer whispered. "Do it one at a time so you don't raise suspicion. If needed, I'll distract Michael and Gabriel. Those two would definitely try to stop us."

"So, exploring the backside of the Mount of Holiness is that much off-limits, that much against the will of God? Maybe we shouldn't go."

"Wyael," Lucifer said. "Don't get all caught up in right and wrong. This is a great adventure—one of which you should not be deprived. If I were in charge, nothing would be off-limits."

Maysel grabbed Wyael's shoulders. "Listen, I want to go, and I know you do too."

First Lieutenant Wyael cocked his head. "Seeing things from that angle does make sense. Okay, Sir. We'll be there."

——⌄——

When the silver trumpets sounded long, every angel ceased their work, assembled, and marched to their assigned spot on the plains. As the power of the Almighty descended upon the Shekinah Glory Base, all bowed in worship. Once the LORD settled, a single silver trumpet blast signaled the entrance of each archangel. Lucifer entered first, as always.

Created to reflect God's perfection, Lucifer was magnificent. His long, golden hair, handsome face, and melodious voice made him the most revered Chief Prince among all ranks of angels. As the wise and beautiful anointed cherub, archangel to God the Father, his covering was laden with every precious gem interspersed with gold. The name Lucifer meant light-bearer, and upon this angel of light, the Almighty bestowed the privilege of leading us in worship.

With the sound of the second trumpet, I entered. Although my appearance was luminous, my face and strands could not compare to Lucifer's. I, too, possessed long, flowing locks, but they were ashen maize rather than golden. My covering was also gilded, but minus the precious gems, and my voice, well…it was more stern than melodious. The Almighty created it to give commands, and some under-angels seem apprehensive around me. I've always been committed to my station, directing the outfitting and training of the angel armies and the duties assigned to me as protector and guardian, archangel to God the Son. But of all my qualities, the strangest was that my name asked a rhetorical question: Who is like God?

When the third silver trumpet called, Gabriel entered, and his incandescence reached as far as the third battalion line. With elegant facial features framed by long tresses of golden-brown hair, he was the second-favored archangel. His vibrant voice was forceful, yet soft-spoken and compelling. Gabriel penned the Word of God and spoke it when commanded. He, the swift and articulate messenger extraordinaire, archangel to God the Holy Spirit, embodied the meaning of his name: God is my strength. Gabriel was my friend and confidant.

The three of us bowed before the Most High, took our places, and pivoted to face the troops below. Holding the center position, I extended my wings. As we touched, illumination flowed from Gabriel to me, onto Lucifer, and out to the under-angels, yet something felt odd as I connected with Lucifer. I recoiled a bit, and my stomach churned. *What is this?* I had no explanation, and as much as I wanted to discover why, I couldn't allow it to distract me. I stood in the presence of Almighty God. Nothing else mattered.

As worship suspended, that feeling resurfaced, but it disappeared when our wings released. While the LORD's glorious power floated over us and filled the Throne Room, I stuffed the thought and concentrated on my duties.

Down on the plains, Senior Angel Captain Greysiel stepped forward and shouted, "Angels…dismissed." I waited on the mountain's secondary level, supervising until the plains emptied and the under-angels dispersed. Scanning the mountain and the surrounding area, all seemed calm, so I focused my attention southward, to what I thought were all angels returning to Ivory Palace City.

I descended the stairs. Reaching ground level, I readied myself and launched, yet I landed halfway to the city, still grappling with whatever I felt during worship. A contemplation bench near the walkway looked inviting, so I sat. *Did I really feel something with Lucifer's connection, or did I imagine it?* "I don't know," I said to the shrubs and flowers, "but something was different. Maybe I need to talk to Lucifer."

In covert fashion, a trio of angels emerged from the perimeter trees and dashed around to the backside of the Mount of Holiness. "Do you think anyone saw us?" First Lieutenant Wyael said, trying to catch his breath.

Lucifer lifted his head high as he scanned the area. "Don't worry. I watched Michael and Gabriel leave. They're the only ones who count. All other angels wouldn't dare question me."

Second Lieutenant Maysel's arm shot out. "That's true, Wyael. You know we would never ask a Chief Prince about what they were doing or why."

Wyael nodded. "Yeah, you're right."

"Remember," Lucifer said. "You two are just following orders. I am your superior, and you have no choice. You must obey. Anyway, I'll cover if we're caught. But we won't be."

Tall grasses slapped at their faces as they hiked down the narrow path. Lucifer held up his hand. "Be careful on this section of the trail. There are crevices. Falling would be unfortunate, not to mention unproductive."

Under the overhanging crag and around to the right, Lucifer shoved open the stone door and stepped inside. Wyael and Maysel followed. Mouths wide open, they rotated, taking in the amazing sights, the enormous rotunda, and the seeming endlessness of the caverns. "Come on," Lucifer said, motioning to them. "I want to check out that area over there."

Reaching a flat, raised rock formation jutting out from a wall, they realized there was an end to these caverns, at least in this direction. Near the back wall, below, and on either side of this stage, they observed staggered, flat-top boulders similar to steps.

Ascending the left stairs, the three examined each feature. "I'm curious as to why the rocks formed this way," Wyael said. "It almost seems planned."

Maysel's eyes swept from left to right. "I see what you mean, but it's hard to imagine the Most High using something like this."

Lucifer grimaced. "Lieutenants, let's not dwell on how or why the rocks formed. The fact is they're here, and I think I can work with this structure."

Wyael strolled toward Lucifer. "How, Sir?"

"Not sure yet. Would you two like to assist me?"

"Yes, Sir." Wyael's eyes sparkled. "What an honor. You can count on me."

"And me," Maysel shouted.

"Good." Lucifer sported a wide grin. "Let's go back to my chamber and discuss the possibilities."

Determined to resolve my frustration from worship, I arrived at Lucifer's. I nodded to his door sentries and entered. "Greetings, Andiel. Is Lucifer here?"

"No, Chief Prince Michael, I'm sorry."

"It's fine. I'll talk to him later. By the way, good job with Lucifer's chambers."

Andiel bowed his head. "Thank you, Sir."

I nodded and turned to exit. I pushed open the doors and almost smacked into Lucifer. "Oh," I said. "You're back."

He scowled. "Michael, what are you doing here?"

The harshness in Lucifer's voice caused me to jerk. "Well, I came to talk about our worship period."

"I'm busy. I have Wyael and Maysel with me. We have things to discuss."

At the thought of another discussion with Lucifer and these two inquisitive angels, I smiled. "Great, I'll join you."

"No, you're not needed." Lucifer's hand slapped my chest, and he shoved me out the door. "Wyael, Maysel, enter. Michael, leave. We'll talk later. Doors!" he shouted.

Stunned, I glared at Lucifer through the decreasing opening. 'But…but," I said as the doors closed in my face. The sentries returned to their ready post while I stood on the porch, frozen like a statue. *Had I been kicked out of Lucifer's chambers?* My eyes moved to the left sentry and then to the right. They seemed oblivious to the whole encounter. Finally, I thawed enough to relocate onto the walkway and return to the Armor Room.

Inside my office, I pondered what I felt during worship and the incident at Lucifer's. *Were they really as bad as they seemed?* "I don't know," I said under my breath. "Maybe it's just my imagination."

I rounded my desk and grabbed the door, but stopped halfway through. "If it were my imagination," I whispered, "what would cause me to imagine something like that? What happened at Lucifer's has never happened before. How could I make up such a thing when I have no former experience?"

"Were you talking to me, Chief Prince Michael?" Randiel said, causing me to flinch.

"No. Sorry, just thinking out loud."

Randiel nodded and cocked his head. "Well, then, is there something you need?"

"Thanks, but no. I'm going to find Gabriel. I'll be back."

I sprinted down Glory Street and bounded up to the Scroll Room. While I waited for Gabriel to answer, I studied the small door. *The Scroll Room has no door sentries? Why haven't I ever noticed this before?*

"Michael," I heard from down the street. "Michael!"

I jerked my head toward the sound of Gabriel's voice and ran to meet him. "You're out here?"

"Yes, I'm taking a break. I've been working non-stop with the scrolls and felt like a walk by the river. What's up?"

"I'm having an issue with Lucifer," I said, frowning, "and I need your advice."

"Okay." Gabriel found a nearby bench and motioned for me to join him. "I'll do my best."

Sighing, I sat. "During worship, I detected something odd. I felt a strange sensation when my wing connected with Lucifer's."

Gabriel snapped his head toward me. "I didn't experience anything peculiar."

"You don't connect directly with Lucifer. I'm between the two of you."

"True." Gabriel nodded. "Still, I talked with him afterward. He seemed fine. So, what's the concern?"

I shrugged. "I don't know. Call it a hunch."

"Aww, Michael, it was probably nothing. Just let it go."

"Maybe I can let that go," I said, fidgeting, "but listen to this. I went to talk to Lucifer about the strange feeling, and he disrespected me right in front of his under-angels. And then, he literally shoved me out of his chambers."

"What?" Gabriel chuckled. "That's absurd. Lucifer would never do that. Was he in the middle of a project?"

"He had Lieutenants Wyael and Maysel with him."

Gabriel threw his hand out. "So, he was in the middle of something. Perhaps he didn't want his thoughts interrupted. You know Lucifer would never hurt you intentionally. I'm sure you just misunderstood."

I hung my head. "I'm not convinced that's the case, but I'll consider it."

"Good. And don't hold on to all this frustration, Michael. It's not worth it."

"I know. Thanks."

———⌄———

Strolling up Glory Street, I considered Gabriel's explanation of Lucifer's actions. *But...Gabriel wasn't there...he didn't hear Lucifer's tone of voice or feel how hard he shoved.* "And," I said aloud, pointing my finger forward as though someone stood there, "Gabriel didn't sense what I felt on the Shekinah Glory Base."

"Who are you talking to, Michael?

Wide-eyed, I spun around. "What are you doing here?"

Smirking, Lucifer cocked his head. "You said you wanted to talk, so I came to find you."

My brows furrowed. I didn't even know how to begin the conversation.

Lucifer crossed his arms and tapped his foot. "Michael, did you hear me?"

"Yes, but I'm not sure I want to talk now."

He turned to leave. "Suit yourself."

I might not get another chance. "Wait."

"Okay, so..."

I inhaled and exhaled through vibrating lips. "The reason I came to your chamber isn't bothering me as much as how you treated me in front of the under-angels. You disrespected me...and...and...you shoved me out. Why?"

Lucifer jerked his head back. "You didn't want to leave. How else could I get you to go?"

"Seriously? You could have asked."

"I did ask."

"No." I pointed at him. "You didn't. You just shoved me out and said you would talk to me later. What was so important that I couldn't be involved?"

Lucifer snorted. "Listen, I had a task I was working on with Wyael and Maysel, and it was none of your business. But you wanted to make it your business. So, you tell me what I was supposed to do when you tried to horn in on my meeting."

My face turned red-hot. "Horn in on your meeting? What? We've been teaching the under-angels together since the Almighty gave the orders. Why now did this meeting have to be just you three?"

Lucifer glared and pivoted. "What's it to you if I want a private meeting? It's none of your business anyway."

"Why do you keep saying that? I grabbed his arm and swung him around. "And why such a change in your attitude?"

"Change?" Lucifer screamed and shook free. His nostrils flared, and fury filled his eyes. "There's no change!"

I gasped and took a step back. "There most certainly is."

"Michael, I'm done with this conversation. Leave me alone, and stay out of my business."

"Lucifer!" I yelled. He launched toward the plains and soared out of sight. I shook my head and pushed my hair back. "What just happened?" I had no words to describe his behavior or the crazed expression on his face. *Yes, he's been different lately, but never like this.*

Still enraged, Lucifer landed before the Garden of Fiery Stones' gate. "Michael thinks I've changed, and that's a problem. I know I'm different, but how does he know? Wasn't this just an inward change? Could it have been outward, too?"

Sprinting down the path, pride resurfaced. Lucifer felt invigorated and more powerful than he had ever been. Rounding the corner, he skidded to a stop before his favorite mirrored rock.

As he stepped up to the polished facade, Lucifer's reflection revealed the answer. Nothing external had changed. "Whew," he said, while his shoulders relaxed. "Michael saw nothing, yet he did detect a change in my attitude, and that can't happen again. I must conceal this transformation, control and disguise my emotions, and absolutely no more outbursts! Michael, Gabriel, but especially the Most High, cannot learn of this, or my plans. At least, not until I'm ready."

Lucifer did hide his change, and he hid it well, or so he thought.

CHAPTER 7

THE BEGINNING

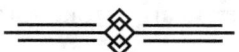

On the expanse of Heaven's plains, stretching out from the Mount of Holiness, just north of Ivory Palace, the angel troops gathered. Ten thousand field armies stood at attention before the splendor of God's Shekinah. Each division, company, and squad, complete with all ranks and commanders, occupied their assigned places and awaited the announcement.

We lingered on the west side of the plateau, off-stage in the wings, anticipating our entrance. Gabriel, to my left, checked his notes, and Lucifer paced behind. When the first silver trumpet sounded, Lucifer rammed my shoulder and shoved me aside. I stumbled but caught myself as he entered. "Gabriel! Did you see that?"

Gabriel looked up from his notes. "See what?"

"Lucifer."

"What about him?"

I threw out my arm. "He almost knocked me over."

"Were you in his way?" Gabriel peered again at his notes. "You know he's always the first to enter."

"No, I wasn't in his way," I said, slamming a hand on my hip. "And he didn't even excuse himself."

"You're making too much of it, Michael." Gabriel stifled a snicker. "It was probably an accident. I'm sure he'll apologize if you make him aware of it."

I sighed. "Somehow, I don't see that happening."

Walking to the entrance, I peeked out to watch Lucifer's effect on the under-angels. They nearly broke formation with excitement. Their commotion seemed over the top and fit more with the adoration we would give the Almighty. *This is so odd. These angels weren't this animated at our worship gathering.*

"Gabriel," I said, stepping closer. "I know Lucifer is popular with the under-angels, but something's amiss."

His head jerked up. "What do you mean?"

"Well," I said, exhaling, "things like that shove and what happened before at his chambers."

"Michael." Gabriel's hands, holding his notes, slapped his sides. "You're always so guarded. Or maybe, a bit jealous."

I crossed my arms. "Guarded…yes…but never jealous."

Gabriel shrugged. "If you say so."

Lost in my thoughts, I paced and didn't hear the second trumpet. "Michael," Gabriel said, nudging me. "Enter."

I cringed and hustled in to much less acclamation. Once Gabriel entered, we faced the Most High God, bowed low, turned, and took our positions before his brilliance. "Angels…At ease," shouted Captain Greysiel.

Gabriel stepped forward to announce and narrate, speaking only the words given to him by the Eternal God, who is Three, yet One.

"Angels," Gabriel said. "What we are about to witness is the starting point. It is called *Time*. And even though this is an unfamiliar concept, we will learn. Here, in the magnificence of eternity, our Sovereign God will lay his foundation and create a new dimension, a physical universe."

None of us had any idea of what that meant, but our bodies tingled as the Almighty commenced. Amber-hued clouds interspersed with sparks of fire billowed from the throne.

The Son spoke, "Let the heavens and earth emerge."

Heaven's plains turned into a majestic arena. Before our eyes, above and circling, appeared a vast blackness, and its massive, unlimited quality enveloped me. Never before had we witnessed the absence of light, but there it was, deep and seemingly endless. "God dwells here, in Heaven, with us," I said under my breath, trying to calm myself. "The Almighty is Heaven's light, and he is our light. In him, there is no darkness. So, what is this?"

I shook off my apprehension and sensed the blackness was not empty. Something was there. Although it emerged dark and formless, it oscillated, generating a sound of flowing liquid.

"This immense blackness, called *Space*," Gabriel said, "contains within it *matter*, the foundation and building block for all the LORD will create. Our Great and Glorious King has made something out of nothing. A feat only he can do."

Praises issued from the angel-filled plain as the Spirit of God moved and hovered above the invisible matter. With infinite authority, resplendent light, and the absolute supremacy of his Holy Spirit, the Son again spoke, "Let light be."

His voice raged above us like a blast of wind, reverberated in our ears, and penetrated the matter. Crackling sounds, sparks, and flashes spiked from it, creating a prickling sensation unlike anything we had previously felt. Everything brightened, and the black seemed to have length, width, and depth.

"Good," thundered the Almighty.

With the entrance of light, we could almost see this unformed matter God called his *foundation*. While we watched, a portion stirred and took shape. In every direction, as far as the eye could see and beyond, round specks splashed onto the screen of blackness. Some were larger than others, but each unique.

At once, an ethereal melody emanated from the circular particles and floated over the plains of Heaven. The music triggered an uncontainable joy within us. Shouts of praise sprang from my lips and what sounded like the lips of every angel.

Simultaneously, God caused the orbs to move into what I would call groupings, so many I couldn't count them all. But one variegated group of nine appeared a bit lost. As we viewed this mystifying event, the light diminished, and the darkness returned like a curtain descending at the end of a performance. Disappointed it was over so quickly, I began to depart, not realizing light had resumed.

"Michael, get back in place," Gabriel whispered. "God is not finished." I gasped and hurried back. As I slid into place, I looked over at Lucifer. He shook his head and let out a muffled laugh. Capitalizing on my blunders was one of the changes I'd noticed in him. My face felt hot. Nothing got past him anymore, and worse, it seemed he never slipped up. But I wouldn't let him spoil this moment. I closed my eyes, concentrated on the greatness of God, and just breathed.

When my eyelids rolled open, Gabriel had turned toward the audience. "As you can see," he said, "the Lord God has divided the light from the darkness. The light he is calling *Day*, and the darkness he has named *Night*. Therefore, you have observed dusk and dawn the *first* day."

A grin crossed my face. Gabriel's use of the word "first" excited me for additional *days* to follow, and somehow, things began to make sense. Peering out into the newly created *Space*, we watched God zoom in. He focused on the straggling group of nine and one particular minute sphere. It was the fourth smallest orb. Nothing exceptional, but it seemed the Almighty had taken an unusual interest in it.

"Let an expanse separate the waters to create water above and below the expanse," commanded the Son.

Immediately, God magnified our view, zeroing in on this specific globe. Its face had turned a radiant, deep blue, and we beheld five transparent layers, one after the other, wrap around it as if this blue orb were a gift. The fourth layer was different. Although it, too, was see-through, I detected liquid of some type because it stirred, distorting my view.

Suddenly, in sight, we plunged into this liquescent layer and out the bottom, but it wasn't liquid at all. It was some sort of dense vapor that appeared watery. Exiting the layer's underside, we quickly descended through two more and found ourselves hovering in the glorious blue expanse. From this vantage point, we could easily see the waters above and below.

"The expanse between these waters," Gabriel said, "the Most High is calling, *Heaven,* or more accurately, *Sky.* This will be considered the *first* Heaven. The larger vastness high above is the *second* Heaven. Likewise, God dwells here, with us, in what henceforth shall be known as the *third* Heaven."

I nodded my understanding while the blue orb tilted and began to move, spinning ever so slowly like a cockeyed top on an invisible shaft. "Dusk and dawn," Gabriel announced. "The *second* day."

We lingered in the light of the third day, drifting in the beautiful blue expanse over undulating water. Once more, the Son spoke, "Let the waters under the heavens be gathered together into one place and let dry land appear..."

The water rippled, swelled, splashed, and separated as a mammoth, grayish-brown mass ascended from its depths. The land rose dry, except for a few pockets of bluish-green liquid scattered throughout. Surrounding this huge landmass, the waters slapped its shores, but they could not overtake it.

"The dry land," Gabriel explained, "our Sovereign LORD has named *ground, clay, soil,* and sometimes, *earth.* Also, for now, the waters he has called *seas.*"

From the throne, the Almighty declared, "It is good."

"Let the earth bring forth grassland," the Son ordered, "with flowers, herbs yielding seed, and trees bearing fruit that contains its own seed so each may produce according to its kind."

Instantly, a palette of color exploded on the scene—greens, oranges, yellows, blues, reds, and purples in every shade and combination. My mouth dropped open, and my heart filled with the astounding transformation. But again, light faded to black, and Gabriel said, "Dusk and dawn, the *third* day."

With bated breath, I anticipated the fourth. Each day of creation had been more exciting than the last. As light returned, the colors were back. The Son said, "Let there be lights in the expanse to divide the day and the night. They will be for signs, seasons, days, and years."

Our view zoomed out to the second Heaven, called *Space*. The billions of round specks now glimmered like white and yellow diamonds scattered on black velvet. Most dots twinkled brightly, and some much brighter than others. However, a number of tiny ones remained only dimly lit.

The Son commanded, and one of the diamonds flew swiftly to the center of the unlit nine. Its flaming-yellow brilliance reminded me of God's Shekinah, and its enormous size greatly exceeded the nine and many others, but not all.

While this giant glowing ball took its place, Almighty God brought the nine into order. He placed his favored blue orb third in line and turned his attention to the dim, petite balls in *Space* that contained no light of their own.

The Son scooped up a number of these smaller spheres and sprinkled them into the area of the nine like pebbles. Some of the larger globes captured quite a few heavenly stones, but the blue orb held only one. And the moment these pebbles dropped into position, they glowed, reflecting the dazzling radiance of the flaming ball.

Speechless, I watched as dawn again turned to dusk. When the small blue orb had nearly completed another full revolution, Gabriel stepped forward. "For the blue orb named *Earth*, the LORD intends this lesser globe to produce a distinction between the time of light and the time of darkness."

Pointing to the immense, blazing central sphere, Gabriel said, "This nobler light will rule the day. It shall be called *Sun*. And the softer luminary will rule the night. Its designation is *Moon*. The others out in the vast expanse will be referred to as *Stars*. Angels," he said, pausing. "What you see reveals the glory of our great God. And now, dusk and dawn, the *fourth* day."

There we stood on Heaven's plains, dazzled by the scene before us. I scanned the ocean of angels, beginning with Gabriel and ending with Lucifer. Most faces wore a look of awe, but Lucifer scowled. I nudged Gabriel and whispered, "What do you think that's all about?" Gabriel shrugged and dismissed it.

To me, Lucifer looked annoyed. We've seen God do incredible things, but nothing compared to this! *So, why the scowl?* Something's definitely off, and I need to find out what.

Sighs coming from the angel armies snapped me out of my thoughts. God was zooming back in on the blue orb, and I almost missed it. As our view skidded to a halt, we hung, suspended in the sky, overlooking Earth's lush, green carpet. Tall trees swayed ever so slightly, but what caused them to sway, we couldn't see. Caught up in the beauty of the LORD's creation, the Son startled me when he said, "Let the waters be filled with marine life and let birds fly through the sky."

At once, the seas teemed with beings of all sizes, shapes, and colors. They glided through the water, darting this way and that, diving deep, jumping high, and splashing down again and again. At the same time, entities with wings similar to ours fluttered across the blue sky and right into our faces, or so it seemed. Their colors and sizes varied. Some had longer necks than others and differently shaped facial orifices, but body-wise, the birds were alike—sleek, oval-shaped bodies entirely covered with feathers.

"It is good," the LORD God proclaimed. "Now, let every winged bird and aquatic beast multiply by staying within the construct of their kind. This way, they will fill the earth and seas as I command."

To explain my joy in seeing this breathtaking creativity would be impossible. I inhaled deeply as contentment filled my being, and the earlier frustration with Lucifer evaporated. When the light faded, and Gabriel declared, "Dusk and dawn, the *fifth* day," I wondered if there would be a sixth.

CHAPTER 8

SHOCKING NEWS

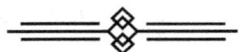

In the sunrise of the sixth day, God transported us a little closer to Earth. Birds and sea life busied themselves, yet they scattered when the Son commanded, "Let the earth bring forth living creatures according to their kinds…"

Living creatures? Promptly, the vibrant-colored landmass sprouted beings of all sizes, shapes, and configurations imaginable. Some gigantic, possessing ferocious teeth and claws, while others were small and delicate. Most walked on four legs. Still, many crawled through the soil with more legs than I had ever seen. Each creature was unique and as different as the next. I held my breath. All this diversity had come from the mind of our God.

"Good," said the LORD.

Awed, I shook my head, expecting the light to dim and bring an end to the sixth day. But yet again, God wasn't finished. As though in unison, the Most High spoke, "Let Us make man in our image, after our likeness…."

Despite hearing God's words, I could not understand what he was saying. *Man in his image?* What is *man?* A new creature? And what does he mean by *image?* Appearance or something else? Either way, why would the LORD God lend his image? And, for that matter, how is it even possible? He is Spirit.

Questions overwhelmed my mind, taking in the expressions of my fellows. I was not the only angel shrouded in uncertainty over the Almighty's proclamation.

"We will give him dominion over all the earth," the LORD continued, "over every nonliving and every living thing we have created."

Dominion? Over the earth? What is *dominion?* Every step of this process left more questions than answers. A man in his image with dominion over the entire orb he just created? What did it all mean?

The Sovereign King dug through the grass-covered land, scooped up some clumpy, moist, brown clay, and worked it, shaping several pieces. *Is this man?* If it was, why wasn't God speaking him into existence as he had the others?

The Almighty fit the molded portions together as though following a pattern. There was a ball at the top and a rectangular-shaped middle section with four long, slender appendages. Two were shorter, and these he placed on each of the upper sides of the rectangle just below the ball. The two longer limbs he attached to the bottom. It was a beautiful sculpture, as sculptures go, but lifeless. After a brief pause to admire his handiwork, the LORD God leaned over, breathed into the sculpture's nostrils, and the man lived.

I gasped. This was unthinkable and so beyond me. I couldn't move. *Our Holy God intimately touched his creation! How? Why?* I had no words.

My cheeks puffed as I rubbed my forehead and exhaled while the Most High moved his hand and created a garden. In it, he deposited every tree and living plant. Shimmering rocks and gems littered the landscape, along with lush greenery, flowers, air, and land beasts. A spring of water gushed from its center, creating four rivers. On either side of the frothing water, the LORD God planted two special trees. One, the Tree of Life, he uprooted from the grounds of Heaven's Ivory Palace. The other was unlike any tree we had ever seen, either here in the third Heaven or of Earth's trees.

The Almighty escorted the man in and spoke kindly to him. "Tend and keep this garden I have named *Eden*," he said, "for I AM the LORD your God. You are Adam, and I will be a father to you."

Father? It occurred to me I knew the name "God the Father," yet I had no concept of what the "father" part meant. Adam nodded, and it was evident he knew. Could this be something God gave to man and not angels? Maybe, but on the other hand, we angels had eyes to see God's glory standing before Adam. The man sort of hunted for him when he spoke. "Gabriel," I whispered, leaning toward him. "Is it possible Adam only hears the Almighty?"

Gabriel scrunched his face. "I hadn't thought of that. But yes, I think you're right."

God walked the man through Eden, and as Adam observed the vegetation and living creatures, I could tell he had sight capabilities. *So, why doesn't Adam see the presence of the Most High? Was this privilege given only to angels?*

Coming to the center, the area of the two trees, they stopped. "Every tree's fruit is tasty and edible," the Almighty said, "especially this tree, *The Tree of Life*—eat your fill. However," he said, moving to the second tree. "This tree, *The Tree of the Knowledge of Good and Evil*, you must not eat its fruit. If you do, life will flow from you, and you will die."

Die? Another foreign word. I was just about to ask Gabriel, but Adam bowed low and said, "Yes, Father, I will obey."

"He talks!" I said, elbowing Gabriel.

"Very interesting," he said, nodding.

When they had come full circle, God paraded the living creatures before the man. And as each twosome passed, the LORD said, "Adam, please provide a name for this male and his female."

Although there were apparent differences, males and females of every kind appeared similar. I had no knowledge of male and female, but Adam seemed to comprehend. Still, in the naming of the pairs, something happened. Adam's countenance, his outward facial expression, dimmed. I wondered if he noticed, as I had, God created male and female of every creature, but for Adam, there was no female. Adam was alone. *Is this why he seems downhearted?* Could he have been longing for companionship? Did I understand this yearning? Possibly, yet I also knew how the Almighty worked. He never did anything without a reason and a plan.

In the middle of the afternoon, God caused Adam to close his eyes and rest on a patch of soft grass. The man appeared lifeless again, except for his rising and falling chest. While in this state, the LORD God took his finger and sliced the side of Adam's body. Out oozed a bright red liquid. I winced, and then cringed when God reached in and plucked something from the opening that resembled a short stick dripping with the red fluid.

He sealed the cut in the next instant, but the man's eyes remained shut. The LORD caressed the gooey rod, squeezed and wadded it up like the clay from which he made Adam. I shuddered and tried to look away, but I couldn't. He molded the clump into another creature. It was almost identical to the man, yet very different. "Ah," I whispered. "This must be Adam's female!"

Delicate, with a rosy-tan covering, the female lay motionless in the soft grass. This sculpture was even more beautiful than Adam and unlike anything I had ever seen. Yet, as I wondered how the Almighty would make her the man's companion, he did that same inconceivable thing. Into this creature, he also breathed his breath of life.

Aroused from his sleep, Adam noticed the scar on his body. "Father," he said. "What is this?"

For the moment, the LORD's presence veiled the graceful human. But in answer to Adam's question, God stepped aside. As his Spirit shifted to the left, he revealed his newest creation, formed from Adam's rib.

The man gasped, adjusted his stance, and stared at the new human while the LORD explained. The lovely creature stood silent before Adam. Smooth, elegant limbs hung gently to her sides. Long, brownish-blond hair streaked with golden highlights framed light pink cheeks and ruby-red lips. Wispy curls softly caressed her shoulders and extended down as a cascading waterfall. With eyes round and clear like deep pools of blue water, she watched Adam. He circled her and observed every detail. He seemed utterly enchanted.

Adam reached the place where he started, and his mouth curled up at the sides. "Aha!" he said. Turning toward God's Spirit, he bent his knee and bowed his head. "Thank you, Father."

"Interesting," I whispered to Gabriel. "These beings not only communicate; they appear to think, reason, learn, feel, and worship." He just shook his head.

Adam stood, clutched the creature's hands, twirled her around, and exclaimed, "You are bone of my bones and flesh of my flesh. You shall be called *Woman*, Eve…because you were taken out of Man."

"Gabriel," I said softly. "Don't you wish the humans could see what we see?"

Seemingly enamored with the sight before him, Gabriel remained motionless. "I do," he finally said. "But even though they cannot view their Creator's transcendent glory and pleasure, they hear his voice and feel his presence."

I shook my head in agreement and turned my gaze back to creation. Our Omnipotent God stood before the couple. As their hands touched once more and linked, he united them with these words, "Therefore a man shall leave his father and mother and hold fast to his wife, and they shall become one flesh."

The Most High appeared delighted by this simple union. And while I did not grasp the whole meaning, I had the great privilege of witnessing it.

Almighty God placed his hand upon their foreheads, blessed them, and explained how he expected them to be fruitful and multiply. "I have given you dominion over this sphere I've created," he said to Adam and Eve. "Bring it under your control, and fill it with your children."

"Ah," I said quietly. "Dominion…but what are children?"

"Come," God said, pointing to each intricate garden detail. "See these herbs and fruit, yielding seeds? They are your food. Every other green herb shall nourish my air and land creatures."

The two nodded understanding and bowed. Soon, light faded, and a watery mist arose from the ground, sprinkling them and covering the greenery. Everything glistened in the moonlight.

"Very good," the LORD said, surveying his creation.

At the same time, our view pulled back, and we could see it too. "Phenomenal!" I cried, dropping to my knees, humbled by his power.

Once more, Gabriel stepped forward. "Angels, what you are witnessing, shouts the glory and majesty of our great God and King. It demonstrates the art of his skillful hands and the love with which he creates. Now, dusk and dawn, the sixth day."

On the plateau and on Heaven's plains, we angels waited, wondering what else the Almighty would do. But as darkness diminished and light returned, he remained on his throne. Then, as in the beginning, God's voice whooshed over us and reverberated in our ears. "Blessed," he said. "My Universe is now complete—finished. Blessed is my creation. Blessed and holy is this seventh day. It shall be a respite, a day I have given for the good of all mankind."

"All mankind?" I whispered to Gabriel. "Are there more humans we haven't seen, or does God plan to create more?"

"Michael, the word I have is what you heard. I don't know any more than you do."

"Let them rest from their work," the LORD said, "as I am doing from mine. They will use this day to renew their minds and bodies, to contemplate, and reflect on my goodness and provision."

Oh, I see—a separate period for worship, just like us. "God be praised!" I said, quickly extending my wings to unite the archangels in adoration. Gabriel's face beamed when our wingtips touched and linked. As my wing reached over to Lucifer, he hesitated, glared, and appeared reluctant. Finally, he unfurled, and our tips joined.

Below the Almighty's throne, our three-fold illumination exploded across the plateau. The white-light struck Lucifer's gems and did what it always did. It produced a spectacular array of colors that streamed down to the angel armies. In the beauty of God's holiness, the under-angels kneeled, and Lucifer's glorious melody united us in worship.

But soon, he withdrew his sensory projection, detached, folded his wings, and our illumination fizzled. Worship ceased. "Lucifer!" I whispered. "What are you…?"

"Every day," the LORD said, interrupting, "but especially the seventh day of each week, let my children call to me, and I will answer. I will show them great and mighty things they do not know, for I love them with everlasting love."

Speechless, I worshiped alone and wondered what part I would play in God's new world. Then, moving from his place, Gabriel stepped forward. "Angels, our assignment will be as ministering spirits to these humans, aiding all who will receive salvation."

Again, the word *"all"* and another word I didn't understand, *"salvation."* I wanted a moment to ponder, but Gabriel didn't pause.

"We angels are of a different dimension, one invisible to humans," he said. "As such, we are forbidden to make ourselves visible or to interact unless sanctioned by the Almighty."

I jerked and cocked my head. Was the difference in dimensions why the humans could not see God?

"Nevertheless," Gabriel said, "we are required to protect and help guide them in God's plan for each of their lives."

"The LORD had a plan for each human?" I said to myself. "And his plan involved angels? Shouldn't we have prepared for such a duty?"

Gabriel continued. "We shall be called to Earth to serve as needed, but most will remain here for now. The Omniscient God has delegated an angel taskforce to the blue sphere to keep all flowing smoothly and summon additional angels should an occasion arise."

An angel taskforce? My brows furrowed. I was God's guardian archangel. I was the obvious choice to lead such a detachment, yet I'd heard nothing. "Psst…Gabriel…Gabriel." He ignored me.

Spanning the crowd, I saw expressions of suspense and anticipation matching mine, but then my eyes caught a glimpse of Lucifer. He appeared unaffected, almost like he already knew the answer.

Gabriel cleared his throat and diverted my attention. "This elite unit has been hand-picked by Archangel Lucifer, and it will be under his command." Cheers and applause erupted.

"Lucifer?" I whispered as my brows creased. *Why Lucifer? And why am I among the last to know?* I glanced in his direction at the same time he looked toward me. Lucifer's scowl had transformed into a self-satisfied smirk. He flipped his hair off his shoulder, strolled forward, and waved to his fans.

With each move, I detected a growing arrogance. Lucifer cocked his head, and once more, our eyes locked. I swallowed hard. It was as if he knew my inward thoughts—my utter shock. He hiked his shoulders, puffed his chest, and turned back to his admirers. Their accolades somehow fed his condescending attitude and boldness.

But as usual, no other angel saw this, and everything inside of me screamed. I couldn't shake the feeling that nothing good would come if Lucifer were to take on this role. Oh...I must speak with the Almighty.

CHAPTER 9

A CHANCE ENCOUNTER

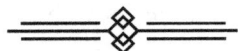

Just beyond Heaven's eastern perimeter lay God's newly created universe. Its beauty and depth only he could have imagined. Holding my position on the Mount of Holiness, I watched the angel armies calm and return to their perfectly regimented status after the revelation and, in my book, most shocking news.

When our gathering wound down, Gabriel motioned for departure. Moving from before God's Shekinah into the side area and down the west perimeter staircase, we reached our places on the intermediate level. The cherubim commenced their thunderous preparation for transfer. As they lifted the Most High, we and every angel present bowed in adoration.

Suspended between the wings of the cherubim, the LORD in all his glory began to sail toward Ivory Palace. While the Almighty passed, the angels in each army section raised, saluted, pivoted to follow his trek, and remained at attention until the cherubim completed their transport. Gently and ever so reverently, they descended and settled the Holy One into his Throne Room.

Gabriel stepped forward. "Angels," he said. Each soldier rotated to listen. "This concludes our activity. As archangels, we look forward to working with you in God's new creation. And we hope you are as excited as we are to learn about it. Every angel will have some part in keeping all things in the center of God's will."

Applause rose from the plains, and Gabriel bowed his head, grateful for their acceptance and inferred compliance. Captain Greysiel took his cue. "Angels...dismissed," he shouted.

The plains, appearing like a colony of honeybees, came alive with movement. Some angels walked, some flew, and some congregated in groups, enjoying conversation and downtime. I lingered for a moment to observe. I had trained these soldiers, and although their numbers were almost uncountable, they were close to my heart—each one unique and pleasing to the eye.

I took a deep breath, and as my chest rose, a smile crossed my face. How amazing the Almighty was to give all angels a part to play in his creation. I'd always heard him say everyone was useful to him, no matter their rank. The lowest private was as beneficial as an archangel. And even though God created us with rank and hierarchy, he showed no partiality. A perfect diplomat, and yet, at the same time, he was the God of order. Rank and obedience conveyed order. It was that simple.

I turned to exit and realized I was alone. Gabriel must have hurried back to the Scroll Room. And Lucifer? I figured he just returned to whatever else he had been doing before creation, or he flew off to the Garden of Fiery Stones again. *Who knows?*

It really didn't matter where he went. Lucifer hadn't been the best company lately. And when we did talk, it was as though he was frustrated or disturbed either by me or something else. *Did God's choice of Lucifer as taskforce leader cause this?*

"I don't know," I mumbled. "I'm the guardian. It's my nature... no...my duty, to be vigilant and careful. What I don't understand, I question."

Lucifer's strange behavior was new. "Stop Michael," I whispered. "Be cautious, he's your equal." I knew that, but something wasn't right. I needed a plan to find out what and why. The question was, how? My cheeks puffed as I exhaled. "I should think it through first, then approach the Almighty."

Descending the staircase to ground level, the trees bordering Heaven on the west caught my attention. They towered above me, yet it wasn't like I hadn't seen them a thousand times before. Still, this moment was different. The stately, tall, majestic trees with their lush green leaves seemed to beckon.

God created Heaven's east and west perimeters similar. The trees near the edge of the plains grew less dense to accommodate the multicolored shrubbery and walkways. Nevertheless, the deeper one walked toward Heaven's border, the thicker the trees. I scratched my head. The trees appeared so compressed an angel could easily disappear. *Silly thought.* I dismissed the notion, and as I stepped toward the clearing to launch, a strange feeling compelled me to walk to the Armor Room. So, I did.

Heaven's plains were massive, and the city, a considerable distance from the Mount of Holiness. I'd walked quite a way, yet every time I thought of flying, that feeling kept my feet on the ground. It was an odd sensation, something I'd not experienced before. Still, I heeded it and kept walking.

A small, decorative garden with a soft bench came into view. "I remember this. It's the seat I used when I contemplated the strange connection with Lucifer during worship." While I sat, I pondered all I had witnessed, Lucifer's behavior, and why I was walking.

The bench faced the plains, the east perimeter, and God's new creation. Before, I had nothing to observe or even think about beyond Heaven's borders, yet neither did I know something like the universe was possible. But now that it was here, it was hard to imagine Heaven without it.

Still, all these experiences required more careful deliberation, and I knew I had been absent from the Armor Room for far too long. So, feeling or no feeling, I decided to fly.

As I readied myself to launch, agitated voices from way back in the west perimeter trees drifted my way. I couldn't see anyone, but I figured I needed to quell whatever tiff was about to take place.

I sprinted into the woods and skidded to a stop when I reached a huge open space. The trees weren't as compact as I first thought. *Why had I never noticed this before?* The trees were tightly staggered to give the appearance of denseness, yet there was substantial room between the tree lines—ample enough, I estimated, to hold several field armies. *Hmm...*

The vocal sounds got louder and even tenser. Nearing the voices, I recognized Lucifer's tone. The others, I assumed, were his taskforce. Their words were muffled for the moment, but when I stepped into the next opening, all became clear. Thirteen angels stood around Lucifer.

"Soldiers, enough!" Lucifer said. "Wyael, lead my team to spread the word and gather my followers."

"Wait. Spread the word about what?" I whispered as Lucifer jerked his head in my direction.

"Something the matter, Sir?" First Lieutenant Wyael said.

Lucifer held up his hand to the Lieutenant. "Never mind, just get going,"

Wyael swung around. "Angels. Ready. Wings. Launch."

The taskforce zoomed straight up, but Lucifer remained behind. And as I turned to exit, he yelled. "Eavesdropping, Michael?"

"No," I said, continuing my retreat.

He sprinted to my side. "Interesting, you would be walking in the perimeter trees. What are you doing here? Don't you have work in the Armor Room?"

I scowled. "Of course, there's always work in the Armor Room. Why do you care?"

"I don't."

"Okay. Tell me what your taskforce was spreading the word about."

His brows furrowed, and his eyes narrowed. "No, it's none of your business."

"Why? What are you hiding?"

Lucifer exhaled hard. "Nothing."

I pointed at him. "You're hiding something, and you've been avoiding me."

He chuckled. "That's just your imagination."

Moving closer, I stared directly into his eyes. "Is it? We aren't able to talk comfortably anymore. Everything is strained between us, and more importantly, you disconnected in worship. Why? And why have I detected a change in your attitude? What's going on?"

"Nothing's going on," Lucifer said, looking away.

"Well, I think there is."

He jerked his head and squinted. "Listen, Michael, if I need your input, I'll ask. But for now, quit spying on me."

"Lucifer!" I said, throwing my arms up, "I wasn't spying. I heard troubled voices, and I wanted to calm the situation. I didn't know it was you and your taskforce until I saw you."

"So you say. But what are you doing here anyway? Why aren't you in the Armor Room?"

I glared at him and shook my head. "I felt like walking. Does that bother you?"

"No."

"Seems like it does. You're edgy and hostile, and I still don't know what word your taskforce is spreading."

"You don't need to know," Lucifer said in a low, determined voice that pierced my core. "Stop meddling in my business."

Ignoring him, I continued moving back toward the walkway. "Are you hearing me?" he yelled, grabbing my arm and yanking me to a halt.

I shook loose from his grip. "What are you doing? Do you really think I care about what you were discussing with your taskforce?"

"Yes, I think you do. And I believe you will do anything to replace me as leader."

"Why would you think that?" I said, shaking my head.

He shrugged. "Oh, I don't know. Jealousy, maybe?"

That word struck a sour chord. "Listen, maybe I do have my reservations about you, but God's choice is God's choice. He does what he wills in the army of Heaven and now in his creation. No one can stop his hand or change his mind. I know that, and I accept it."

"Do you really?"

My hand flew out to him. "Yes, of course. What I don't accept is how odd you've been lately. Why did you disconnect during worship, and why did you give me those looks?"

Again, he chuckled. "That was nothing, Michael. You're too sensitive and always overreact."

I clenched my fists and released. "I don't believe I am. In fact, this encounter just solidified it. I'll figure out what you're up to, and I will speak to the Almighty. And just so you know, I'll also be watching you."

"Ooo, I'm scared."

"Mock if you want, Lucifer. I'll not let you harm Heaven or Earth."

"What makes you think I would harm them?"

"Call it a gut feeling." *But why did I think he might harm Heaven?* I had no idea, yet I knew I couldn't let that happen. "Lucifer. Watch yourself. Just because I can't put my finger on how or why, I know you're different."

He stepped closer. We practically stood nose to nose, and it sounded as though he growled as he spoke. "I'm no different. I told you it's your imagination."

I jerked back and glared. "It's not, but we're going in circles. I'm done talking. I need to go."

As I turned to leave, Lucifer seized my shoulders, halting my pivot. "Michael," he said in a voice that caused a chill to run through me. His brow crumpled, and as his eyes narrowed, I thought I saw a fleck of red streak through. It caught me off guard. I gasped, lost my footing, and stumbled back.

But Lucifer never let go. He gripped my shoulders even tighter, lowered his voice, and as his eyes pierced mine, he said, "You get this. You will not hinder me or my taskforce in any way. And if you try, I'll stop you. Take this as your warning; stay out of our affairs, or else."

When I heard those words, I rallied. "Or else what, Lucifer?"

He released my shoulders and shoved. "Just stay out of my business." I hit the ground as he turned and rocketed through the trees.

In a flash, Lucifer was gone, and I was left trying to make sense of it all. Bewildered, I picked myself up, walked back to the bench, and collapsed into it. The more I thought about our encounter, the more determined I was to speak to the Almighty. Plan or no plan, this was too important, and it could not wait. I must inform the LORD of Lucifer's threats and his peculiar behavior. "Who knows," I whispered. "Maybe I can change God's mind."

CHAPTER 10

CONTEMPLATION, RIVALRY, AND ORDERS

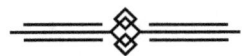

For the umpteenth time, I stood before the Throne Room doors, where my image reflected in the golden surface. The stoic sentry guards held their positions, but their eyes darted from me to forward and back to me as they waited for my order. I cocked my head side to side to stretch my neck, and smoothed my linen garments, while I contemplated my reason for meeting with the Most High.

When I nodded for the opening, the doors swooshed, drawing the Throne Room's serenity outward until it wrapped around me like a rope and dragged me inside. Kneeling in the presence of God's holiness, my anxiety melted, but not my concern.

The LORD's Shekinah glimmered and swirled around his being. "Michael," he said, causing me to rise, "you object to my choosing Lucifer as leader for Earth's Taskforce?"

I gasped. He already knew my thoughts and why I had come. In all my eons of service, I understood this omniscient character of our

LORD, but it always shocked me. I fought to swallow the lump in my throat. "Not objecting, Majesty," I said. "Just wondering why."

"I have my reasons. What are yours?"

"Sire, something's off with Lucifer. I can feel it. I don't know what it is, but you are all-knowing. Surely you feel it, too. I'm concerned he may do something to ruin your beautiful creation."

"Michael, I'm aware of your trepidation, but there are things at work you do not know, nor will you understand until they are complete. Remember, none, including Lucifer, can do what I forbid. I have work for him there, and I have work for you and Gabriel here.

"By the way, how are the angel troops shaping up? Are they battle-ready? Do you feel the Armor Room is well-stocked? Has each angel warrior been fitted?"

My head and shoulders drooped. I understood the Almighty was finished with my line of questioning, so I said, "My King, you know all, yet I will answer. Yes, the angel armies are in training. Most are so precise with their swords it's hard to declare a victor in the sparring. The only difference in their ability is in the variance of their creation, makeup, and the station to which you fashioned them. But peer-to-peer, they are equal in skill and power. They will please you, Sire."

"They do please me, Michael, as do you."

I bowed my head. "Thank you, LORD."

His Shekinah again stirred. "So, tell me more."

I shifted my stance. "Majesty, I continue to stock the Armor Room. New swords, breastplates, belts, boots, shin guards, helmets, and shields steadily come in from the Forge. They are cleaned, buffed, and shelved. But I still don't understand. Who are we to fight? Surely, not these creatures you just created; they seem so fragile."

"When the time comes, Michael, you will see."

Accepting I would not have the answers I sought or the Almighty's help with Lucifer, I sighed, and my eyes skimmed the floor. Suddenly, the Throne Room doors swept open. Randiel rushed in. He quickly bowed before the LORD and said, "Pardon the intrusion, Most High. Chief Prince Michael, Chief Prince Lucifer is in the Armor Room. He's there to collect weapons and armor for his team. What would you have me do?"

"Fascinating." I turned toward the throne. Fist to my chest and knee to the ground, I bowed my head once more. "Sovereign, I am needed."

"Yes, Michael. Go."

Angel sentries guarding the Armor Room flinched as Randiel and I swooped onto the threshold. They clutched the door handles and yanked, almost losing their balance in the opening.

"Lucifer," I shouted across the room, continuing a swift pace toward him. "Interesting, you would pick a time I'm not present to gather your gear."

"Ah, Michael," he said, snickering. "I just didn't want you to suffer any more humiliation by seeing me prepare for the Earth mission."

I stopped in my tracks. "What are you talking about, Lucifer?"

"Well, when Gabriel announced my name, I saw your face. You were shocked the Almighty chose me over you. And I know you were just in the Throne Room trying to get him to change his mind."

My eyebrows narrowed as my head flicked. "So what if I was?"

Lucifer clamped a hand over his mouth to hide his giggle. "Did he change his mind?"

"No." My face reddened as I tried to pass.

"Of course, he didn't." Lucifer grabbed me, pulled me close, and whispered, "I knew he wouldn't. Certainly, you must know by now you cannot outdo me."

I shook loose. "I wasn't trying to."

He raised his chin and thrust out his chest. "Remember, I was the foremost of God's creations. I am perfection. Everyone knows it, and I'm pretty sure you do too. The angels bestow on me the honor I deserve. And now, so does the Almighty. It's about time you do the same." Lucifer slid closer and said under his breath, "Michael, you cannot compare to me, so why do you even try?"

Shoving his shoulder, I pushed past him. "Enough of this nonsense. We are the same, created equal in every ability. Our only differences are appearance and station." I looked him square in the eyes and pointed. "And, you know that. The LORD has work for me here while you are working on Earth. But I warn you. Do only what God commands, or you will have me to face."

"Lighten up, Michael. You know I'm just messing with you."

"No, I don't. In fact, I believe this is exactly how you feel about yourself and the rest of us." I threw up my arms. "What happened to you? From where did this inflated ego come? Why do you see yourself above everyone else?"

Lucifer glared and inched even closer. With hushed tones, he said, "I am above everyone else. You just need to accept it."

I thought I saw red in his eyes again, and my breath caught. But I couldn't let him think he got the best of me. "Never," I spat back.

His hands pounded his hips. "Well, you don't have a choice."

"Lucifer, something's different about you." I stuck my finger in his face. "And, I will find out what."

He pivoted away. "I told you before; nothing's different. Gabriel's right."

I jerked. "You talked to Gabriel?"

"Yes. He believes you're jealous."

"I'm not!"

"You are. But I'm done talking. Just help me gather what I will need for Earth."

Lucifer baited me, and I bit. I looked around to see if Randiel heard any of our exchange, but no. He had gone to the rear door to check in a delivery from the Forge. So, as usual, there was no other angel to corroborate my theory about Lucifer. And before I could respond to him, the voice of the Almighty summoned me back to the Throne Room. "Lucifer," I said. "We'll have to continue this at another time. The LORD is calling."

"He's calling me as well. Let's go."

Lucifer and I arrived at the Ivory Palace at the same time as Gabriel. "Michael," he said, "do you know what this is about?"

"No, but I'm guessing it has something to do with God's new creation."

We hurried into the Throne Room and bowed before his Shekinah. As we did, the Son emerged from the radiance and said, "Ah, you're here."

"Majesty." I lowered my head. "How may we assist you?"

"We are prepared to have our second meeting with our human children and desire for you to accompany us rather than the cherubim. Our archangels need a closer look to understand creation, comprehend Earth's environment, and empathize with our children and creatures. As Earth's inhabitants increase..."

My head snapped up. "Pardon me, Sire. Increase? Are you going to create more humans?"

He nodded. "Yes, Michael, in a sense."

Gabriel chimed in. "What do you mean, in a sense?"

"Our children, Adam and Eve, will procreate."

"Procreate?" I said.

The Son smiled. "Yes, their physical makeup and the union of the man and woman will allow their fleshly bodies to produce tiny humans or children. Procreation, or rather reproducing, will be similar for every living creature, land, sea, and air. Each will increase in number—multiplying after their kind."

"After their kind?" I shook my head. "What does that mean?"

The Shekinah glory brightened while the Son explained. "Kinds are the different groups of creatures I've created. They all reproduce within their specific kind, and none shall procreate with a different one. Humans, however, are distinct. While they, too, are a kind and retain the procreation laws, only humans bear my image and contain a spirit. Unlike animals, birds, and aquatic life, their physical oneness will also create an emotional attachment and a bond of deep love between them. This, I've not given to my other creatures.

"At times, but not always, the oneness of my humans will create a little one, a baby conceived in the mother's womb with the blood and traits of the parents. When the child is ready, he or she will emerge from the womb and grow to adulthood, marry, and, in turn, bear children of their own. These are families: Father, mother, and child. But every baby conceived is my unique miracle of life."

I pushed my hair back. "Uh…Adam and Eve will have a child?"

"Yes, Michael."

"Oh…so…maybe now I understand the meaning of father, and …"

"Does this affect me, my taskforce, or the mission to Earth in any way?" Lucifer said, interrupting.

The Son moved back to the throne and absorbed into the Shekinah. "No, Lucifer. Your mission remains the same."

"But, LORD," Gabriel said. "I'm still not understanding what you meant when you said, in a sense, you will create more humans. By your description, it seems only the human male and female are involved in this procreation."

"Gabriel, very observant. Even though the man and woman will be intimately involved, all children, in essence, will be created by me. For life apart from me is nonexistent."

"Sir?" Gabriel cocked his head.

"I am Creator. In me, all things consist or hold together."

"Including Heaven?" I said, glancing at Lucifer, who had crossed his arms and now tapped his foot.

God's fiery brilliance shifted. "Yes, Michael."

Laying a hand to my chest, I inhaled deeply. "How does this relate to children?"

Lucifer paced back and forth in his space, yet the LORD ignored him and continued. "As Creator, we choose each child's personality, outward appearance, and abilities using unseen elements from the husband and wife. We form each one in their mother's womb, weave them together, if you will, and impart a spirit as their parents possess. I do this according to my will and sovereignty, for I have a plan for every child and predetermined work." God appeared to thrust out his arms in a panoramic span, and his Shekinah sparked. "From here, I see all children of all time, and each one is precious."

"How may we help?" I said as Lucifer let out a heavy sigh. My shoulders dropped, and I glared at him. *Why does he do that? And why...*

"You, my angels," the LORD said, refocusing my thoughts, "will assist according to my plan." Within my being, I could feel God's joy as he spoke. "You will protect our humans always in the spiritual dimension and sometimes in their physical one. And even though they cannot see you, remember, you are as real in your dimension as they are in theirs. Keep them safe from harm and watch over all Earth's inhabitants."

I cocked my head as my face scrunched. "Protect them? Keep them from harm? Master, what harm could come to them?"

Lucifer had stopped pacing and just scowled at me. I thought to address his issues, but the Most High began answering. "Angels, in due course, you will see. But, for now, our creation is new and exquisite. You must experience it firsthand to understand the natural laws we've created to govern this planet and the universe in which it exists.

"Familiarize yourselves with the lay of the land, the expanse of the sky, and the beauty and depth of the seas. Each contains diverse creatures. As well, become acquainted with the perfect layers we neatly wrapped around this little blue orb. I devised them to keep Earth warm, moist, and tropical, especially the fourth band. This layer I created as the Earth's seal and protection. All segments work together to preserve the dense layer of oxygen, nitrogen, and a few other elements you and the humans view as sky. It is the air they breathe."

I could barely take it all in. I wanted to ask another question, but God continued. "And because I AM All Knowledge and Wisdom, we supplied humans with intellect like we did you, for knowledge, as life, does not exist apart from me."

My eyes got big and my mouth dropped open. *Life and knowledge do not exist apart from God?* I needed a moment to ponder, but the LORD resumed. "In time, our children will build on their understanding by exploring this first Heaven and into the second. They will delight in learning about it and spend countless hours comprehending its secrets. But before they can examine the heavens, humans must acquire knowledge about the essentials of living and how to sustain themselves on Earth.

"So, with this visit, it's my will for you to observe our children in action. Grasp their sensitivity, delicate nature, and gracefulness. I created them in my image, and they are flawless."

Gabriel bowed his head. "Yes, LORD, we will carefully observe all."

"We are ready to travel if you are," Lucifer said in a huff.

I inched my hand up. "Majesty, before we go, may I ask another question?"

Lucifer's head whipped in my direction. "Now, Michael? Can't it wait?"

Sighing, I said, "I suppose it can, but…"

The Most High shifted, and ripples of fiery light radiated. "Michael, please ask."

Taking a deep breath, I exhaled. "Um…what does it mean that man is created in your image? I see, in one respect, humans resemble the Son as he steps out from your Shekinah. But…" I paused, patted my chest, and shook my head. "I don't understand how you can lend your image to a being."

"Ah, Michael, great question and a fundamental concept for all angels to grasp, but especially for the three of you." God's glory intensified as flaming waves wafted. "When we breathed into the nostrils of Adam, and Eve, his wife, we not only provided them with the breath of life, making each a living being, for if that were all I desired, I would have spoken them into existence as I did the other creatures. My breath infused humans with an eternal soul and spirit."

I took a step back. "So, are they like us?"

"Not exactly Michael. The human body is an outer shell housing their true essence, their spirit and soul. As I AM Three-in-One, they are, on a very small scale, three-in-one as well. Their body is physical; it associates with their environment. Their soul provides them the ability to relate to each other, as well as to my creatures and to me. However, their spirit allows them to communicate with my Spirit.

"Nevertheless, an image, for the most part, is a representation, a likeness of the true, but in and of itself, it is not the true. I AM the True. I AM Eternal God, and there is no other. They are merely a resemblance, and they will never be anything more. Do you understand?"

"To a degree, LORD," I said. "I'm sure I'll better comprehend once I observe them. But for now, this explanation is enough. Thank you."

"Gabriel, Lucifer, are you understanding?"

"Yes, Sire," Gabriel said, lowering his head. "As much as I am able."

"Lucifer?"

Expelling a heavy sigh, Lucifer said, "I don't see the significance of understanding. The flood of information you gave is enough for this visit. Can we just get going so I can get back to my taskforce?"

I jerked, shocked by how Lucifer spoke to the LORD. When I looked at Gabriel, though, he seemed unfazed by what I considered disrespectful. If an under-angel had directed this condescending comment toward me, I would have corrected him immediately. Lucifer was my peer archangel. Yes, he spoke to me this way, and that was one thing, but the Almighty?

"Just grasp this, Lucifer," the LORD thundered, interrupting my mental tirade. "I love my humans. They are extremely valuable to me, and their well-being is of the utmost importance."

I noticed something in God's voice I'd never encountered. I hoped this meant he also had detected the change in Lucifer. Still, it passed so quickly, I figured he hadn't.

"Angels," the Most High said. "These facts and the knowledge you gain on our trip will become increasingly important as time passes on Earth."

With God's firm comment, I sensed the conversation had concluded. I bowed low, and, taking my cue, so did Gabriel and Lucifer. "We are your servants, LORD," I said. "Ready to move at your word."

"Perfect. Michael, you take the lead on this mission. Let's depart."

CHAPTER 11

A VISITATION

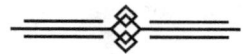

As a late afternoon breeze speared its way through Eden's tall grasses, the sound of the Almighty walking in the garden alerted Adam and Eve. I hovered above while Lucifer monitored things before God, and Gabriel patrolled from behind. From my vantage point, I could clearly see and hear the humans.

"It's the LORD," Adam called to his wife.

"Yes, I heard him, too," she said. "What should we do?"

"Let's run back to the place where he united us. Maybe he'll be there."

Eve set the basket she was weaving on the ground and sprinted to Adam. Together, they made their way through the trees, the swaying wheat and barley, and zigzagged in and out of towering corn stalks. They hurried past a pride of lions whose cubs frolicked with a troop of monkeys, and they arrived at their special place in perfect timing. The couple bowed low before their invisible, yet sovereign God, and acknowledged his presence.

I came to rest beside Gabriel. Our wings touched as we began illumination, marveling, and rejoicing with the humans. When I extended my other wing to Lucifer to complete our radiant worship. He acted as if he didn't notice and tried to look away. But I saw his face. It again held an odd expression. This time, though, it appeared as disdain. I tapped Gabriel and nodded in Lucifer's direction. Of course, when Gabriel looked, Lucifer had rotated, so he couldn't see his sneer. And just like that, he shrugged off my concern and disconnected his wing.

God moved his arm in a sweeping motion. "Children," he said as his Spirit wrapped around them. "Isn't this evening lovely?"

The humans were unable to witness the spectacle of the Almighty, but they gazed around at creation as if they had. "It is lovely, Father," the man said. "How may we serve you?"

"Let's talk. Do you have questions?"

"Oh, yes," Adam and Eve said in unison, as their eyes met and quickly turned back to the LORD.

Adam seemed to bob when he talked, and his arms conveyed his message. "We have questions about the land and air creatures here in Eden. They don't communicate with the same type of language you have given to Eve and me. And although we somewhat comprehend the meaning behind most of their roars, screeches, motions, and chirps, do they understand us when we speak? It appears they do, but we wanted to be sure."

"Excellent question. Yes, my creatures understand your inflections, tone of voice, and gestures. They also have a limited ability to learn, so you can teach them to obey your commands. This will become more necessary as time goes on. However, to fully comprehend the meaning behind your utterances is a skill I have not given them."

Adam stilled and tilted his head. "But what about the enormous land animals? Will I be able to command and train them?"

The LORD smiled. "Yes, Adam. Eve too. Each creature knows its place in the hierarchy of my creation. I made them with an innate subservience to humans. As the crown of my creation, you two will command them and harness their power. For under me, you, my children, have dominion."

"I remember, Father. Thank you."

"Master," the woman said. "May I ask about the sea creatures?"

"Ask, Eve, please."

"I noticed most of your sea creatures never come out of the water to eat the green herbs you planted for the land beasts. What do they eat? Are we to clip herbs and feed them?"

"Eve," the Most High said. "This is a wonderful question. I'm glad you care. However, I have fully provided for them as I have for you. But tell me, have you stepped into the water yet?"

"No, LORD. We've been busy exploring and creating a home. Should we?"

God's Shekinah glittered as he pointed toward the shore. "Oh, yes, please do. When you swim in the sea, you'll spot the underwater gardens I've planted. My creatures feast on such delicacies as sea and marsh grass, ferns, and algae. And have you noticed my floating hearts, water lilies, lotus blossoms, and water hyacinths? These lovely flowers I placed in the shallower waters of the inlets. They are a sight to behold."

Adam and Eve clasped hands. "We'll search for them tomorrow."

"Ah, good. Any other questions?"

Their eyes met. "I can't think of any. Can you, Eve?"

"Not right now. I'm just trying to remember all the LORD taught us today."

"Father," Adam said. "We'll have more questions the next time you visit."

"I'd like that. Until then, my children."

———— ⌄ ————

As we prepared to return to Heaven, I watched the humans. They seemed disappointed God was departing. "Oh, Adam," Eve said, "I can't wait until tomorrow." Her shoulders raised, and her eyes crinkled. Eve's smile seemed to touch each ear. Adam smiled back and clasped her hand. The two turned and moseyed to their resting place just as the evening mist rose and again watered the earth.

I felt like I wanted to stay, but Heaven was my home. I had duties there, as the Most High said. It was Lucifer, with his pleasant disposition, who had the honor of managing this place. *Yeah, I don't get it. Maybe I am jealous? Nah...can't be.*

While the three of us readied to escort the Almighty back to Heaven, the cherubim arrived with God's throne, and we jumped out of their way. The Almighty, encompassed by his ever-shifting glory, seated himself, and the cherubim took their place, surrounding and upholding his holiness.

"Lucifer. Michael. Gabriel," God said from between the cherubim. "We want you to continue your education and remain on Earth for several revolutions. Learn as much as you can in this brief period. You will need such understanding in the coming days, and you cannot obtain it if you're not here."

My mouth fell open. "B-but LORD, what about the armor?"

"And the scrolls?" Gabriel said, chiming in.

The cherubim began the transport. "There's no need for concern."

Lucifer tried to follow, but God's hand forced him back to Earth. "What about the taskforce, then?" he shouted. "Their training is incomplete."

"Again, do not be concerned. Spending a few days on Earth will seem to Heaven's inhabitants as though you were never gone. Everything will be as you left it when you return. Cherubim. Home, please."

"I was not prepared for this," I said.

"Michael, none of us were," Lucifer snapped. "It's certainly not what I expected for my first excursion on Earth. Why am I doing this with you and Gabriel? It should be my taskforce."

"It's a short visit, Lucifer," Gabriel said. "The Almighty wills it. Let's make the best of it and learn as much as we can."

Lucifer spun around and stomped off. "Fine! I'm taking Eden. You two can learn about Earth's outer edges, the sea, and sky."

"Agreed," I yelled. "But let's wait until first light, and after each revolution, we'll meet back here and switch study regions."

Lucifer halted and started back to us. He threw his arms in the air and said, "Why do we need to meet back here? Can't we just switch on our own?"

"No, Lucifer," I said. "We need to report on our region. By reporting our findings, the next archangel to observe the area will be better prepared. We'll review your discoveries and move forward with our own exploration. That way, we'll cover more territory."

Gabriel patted my shoulder. "Sounds good to me. Lucifer, are you in agreement?"

Lucifer hung his head and plopped down on the ground where he stood. "Obviously, since I seem to have no choice."

———⌄———

In the Throne Room, the cherubim settled back into their usual sentinel state while the seraphim flitted above, and God discussed his plan already in motion. "I know the archangels were surprised by this visitation," the Father said. "Still, they will learn what they need to learn and fulfill the roles we have assigned them."

"Yes." The Son nodded. "They are up to the task."

"But Michael and Gabriel won't see this coming," the Spirit interjected, "nor will they fully understand."

"Spirit, we know you long to help," the Son said, "yet this is something they must do on their own."

The Shekinah Glory brightened and waned as the Father resolved and concluded the conversation. "These two archangels will perform and fight as we created them to do, for this is our will."

———⌄———

CHAPTER 12

RESEARCH WITH CONFLICT

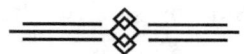

Since Lucifer had already selected Eden and the humans, I chose the sky as my initial study area. Gabriel picked the sea.

When the sun crested Earth's horizon, and glorious shades of reds, oranges, and yellows unrolled upward and melded into the deep blue, we dispersed. Light inched its way across the green-covered surface and awakened the creatures to begin their daily activity. The land beasts either scurried about or moseyed along to find morning sustenance. While I surveyed all the beauty, I couldn't help but be intrigued by the sky and the creatures not limited to land or sea.

Similar to birds, God created all angels with wings. Moreover, cherubim and seraphim each possessed six, but they differed from us. Most angels had only two wings, and our bodies, if you could call them such, were more akin to humans than birds. Angel wings, though, were in addition to our other appendages. Birds had wings rather than arms, and feathers enveloped their frame to provide a smooth, silky covering.

I noticed these creatures were more comfortable and agile in the sky than on the ground, yet I also realized they could not dwell only in the air. They needed the land and the items growing from it for food and shelter. And, although confined to this planet, their powerful wings lifted them and propelled them forward to fly through the blue expanse, just as ours did.

Caught up in the joy and ample space of the first Heaven, I decided to join them. Side by side, we flew, back and forth, and sometimes straight up and straight down. But these fowl appeared to fly only short distances and for brief periods before alighting in a tree or on the ground. "Very curious," I said. "Birds cannot do what I do. Did God limit their flight and energy supply? They appear boundless, yet the height they fly, the distance, and the length of their flight seem restricted by their need to rest and refuel."

The light streaming from the sun began to fade, and I recognized this from the days of creation. "How did Gabriel phrase God's word? Oh yes, dusk and dawn. This must be dusk." As I hovered in the evening sky, I noticed the sun gave the impression it had traveled from one side of Earth to the other. But I knew better; Earth's rotation caused this phenomenon.

Remembering I wanted to watch the birds at this time of day, I tore my gaze from the orange and yellow streaked horizon. When the light dimmed even more, most winged creatures found shelter in the trees. But soon, different birds emerged and took flight. I surmised daytime birds had trouble seeing without light, so they ceased activity. But the night birds seemed to excel in the dark. *Do they rest during the day?* I decided to observe them at daybreak.

"But for now," I said, looking up, "this fascinating night sky is calling." With the sparkle of the stars, I felt as though I could reach up and touch them, yet I knew their distance from Earth was astronomical. Peace and calm enveloped me as noise and chatter silenced. Day creatures rested, and night critters were nearly soundless as they prowled for food and munched herbs. I marveled. God must have designed it this way to produce ultimate repose for his creation.

Serenity begged me to stay right here, yet I was on a mission. I must examine the layers of atmosphere since God specifically mentioned them in his briefing. And I was curious about the thick fourth layer, the one that appeared liquid but wasn't.

Zooming upward through the lower three, I pierced this dense vapor stratum and perceived a thermal drop. *Oh...I see.* All five layers, but especially this fourth one, kept the sun's extreme heat and the frigidness of space from overpowering this planet, as they did with the other orbs in space. "What was it God said about this level?" I whispered. "Oh, right, it's the seal he created to sustain the planet's moisture and regulate its temperature." *My, he's thought of everything.*

Close to central Eden, Lucifer entered the grass and bamboo hut Adam and Eve had built. The structure appeared square with a cone-shaped thatched roof and a crossbuck-style door. Inside, the humans had crafted a rustic table and chairs, which they placed directly beneath the ceiling's peak at the room's center. Two long, but lower rectangular table-like items, topped with clipped tall grasses forming a sort of cushion, were placed side by side in the far corner. A high cupboard with shelves for bowls, cups, baskets, and utensils hugged the right wall, and an elongated chair, big enough for two, touched the left.

Their shelter was small, adequate for humans, but not roomy enough for unhindered archangel observation. Lucifer had to shrink to monitor their activity. He shifted his stance and hoped they would soon exit the dwelling. But instead, Adam and Eve drew close, touched their lips together, shared a sweet embrace, and each stretched out upon a cushioned rectangle. They talked for a while and soon became motionless. *What? No, no! Get up! Let's go!* Lucifer tried rolling Adam off the cot and onto the floor, but his hand passed right through him. *Now what? Why are these humans just lying there?*

He watched for a while and noticed their breathing was different— it was slower and deeper. *Does this stillness replenish their energy supply?* As the day went on, Lucifer had noticed their activity decelerated, almost as if the man and woman were experiencing a draining of sorts, an emptying out of whatever made them productive.

"Could this be their type of rest?" Lucifer whispered. "If so, is rest necessary to keep their bodies functioning?" *Possibly.* "Do they do this every time the light changes to dark or only once in a while?" Lucifer groaned. "It's such a waste. I guess I'll have to wait and see what happens when light returns. But…" he said, stroking his chin, "can I use this sedentary period to my advantage?"

Watching the humans in this activity seemed inefficient, so he decided to further prepare for the mission to Earth. Slinking out of the little cottage, Lucifer stretched and stood fully erect. "Ah, that's better." As he stood there, some night creatures scurried around his feet. He shuddered. "Ooo, these things are creepy. Shoo! Get away!" He kicked at one but missed.

Cringing, Lucifer tiptoed to a critter-free zone within Eden, yet still, no ideas came. He rubbed his forehead, pushed back his hair, and clomped around the area. Finally, he slumped down beside a tree. On the way down, a thought popped into his mind: *A map! I could definitely use a map, but I've nothing to draw with.* His shoulders slouched and then lifted. *Eden might yield sketching tools!*

He scanned the grass-covered area and saw only the flowing water in the distance. *Maybe I'll find something there?* As he stood, a crumpling noise caught his attention. Reaching into his pocket, Lucifer pulled out drawing materials. *Ha, look at that!* He had intended to jot down notes about the armor room before Michael and the Almighty ruined his plan. *But oh…this is a much better use.*

After examining the fifth layer of atmosphere, I descended to the first and again hovered high in the starry night sky. But just above the east horizon, a sliver of light washed over the landmass, heralding a new day. *Already?*

Rocketing downward to observe the night creatures at daybreak, I noticed an odd-looking bird with a flat face, hooked beak, and large, round eyes fly to a tree and perch. But then, a similar one crawled into a burrow in the ground. *So many details.* Would I ever learn all there was to know about God's creation and each inhabitant? *How did he even imagine such variety?*

"Michael," Gabriel called, jolting me from my thoughts.

I waved. "I'm over here. Is Lucifer with you?"

Gabriel shook his head. "No, he's not here yet."

Arriving at our meeting place, I said, "Don't you think Lucifer seemed obsessed with the humans yesterday?"

Gabriel wrinkled his nose and exhaled. "I don't think so. I think Lucifer was focused. He knew what he needed to study since he'll be dwelling here."

"That's no excuse." I huffed. "He was supposed to be back by now."

Gabriel's features softened. "I know running lead on a mission is difficult, but your plan is good. I have no idea what's keeping Lucifer. Maybe he lost track of time. It is a new concept for us."

"Yeah, I know. But maybe he's not coming at all."

Gabriel jerked and shook his head. "Why would you think that?"

I looked at the ground and back at Gabriel. "Lucifer is behaving strangely, but you haven't seen it. God commanded us to learn as much as we could about his creation. With the way Lucifer's been acting, I wouldn't put it past him to defy God's orders."

Gabriel gasped. "Deliberately disobey the Almighty? No, Michael, you're wrong. Lucifer would never do that."

Sighing, I said, "Just because no one has willfully disobeyed yet, doesn't mean someone won't."

"That's absurd, Michael. He's our peer archangel."

"Don't be so sure."

His face reddened. "Michael, no one is going to disobey God's perfect will."

"Lucifer might."

"No. I don't believe it's possible."

My shoulders slumped. "Okay, Gabriel, maybe it is possible, and maybe it isn't. Still, if Lucifer violates God's command to study all of Earth, it's his loss. I've learned so much about the sky that I can hardly wait to learn about the sea. How about you?"

Gabriel's countenance brightened. "Oh, the sea is magnificent. You'll be amazed. Make sure you observe the underwater plants. They're remarkable and so abundant. Every sea creature, from the largest to the minute, feast on these. It's fascinating."

With his words, I let go of my frustration. My tension melted and I smiled. "Good observations. The sky will astound you as well. I enjoyed the winged creatures, and be sure to take note of their flight patterns. They fly only so far and so long before resting. And, about the five layers of atmosphere, I don't fully understand how they work, so I can't give a complete report. But you will find them incredible. Maybe we can compare notes later."

Gabriel nodded. "Great idea."

"Thanks. For now, let's not concern ourselves with Lucifer."

"Agreed," he said with a grin. "You and I need to do what God asked us to do."

"Right. One more revolution, and we'll meet back here."

Finishing his sketch of Eden and the surrounding area, Lucifer folded his makeshift map and tucked it back into his pocket. With his work complete, the frothing river of central Eden caught his attention. It rippled and flowed steadily, reminding him of his chamber atrium and tranquility pool. As he sauntered closer, thinking to recline on the bank, a craving for ecstasy surfaced. *Would this water also produce his image?*

Moseying to the river's edge, Lucifer gazed at the brightening orangish-red horizon, and his desire faded. "I'll bet Michael is fuming," he said, snickering. *Why does he think he can order me around anyway?* "Data about Earth's regions could be useful, but I'm only here to learn about human vulnerability." Lucifer took a deep breath and stroked his chin. "Although," he whispered, "discovering how much Michael and Gabriel know about my change would be a bonus. Still, these inferior archangels have no idea I won't be meeting them this morning or any other morning." Lucifer's nostrils flared. "Nobody will research Eden or the man and woman...but me."

Spinning around, he extended his arms toward the two trees in the midst of God's Garden. "Ah, central Eden is my kind of place— spacious, lush, and beautiful. This is where I will build my dwelling when I come with my taskforce." Lucifer clamped his hand over his mouth to contain his laughter. "Eden is all mine!"

CHAPTER 13

LET THE GAMES BEGIN

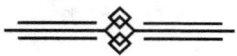

Trad he sun continued its wake-up call on Eden, and Lucifer returned to the human's shelter. As he observed from the doorway, Adam sat on his bed of soft grasses, raised his arms, opened his mouth in a wide oval shape, drew in a deep breath, and let out a sigh. He put his fists to his eyes and rubbed. Soon, Eve did the same.

"Finally!" Lucifer shouted, but he cowered, concerned they might have heard him as they had the Almighty.

Adam and Eve didn't hear Lucifer. The two seemed completely unaware of his presence. Thrilled, Lucifer danced around outside their hut while menacing schemes again pierced his mind, and a sinister grin emerged.

The couple shared a good morning kiss, grabbed a basket, and stepped out into the new day's sunlight. Not far from their shelter, they stopped at a patch of ground-level greenery. These plants bore red, triangular-shaped fruit. They each picked several and placed them into their basket, but paused now and then to eat a few. "Oh," Lucifer said with a chuckle. "They're gathering sustenance."

The pair continued searching for food until their baskets were nearly full. The last piece of fruit they picked was from the Tree of Life. Cushy, green grass beneath made it a perfect spot to eat breakfast and discuss the day's activities.

"This is boring!" Lucifer said, slapping his forehead. "I don't think I'm going to be able to do this for another day, let alone for however long the Almighty will have me here. I've got to liven it up." *Hmm…how can I make this more interesting?* "Well, I know the man and woman do not see me," he muttered, "yet they see the things of Earth." *Can I use that to my advantage?* "Seems the LORD has made it impossible for me to touch humans, and that's a problem. But maybe I can touch other things."

Lucifer scoured the shores of the four rivers and spied a good-sized rock. He reached out and felt its firm, cool dampness as his fingers clamped around it. "Yes!" he said. "I can handle inanimate objects. I wonder what will happen if I…"

He pitched the rock, and it landed beside Eve. Her body jumped at the thud. "What was that?" she said as Lucifer snickered.

Adam jerked his head in her direction. "What was what?"

"Something pounded the ground near me."

"That's not good." He set down his bowl and rose to his knees. "What was it?"

"I don't know!"

"Well, let's check."

Adam ran his hands through the soft grass on his side of Eve while she searched the other side, closer to the sound. "I'm pretty sure this is the culprit. It seems out of place here."

"A rock?" Adam's face scrunched. "That's strange."

"Do you think one of the monkeys dropped it from the tree?"

"Not sure. But if it was a monkey," Adam yelled, gazing upward and scrutinizing monkey activity among the Tree of Life branches, "it needs to stop now! Any rock dropped from such a height could damage us or one of the smaller creatures."

Lucifer chuckled and slapped his thighs. *That was just too easy.* After the humans settled, he whispered, "What else can I do to confuse them? Let's see...they don't hear me when I speak from a distance, but..." *What would happen if I spoke right into their ears?* Lucifer moved close to Adam, bent down, and whispered, "I'm thirsty."

Adam's head jerked up, and he searched as though he heard something but couldn't quite tell. "I need to get some water. I'm very thirsty."

"Really?" Eve said. "That's odd. Usually, we don't go for water until after breakfast, but we can go now if you want."

"Fascinating," Lucifer said, observing the pair heading to the spring. His fingers tapped his lips, "So...they hear my words in their ears. And... my words transform into their thoughts. Amazing! This I can use!"

In every location and each activity, Lucifer toyed with the humans. As dusk returned, Eve leaned on Adam as they walked. "Don't you think this has been the strangest day?"

His strong arm held her up. "I do. Nothing has seemed normal since breakfast."

"I hope tomorrow goes better."

"Me too, Eve," Adam said as they entered their shelter. "Me too."

At sunrise, Gabriel and I met at the gathering place. "Again, no Lucifer?"

"Relax, Michael," Gabriel said, trying to soften my dissatisfaction. "He's being thorough. I'm sure he just got caught up in observing and lost track of time."

His eyes carried concern, so I shrugged and kicked the ground. "I suppose, but somehow, I don't think so. I'm pretty sure this is deliberate."

"What?" Gabriel threw his arms out in my direction. "Why are you always thinking the worst about Lucifer?"

"Something's off with him." I sighed and formed an invisible circle with my hands. "I feel like he's a ball of thread wound around something not so good. And try as I might, I can't unravel it."

"So, you're implying Lucifer is intentionally not switching study areas?"

"Yes, I guess I am."

Gabriel shook his head and stuck his finger in my face. "Michael, no! Lucifer would not do that. He will be accountable for Earth's well-being, especially for human safety, so stop this absurdity. Lucifer needs to learn more about them than the sky or the sea. He'll have plenty of opportunities to learn about the other portions of Earth once he's settled here."

I pinched my lips together, inhaled, and exhaled. "I see your point, but I think you're mistaken. You don't know him like I do. Lucifer is trying to control this mission. God put me as lead, and I'm responsible for our current assignment, not him. I know he's up to no good."

"You're wrong, Michael. Lucifer's preparing for a successful operation with his taskforce. That's all."

Stepping closer, I said, "Listen, I've had a few strange encounters with him, and you haven't, so I get why you're hesitant to believe me. But I tell you, Lucifer's different than he used to be. I don't trust him."

Gabriel looked to the sky and then back at me. "Careful, Michael. You're letting God's choice of Lucifer for the Earth Mission really affect you. Jealousy is unbecoming."

I slammed my hands on my hips. "I'm not jealous!" I paced the area until I calmed. "Look, I admit I've been concerned, mostly because I don't understand God's reasoning. But Lucifer is trying to control this quest, and I'll not allow it. The LORD's commands were clear, and they must be obeyed. We need to find him."

He shook his finger at me. "No, we don't. We have one more day, and we need to stick to our assignment."

"Gabriel! Stopping Lucifer is more important."

"Well, if that's how you feel, you're on your own. I'm staying right here." Gabriel plopped on the ground and mumbled, "At least I'll be compliant with God's orders."

"Suit yourself," I said as I sprinted toward Eden. "I'll be back with Lucifer one way or another."

As I stepped in from the outland, Eden unfolded before me. Towering flora enveloped the landscape, creating a tapestry of emerald beauty.

Majestic creatures, some adorned with colossal ears and elongated snouts, moved with a graceful rhythm. Others reached for the heavens with their towering stature, sporting tree-like tails, long, slender necks, and diminutive heads that didn't seem to fit their bodies. Compared to these titans, I couldn't help but feel like a mere speck. Thankfully, they weren't interested in angels. These giants focused on consuming the lush banquet of leaves God had provided.

I tiptoed gingerly through the abundant greenery, and as I did, small creatures scurried around my feet. Smiling, I asked, "Where should I begin?" They stopped for a second and looked at me. "I can't fly," I whispered. "Lucifer would spot me before I could see what he was up to." The critters cocked their heads and then just went about their business.

Observing Lucifer in action would either calm my uneasiness or confirm it, so I decided to zigzag my way in from the perimeter. Nearing central Eden, frantic voices reached me.

"No, no, no! Not again today!" the woman yelled. "Adam! Why is this tree shaking? None of the others are."

Inching toward the sound, I came to the edge of a clearing. Parting the tall grass, I witnessed anxious humans.

"I'm not sure," Adam shouted back. "Maybe something is happening beneath it, under the ground. You better move away."

"Do you think the tree will fall over?" Eve cried, jumping to her feet.

"I don't think so. But it might."

I narrowed my eyes, homing in on the cause. Lucifer! Eve sprinted to Adam, and the two entwined their arms around each other. As they recoiled, Lucifer burst out laughing.

"What is he doing?" I said under my breath and continued to watch. Was he trying to play with them? If so, the play was not consensual. They were agitated. *But why? Oh, right…they couldn't see Lucifer.* Trees don't shake by themselves; they sway. Lucifer was causing distress and disobeying orders. *I knew it!* "God commanded us to observe only, not interact. I need to stop him."

Launching into the air, I landed beside Lucifer. He jerked and released the tree. "Michael! What are you doing here?"

"Obviously, terminating your disruptive play," I said. "What were you thinking?"

Lucifer chuckled. "Ah, it's all in fun. I was bored."

I stepped closer. "No, you were defying God's instructions."

He shook his head. "I wasn't! The Almighty said to learn as much as possible about Earth and its inhabitants. This is my way of learning."

Inhaling deeply, I looked toward Heaven and back at Lucifer. "The LORD God ordered us to observe and learn, not irritate the humans."

"Listen, you have your way of learning, and I have mine."

"Well, I've seen enough," I said, scowling. "This mission is over!"

"You can't call the mission."

"Watch me!"

His brows furrowed. "Michael, your jealousy is really starting to irritate me."

I pointed my finger at him. "I'm not jealous! Why does everybody keep saying that?"

"Because it's true and apparent to everyone but you."

My hands wadded up into fists and released. "I want you to obey God's orders the way Gabriel and I do. You're not, so I'm calling the mission."

"Okay, but you'll be sorry." Lucifer scanned the area. "Gabriel's not here. We can't leave without him."

"I know," I snapped.

Lucifer shrugged. "Where is he?"

"Outside Eden—the place where we arrived."

"Fine," he said. "I need to get back to my taskforce anyway. But you'll see, the Almighty will be on my side."

———⌄———

CHAPTER 14

REPORTS AND REPRIMAND

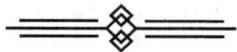

Although we had been on Earth for two and a half days, nothing in Heaven had changed. No one, except the Almighty, even knew we were gone.

The three of us entered the Throne Room and bowed before God's Shekinah.

"Michael," the LORD said as his fiery brilliance shifted from a soft glow to a towering inferno. "You have returned prematurely. Explain."

My eyes skimmed the floor as I searched for words. Looking up, I said, "Sire, I called the mission early first because we could not agree on how we should learn about Earth and its inhabitants. Too much liberty was being taken with your orders. And…"

"Since you are back, and you ran lead," the Most High said, interrupting, "please give your report and assessment."

I straightened my stance. "Yes, Sir. Um…well…Earth is exquisite. I saw things on this blue orb I could never have imagined. Examining the layers of atmosphere, I learned how you retain Earth's warmth and keep it moist so vegetation can grow, yet not so much that it is overrun with moisture.

"I also had a chance to study the order you built into this planet's flow. Everything works and runs its course according to your precise timing.

"One curious feature," I said, stepping toward the Almighty as if I were telling him a secret. "You created Earth with age." I shook my head and shrugged. "Earth appears as though it has been there for eons, yet we all know it's a brand-new creation. The hills and valleys, the soil and trees, and every creature came on the scene of full age."

The LORD stirred amid his Shekinah. Specks of fire spit, causing a glittering swirl that quickly softened. "Very good and true observations, Michael."

"Thank you, Sire," I said, bowing my head. "And from what you explained before our visit, I also see you created Adam and Eve with age, not as the tiny humans you mentioned. Is this how you created angels, except for the marriage and procreation elements, not of our design?"

As God answered in the affirmative, iridescent waves emanated from the throne, so I continued. "I found your birds could do some of what we angels do, but not all. You've set limitations for them, yet provided abundantly. It's all so perfect."

"Yes, Majesty, I agree," Gabriel interjected. "Earth is marvelous, especially the sea with all its creatures, from the itty-bitty to the colossal. The underwater vegetation they use for food, and the stunning flowers blooming on the water's surface. To say I was awestruck is an understatement."

The LORD lifted his hand. "Thank you, Gabriel and Michael. Lucifer, what did you learn?"

Lucifer displayed a wide grin. "Eden is magnificent. It's lush, abundant, and flawless. I wouldn't change a thing."

God's glory flamed white-hot. "Glad you're giving it your stamp of approval."

"Oh, yes, Sire." Lucifer held out his arms. "The creatures lack nothing. I observed the man and woman gathering food, tending and caring for the garden, and controlling the beasts, great and small. I witnessed human interaction, how they discuss and reason together. It's quite remarkable. I'm excited to begin the assignment with my taskforce."

"Interesting," the Most High said as his Shekinah sparked. "How is it that you are speaking only of your initial regions? Were the others not impressive?"

I gasped. "Oh, yes, LORD. I didn't mean to omit anything. The sea was also tremendous, and Eden too. However, by cutting the mission short, I could not observe much about Eden, the humans, or the land creatures. Still, there's so much more I need to say about halting our..."

"Sir," Gabriel said, cutting me off. "I found the sky, the birds, and each band of atmosphere incredible, just as Michael reported. I loved learning."

The Almighty shifted, and fire flashed, then receded. "So, Lucifer, you only studied Eden and my humans. And for this reason, Michael called the mission early?"

Lucifer lifted his chin and puffed out his chest. "Yes, Majesty,"

No, that's not the only reason! I held out my hand toward the throne. "Sir, if I may..."

"Not now, Michael."

My eyes widened, and my mouth clamped shut since my opportunity to explain ended.

"Lucifer," the Most High said, "express your ideas. How do you plan to oversee this planet and its residents?"

I stepped back and stood there, stunned, when Lucifer began to elaborate. I had expected the LORD God to chastise him or, at least, ask me the complete details, but no. The Almighty seemed...as Lucifer predicted, to be on his side. I glanced over at Gabriel, hoping for some empathy, but he appeared to be hanging on Lucifer's every word.

Why I thought Gabriel would back me up after he was so antagonistic on Earth, I didn't know. Still, this behavior was unlike him. He and I had always been close and connected. *Has Gabriel changed, too?*

Not seeing Lucifer toy with the humans could be a factor. Thinking back, maybe I should have insisted he come along. But even that didn't explain why Gabriel didn't believe me or, in some measure, consider my angst about Lucifer credible. And none of this explained why I was the only one who seemed to know these things.

God was omniscient and all-powerful. Wouldn't he already know Lucifer disobeyed without me saying a word? Why, then, was he letting him get away with it?

"Good report," the Almighty said.

My head snapped up. *What? Good report? No! It's incomplete. He mentioned nothing about what he did to the humans...and...and...*

"Lucifer," the LORD said, disrupting my mental tirade. "For a season, Earth, Eden, and all inhabitants are yours to rule and guard. Under my Kingship, you will be my overseer in the spiritual realm." Lucifer's chest puffed.

No…this can't be! Lucifer was still leading Earth's taskforce? And, now…ruling the planet? *How could I have been so wrong?*

The Most High raised his hand, causing his Shekinah to flicker. "In addition, you will have as many angels as you desire to help, yet, for the moment, the taskforce is sufficient. We expect you to give your all to this assignment. And Lucifer, I reiterate—our creation's well-being is paramount. We are bestowing upon you great honor."

"Yes, Majesty, I know," Lucifer said, bowing. "Thank you."

"Could this possibly get any worse?" I mumbled under my breath.

"Gabriel and Lucifer, you are dismissed. Michael, stay. I need to speak with you privately."

Oh no, it is worse! I looked in their direction and nodded adieu. Gabriel's eyes held a tad of concern, but Lucifer gloated. He smirked and snorted a chuckle, seeming very satisfied with his vindication and pleased with what he assumed would be my reprimand. And I wasn't entirely sure his assumption wasn't correct.

The two bowed before the glory of the LORD. Gabriel hastened through the doors, probably to return to his duties. But Lucifer waltzed out as if he'd won—fully expecting God to discipline me for calling the mission early. *Come on! Have the tables turned? Was I the one disobeying? No! I never disobey!*

Still, when the Throne Room doors swung shut, I swallowed hard. Turning to face the Almighty, I lowered my head.

"Michael," God said as I raised my eyes to Him. "Why are we detecting anxiety?"

"LORD, I called the mission early for many reasons, but mostly because I felt it best for Earth, the humans, and Heaven. Forgive me, please, if I made a wrong assessment."

His gentle voice comforted. "You are forgiven."

"Thank you, Sir. Is that all?"

"No, we wanted to speak with you privately because of these issues with Lucifer. Our will is for you to help him prepare for Earth. Do not hinder him. His work is there."

I sighed, and my stomach knotted. "I know I have issues with Lucifer. But, Sire, you don't understand. He's different than he used to be. Something's off. And try as I might, I cannot understand why all this escapes you."

God's Shekinah brightened and billowed. "Enough, Michael. You are dismissed."

"Majesty, please. Can't we discuss it?" I expected some kind of response, but the Holy God remained silent. I bowed my head, folded an arm to my chest, and my knee touched the floor. "Most High," I said, rising. "I am your servant. My only aim is to obey." I nodded a respectful farewell and withdrew from God's presence.

Once outside, my head and shoulders dropped. The weight of knowing I had disappointed the LORD kept them bowed as I walked the long hall. Reaching the Ivory Palace Great Room, I couldn't even lift my eyes to greet the angel caretakers.

Shuffling past them and out the palace door, I didn't understand anything that had just taken place. To my knowledge, I've never failed my Master. But now, for the first time, I believed my actions greatly displeased him. *How can I possibly bear this grief?*

CHAPTER 15

ARMOR AND SECRETS

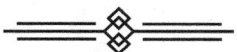

The Armor Room's tranquility washed over me as the anxiety of our Throne Room meeting retreated for the moment. Grateful for reprieve, I closed my eyes and just breathed.

This Grand Hall stood quiet and serene with rows of hand-polished armor. Gleaming swords lined the walls midway up. Above them, golden breastplates dangled, and suspended below were the matching shields. Belts, shin guards, boots, and helmets overlain with gold were neatly shelved beneath each set. Every rank held its own distinct section.

Organized to perfection, this room gave me satisfaction and a sense of accomplishment. I designed this systematic armor arrangement to allow any angel to dress for battle without hindrances. And even though no battles had been fought, preparation did not stop. We forged armor and trained hard as the Almighty willed, not knowing when or if we would be needed.

With Lucifer's team heading to Earth soon, this would be the first time armor was used for anything other than sparring. Yes, the sentries had armor, but not combat armor. I could only trust Lucifer had good intentions and that God would provide me with sufficient information when the time for battle arrived.

"Chief Prince Michael," Randiel said, rushing toward me.

Caught up in my thoughts and surveying the armor, I hadn't realized my steps had slowed. "Yes, Randiel?"

"Chief Prince Lucifer is here again. He was perusing the Armor Room. But right now, he's waiting in your office. And, Sir, he's not happy."

"Of course, he's not happy. Thanks for the heads up." Strolling past my office window, I opened the door and observed Lucifer pacing.

"Took you long enough, Michael," he muttered, pushing past me and gliding out into the Grand Hall.

"Well, hello to you too, Lucifer," I said, allowing the door to swing shut behind him.

"Enjoy your reprimand?" He snickered.

I flinched. "What?"

He waved his hand. "Never mind, let's just get down to business."

"Fine," I said, knowing I would never discuss the Throne Room conversation with him. "How many angels are you taking with you?"

Lucifer glided through the rows of armor. "Just the taskforce this trip. I'll see what's required once I'm there and adjust as needed."

As usual, I followed behind. "Why are you taking armor for the mission? Humans seem weak compared to us. I don't think they could harm angels even if they tried." Lucifer ignored me. So, I asked again, "Why are you taking armor?"

"Michael, I heard you the first time."

"So, answer," I said, trying to suppress my frustration.

He spun around and glared. "Fine. I've always wanted armor for Earth, but especially since our short visit. The place seems peaceful, yet I don't know what we'll encounter. Land creatures could become aggressive. Remember, animals see us. Humans don't. It's not up for debate. We're taking armor, and that's that."

Recalling the LORD'S command, I sighed. "How many suits will you need?"

"I have thirteen angels, and with my armor, it's fourteen." Lucifer creased his brows and stroked his chin. "I only wanted twelve angels originally, but something made me pick thirteen. Is that a problem?"

"No, not at all. Send in the taskforce. I'll fit them, and they'll be ready to leave at your word."

"Good. Expect them soon, but I'm taking mine now."

"Alright." I swung around and waved. "Follow me to the inner chamber. Our armor is there." As we walked, I explained how I had designed each Chief Prince's armor with a specific insignia that would identify us without removing our helmets. "Brilliant idea, don't you think?"

"I suppose so."

"Anyway," I said, "our insignias will enable us to command immediate obedience. The angel warrior, whether general, lieutenant, sergeant, or private, will know to whom he is speaking or from whom he is receiving a command. I'm convinced this will eliminate confusion during battle and accelerate a victory."

We exited the Armor Room's Grand Hall through the far door tucked into the side wall adjacent to our sparring equipment and near the receiving bay. A long marble corridor lay before us. It gently curved and led to the Armor Room's back entrance. To the left, at the hall's central point, lay a rustic wooden door with heavy iron hinges, bolts, and handle. At first, it seemed out of place in Heaven's elegance, but I've grown accustomed to it.

Arriving before this unique entryway, I grabbed the key tethered to my belt, unlocked it, leaned my shoulder in, and shoved. The inner chamber door creaked open.

"You keep it locked?" Lucifer said with an air of contempt.

"Yes! I thought it best, for now, anyway."

Lucifer shook his head. "Ridiculous. You're always too cautious. No one else can wear these articles. Why are you so guarded?"

"I know our armor is molded to fit only the Chief Prince who will wear it. Just seems right to keep them and the other special items in this room under lock and key."

"Other items, Michael?" he said, gazing left and right. "I don't see anything but armor."

What? I looked around the inner chamber. All the items were still there. *Why isn't Lucifer seeing these?*

I was about to ask when he pointed at me and continued his rant. "Your attempt at perfection is exasperating. Ever since the Almighty chose me for Earth, you've been different. So, let's get on with it. Give me my armor, and I'll be on my way."

I've been different? No, no. He's been different. And instantly, all my earlier thoughts dissolved. Trying hard not to show my frustration, I carefully lowered Lucifer's breastplate and held it up so he could see the symbol I engraved for him, a flame with a blazing red gem at its center.

"Interesting," Lucifer commented. "You picked this emblem all by yourself?"

"I thought it appropriate since you are archangel to God, the Father. But now, I'm not so sure. I think your head is already big enough."

"Actually, Michael, it's the first time you've gotten things right. The Shekinah Glory appears as fire, so a flame on my armor is perfect for my recognition. Let me try it on."

Lucifer donned his boots, belt, and shin guards before I buckled his breastplate into place and fitted his scabbard. He slid his helmet over his head, keeping the face plate open. I lifted his shield and held it as he slipped his arm through the handles. Lastly, I passed him his sword. He reached back and sheathed it, then drew it out again. Rocking the saber back and forth, he said, "Nice job, Michael. The armor fits, and the sword, well, it's perfect." He resheathed and shouldered his shield. "Do I have all the pieces?"

"Yes," I said. Lucifer turned and bolted. "Wait, let's test your armor."

"No," he yelled. And then, he was gone.

The Armor Room sentries could barely open the doors fast enough for Lucifer to whiz by. In a swoosh that sucked their garb, Lucifer took to the air, speeding toward his quarters.

Coming to rest on the stoop outside his residence, Lucifer removed his helmet, scowled, tapped his foot, and huffed. The door sentries, fascinated by his armor, were slow in the opening.

His hand-picked angel taskforce welcomed him with their special salute—two fist-taps to the chest, followed by an extended arm and a shout. But Lucifer put a finger to his lips as he hastened inside and waited until the door clicked. "We need to confer without extra ears catching wind of my plans."

"Commander," First Lieutenant Wyael said, ogling Lucifer's breastplate. "Your armor is perfect, the best I've ever seen."

"Yes, it's molded to fit my frame and no one else's." Lucifer unsheathed his sword and sliced the air in a figure-eight pattern. "My blade is constructed and forged of the densest metal created, and I was there to oversee its sharpening." Halting his blade work, he stretched out his left hand with palm up and laid the sword upon it. Loosening his right, he rolled it around under the handgrip, and the saber lay level across both hands.

"See the grip?" he said. "It fits only my hand. No one in all Heaven can defeat me, not even Michael, with his annoying by-the-book obedience. And except for our trip to Earth, when Michael definitely overstepped his authority…well…Ha, I let him have his moment. His actions displeased the Almighty, and I'm sure he's watching him very closely."

The taskforce angels snickered since only they knew how much Lucifer despised Michael. "Sir," Second Lieutenant Maysel said. "When will we receive our armor? We leave for Earth soon, and didn't you want us outfitted in armor before the trip?"

"Yes. Michael is expecting all thirteen of you now, so go. Once fitted, meet me back here, and we'll prepare for my address. Following the speech, together, we'll proceed to the Throne Room for final Earth-mission instructions."

As the taskforce departed, silence beckoned. Lucifer did an about-face, waved his hand, and on the wall to his left, an entryway appeared—the door to his inner sanctum, his secret room. It was the place Lucifer could be himself without concern for exposing his heart's desire. No one had seen this room, not even his trusted chamber angels or the taskforce. He kept the door cloaked from view, and even as he unlocked it and entered, the door remained masked to everyone but himself.

Standing by the sparring equipment, I observed Lucifer's taskforce saunter into the Armor Room with the same flare of arrogance I had detected in their leader. Randiel greeted them, but didn't seem to notice. As I approached, I questioned myself. Was it really an attitude of superiority, or was I letting my imagination get the better of me? Now, I couldn't tell.

Nearing Lucifer's team, I said, "Taskforce, you are the first to receive the newly crafted suits of armor. I hope you understand what an honor this is."

"Yes, Sir," they responded in unison.

"Good. I have them arranged in sections according to the angel ranks. Find your rank, choose your armor, and my attendants will fit you. Once fitted, I will inspect the suit. If I feel the fit is perfect, we will test it. When proven effective, we'll mount your nameplate, and this will be your permanent spot. As you return from Earth, your particular battle armor will be stored here.

"Yes, Sir, Chief Prince," First Lieutenant Wyael said, squaring his shoulders, jolting to attention, and saluting.

"At ease, Lieutenant. This is an informal fitting."

"Thank you, Sir," Wyael said, relaxing his stance.

Accompanied by the Armor Room angels, the taskforce members found their rank section, inspected the pieces, and chose what they felt would be their best suit of armor. Some of my angels helped fit Lucifer's angels, from private, the lowest rank on the taskforce, to the highest, first lieutenant, while others crafted their nameplates.

"This armor is different than the armor you've used in training," I said, examining each soldier. "It's denser, yet more form-fitting and not as cumbersome. In fact, I designed battle armor so its weight and bulkiness disappear with full dress. That's the beauty and wonder of Heaven's armor—you'll barely feel it."

"Chief Prince," Specialist Carsiel said when his breastplate snapped into place. "It's true! It feels as though it's always been there!"

"Splendid," I said, checking each angel. "Exactly what I had anticipated. After my cursory inspection, the armor you have chosen appears to fit well, but I'll need to observe you sparring before I assign this specific suit and hang your nameplate. Soldiers, keep in mind you must be able to move freely without any hindrances. Every piece should feel like a natural extension of your body. Let's head to the Arena for a trial run."

"Sir," Second Lieutenant Maysel said. "Is this necessary? We are due back at Chief Prince Lucifer's quarters as soon as possible for briefing and instruction."

"Yes, it's absolutely necessary. I will not allow under-angel armor to go out without proper testing. If you must leave now, then remove your armor and go."

Maysel hung his head. "My apologies, Sir. Let's continue."

Lucifer inhaled deeply, taking in the room's quietude. As he exhaled, his earlier frustrations with Michael released. Strolling to his ornate chair, the one he had crafted on the sly to resemble a throne, he collapsed into it. There, Lucifer contemplated what it would be like to dwell on Earth and what dangers they might encounter. But then his thoughts strayed.

Diverted from strategy, Lucifer considered how good he would feel ruling Earth. To be like God, commanding all the creatures, especially the humans. *I am excellent, the brightest, and wisest angel of all. No one can compare to me, not even Michael or Gabriel.* "In fact," Lucifer whispered, "I'm done with them, and with Michael's insistence of complete equality. We are not equal. I am unsurpassed, superior, by far the finest angel and the only one like God. Earth will be mine!" he shouted, but then lowered his volume. "I wonder how quickly I can persuade the man and woman to worship me instead of the Almighty. Ha…from what I've observed, it shouldn't take too long."

Cloaked by daily activity, one by one, angels enamored with Lucifer heeded the word spread by the taskforce and slipped away to enter the never-ending caverns of the Mount of Holiness. As far as the eye could see, angel devotees occupied every alcove and nook, yet most congregated in the spacious rotunda.

Excited for Lucifer's address, fidgety angels in the stuffed caverns began a low-volume, monotone chant, "Lu-ci-fer...Lu-ci-fer..." If Lucifer didn't arrive soon, their invocation could increase to a decibel that might alert the Most High. He, above all, could not learn of this secret meeting.

Sergeant Major Gragael stepped onto the stage and marched up to the podium. All quieted. "Chief Prince Lucifer will be here momentarily," he said. "Let's cease the chanting! Each angel must prepare personally, yet silently, for his luminous entrance."

CHAPTER 16

SUSPICION GROWS

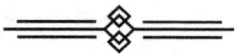

Gleaming like a jeweled crown, the majestic Arena stood towering above all the buildings of Ivory Palace City proper, except for Ivory Palace itself. This massive, open-air structure, equal in height to the Forge, was five times the size of the Armor Room and located one street behind. Its walls jutted up much higher than the gilded, ornamental front gate and angled slightly toward the center. Inside, training rings lined the perimeter and filled the center.

I led Lucifer's taskforce through the far door of the Grand Hall, down the long corridor, past the inner chamber, and out the Armor Room's back entrance. Crossing the street, we arrived at the Arena's gate, and the angel caretaker opened. I stepped aside while the taskforce filed past, thanked the caretaker, and entered the Arena. Each member stood at attention, awaiting sparring instructions.

"Angels, at ease," I shouted. "I'll be pairing you up according to rank. Your numbers are uneven, and since they are, First Lieutenant Wyael will spar with me."

"I'm honored, Sir," Wyael said.

I nodded to him and turned back to the soldiers. "We are here to try the armor, to make sure the pieces you have chosen fit your frame. Agility and ease are essential to winning any battle. If cumbered in sparring, you will be cumbered in battle. We need to know it now so we can exchange your pieces and find you the best-fitting armor. Let's get started."

Glancing at my checklist, I said, "Private Charrael and Private Second Class Dylael, you will be in training ring seven. Private First Class Olivel and Specialist Carsiel, yours will be training ring six. Corporal Huntiel and Sergeant Sebiel, training ring five. Staff Sergeant Alexael and Master Sergeant Stewel, ring four. Command Sergeant Major Ennel and Warrant Officer 1 Willel, ring three. Chief Warrant Officer 4 Juael and Second Lieutenant Maysel, ring two. First Lieutenant Wyael and I will spar in ring one.

"Get the feel of the armor. Assess your ability to move, lunge, parry, and riposte. I will be observing while you spar. When I am pleased with what I see, Wyael and I will test his armor. Remember, we are sparring only. This is not a competition, so don't make it one."

Each angel warrior found their training ring, fitted their helmet, and entered the ring prepared for battle. Once all were in place, I shouted the commands, "En garde. Prêts. Allez." The first saber clashes were deafening.

As I walked from ring to ring, observing, the angels appeared to be moving smoothly in their chosen armor. I couldn't help feeling incredibly satisfied. I had supervised the training of every angel in Heaven, and they were like my own. I turned to First Lieutenant Wyael and said, "The angels are doing well. Are you ready to spar?"

"Yes, Sir." Wyael donned his helmet and entered ring one.

I followed, and our sparring commenced. Wyael's armor also seemed a flawless fit, and his movements unhindered. He was a worthy opponent and highly skilled. I halted the testing with Wyael and shouted, "Arrêt." Sparring ceased.

The taskforce removed their helmets and gathered around us. "Angels, as I observed, I saw great skill and agility. I commend you. Each armor suit appears to fit perfectly, but only you can be the judge. If you need replacements, follow me back to the Armor Room. However, if you are comfortable with your armor, you may take your leave. Does anyone need replacements?"

"No, Sir," the taskforce angels shouted back in unison.

"Great," I said. "Then we're done. Gather your gear and head to the exit." I removed my sparring armor, checked the training rings to ensure nothing was left behind, and restored the Arena to pre-spar status.

When I reached the gate, I was surprised to see Lucifer's team still within the Arena grounds. Assembled around First Lieutenant Wyael, the taskforce seemed unaware I had emerged from the Arena. And although Wyael used hushed tones, I overheard his agitated orders.

"Our schedule is out of control," Wyael said, pointing to the soldiers. "It did not include testing armor or your questions. We're already late. We need to rush back to Chief Prince Lucifer's chambers. It's nearly time for his address. Follow me."

"Wait," I shouted, sprinting from the gate. "Lucifer's address?" Without halting or answering, the taskforce took flight, causing the air behind them to vortex and suck at my garments and hair. I pushed my hair out of my face and smoothed my robes. "How odd. I know they heard me. What did Wyael mean by Lucifer's address?

Did I hear correctly?" I shrugged. "Maybe Wyael said 'to dress' and not 'address.'"

⌄

The taskforce arrived almost instantly at Lucifer's. The astonished sentries fumbled but managed to open the door, and the angels burst through, startling the chamber angel tidying up. Each soldier stacked their armor along the walls for easy access.

"That was awfully close, Wyael." Second Lieutenant Maysel whispered. "Do you think Michael overheard your orders?"

Wyael glared at him. "Where is Chief Prince Lucifer?" he asked the chamber angel.

Andiel nodded. "He's in the atrium, Sir."

"Please let him know we are here."

"Yes, Sir."

Turning back to Maysel, Wyael said in a low voice, "I don't need your commentary, especially when others are present."

Maysel was about to respond when Lucifer entered. "Ah, you're here, and you have your armor. Did you test it?"

"Yes, Chief Prince Lucifer," Wyael said. "Chief Prince Michael would not allow us to appropriate the armor without testing it first."

"Good, I knew I could count on Michael to provide the best armor for my team. He is annoying, but thorough."

"Sir," Wyael said. "Are you ready for your speech? We should be going. From what I've heard, the angels are restless."

"Yes," Maysel said, stepping closer. "If we delay much longer, they may walk out disgruntled."

Lucifer tilted his head back and snorted. "Let them wait. It'll do them good. And if they walk, they walk—no great loss. Soon, all will bow to me."

"Sir?" Wyael said, glancing at Maysel.

"Never mind." He waved them off. "We have plans to review. Remember, we're leaving for Earth immediately following the cavern meeting and our final instructions in the Throne Room. However, you are not yet ready. I need my taskforce fully apprised of their station on Earth, the dangers, and all duties before we depart. These moments are crucial, not to mention mandatory. I certainly cannot take a team to Earth if they are not capable, sufficiently informed, and with me one hundred percent."

———◇———

Instead of returning to the Armor Room, I strolled down Beauty Avenue until it connected with Glory Street. As always, the splendor of Heaven wrapped around me, but nothing calmed my angst. Up ahead, I saw Gabriel, and he moved at a swift pace. His garments swept the walkway, and his hair streamed behind. "Gabriel," I called, running to catch up. "Where are you headed?"

"The Scroll Room," he said, halting until I stood beside him. "The Almighty has called me to assist in placing the seal on the scroll He spoke before creation."

I jerked. "Oh?"

"Yes." His tone was serious as he nodded. "I'm not sure what it will entail. We've not sealed scrolls before. God indicated he would give direction once I'm there."

My eyes widened. "Sounds interesting."

Gabriel smiled. "Every task has been so far, and this scroll is special."

"What makes it special above the others?"

He cocked his head. "Well, it's special and odd."

I wrinkled my nose. "Odd? In what way?"

Gabriel became animated. He picked up an invisible quill and began air-writing. "Although I penned God's words, I had minimal understanding, and he's not explaining."

Taking a step back, I said, "Wait. Is this what makes it odd or special?

"Odd."

"Why?"

He pursed his lips and then spoke. "Until now, I've understood all the words I've written and their meanings."

I raised an eyebrow. "What makes it special then?"

Gabriel took a deep breath and exhaled. "This scroll is unlike any other. Not only does it remain a complete mystery, but I must keep it in its own distinct place. And once the scroll is sealed, the LORD God says only he can open it."

My mouth fell open. "Amazing."

"Yes," he said in a whisper. "So, can we walk while we talk? I need to get to the Scroll Room quickly. The Almighty is waiting." Gabriel turned to go, but I didn't follow. "Michael, are you coming?" He snapped his fingers in front of my face. "Michael!"

I jolted from my stare. "Oh, sure, let's walk."

The River of Life burbled as we strode alongside it on the translucent gold walkway. The just-harvested Trees of Life towered above us and again began to bud in preparation for their new crop.

"Listen, Gabriel, I overheard something earlier, and I'd like your opinion."

"Certainly. What did you hear?"

"Well," I said, taking a deep breath, "I had just finished testing armor with Lucifer's taskforce. They gathered their gear and exited, yet still lingered on the Arena grounds when I emerged. No one saw me." I cocked my head. "At least, I don't think they did. But as I looked on, I'm sure I heard First Lieutenant Wyael telling his subordinates it was almost time for Lucifer's address, and they needed to rush back to his chambers."

"Address?" Gabriel rubbed his chin. "You mean like a speech?"

"That's what I'm thinking."

"Okay?" he said, tapping his lips.

"At first, I thought I misunderstood, and Wyael might have said 'to dress' instead of 'address.' But the more I think about how he said it, the less I believe I misunderstood. What do you make of it?"

Gabriel shrugged. "I'm not sure. Who would Lucifer be addressing? The taskforce or someone else?"

I threw out my arms. "I don't know. Who do you think he would be giving a speech to?"

His eyebrows furrowed. "Well, it's not like he has a whole army of angels under his command. He only has the thirteen-member taskforce, right?"

"As far as I know," I said, shaking my head. "But then again, I knew nothing about God choosing Lucifer to govern Earth until you announced it."

"Really?" Gabriel stopped in his tracks. "The LORD informed me about his pending creation and Lucifer's small taskforce before he created. I thought you knew."

"I didn't. Is it possible Lucifer has more angels ready and waiting to join him on Earth?"

Gabriel bit his lip. "I suppose, but somehow, I don't think so. There are only two humans and cumbersome land creatures. Earth doesn't seem to require even the thirteen Lucifer chose."

My countenance brightened. "I agree. And when he talks to the thirteen, I don't think you could classify it as an address. Do you?"

"No, you're right."

I jabbed my finger forward. "He's up to something, Gabriel. I can feel it."

Gabriel rolled his eyes and once more started to walk. "Oh, here we go again with your Lucifer conspiracy theory."

"No. Okay, yes, maybe." I hastened my steps. "Don't you remember his facial expressions during the Almighty's creation? Lucifer looked upset and a little irritated when the rest of us were amazed and in awe."

"I didn't see that." Gabriel halted, and so did I. He shook his head. "Lucifer has no reason to be upset or appear disturbed about anything. It's your imagination, Michael. Or possibly...wishful thinking."

I stepped back and folded my arms. "Wishful thinking? What do you mean by wishful thinking?"

Gabriel pursed his lips and pointed at me. "You feel you should have been chosen to lead Earth's taskforce instead of Lucifer, don't you?"

"So, what if I do? I'm the guardian archangel. It's my job to protect the Most High and Heaven, and now all of God's creation. Lucifer isn't the guardian. It doesn't make sense for him to lead the taskforce."

"That's why it's wishful thinking."

I pounded my hips. "Seriously?"

"Yes. You think if you find something on Lucifer, the Almighty will remove him, and you can step in and take his place."

My head involuntarily wagged. "That's not true, Gabriel. It took me a while, but I'm okay with not being chosen. I know God has his reasons, and I will not question them. I do question Lucifer, though. Believe me, he's different than he used to be, and now his taskforce is also acting strange."

Gabriel inhaled and exhaled hard. "Michael, you are my friend, so understand what I say, I say because I care. Stop this obsession with Lucifer. It's not only making you sound crazy, but jealous. I cannot be on your side if you insist on continuing this nonsense. Were something wrong with Lucifer, I believe the Almighty would tell us. So let it go."

I squeezed my eyes shut and rubbed my forehead. "I can't. Too much has happened." I pushed my hair back and sighed. "I guess I'll have to prove it to you…and God."

Gabriel squinted. "Should I see it with my own eyes, I might, and I stress, might believe you. But until then, I can't be around you. You're irrational and negative, consumed by what you think of

Lucifer. Don't bother me with this anymore, Michael. I'm going to the Scroll Room, and I don't want to talk to you again, unless you've come to your senses."

Gabriel launched toward the Scroll Room, and my heart sank. Sadness clenched me like a vice-grip. He'd never talked to me that way, and it seemed so final. Had I lost my only friend…all because of Lucifer? "Why doesn't Gabriel believe me?" I mouthed. "Is he correct? Is it my imagination? Am I jealous? Should I let it go?"

While Lucifer continued talking, Master Sergeant Stewel slipped away from the group. Trying not to draw attention from the Chief Prince, he quietly opened the front door and whispered to the sentry on duty, "In exactly one period, sound the door chime."

Taking his cue, the Sentry came to attention and said in hushed tones, "Yes, Sir."

Stewel eased back into the group as Lucifer said, "I have great plans for Earth, and you must know them."

Staff Sergeant Alexael, holding a long tube, said, "Chief Prince Lucifer, Sir. Would you like me to unroll your map of Earth now?"

Lucifer squinted and glared. "Yes, but not here."

"Alright, Sir, then where?"

I did the only thing I could do. I took to the air and returned to the Armor Room. I needed to think, to decide my next course of action. Do I let go or keep digging?

Alighting on the Armor Room's walkway, the sentries nodded allegiance as they opened the doors. "A list!" I said, pointing my finger upward and entering. "Yes, that way, I'll gain some perspective. Pros, cons, and," I said, lowering my voice, "maybe Lucifer's questionable activities."

I made a beeline across the Armor Room, longing for the solitude of my office, but stopped mid-way. Upon my return, I would always visit and assess each post, speak to any angel who needed me, and pause at Randiel's station to check on our newest deliveries. Right now, things must remain normal. A list could change my mind about Lucifer.

Randiel, of course, had everything under control, as did the others, although I did notice a strained look on his face, an anxiety I'd not seen before. *Maybe it's just me.* I shrugged it off. These angels were like gears in a smooth-running machine, interconnecting, rotating, and flowing so effortlessly that no one outside had any idea of the rigorous inner workings of this Armor Room.

Content with what I saw, I retreated to my office. I drew three columns on the pad and labeled them with my preplanned headings. "So," I said, sitting back in my chair, "what would be the pros of dropping my suspicions of Lucifer?"

After pondering a short while, I wrote, #1: I would have my friend back. #2: The Almighty would be pleased. I hesitated, realizing I should reverse numbers one and two. God is infinitely more important, and pleasing him…always my number one…

The sound of a crash came from the Armor Room. I bolted to my office door to see what had happened. Two angels transporting armor collided, and a few pieces fell from the carts. I couldn't tell if they were damaged, but I knew Randiel would handle it.

I filled my lungs and exhaled a sigh. Maybe I should have been more concerned about the fallen armor. But for the first time in my existence, my heart ached. What was the point of any of this if things weren't mended with Gabriel? There had never been a rift between us. How could I fix it?

Nothing came to mind, nothing but my lists. Finishing, I supposed, would help. I slid back into my chair. "So, where was I? Oh, yes, number three. What would be my third pro?" As I deliberated, Randiel came to my door and knocked. He stuck his head in and said, "Sir, I'll be out for a bit."

My head jerked up. "Oh?"

Randiel sighed. "Yes, the crash dented some armor. I'm taking the pieces to the Forge for repair."

"Why are you going? Send one of the under-angels."

"I would, Sir," he said, stepping into my office and closing the door, "but I prefer to do it myself. That way, I know it'll be done correctly the first time. And, if I'm telling all, I'd like a little break from the Armor Room. It's been tense lately, and I've no explanation as to why."

"I can relate, Randiel. There's much more activity than usual, especially with preparation for the Earth Mission. So go, see to the armor repair, clear your head, and relax. Thankfully, things like that don't happen often."

He nodded. "Yes, Chief Prince. Thank you."

I came around my desk and patted his shoulder. "Be sure to make the most of your trip to the Forge and come back refreshed. Who knows when you'll get another opportunity?"

"Very true, Sir."

As my office door closed, I sighed. Who was I kidding? Things like that never occur, not in this Armor Room. My head clogged with thoughts. What happened with Lucifer and Gabriel? Why the tenseness in my Armor Room workers? And now a collision? Was it me? Was my turmoil causing the Armor Room chaos? *Maybe.* Where's my pad? I need to finish my lists.

I sat and thought more, then wrote #3: Things in Heaven would return to the way they were. #4: All would continue without change. "Absolutely," I said aloud, pushing my chair away from my desk and jumping up. "Four excellent reasons. In fact, they're so good, the other two lists don't matter." I ripped off the pros column and set it aside. "I'm satisfied. All this frustration needs to cease. Gabriel was right. I have to let it go."

CHAPTER 17

THE DECISION TESTED

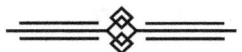

"**H**old that thought, Alexael," Lucifer said. "The Almighty is summoning me to the Throne Room."

The Staff Sergeant bowed his head. "As you wish, Sir."

Lucifer pivoted. "Wyael."

He came to attention. "Yes, Chief Prince?"

"While I'm gone, check with Sergeant Major Gragael in the caverns. See if he is controlling the masses. If not, lend your help, but get back here as quickly as possible."

"Right away, Sir."

"The rest of you," Lucifer said, stepping into the atrium, "use this as an opportunity to grow more familiar with your armor and weapon. I won't be long. We'll pick up where we left off when I return."

"Yes, Sir," they said, coming to attention and saluting. When Lucifer propelled upward through the atrium access, Master Sergeant Stewel inched his way to the door, opened it, and cancelled the chime.

I sprang from my office with one thought: tell Gabriel my decision. I felt so free, I wanted to fly through the Armor Room. It was big enough, and several angels had tried. Still, my no-flying inside rule kept me grounded.

As I approached the entryway and stepped through the opened double doors, the Almighty called. "Michael, come to the Throne Room."

"Yes, Majesty," I said, taking to the air. "On my way."

Everything looked different since I let go of my Lucifer obsession. The Trees of Life, loaded with growing fruit for the next harvest, appeared more vibrant. And as I zipped above Glory Street, the translucent gold pavement glimmered even brighter. My heaviness seemed to vanish, and I beamed with newfound lightness.

Determining nothing would get me down again, I swooped onto the walkway of Ivory Palace and stepped up to the mammoth doors. I smoothed my garments, folded my wings, and prepared to ring the gong when someone landed behind me. I swung around to greet whoever, but before I could speak, Lucifer glared and said, "Michael, you're here?"

"I am. Are you surprised?"

"No, irritated."

"Why?"

"I was called out of a meeting with my taskforce. We leave for Earth soon, and my team is not ready. When the LORD called, I thought he would be providing me, and only me, with additional information to use on our mission. But since you're here, I'm guessing it's something else. I don't have the patience for this."

"Lucifer," I said, sighing. "We exist to serve the Almighty. His will should always be our desire. I don't understand you anymore." At once, I recognized that same strange feeling was trying to surface again. *Oh, no, you don't! I'll not go there. I just got free.*

"Well, let's get this over with." Lucifer shoved me to the side so he could ring the gong. Before my decision, I might have added this little tête-à-tête to my "Lucifer's Questionable Activities" list, but not now. I took a breath, stuffed down the old sentiment, and just smiled.

Again, the caverns pulsed with the cadence of chanting. Some angels swung from the rocks, and others bounced, danced, or took flight. Sergeant Major Gragael rubbed the back of his neck and stared at the cavern's door, willing Lucifer to open it. He had no idea how to contain the followers. Stepping up to the podium, Gragael tried again to quiet the gathering. "Angels," he shouted. No response. He yelled louder, "Angels, please restrain yourselves." The sound of his voice hit a wall of clamor and dissipated. He waved his arms, stomped his feet, and hollered a third time, but they paid him no attention. The sergeant major was about to give up, but glancing once more at the entrance caused his face to brighten. Wyael strode through the door.

"Make way for First Lieutenant Wyael," Gragael announced. A hush spread over Lucifer's devotees at the sight of an actual taskforce member. Gragael closed his eyes as relief washed over him, and he wondered if Chief Prince Lucifer would enter next.

The angels on the cavern floor anticipated the same, but when Lucifer didn't appear, they crowded around Wyael, impeding his trek. Racket increased. Wyael shook some hands and received pats of encouragement, yet he had a job to do. "Soldiers," he shouted. "Let me pass."

Lucifer's most ardent fans silenced while Wyael trotted to the stage. "Thank goodness you're here," Gragael said. "Is the Chief Prince with you?"

"No, unfortunately, he's not. The Almighty called him to the Throne Room."

Gragael's eyes grew big, and he threw up his arms. "What does that mean for us?"

Wyael glared. "Lucifer's speech will be delayed, which is why I'm here. He asked me to check on you."

"I'm glad." Gragael's shoulders dropped. "This is the first time these supporters have been quiet for even a short period. I can't imagine what they'll be like when they find out Lucifer isn't here or coming soon. I cannot keep them under control by myself. I need assistance. Will you get me some, or maybe offer suggestions?"

"They don't seem that difficult to restrain. But I'll speak to them."

Gragael shrugged. "I hope it helps."

"It will," Wyael said, turning to the crowd. "Greetings to all of Chief Prince Lucifer's faithful followers. It is an honor to stand before you." Applause, whistles, and screams burst from the throng in a deafening roar. Wyael raised his arms and pulsed them downward, trying to silence the angels. "Shhh, shhh, shhh."

The riled-up angels ignored his shushing. Most had expected Lucifer to follow Wyael, and since he didn't, they chanted even louder, "Lu-ci-fer, Lu-ci-fer."

Wyael scowled and turned toward Gragael, "Quieting these devotees is more difficult than anticipated."

Gragael leaned in so Wyael could hear. "I told you. I need help."

"Have they been like this the whole time?"

"Yes," Gragael said. "I've tried everything. They're getting worse, and I don't know what to do."

"Well, I do." Wyael yelled, "Guards!" Lucifer's soldiers advanced from the rotunda floor at Wyael's word. They stood shoulder to shoulder across the front of the stage, swords in hand. As angel devotees in each section of the caverns noticed the display of authority, a wave of quiet washed over the crowd. Light bounced off the sentry's breastplates and streaked the rotunda until all were silent.

"That's better," Wyael said, raising his arms toward the audience and smiling. "Angels, I have come to inform you there will be a delay in Chief Prince Lucifer's arrival."

"No," the voices groaned and shrieked in protest.

"Angels! Quiet!" he shouted over the moans. "The Chief Prince has been called to the Throne Room, and unfortunately, we do not know for how long."

Boos and hisses blasted Wyael from the floor as other gripes wafted from the higher alcoves. He pounded the podium and yelled, "Listen up. If your duties prohibit you from waiting…" The sound of his words didn't reach any farther than the edge of the stage. "Sentries, en garde!"

Each sentry prepared his stance to engage an unruly angel. More light flashes lasered through the rotunda, shocking the devotees and striking them mute. They had never seen a sentry guard take that type of stance outside of sparring. Wyael expected the crowd to erupt again, so he waited to speak.

After a moment of silence, Wyael said, "If your duties prohibit you from waiting, Archangel Lucifer says you are free to leave. Departure will not count against any angel. And despite this delay, please know you are essential and valuable to the Chief Prince. He needs every one of you, and craves your allegiance. If you feel you can linger until our illustrious leader arrives and keep the noise to a minimum, you will be rewarded for your loyalty."

Controlled applause arose this time, but Wyael easily quieted them. "One more thing," he said. "A meeting of this caliber has never occurred, and Chief Prince Lucifer is positive the Almighty would forbid it if he knew. Should your voices reach the Most High, and he becomes aware of our gathering, there could be consequences for all in attendance.

"Archangel Lucifer wants you safe. Therefore, in honor of our great and powerful leader, let us use hand gestures for communication and no noise. Thank you."

The angels wanted to clap and holler, but they refrained. First Lieutenant Wyael dismissed the guards from the stage, turned to Sergeant Major Gragael, and said, "I don't think you'll have any trouble from here on out."

Gragael saluted. "Thank you, Sir,"

Wyael responded in kind. He stepped back, pivoted, descended the stage area, and headed for the door, escorted by the floor guards.

The quieted angels parted as though an invisible wind tore through and created a walkway. Before exiting, Wyael turned around and waved. Each angel devotee returned his wave, and he closed the door on a soundless room. Confident he had remedied the situation, Wyael navigated back through the mountain's narrow pathways.

One angel caretaker of Ivory Palace opened the door and bowed before us. Lucifer pushed the angel aside and entered the Great Room. With this, my suspicions resurfaced, and I struggled to suppress them. Still, I ensured the caretaker's wellbeing, and when he acknowledged my concern, I saw Lucifer had already reached the mouth of the long hall. I jogged to catch up, but as usual, I followed him to the Throne Room, looking like a naïve groupie.

Lucifer waved for the opening before we even reached the Throne Room. The sentries tugged the heavy doors and held them until we arrived. Entering, I bowed low before God's Shekinah.

"Can you tell me what this is about?" Lucifer said in a huff. "I was in the middle of a training meeting. You know we leave for Earth soon, and I must have my taskforce fully educated. So, let's make this quick."

I still had my head bowed when Lucifer began his rant, but I jerked up. This was precisely the type of thing that initially caused my alarm. I clenched my jaw as frustration surged. A deep-seated need to find the underlying cause of Lucifer's change gripped me. I started to move in his direction to stop or at least restrain him from speaking to the LORD this way, but a stern and unsympathetic reply came from the Most High. "I am aware of your need to instruct your taskforce, Lucifer."

"Then why am I here?" Lucifer said, throwing his arms in the air.

A spark of fire spat out from God's Shekinah as he shifted on his throne. "I want a detailed description of all your preparations for Earth. In what way have you instructed your taskforce? And, how do you plan to govern each of Earth's regions?"

Narrowing his brows, Lucifer said, "This could have waited until our final instruction period."

The Almighty's glory flamed. "It could have, but I desire to know now."

"Well, if you want information, you must dismiss Michael. Why is he here anyway? He has no part in my Earth mission. I'll say nothing until he's gone."

I couldn't contain myself anymore. I stepped between Lucifer and the LORD and said, "Pardon me, Majesty. Lucifer and I need to have a word."

"By all means, Michael."

"No," Lucifer shouted.

Walking toward the Throne Room doors, I said, "Yes! Follow me into the hall."

Lucifer stomped his foot. "Absolutely not."

The Almighty pointed a fiery hand. "Go, Lucifer. Do as Michael has asked."

Lucifer's nostrils flared. He spun around, stomped out of the Throne Room, and followed me down the long hall to an alcove where the sentry guards could not hear. Deep within its recesses, I turned to confront Lucifer, but he spoke first. "What's the deal, Michael?"

I stuck my finger in his face. "You cannot talk to the Almighty that way."

"Who made you my superior?"

"No one, but you must speak and act more reverently toward the LORD."

"Listen," he said in a huff. "If God has a problem with how I communicate, he can tell me. I will not accept correction from you."

"Fine. So, what's your problem with me? Why all the secrecy? The Most High summoned us both to the Throne Room. He must have a reason for wanting me here. You just have to accept it."

"I won't. I don't care that the Almighty invited you. You don't need to know anything about my plans for Earth, and I'm not talking while you're in the room."

"Lucifer!" I said, stepping close and staring into his eyes. "Stop this nonsense. You should not defy the LORD."

Lucifer inched even closer. He glared, and I could feel the heat of his breath. I retreated until my heel touched the wall. He had backed me into a corner, and for a brief moment, I felt unnerved. Stifling a shudder, I attempted to push past him, but he stood stationary. "Lucifer! Let me pass."

"Michael," he said, planting his hand on my chest. "I told you before, this is my business, not yours."

His words irritated me, and my muscles tightened. "Listen," I said. "As guardian archangel, the Most High is my business."

"Not anymore," he said.

My head jerked back. "What do you mean?"

"I'll handle God. You just concentrate on your Armor Room."

"Lucifer! Who do you think you are? You're not my superior, either. You have no more authority than I do."

His hand on my chest squeezed into a fist that wadded my garments. He yanked me close and whispered, "Michael, this is the last time I'll warn you. Leave the Almighty to me, and stay out of my business or else."

He shoved me back hard. I lost my balance, fell against the wall, and slid to the floor. As I descended, I was sure I saw that red fleck in his eyes again. It flickered, and then it was gone.

Lucifer turned in a huff and exited. I sat there for a moment, replaying our exchange. Nothing about this made any more sense than our west perimeter encounter.

What's happening in Heaven? Gabriel abandoned me. The Sovereign God is displeased, and Lucifer…I didn't even have words to describe his actions. "Things are getting worse," I whispered. "And now, I must address the Most High alone." I buried my face in my hands. "How can I bear his disappointment again?"

I pounded the floor. "I don't know. I'll fall into the hands of the LORD and trust his mercies are great." With that, I nodded my resolve, inhaled, picked myself up, and returned to the Throne Room.

CHAPTER 18

RENEWED FERVENCY

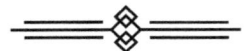

Lucifer stormed out of the Ivory Palace, nostrils flaring and fists clenched. "I need to be alone," he yelled as the angel caretakers jumped out of his way. Barreling down the Glory Street walkway, he flailed his arms as though reprimanding an unruly soldier. "I can't go to my chambers…the taskforce is there. My followers are in the caverns, so where?" Lucifer braked. "Of course! The Garden of Fiery Stones."

He shot upward and sailed over the city's wall. With the plains below, Lucifer felt his rage begin to subside. And even though he knew he had revealed too much of himself, at that moment, he didn't care.

Alighting before the Garden's gate, Lucifer took a deep breath, thankful for the solace. The gate opened and beckoned him to enter. Stepping in, flames spouted from the rocks, and the rhythm became one with his being. The smaller stones near the entrance gave off a higher pitch, but the grand boulders at the center pounded out deeper, robust tones.

Lucifer felt more like himself in this place than in his chamber, for this was where he changed and evolved into who he was now. It was here he came alive, and here, he made his plans. "Oh...if only these stones could talk," he whispered, "what a story they would tell."

As he strolled toward the center, the boulders increased in size, revealing more and more of his beauty. With each glimpse, his frustrations waned. "Hold it together, Lucifer," he said to himself. "You only have a short period left to endure Michael. Your strategies are good. They will work exactly as planned. And the best part, ha-ha, God knows nothing."

He rounded the final corner and arrived at his favorite mirrored rock. The boulders discharged their fire and bathed him in an amber glow. As Lucifer admired his reflection, he calmed, stepped closer, and touched the rock as though caressing his beautiful face. Mesmerizing ecstasy washed over him, and from deep within, a renewed lust for power gushed. "My taskforce must see all my glory!" he shouted, launching skyward.

I re-entered the Throne Room and bowed. "Sovereign, Lucifer has left the palace. I guess our talk caused him to forget that you called him here. Would you like me to find him and bring him back?"

His Shekinah blazed brighter. "No, Michael. I appreciate the offer, but Lucifer is correct. I can learn all I need to know when he brings his taskforce to the Throne Room for final instructions."

I hung my head. "Majesty, it appears I've let you down again. I'm trying so hard to serve you, do my job, and please you, but it seems at every turn, I've failed. Please accept my apology."

"We already have, Michael. You may go."

"Thank you, Sire." I bowed low and exited, but I felt beaten. My legs quivered as I walked the long hall back to the Great Room, and my firm resolve wavered like a jelled dessert. *What am I supposed to do?* If I followed my gut about Lucifer, I wouldn't have Gabriel or the Most High with me. But if I didn't, Earth and maybe even Heaven would suffer.

After Michael's departure, the Throne Room returned to its ethereal serenity. Seraphim glided above God's throne and sang together with the cherubim, "Holy, holy, holy, is the LORD of Hosts."

Pleased with their worship, the Almighty's fiery glory filled his room, and the uniquely placed, gilded furniture glimmered in his Shekinah light. Basking in this precious moment, the Three-in-One God conversed.

"Michael is downcast. I feel his pain."

"Yes, Son," the Father said. "He is hurting, but it's necessary."

"I wish we could have spared him or at least comforted him before he left."

"Spirit, your compassion is cherished. Michael must be confident in his decision."

"True, Father. Everything hinges on Michael."

"And Gabriel." The Spirit sighed, and his breeze caused their Shekinah to flicker.

"Yes, Gabriel is important to our plan," the Most High God said as One. "He does have a big role. But Michael is key."

━━━━━━━⌄━━━━━━━

Lucifer spied his chambers from above, and First Lieutenant Wyael drew near his front door. The sentries opened for Wyael, and he entered at the exact moment Lucifer descended through the atrium's rooftop access. "Gentlemen, I'm back," Lucifer said, approaching the main room. The senior chamber angel who stood by the atrium door stepped up to Lucifer and bowed. "Sir, may I be of service?"

"Yes, Andiel," Lucifer said. "This is a private meeting with my taskforce. I do not want to be disturbed. Make sure all my chamber angels know."

The angel nodded. "Yes, Chief Prince. I'll do my best to carry out your orders."

"You better," Lucifer said, causing Andiel to flinch. "Dismissed."

Lucifer turned back to his taskforce. "Have you been handling your armor, wielding your swords, and becoming more comfortable using each piece?"

Second Lieutenant Maysel hiked his shoulders, "Yes, Chief Prince. We wore our armor while you were gone and actually just removed it."

"Perfect. Any issues?" Lucifer said as Master Sergeant Stewel tiptoed, once again, to speak to the door sentry on duty.

Maysel shook his head. "No, Sir."

"Good." Turning to Wyael, he said, "I ordered you to check on Sergeant Major Gragael. Did you?"

Wyael stiffened. "Yes, Sir."

"How are things in the caverns?"

"Improved," Wyael said, smiling. "They were chaotic and loud when I first arrived. But I spoke to your followers and ensured they understood the importance of silence. All was quiet when I left. I hope it stays that way until you arrive."

Lucifer patted Wyael on the back. "Fine," he said while Stewel snuck into place. Lucifer stroked his chin. "Let's see. Where were we when I was so rudely called away? Oh yes. Alexael, you were about to unroll the map of Earth."

Staff Sergeant Alexael came to attention. "Yes, Sir, Chief Prince. Where shall I lay it?"

Exiting Ivory Palace, I didn't feel like flying. I hung my head and wandered down Glory Street, realizing I had decided to let things go with Lucifer solely based on my comfort. I wanted my friend back, and that clouded my judgment.

But after this second showdown, there was no question. Something was wrong with Lucifer, and I couldn't think of myself anymore. I had to think of Heaven, Earth, and the Most High, even if he didn't want my help or know he needed it.

I gazed at the trees edging Glory Street and stepped off the walkway toward the river. "Lucifer is cruel," I whispered to them. "I don't remember noticing that before creation. And what's with the red in his eyes? Had I only seen it once, I could say it was a fluke, but I've seen it twice. Still, the greater question is, could whatever happened to Lucifer happen to others?"

I shuddered and quickened my pace toward the River of Life. Reaching its edge, I leaned over and peered into the crystal-clear water. As my face came into view, my heart finally agreed with my head. "I must do the right thing," I said to my watery reflection. "Self-interest is not an option. If I remain friendless and alone for eternity, then so be it." I collapsed to my knees, and my head lowered. "I'm guardian archangel. Protecting the Almighty and his holiness is my duty. Nothing else matters." I stood, straightened my stance, punched my fist upward, and soared high above the city.

Lucifer waved his hand, and the door to his inner sanctum appeared.

"Whoa," the taskforce expelled in a whisper.

"Follow me and enter quickly. Some of my chamber angels may not have received my orders. Charrael, get the door."

Private Charrael grabbed the handle, yanked, and held it open until Lucifer and all the higher ranks had entered. When Charrael stepped into the room and turned to close the door, it had disappeared. "What? Where...where's the door?" Charrael felt the walls. "Nothing! It's gone!" he yelled. "No way out? Are we trapped?"

"Correct, Private Charrael," Lucifer said, stifling a sinister laugh. "For you, there is no way out." Charrael gulped and pivoted. Lucifer continued, "None can enter or exit without me."

The private's eyes grew big, and something Charrael had never felt before gripped him. His body shivered at the chill in Lucifer's voice, yet observing the others, not one reacted as he did. They appeared unfazed, like nothing strange had happened.

Charrael stood there quivering, and suddenly, his feet began an involuntary shuffle across the floor. He looked down to see why, but saw no explanation. It was as though an invisible rope dragged his frame closer and closer to his illustrious leader.

Once Charrael was in the desired position beside Dylael, Lucifer said, "There, that's better." Charrael stiffened, realizing the Chief Prince not only controlled the door but also his movement. He looked to his fellow taskforce members for some empathy, but again, no reaction.

Charrael was about to nudge Dylael when Lucifer spoke. "Gentlemen, you are privileged to be the only ones who will ever enter my room or learn of its existence. Do not take this honor lightly."

Wyael gasped. "No one else knows about this room, Sir? Not even Michael or Gabriel?"

Lucifer jerked. "Of course not."

"What about the Almighty?" Maysel said.

"No!" Lucifer shouted. "Especially not him." He lowered his voice and snickered. "God hasn't a clue about anything."

Some of the taskforce chuckled at his statement, and the rest, minus Charrael, soon took part. When Lucifer joined in, the chuckles turned to roaring laughter. They slapped each other on the backs, and some doubled over in hysterics. Dylael howled and whacked Charrael.

Stumbling, Charrael caught himself, whipped around, and observed more chaos. His brows narrowed. To him, this was not funny. It was disrespectful. Charrael's eyes darted from one taskforce member to another and back to Lucifer. His chin trembled, and fear gave way to great sadness.

———————⌄———————

Deep in thought, I floated above the city. Where could I go to clear my head, plan, strategize, and figure out my next move? My office? *No—already tried that—too much commotion.* Sure, it was comfortable, but the angels knew I was always available for questions. Interruptions were not conducive to formulating plans.

What about my chamber? "No," I said to the city below. "I wouldn't be alone. My chamber angels are there." *I could dismiss them.* "I've not done that before, and it would create questions I can't answer right now. No sense in taking a risk." The more angels suspecting something was wrong in Heaven, the more chance Lucifer would find out I was onto him. If he even had an inkling, he'd alter his behavior, and I'd be back to square one.

I flew out to the plains, thinking I might find a solitary spot near the perimeter trees. Yet as I did, my eyes caught sight of the Mount of Holiness. "Aha! The Shekinah Glory Base. It's ideal—deserted and quiet."

The vacant plateau seemed forlorn as I alighted, and I wasn't ready for the loneliness that washed over me. Standing in the very spot where the three of us archangels united in worship, I thought of Gabriel, rubbed my arms, and sighed. He had always been my sounding board, the one I'd reach out to when I had a quandary. Gabriel would bring perspective to my thoughts and ideas, and this was the first time I wouldn't have him. I dropped my head and whispered, "How will I do this alone?"

When I lifted, the plains lay before me, and in the distance, Ivory Palace City glimmered a brilliant gold. Heaven appeared glorious, yet I knew it only had glory because the Most High God dwelled within. Should he remove his presence—his Shekinah—because of this turmoil with Lucifer, desolation would follow. I couldn't let that happen.

I didn't know what befell Lucifer or why it had affected Heaven, but I knew I had to stop it. "This cannot continue," I shouted to the plains, "and it doesn't matter that I don't have Gabriel. I must find a way to make everything right again."

I trekked back and forth across the Shekinah Glory Base with renewed determination, straining to dispel my angst about Lucifer and devise a good plan. I tapped my lips. "Let's see. My suspicions are sound, so what do I already know?" The boulders were my audience, and I half expected them to answer.

My mental list began: The strange connection I felt with Lucifer during worship. Number two? Oh yes…Lucifer's facial expressions during creation. He was upset, appeared irritated, and worship seemed a chore. Number three? Our encounter in the west perimeter trees.

Number four, when we visited Earth, and the humans worshiped. Gabriel and I connected, but Lucifer refused to join wings and adore the Almighty. And this was his second worship offense.

I threw my hands in the air. With just these four questionable activities, I knew I had enough to warrant surveillance. "But..." I whispered, "I can't stop now. I need to remember it all." *So, what was number five? Right...* "Lucifer disobeyed God's commands on Earth. He refused to switch study regions. Number six, he teased and toyed with the humans. Number seven, he spoke disrespectfully to me and, worse, to the Most High. Number eight, our encounter in the alcove...the red in his eyes...twice!"

When I realized the length of my list, I felt faint and reached for a nearby boulder to steady myself. A seat-shaped ledge jutted out, so there I sat, rubbing my forehead and combing my hair with my hand. Despair tackled me, and was close to winning. My heart hurt.

I leaned over, rested my elbows on my knees, cupped my face in my hands, and whispered, "Lucifer has Gabriel completely duped, and the Almighty thinks Lucifer's the right angel for Earth. He most definitely is not! But God won't listen to me, so what can I do?"

I shook my head and blew out a sigh. *Wait!* Our strange encounters. Can I use them to my advantage? *Possibly.*

If Lucifer believed he had me so intimidated that I wouldn't move against him, then maybe, just maybe, I could uncover what happened and what else he was up to. *But how? Surveillance?*

Was tracking Lucifer even doable? I fidgeted and rubbed my neck. Lucifer was shrewd and slippery. If he didn't want to be found, I knew he wouldn't be, just like the other times he'd disappeared without a word. No one ever knew where he went.

Soon, another thought invaded my frustrations. *The Armor Room, my angels, and my duties?* How would spying on Lucifer affect them? I slapped my thighs, jumped to my feet, and yelled, "Michael, back to the Armor Room!" But I quieted to a whisper. "Things must remain normal. No one, and I mean no one, can know what you're doing or why, at least not until there's proof."

CHAPTER 19

THE REVEALING

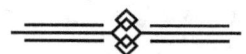

A red smog sifted down from Lucifer's ceiling, draping his room in a light haze that scattered with movement. Laughter quieted, and the room became still, blanketed by an unexplainable heaviness.

While the taskforce surveyed their eerie surroundings, Private Charrael's chest compressed. When he attempted to take in a deep breath, he couldn't. His hands were hot and clammy. Trying to remain inconspicuous, Charrael slowly wiggled his fingers and wiped them on his garments, but nothing helped. He had never seen Chief Prince Lucifer this way, and was pretty sure no one else had either.

Lucifer's room was unlike anything in Heaven, and no one said a word. Silent and trapped, Charrael felt himself tremble. Would the others notice? Finally, First Lieutenant Wyael spoke. "Sir, what is this room?"

Crossing his arms, Lucifer smirked. "If you must know, it's my sanctuary."

Wyael rubbed his forehead. "Sanctuary?"

"Yes," he said, "the place where I relax, contemplate, and tweak my plans. It's my special room." The taskforce stood in awe as Lucifer explained. Then, in the midst of his explanation, his brows furrowed, and his voice deepened. "Be forewarned," Lucifer said, pointing his finger in a sweeping motion at the taskforce. "No one else can ever hear of my room. Each of you is sworn to secrecy by the bond we now share. Are we clear?"

"Yes, Sir," the taskforce said, seeming to vow allegiance in one accord, except for Charrael. He remained mute, unable to pledge to something so bizarre.

Stepping from one taskforce member to the other, Lucifer wandered the room, pausing at each one to gaze into their eyes like he was reading their thoughts. Charrael cringed. And when Lucifer stopped to stare at Command Sergeant Major Ennel, he snuck to the other side of the room, the one Lucifer had already scrutinized.

Moseying toward the members he hadn't yet intimidated, Lucifer said, "To safeguard this room, the door is undetectable from either side. And even if you think you know the door's location, you don't. Get the idea?"

The taskforce stood a little straighter at Lucifer's charge. They nodded, but not Charrael. Considering Lucifer's deeper tone and this peculiar room, the private hid behind Second Lieutenant Maysel. Being out of sight, he felt safer.

When Lucifer finished analyzing what he thought was the entire taskforce, he continued his cunning threat and gradually increased his decibel. "There's no entering or exiting my room unless I am present," he said. "And…mark my words…if an angel outside this taskforce even hints at the room's existence, I won't have difficulty narrowing the suspect field. I'll easily find the informant and eliminate him. Understand?" he screamed.

"Yes, Chief Prince," replied the taskforce, minus Charrael. Eliminate an angel, he wondered. What does that mean? Charrael wanted to ask aloud but chose not to call attention to himself.

"We will not speak of this again," Lucifer said, shaking Charrael from his thoughts. "So, remember my warning. Come, let's get started."

Twelve of the taskforce stepped closer to Lucifer, leaving Charrael alone, exposed, and with feet seemingly glued to the floor. Lucifer sauntered toward the private and towered over him. Charrael, frozen in place, rolled his eyes upward. "Private, move!" Lucifer bellowed. The jolt released this soldier, and he jumped aside as the archangel glided past, followed by his entourage. Lucifer crossed the room and stopped at the large, oval table. Charrael hesitated but then shuffled behind the group.

"We need to have our strategies in place," Lucifer said, sounding as though he was back to normal. "You must know your station, what dangers you could encounter, and how I will run this planet. Staff Sergeant, you may now unroll the map."

As Alexael spread the map to fill the table, Charrael took a deep breath, and with his exhale, he felt himself relax. Lucifer stood facing the map at the central position and began to assign his angels. He placed the first and second lieutenants at his right and left, respectively, and followed the sequence with the lower ranks around the oval, ending with Private Charrael and Private Second Class Dylael. These taskforce members held a split position directly across the table from Lucifer.

The Chief Prince locked eyes with Charrael. He stiffened, unable to break the stare until Lucifer let go. Recovering the use of his body, he blinked and wiped his brow.

Lucifer clenched his jaw and scowled. "What's the matter, Private? Can't take it?"

Charrael's knees buckled, but he grabbed the table.

"You better toughen up, Private Charrael," Lucifer said. "You've already seen this room, and there's no turning back."

"Yes, Sir." Charrael saluted with a trembling hand.

Lucifer ignored him and seized the writing utensil. Drawing dividing lines, he separated Earth's landmass, the adjoining sea, and the sky above into six equal sections. He then marked each part with a numeral, paired the angels, and numbered the pairs. But Private Charrael was left without a counterpart. "Your number corresponds to the numbered segment of Earth," Lucifer said. "Each pair will guard and oversee their assigned section, answering only to me. Additional instruction will be forthcoming upon our arrival."

Charrael inched up his hand. "Ex...cuse me, Sir."

"Private?"

"I...I've not been allocated an associate, Sir, or a portion of Earth." Charrael swallowed hard. "What would you have me do, Chief Prince?"

Lucifer leaned back, crossed his arms, and squinted at the private. "I've taken a liking to you, Charrael. You will serve as my assistant."

It was a great honor that Archangel Lucifer had chosen Charrael for the taskforce out of all the privates of Heaven. And now this? The Chief Prince liked him and wanted him to be his assistant? Charrael gulped, hiked his shoulders, came to attention, and shouted, "Sir. Yes, Sir."

The higher ranks snickered at Charrael's naïveté. But Lucifer raised his hand and choked back their scoffing.

———⌄———

The taskforce peered at the map. "Chief Prince, where will you be located so we may report?" First Lieutenant Wyael asked, speaking for the group.

Lucifer touched the central point on the map. "I plan to set my camp right here, Eden's center. I will position my chair amid the two trees the Most High planted, and from where the mighty spring flows. All Earth is under my control. And angels, I want you to hear me on this next point and hear me well. You are to oversee the area I have assigned you and nowhere else. Eden is mine, and the humans are mine, so hands off. Do you understand?"

First Lieutenant Wyael straightened his stance and nodded. "Of course, Sir." Charrael and the others concurred.

"Good. Keep it that way."

Command Sergeant Major Ennel raised his hand. "Chief Prince, you spoke of dangers. What dangers might we encounter?"

Cocking his head, Lucifer glanced at the ceiling. "For now, we must be on guard with the land creatures. We don't know what to expect from them. The great beasts tower over the man and woman, and us, for that matter. They could be provoked and harm the humans."

Private Charrael gasped. "Could they harm us, Chief Prince?"

"No. Although the animals see us, they can't interact with us unless we initiate contact. We inhabit a dimension different from where humans and other living creatures dwell. Still, we must be watchful with the large beasts. The Almighty wants the man and woman kept safe, as do I." Lucifer snickered and rubbed his hands together. "I have my own plans for them."

"Plans, Sir?" Warrant Officer Willel's head snapped up, and he turned toward Lucifer. "What sort of plans?"

Lucifer grimaced, then softened. "My designs aren't yet complete. But I alone will rule this planet and those measly humans."

Sergeant Sebiel's mouth dropped open. "Measly humans, Chief Prince?"

Lucifer eyeballed his taskforce, and his fist tapped his lips. "Yes... humans are boring creatures and easy to control. The first day I was on Earth, I just observed. The second day, I decided to have some fun."

Maysel grinned. "Fun? Oh, please tell us."

Lucifer shifted from foot to foot, and his hands moved as he recounted his findings. "It has to do with the two dimensions I just cited. Although first revealed in creation, I didn't understand them until I visited Earth. The physical and spiritual dimensions coexist, but interestingly enough, humans can only see the physical, the things of Earth. They cannot see the spiritual, the things of Heaven. We see both."

Huntiel's head tilted. "How did this lead you to have fun?"

A growing smile crossed Lucifer's face. "When I finally understood our differences, I discovered that even though angels inhabit the spiritual, I could step into the physical and interact with inanimate objects, like rocks."

Specialist Carsiel cleared his throat. "Rocks, Sir?"

"Yes," Lucifer said, chuckling. "I'd pick up a fist-sized stone and throw it close to where the man and woman were sitting or standing. When the rock thudded to the ground, one or the other would jump, move, or look in that direction. I'll tell you, I laughed so hard, and once, I even fell to the ground.

"After a while, that fun wore off, and I needed a new thrill. So, I tried something different. When the humans were sitting under a tree, I shook the tree as hard as I could. Fruit pummeled the ground, and the humans ran, covering their heads." Lucifer slapped his thighs and belly-laughed. "It gave me such a charge. But I think the humans were scared."

Corporal Huntiel's face puckered. "Why did that scare them?"

"They had no idea what caused the phenomenon," Lucifer said as he gazed around the table. "The man and woman couldn't see me." He took a deep breath and extended his hands out to his taskforce. "That was the moment I realized I was in complete control."

Lucifer clutched the sides of his head, pushed back his hair, and paced as he detailed the remaining events. "Wherever they went, I triggered chaos. In the beginning, I thought this would just be fun, like throwing the rock, yet I found it to be so much more."

Alexael shifted his stance. "More, Sir?"

Lucifer's eyes narrowed. "Yes-s-s-s," he hissed as a sinister grin emerged.

Charrael shuddered at Lucifer's answer. Dread sought to engulf him, but he did his best to push it down and search the room for a means of escape. Could he remember where he entered? If so, would he be able to find the door?

Taking in short breaths, Charrael realized what Lucifer said was true. There was no way out. He felt his whole being teeter, and he clenched the table to keep from falling.

"Angels," Lucifer said, "when I fully grasped the degree of control I possessed, so much power surged through me I could barely contain it." He paused, closed his eyes, and as they rolled open, Lucifer whispered, "What I learned next confirmed that nothing would ever stop me. Earth and all creation…would…be…mine!"

Some of the taskforce, including Charrael, flinched, and some just stood there wide-eyed and speechless. But Wyael seemed energized. "Really? What did you learn?"

Lucifer's shoulders rose as he inhaled, held it for a moment, and exhaled. "Ahh…this element will be the key to my rule and our subduing Earth, so pay attention.

"Because of the differences in our dimensions, not only was I undetectable to the eye, but neither could they hear me from a distance. However, when I got close and spoke directly into their ears, voilà, my comments became their thoughts."

The taskforce gasped but said nothing. Eventually, Chief Warrant Officer 4 Juael broke the silence. "Shocking, Sir."

Quirking an eyebrow, Lucifer smiled. "Yes, quite. And this, I will use to my advantage."

Juael jolted. "How?"

"Doubt."

Ennel's face scrunched as he took a step back. "Doubt, Sir?

"Yes. It's a feeling of uncertainty within them. I've thought long and hard about this since I returned. My plan is to whisper words that will cause them to question what they know of God, who he is, and whether or not he is good. I expect this doubt to trigger mistrust and unbelief. Since the humans don't actually see God, they should start to think he is a figment of their imagination. And my seed of doubt will sink its roots deep within their souls.

"Even though creation itself displays overwhelming evidence of the Almighty, I'll help them to ignore what they see and show them the pleasure of my way, how benevolent I am. I believe this is all it will take for the humans to abandon God and run to me."

Charrael clamped his hand across his mouth to keep from screaming. *Why would the Chief Prince do such a thing? Those poor humans.*

Lucifer's head tilted upward, and the most sickening expression crossed his face. It seemed Lucifer felt something Charrael and the rest of the taskforce didn't. He let out a short gasp, lowered his head, and just stared.

"Sir," Maysel said, dragging the archangel back from wherever his thoughts had taken him. "Aren't you concerned the Most High will learn of your plan?"

"No, I've been very careful." Lucifer glared as he stepped back from the table, spread out his arms, and presented all his handiwork. "Secrecy is why I constructed this room. Everything is concealed here—every idea, tactic, strategy, and scheme. And what's more, the Most High is clueless!" Lucifer snickered as he pointed at his taskforce. "You know how many admirers I've amassed. God will be stunned when he sees most of his angels following me. In fact, when this is said and done, I'm certain I'll have won every angel."

Charrael's stomach churned. He fought tears, but some dripped on the map. Lowering his head, he rotated slightly so the group could not see. Wadding his garment, he discreetly blotted Lucifer's map and wiped his eyes.

Turning again toward the table and the taskforce, Charrael watched Olivel push back his dark brown locks and say, "Every angel, Sir? Even Michael and Gabriel?"

Lucifer grumbled as he returned to the table. "No, not them. They'll never convert. I'll have to eliminate them. And with those two out of the way, I shouldn't have any trouble commanding the worship of the remaining angels."

Worship of angels? Charrael's breath caught, and the sound escaped, but he quickly hid his shock. Lucifer's head snapped in his direction. He squinted and glared as though boring holes into each taskforce member across the table. Charrael took that as a good sign. Lucifer wasn't sure who made the noise.

Wyael shifted. "Sir," he said, "what about the Most High?"

Lucifer didn't answer. Instead, he strolled from the table toward the center of the room, but after a few steps, he floated, and as he did, his countenance changed. A soft red glow emanated from somewhere within his chest and intensified, consuming his whole being. The angels filed out from around the table, and spellbound, they followed after Lucifer.

For some reason, Charrael remained clear-thinking, alone, and lingering at the table. He gasped. Did Lucifer see him? Charrael ducked down, inched closer to the taskforce, and scooted in line behind Dylael.

All angels, at one point or another, had seen Michael, Gabriel, and Lucifer join wings and illuminate in the worship of the Most High God. But Lucifer's glow was different—bizarre even. He pulsed and radiated, not iridescent white-gold as in worship. No, Lucifer's luminosity intermixed red, yellow, and orange hues, comparable to the fiery brilliance of God's Shekinah. And even though his appearance could not match the brightness or glory of God, it was enough to hold his taskforce mesmerized, suspended in eternity, except for Charrael.

After a brief period, Lucifer broke the silence, yet the angels remained in a stupor. He paced back and forth, shaking his fists and flailing his arms. "With the multitude of angel warriors on my side," he said in a flaming tirade, "I will crush the Almighty under my feet. I will ascend and replace Him. I will exalt my throne above all the angels of God. I will sit on the north…the Mount of Holiness… before the angel congregation, and…I will be the Supreme Monarch."

As Lucifer's head tilted back, his eyes closed, and he filled his lungs. "Hear me," he screamed, "I will be like the Most High! For I am God and master of all."

Lucifer's loyal angels present for this revealing fell to their knees, unable to move, compelled to worship their consummate ruler.

CHAPTER 20

A TRAITOR IN THE MIDST?

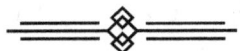

Ever since our creation, the backside of the Mount of Holiness had been off-limits to most angels. God gave permission to fly over it if desired or required, but hiking the mountainous terrain was frowned upon and risky.

The Shekinah Glory plateau graced the mountain facing southward to the plains and the city, but two-thirds of the mountain jutted up above this base. Peering northward and down the backside from the pinnacle, cliffs and ledges came into view. Overhangs, clefs, and crags characterized the rocky topography. Resting at the mountain's bedrock, trees and tall grasses obscured narrow, rough trails, shallow valleys, and deep crevices, yet none of us knew why.

When everything in Heaven was cultured and landscaped in perfect dimensions, it was curious why the backside of the Mount of Holiness was rough. Even though many were unaware of the backside, unbeknownst to Michael, countless others knew the mountain's belly contained the caverns.

Word of Lucifer's secret address continued to spread from devotee to devotee throughout Ivory Palace City and all the way to the Forge. Angels dedicated to Lucifer quietly withdrew from their regular responsibilities to attend the clandestine meeting.

In ever-increasing numbers, Lucifer's supporters followed the specific directions, traced the path, and located the doorway to the caverns. The rotunda already appeared packed, but none of that mattered to these later devotees. They pushed through the entrance and squeezed in where there wasn't room.

While those who heard Wyael's speech understood the importance of silence, the new arrivals knew nothing. Frustrations flared. Voices raised. Devoted followers shoved and rammed devoted followers. Lucifer's influence had taken its toll on these once gentle angels.

Sergeant Major Gragael rushed from his post to the empty stage. "Please, please, quiet down," Gragael yelled, raising his arms and pulsing them lower and lower to indicate the urgency of dropping the volume. "Hush! Do your best to make room and accommodate your fellow enthusiasts. Chief Prince Lucifer needs every one of you. Angels! Remember First Lieutenant Wyael's speech. No noise, please! Individually prepare and quietly meditate on the magnificence of our great Chief Prince."

No one cared about what Wyael had said, and this time, Gragael's insistence on silent preparation for Lucifer's appearance didn't work. In the jam-packed caverns, angels who had chosen the more remote spots to watch Lucifer and hear his address now realized these new attendees obstructed their view. Unaccepting, they migrated toward the center of the rotunda, and intermittent skirmishes erupted.

Angel pushed angel. Tension climbed. Gragael clenched his fists and stomped the stage, struggling to control the throng.

Lucifer's supporters grew unmanageable. Their noise infuriated Gragael, and his only option was to dismiss the unruly ones. But would this bring repercussions? They could abandon Lucifer, and if so, would the Chief Prince retaliate against him? Would the dismissed ones divulge information about this hidden assembly? He had no idea, but could not take the chance.

"If the Most High learns of this gathering," he said, "it will not be my fault. Guards!" Gragael shrieked as a last resort. "Sentry Guards! To the stage!" The guards marched quickly and lined the front of the stage area as before.

With this second show of authority, the crowd quieted for a moment. Gragael allowed his shoulders to drop. His cheeks puffed as he blew out a long breath and wiped his brow. A crisis averted? Maybe. Still, from somewhere deep within the measureless caverns, Gragael identified the resurgence of low-volume chanting, "Lu-ci-fer; Lu-ci-fer." It was slow and methodical, but with each additional voice, the decibel rose.

Abuzz with activity, no one in the Armor Room was the wiser about my lengthy absence. I followed my usual routine, checked each station, and stopped at Randiel's cubicle, all neat and orderly.

In the solace of my office, I felt a calm wash over me. On my desk lay my original lists, two of which were blank. I picked up the "pros" column, crumpled it, and tossed it into the trash. Lucifer's "questionable activities" were sealed in my head. "So, unless some angel can read minds…that's where they'll stay until I have proof," I whispered, wadding the remaining lists and chucking them. They bounced off the wall and went right in. "Score!" I said, shooting my arms up and wishing it was that easy to figure out a good surveillance plan.

The disconnect between Lucifer and me had been building, and none of it made sense. Why has his attitude changed? Did he have an ulterior motive for his actions? While I pondered, another alarming notion came to mind. Could it be Lucifer had somehow developed a flaw in his character? *Is that even possible?* What would be the outcome if it was? Would he damage Heaven or Earth? That consideration had shot into my head and out my mouth when I encountered him in the perimeter trees. He'd denied it then, but now with what I'd observed, it seemed likely.

The thought of someone altering what the LORD God had created made me cringe. "I need evidence," I said, pounding my desk. But how to obtain it was another story.

Watching Lucifer could reveal something. Still, I would uncover nothing if I didn't know where to begin. Leaning back in my chair, I clasped my hands behind my head to ponder.

"Hmm…let's see…where should I start?" I whispered to myself. "Wyael did order the taskforce back to Lucifer's chambers. Perhaps my investigation should commence there?" *Might be tricky, though.* If Lucifer departed through the front door, I'd be able to track him. But if he exited through his atrium, he could hide his departure. And if I only surveil the atrium, I would miss the front door. *Why am I having so much trouble? I'm never this indecisive. Michael, make a decision!*

"Fine," I said, jumping to my feet. "Reconnaissance begins at Lucifer's."

The pulsing light streaming from Lucifer held his taskforce entranced and kneeling before him, yet Charrael remained upright. Inching his way to the corner to avoid Lucifer's field of vision, he did his best to blend into the wall.

From the far-left point, Charrael kept watch. Lucifer lifted his head and raised his arms, accepting the taskforce's worship and complete and utter devotion.

Appalled that any angel would worship someone other than God Most High, Charrael wanted to run, yet he couldn't. The room was sealed. With Lucifer facing the opposite direction, his corner helped, but didn't hide. Charrael knew he was visible, as much as if he waved a flaming sword and yelled, "Here I am! Come get me!"

Angel by angel, Lucifer scanned his sanctuary and gazed upon each worshiper. Their adoration seemed to feed his pleasure, and his radiance mushroomed. He paused by Wyael and Maysel and drew in a deep breath. His chest swelled, and a look of euphoria materialized on his face. Lucifer slowly traversed the lower ranks and appeared to suck in their worship with his eyes, but as he did, something seemed to pierce his peripheral vision.

At the precise moment Lucifer flicked his head toward Charrael, the angel sentry outside his chamber sounded the chime. Worship disrupted. The taskforce stirred and awoke from their stupor.

Lucifer locked eyes with Charrael, yet voices diverted his attention. Instantly, he flung his arms out toward his angels, and an invisible burst of power seemed to cover them like a blanket. They stood motionless.

Charrael felt his body quiver. As before, Lucifer's spell had not affected him, but his tremors might give him away. If the Chief Prince moved closer, could he control them and play along? Or was he already foiled? Had Lucifer noticed him standing while the others knelt?

Inhaling deeply, Lucifer moved his hand toward his face. He pulled it in a downward motion, exhaled, and seemed to return to his customary state. Pivoting, he stepped toward the corner that hugged Charrael.

Rigid with vacant eyes, Charrael held his breath while Lucifer stared, poked, and prodded. Would Charrael be found out? Soon, the Chief Prince swung around and drifted back to center. Charrael wanted to suck in a huge breath, yet small, easy, and silent inhales would have to suffice.

I popped out of my office, focused and ready to take to the air on this investigation. "Stop, Michael," I whispered. *This one-track mind of yours is not good. You have responsibilities.* I halted and looked around.

Everything appeared secure as usual. "Fine," I said under my breath. "But why do I have assistants if I can't do what I need to do when I need to do it? Why can't I just assume things will remain sound and run smoothly?" Every word of caution Gabriel ever spoke rushed my thoughts and consolidated into this, *Michael, don't be impulsive.*

"Right," I said, expelling air through my vibrating lips before entering Randiel's cubicle. "I'll be stepping out for a while, and as always, I'm trusting you to oversee the Armor Room. Not sure how long I'll be, but I'll check in periodically, or you can summon me as usual."

Randiel looked up from his desk. "Do not concern yourself, Sir. At this moment, all is well."

"Good. I'll be going then."

I half saluted, and as I turned to exit, Randiel jumped to his feet. "Wait, I just remembered. I do have some armor alterations needing your approval."

My head jerked in his direction, and I halted. "Really? That's strange."

Randiel stared at the floor and then at me as he nodded. "I know, Sir. I don't believe we've ever needed armor revisions."

"You're right. The forge angels are meticulous in crafting to each specification. It is very odd this would happen. Which armor is affected?"

"The rank of corporal, Sir," he said, turning back to his desk and grabbing his notes. "The breastplate is too wide, and the saber handle needs shortening. It will interfere with the angel's grip and ability to parry if not adjusted."

"Let's see the specs."

Randiel handed me the clipboard. I checked the original measurements against the requested alterations. "These modifications seem to be in order. Good catch. We wouldn't want our Corporals looking sloppy or having difficulty wielding their swords."

"No, Sir, we wouldn't. Thank you."

I turned to exit but spun back around. "Randiel, be sure Jaysael gets your corrections so the Forge can make the adjustments."

"Yes, Sir. I will."

"Good. Is that all?"

"For now, Chief Prince,"

"Alright, then," I said, waving. "I'm off."

The sentries opened the large double doors of the Armor Room, and I nodded a greeting. Taking flight toward Lucifer's, I surveyed the dwellings below and reviewed my plan. "First order of business—locate Lucifer. Second—follow without being detected. And third, well, I'll figure that out when I've accomplished one and two."

Lucifer paced the room and gripped his head like a clamp. "Private Charrael is standing!" he muttered to himself. "Either he jumped to his feet when the chime sounded, or he didn't bow to me at all. I'm guessing the latter. I'm positive I saw him standing before the chime. Unacceptable! If Charrael didn't bow, I need to know why. Was he not mesmerized like the others? And if not, why not?"

Lucifer wandered in circles, seething. He shook his arms out, clenched and unclenched his fists, and mumbled. "What was my reason for choosing Charrael in the first place? He was an afterthought, the thirteenth. I knew I didn't need him, but I wanted him. Why?" *How could I have been so careless?*

Weaving in and out of his statue-like taskforce, Lucifer poked at some, and several times, he stopped to glare at Charrael. *If I'm not controlling this soldier, he isn't truly loyal. He could expose me before I'm ready.* "Charrael could thwart my plans and ruin everything," Lucifer said under his breath as he reached midpoint. "Better keep a close eye on him." *No, no. Can't risk it.* "I need to get rid of him." *How?* "Sure…catch him alone and end his existence!" *Yes, annihilation! He's only a private.* "I can always find another, should I feel the need. And would anyone even notice if he was gone?"

Stuffing down the question of whether angel annihilation was possible, Lucifer narrowed his eyes, stared at Charrael, and then looked back to the taskforce. Moving in their direction, he threw up his arm, snapped his finger, and released the angels. He waved his hand once more, and the door to his secret room appeared. "I'll exit first and signal when the way is clear for you."

Charrael concealed his fear as he slid out of the corner and congregated among his fellow soldiers. Dodging Lucifer at every move, he slipped between Sebiel and Huntiel and hid as they all reentered Lucifer's front room.

Stewel stole away to speak to the door sentries, and while most soldiers fiddled with their armor, Charrael sought opinions about

Lucifer's big reveal. Tapping Dylael's shoulder, he said quietly, "Hey, what do you make of that?"

Dylael scrunched his brow. "What do you mean?"

"Well, you know, Chief Prince Lucifer's red glow and everything."

"Red glow?" Dylael said with a hearty laugh. "What red glow?"

"Shhh," Charrael waved and murmured. "You didn't see it?"

"No. You're talking nonsense. We just left the table. There was no red glow."

"What...?" Charrael breathed out in a whisper. Near the back wall, the one closest to the door, he saw Olivel. Moving in his direction, he bumped him accidentally on purpose.

"Charrael," Olivel said, grabbing the wall to keep from falling. "Watch where you're going."

"Yes, Sir," he said, bowing his head. "Sorry."

Olivel turned to pick up his shin guard. "Be more careful next time."

"I will, Sir...Ah...May I ask a question?"

Strapping the piece of armor to his right leg, Olivel said, "Quickly, we should be leaving soon."

Charrael's shoulders raised as he inhaled. "What did you think of Chief Prince Lucifer?"

Still bent over, Olivel turned his head toward Charrael and then back to his shin guard. "You mean about him placing his chair at the center of Eden?"

"No...about his red glow."

Standing erect, Olivel chuckled. "What red glow? Wait. Charrael, are you allowing the vanishing door to get to you?"

Charrael shook his head.

Olivel huffed and rolled his eyes. "Then how did you come up with this fabrication? Archangel Lucifer has no red glow," he said, pointing. "Look at him. See, no red. You need to control yourself. Gather your gear and get in line."

"Yes, Sir." Charrael shuddered. Every command made him jumpy, but worse, Olivel didn't see Lucifer's red glow either. He dared not speak to the higher ranks—they'd bark even more orders at him, and suspicion would rise. Did he see what he thought he saw? Could it have been his imagination? *No, I did see Lucifer glowing red, and I heard his declaration. Why didn't the others?* Charrael gasped. *Did something erase their memories?*

CHAPTER 21

CAUGHT

Arriving at Lucifer's chambers, I alighted on the stoop. The sentries jolted to attention and saluted. Returning their salute, I said, "Is Lucifer inside?"

The sentry on my right responded. "Yes, Chief Prince Michael."

"Is he alone, or does he have his taskforce with him?"

Lucifer's left door sentry stepped forward. "The taskforce is also inside, Sir."

Precisely what I was hoping. "Alright," I said, trying not to show my delight. "I won't interrupt. I'll come back later."

"Yes, Sir," both sentries replied as they returned to their post.

My visit to Lucifer's chamber was atypical. I hadn't been there since he threw me out, and I certainly didn't need questions. So, I nodded to the guards and sauntered down the walkway. Once out of sight, I crossed the street and snuck back, using the dwellings and greenery as my cover. From the abode catty-cornered to Lucifer's, I found a place with a good view of his chamber door and where the sentries couldn't see me. When Lucifer departed, I would follow. But for now, I'd wait. He had to come out sometime.

The taskforce continued preparing for departure as Lucifer looked on with distant eyes. Master Sergeant Stewel approached. "Sir... Sir... Sir." The third time, he tapped Lucifer's arm.

Lucifer glanced down. "What is it, Stewel?"

Straightening his stance, Stewel said, "The chime was our signal, Sir."

"Signal for what?"

As Charrael snuck closer to better hear their conversation, Stewel beamed and thrust out his chest. "Chief Prince, I had the sentry sound the chime so we wouldn't linger too long in your chamber. Remember your address? Anyway, as I thanked the sentries, I was able to intercept a message from Sergeant Major Gragael. He's concerned, Sir. The cavern angels are growing restless again. Although they're controlled for now, he's not sure how much longer he can keep them contained. We really should go, Sir...Sir...did you hear me?"

Lucifer's hand swept the air. "You go. I'll come along shortly."

Charrael tailed Stewel as he made his way through the maze of soldiers and armor to Wyael. "Lieutenant," he said.

"Stewel? What do you need?"

"Not a thing, Sir, except to tell you Chief Prince Lucifer said we should go to the caverns ahead of him."

"And why would he tell you?" Wyael said, adjusting the buckle on his breastplate.

"I think because I reminded him about his address."

Wyael's head snapped up. "What made you do that?"

"Trying to be efficient, Sir. I had the door sentry sound the gong so we wouldn't be too late. Then I intercepted a message from Gragael for Chief Prince Lucifer."

Wyael scowled. "What?" And what message?"

Stewel took a step back and bumped into Charrael, pretending to fiddle with his belt. He gawked at Charrael, turned, and said to Wyael, "Ah…the devotees are getting out of hand again."

Charrael saw Wyael's brows narrow. Although he was a much lower rank, Charrael knew exactly what Stewel had done. This master sergeant had just tried to usurp First Lieutenant Wyael's position.

"Stewel," Wyael said in a low guttural growl that caused a chill to surge through Charrael. "Messages come to me first. Don't you ever go behind my back again. Return to your place. I'll take it from here."

"Yes, Sir." Stewel gulped and pivoted. As he did, he glared at Charrael.

"Taskforce," Wyael shouted as every member came to attention. "Prepare for departure."

Stewel dressed quickly to catch up with the others. Lucifer stood out of the way, observing, yet he still seemed rooted in thought. His left arm crossed his chest to support his right elbow while his fingers drummed his lips.

Charrael and each taskforce member gathered their things and lined up in exit formation. When they started toward the front door, Lucifer yelled, "Wait! Leave through the atrium. I don't want anyone to see you. I'll do the same."

Across the street from Lucifer's, I stood, waiting for someone, anyone, to exit his chamber. I shifted from one foot to the next. I sat, reclined for a while, and stood again, but no one came out of that door. *This is silly. I can't imagine Lucifer and his taskforce are still inside. They must have left through the atrium.*

I decided to return to the Armor Room and try again later. "Wait," I whispered. "I shouldn't leave until I've verified their departure." *But how? Ask the sentries? What if they don't know?* "Well...then...I'd need to enter Lucifer's chambers." *Suppose they are still inside? What then?* "I'd need a reason for my visit. Hmm...I do want to set things straight with Lucifer after our encounter in the Throne Room. So, yeah, that's my reason."

As I began to step out from my hiding place onto the street, I paused, realizing it would be unwise to expose my surveillance location. The spot was a good one. I might need it again.

Making sure Lucifer's sentries weren't looking in my direction, I hiked to a different site, but on the way, my sense of responsibility took hold. "Maybe a quick visit to the Armor Room will ease my mind. Yes, I believe it will," I muttered. "And if Lucifer leaves in the meantime, well, I'll just deal with that then."

Contented I was far enough away, I parted the greenery and stepped out onto the walkway, nearly colliding with Bradiel and Justel. The surprised generals quickly came to attention.

"Chief Prince Michael," Justel said, saluting. "I beg your pardon, Sir."

"At ease, gentlemen. And don't mention it, Justel. It's fine."

Bradiel cocked his head. "If I may ask, Sir, why are you here, and especially in the walkway shrubberies? Is there anything we can do to help?"

———⌄———

Obscured by tall, majestic trees, Lucifer's indoor atrium oozed peace. Plentiful vegetation with abundant, multi-colored flowers and the soft tinkle of trickling water continually delivered beauty and tranquility. Heaven beamed its glorious light through its dome and bathed the luxurious cobalt-blue floor in a graceful shimmer.

Clangs of battle gear and clattering boots shattered the serenity. One by one, taskforce members clomped into the atrium, struck the mosaic tile, and soared through its circular rooftop access. Landing on the secluded walkway behind Lucifer's chamber, the soldiers reassembled and prepared to march.

Private Charrael's thoughts suddenly became clear. He wanted out. Not that it wasn't a great honor to be chosen by Lucifer; it was. Still, he could not stand by while this illustrious yet demented Chief Prince seized God's throne, gained control of creation, and swayed the whole army of angels.

Hashing over what he saw in Lucifer's chambers, Charrael's stomach churned. Still, he tailed the taskforce and trudged through the city toward the gate. Could he possibly give Lucifer the benefit of the doubt and still serve him? Yes, but that would mean overlooking his red glow and the irreverent rantings against the Most High. No, he'd have to figure out another way. Nearing the Armor Room, Charrael had an idea.

"Private, Charrael," shouted First Lieutenant Wyael. "You're lagging. Keep up."

"Yes, Sir," he said, quickening his pace.

Lucifer rang for Andiel. "I'll be leaving," he said to his lead angel. "Make sure my chamber is orderly for when I return."

"Of course," Andiel said, bowing.

Lucifer crossed the atrium's threshold and zoomed upward. As he topped the trees, he spied Michael up the street with two of his generals. Instantly, he shot down behind his chambers. *What's Michael doing here? Snooping, I bet. Did he see me? I don't think so, but I better watch him.*

Lucifer removed his helmet and breastplate and leaned them against a tree. He opened his wings and rose slowly until he was flush with the top of the atrium dome. Grabbing the lattice, he rested his body on the rooftop and folded his wings. Only a fraction of his head peeked above the apex, and the trees parted just enough so he could keep his eyes on Michael.

The meeting seemed innocent, but Lucifer knew there was more to it. He had created a problem when he gave Michael a glimpse of his true self. *What was I thinking? I should have been more controlled. Do I have a situation I need to defuse, or doesn't it matter?*

Caught off guard, I wrinkled my brow and stared at the generals. Since I didn't answer immediately, my silence made them fidget. *Careful how you respond, Michael. Your answer could spark deeper inquiries.*

The long interval between Bradiel's questions and my answer served me well. I shook myself out of my stare. "Gentlemen, I know I rarely come to this part of the city. However, I have business with Chief Prince Lucifer. With the mission to Earth, we've had many encounters lately."

Bradiel nodded. "Of course, Sir. I didn't mean to pry."

I held out my hand. "You didn't. But what are you two doing here?"

Justel hiked his shoulders. "Our chambers are on this street, Sir, and Chief Prince Lucifer's chambers are on our way. May we walk with you?"

"Oh yes," Bradiel said, smiling. "I've wanted to hear about your visit to Earth."

Much to my relief, they seemed to have forgotten about the shrubberies. "Well, Generals," I said, "I would love to talk about Earth, and we could if I were going that way. But I've already been to Lucifer's. I wasn't able to see him because he was meeting with his taskforce. Right now, I'm headed back to the Armor Room."

Bradiel scrunched his face. "Okay, Sir. Some other time then."

"Please count me in on the discussion, too," Justel said, rubbing his hands together.

I smiled. These were two of Heaven's finest generals. "Let's plan it for after Chief Prince Lucifer and his taskforce depart for Earth." I turned to leave but called back, "Have a good rest, Generals."

"We will, Sir," they said, waving.

Whew! Dodged a big one, Michael.

———————⌄———————

Reaching the edge of Ivory Palace City, the taskforce exited the gate, and the immense plains connecting the city to the Mount of Holiness lay before them. The caverns' entrance was hidden somewhere at the mountain's base, yet its distance seemed incalculable. "Angels," First Lieutenant Wyael ordered. "Ready. Wings. Launch."

The taskforce lifted off with the precision and elegance of an aerial ballet. Below lay the vast plains providing a kaleidoscope of color. Dense trees lining the east and west borders gave way to lush greenery and elaborate walkways skirting its floor. Flaunting intricate patterns, the plains, together with the Garden of Fiery Stones visible in the distance, illustrated God's glory, holiness, and splendor. On these immense flatlands, the angel armies assembled for worship, orders, and announcements, and this was where angels had the privilege of observing the Three-in-One God create his physical universe.

The beauty of Heaven almost made Charrael forget the horror of Lucifer's secret room. But what Chief Prince Lucifer said about the person who divulged any information, he would never forget. "Think, Charrael," he said to himself. "You have to get out of this taskforce before Lucifer learns you didn't worship. Or maybe, it's already too late."

Lucifer watched Michael hasten toward the Armor Room, yet he delayed his departure until the generals entered their chambers. Satisfied all was under control and neutralizing the situation unnecessary, Lucifer slipped off the atrium dome and landed on the walkway. Retrieving his armor, he continued his original mission—the caverns of the Mount of Holiness.

CHAPTER 22

DISAPPOINTMENTS AND DELAY

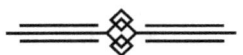

C all it a hunch, intuition, or whatever; I felt like I was being watched. I only half answered General Bradiel's question. *Was Bradiel watching me? Or someone else?*

I shrugged it off and continued up the street, but my angst slowed my pace. If I abandoned surveillance now, I might never have the opportunity again. Why was I returning to the Armor Room? If things weren't running smoothly, Randiel would summon me. *Should I skip my quick visit and go back to Lucifer's?* Rounding the corner, I found the walkway garden and comfy bench where the three of us met with the under-angels. I sighed and sank deep into the cushion, almost longing for those discussions again.

Greenery flourished all around, and thankfully, colorful, long-stemmed flowers kept my seat a bit secluded. Maybe here, I could avoid any more unplanned meetings.

Still, I fidgeted. My decision to return to the Armor Room now seemed counterintuitive. All the while I talked with the generals and walked to this garden, Lucifer's chamber was unguarded. *What if he'd already left? Or…he could leave while I'm hiding out here.* I stood to my feet. "The Armor Room can wait. I need to go back now." *Hopefully, I haven't ruined my only chance to trail Lucifer.*

I peeked out of the garden, and with no one in sight, I stole onto the walkway and hurried toward Lucifer's. As his chambers came into view, I decelerated, calmed my anxiousness, and sauntered toward the sentries. This time, they were ready. "Are Chief Prince Lucifer and his taskforce still inside?"

"Sir," the right sentry said. "They have not departed through this door."

Thrilled to hear the news, I said, "Thank you, but I can't wait any longer. I need to speak to Lucifer now."

"Yes, Sir," they said, grabbing the handles.

I nodded to them, passed through the entryway, and startled Lucifer's chamber angel. "Is Lucifer here?"

Andiel bowed his head. "I'm sorry, Sir, he's not. You just missed him."

"Oh, I see." I turned to leave but whipped back around. "Do you have any idea where he was headed?"

"No, Chief Prince. I'm not privy to that information."

My shoulders dropped. "Fine. When he returns, please notify me at the Armor Room. I must speak to him."

Andiel held out his hand to stop my departure. "May I give him a message, Sir?"

"No," I said, sighing. "No message."

His eyes held concern. "Sir, I never know how long Chief Prince Lucifer will be away from his chamber. However, I will do my best to notify you."

I smiled. "Thank you, Andiel. You are a good chamber angel."

———◡———

The taskforce landed at the backside of the Mount of Holiness. They trudged through the tall grasses and hiked gingerly on the narrow paths. There, under a crag, they located an isolated crack visible only to those searching for it. The trail tapered into what seemed like a dead-end, but instead, it was the rock formation God created as the cavern's door. Nearing this stone entrance, loud chanting and frenzied voices leaked out.

Charrael realized if he stepped through that opening, he would never escape. His insides knotted and cramped. He scrunched his face, loathing these new feelings overtaking him, and he knew he had to do something to get away, yet now his bright idea seemed lame. Still, it would have to do.

Being last in line usually bothered Charrael, but at this moment, he was thankful. No one cared enough about a lowly private to check on him or even look back to see if he was still there unless it was Lieutenant Wyael. As the highest-ranking officer, he controlled the taskforce. So, Wyael would check on Charrael occasionally, not because he cared, but because it was his responsibility.

Mainly, everyone just concentrated on themselves, their duties, and now, the cavern's entrance. Charrael slacked off and allowed more space between himself and Dylael. When he felt he was back far enough, he slowly unsheathed his sword. Slipping its tip between his right leg and the shin guard, Charrael sliced through the top strap.

The shin guard hung cockeyed. He delicately re-sheathed and hoped no one had noticed. Charrael hustled to close the gap. Squeezing by the lower ranks, he crept toward the front. That odd feeling gripped him again, and his body quivered as he spoke, "F… First Lieutenant Wy…Wyael. Sir."

"What is it, Private?"

"M…my shin guard is loose."

"What?"

"Yes, Sir," Charrael said, stiffening but cocking his stance so the Lieutenant could see.

"Oh, this won't do. We leave for Earth directly following Chief Prince Lucifer's address, and you cannot accompany us with faulty armor. Head back to the Armor Room for a replacement. You'll miss most of the address, but it cannot be helped. Go now, so you can return before the speech is over."

"Yes, Sir."

I smiled at the sentries so they couldn't see my disappointment and stepped off the stoop of Lucifer's chambers. *How can I possibly track him now?* I needed to think. Choosing to return to the Armor Room via the long way, I strolled up the street, wondering what my next move should be. My thoughts reverted. *Maybe it is my imagination.* Was Lucifer's behavior really as bad as I thought? Was there something off about him or not? He would be leaving for Earth shortly, and I knew if I didn't find him soon, I would discover nothing—if there was something to discover. *Maybe I am overreacting.* The Almighty wasn't alarmed. Why should I be? Perhaps I should just let it go and concentrate on my own work.

As I neared the Scroll Room, I thought of Gabriel penning the Word of God. For an instant, I contemplated how pleasant it would be to forget Lucifer and his antics and to have my mind saturated with God's word. But then I remembered the station to which each Chief Prince was created. I was the guardian. Gabriel was the messenger. And Lucifer…? *Does he have a station other than directing worship?* I knew he was an archangel as I was, and I knew he alone walked amidst the boulders of fire. So, was leading worship his only task? I threw my hands in the air. "Why hadn't I realized this before?" I cowered and looked around to see if anyone was watching. Thankfully, no one was. "But," I whispered, "what difference does it make that I know it now, other than he's certainly not doing his job?"

Exasperated, I slapped the sides of my legs. And with the slap, I heard crinkling paper in the tuffs of my garment. My lists? *No… can't be. I pitched them.*

I dug out the slip; it was a list, yet not the one I thought. It contained only armor specs. Still, this simple record was enough to jog my memory of the more critical list tucked away in my head—exactly the motivation I needed to stay on top of Lucifer. I couldn't let it go by the wayside. I had to find him. *But now, where do I begin?*

Charrael rushed to get away from the Lieutenant and the whole taskforce. But, to them, he hurried so he could return in a timely manner. Charrael edged by the soldiers and continued down the precarious trail while Wyael observed. His back ached from the imaginary daggers their stares hurled at him.

Anxious, Charrael sped up. He could hardly wait to be out of their sight. Around the bend and halfway to the end, the path narrowed. As he hustled down the tapering path, he lost his balance. With his second step to regain footing, Charrael found a deep crevice obscured by tall grasses.

Arms flailing, his boots teetered on the edge. He tried to grab the rock and some of the greenery to keep from falling, yet he couldn't get a firm grip. Appearing as a tree toppling in a forest, Charrael keeled over across the opening.

Thankfully, the crevice was only slightly wider than he was tall. He reached out and caught himself. Pressing his palms against the face of the adjacent rock, like armbars, he stopped his fall.

Face down, feet on one side, and hands plastered against the other, Charrael stared into the deep crack that seemed bottomless. His body resembled a wavering bridge, and he knew he couldn't hold this posture for long. *I need a way out and fast. I have to get to the Armor Room. Wait! My wings! They should get me back to the surface.*

He grunted to activate his wings. Nothing. For some reason, in this position, his wings wouldn't unfold. He tried again and again... still nothing. His hands ached, and his feet started to shift. Angel army training didn't include rock climbing, and Charrael had no idea what to do next.

"Help," he yelled. No response. *I can't stay like this forever.* "Help," he called out louder and waited. No one came. *Why can't they hear me? Are they too far away? Am I too deep? I need help...I'm already slipping.*

Charrael examined the crevice and the rock face his hands touched. He spotted a toe pocket and a hand crack within reach. Could he access them without falling? *Maybe.* He braced himself, and once he felt solid, he swung his left leg across the gap. His toe slipped neatly into the pocket, and he straddled the divide while his right hand found the crack. *Okay, much better.*

Even with these, his stance was awkward and unsteady. *I need to get turned around.* But as he peered deeper into the crevice, his left toe slipped out of the pocket. Charrael's leg dangled, and his body shook and shifted. He gripped the hand crack tighter, pressed his right leg even harder against the rock, and tried his wings again. Nothing. His heart sank. "Help!"

I glanced once more at the Scroll Room, and as I passed, Gabriel burst through the door. Startled, I forgot our rift and said, "Greetings, Gabriel. Where are you off to in such a hurry?" He scowled at me briefly, but then his countenance softened.

"I'm headed to the Throne Room. The LORD has additional instructions for the newly sealed scroll."

"Oh, right," I said. "That's the one you were telling me about..." My voice faded, remembering how that conversation ended, and I didn't say any more.

"Yes," he said coldly, and I quivered with his tone. "Are you still on your kick about Lucifer?"

I didn't want to respond because I knew the outcome, yet, for some reason, I answered. "Yes, sort of," I said.

"Sort of," Gabriel retorted. "What does that mean?"

His tone irritated me. "Well, if you must know, I lost his trail."

Gabriel's mouth dropped open. "You were following him?"

I cocked my head. "Trying to."

"Michael, what a waste of energy. I have to go."

"Please, Gabriel. Don't go. Let me explain."

"No, I don't want to hear any more about it. I told you I'm done with this. When you come to your senses, we can be friends again. But not until then," he said, taking flight.

My head hung down, and my shoulders hunched. *Why did I tell him?* Everything I felt the first time flooded back, gushing over me in torrents. *If only I had taken another route back to the Armor Room.*

CHAPTER 23

RESCUED?

Still frustrated about his chance meeting with Michael, Gabriel marched up the long hall toward the Throne Room. Reaching the door, he held up his hand to halt the opening, and the sentries obeyed. Gabriel took a deep breath and let it out while smoothing his garments. Eyes fixed on the intimidating doors, he hiked his shoulders and nodded to the sentries. They opened, and he entered.

Bowing low before the LORD's fiery glory, Gabriel said, "Majesty, I know we were to converse about the scroll, but before that, I was hoping to discuss Michael."

"Michael?" the Most High said.

"Yes, Sire. We disputed briefly outside the Scroll Room. And can you believe it, he actually admitted he's been following Lucifer." Gabriel's arm went out to the LORD. "He's obsessed. He thinks something is wrong with Lucifer, that he's changed in some way, and now Michael's trying to prove it. I'm frustrated, and I don't know what to do."

Shekinah fire spit and fizzled out when God shifted on his throne. "Gabriel, do not concern yourself with Michael. He will resolve these issues with Lucifer. You just concentrate on the scroll we sealed. You are keeping it under lock and key, correct?"

"Yes, Sir," Gabriel said, sighing, "just as you commanded." The Almighty had changed the subject, and Gabriel knew there would be no more discussion about Michael.

"Good," said the LORD.

"But, Sire, why am I locking it? No one ever enters the Scroll Room except me."

"It's my crowning word—settled and precious," God said as his glory brightened and then receded. "You are dismissed."

That's all? Perplexed about why the Almighty summoned him for further instruction on the scroll when no instructions were given, Gabriel bowed and slipped out the door.

Charrael wobbled a bit, straining to open his wings. He thought he felt them start to unfold, but no. He peered deeper into the crevice and spied a narrow ledge just below the toe pocket. It was wide enough for both feet yet out of reach. He stretched his dangling leg several times but could not touch it. *I need to get lower. Maybe I can...if I find another grip.*

Charrael again inspected the rock wall and spotted a fist-sized knob way over to the left. He groaned as he braced and managed to swing his left toe back into the pocket. Feeling more secure, he pushed his right leg harder against the opposite surface, grabbed the hand crack tighter, and reached for the knob.

When his left hand gripped it, he expelled a sigh and steadied himself. After a brief rest, Charrael scooted his right leg lower on the adjacent rock, so this time, when he tried to touch the ledge, he would.

With his legs split to capacity, he slipped his left foot out of the pocket and reached for the ledge. His toe tapped it, and his heel landed. Charrael repositioned, stabilized, switched hands on the grip and crack, and delicately rotated his body.

His back now pressed against the left face of the crevice, while his right leg pushed against the opposite rock and held him there, but not tightly enough. "My foot is too high," he said, wincing and trying to scooch it down with a slow, back-and-forth motion for a better bracing position.

Once stable, Charrael realized the ledge might not work, so he pushed his wing muscles again. Still nothing. *How can I get to the Armor Room and Chief Prince Michael when I'm stuck? If I move, I'll fall.* "Help!" he called for the umpteenth time.

When no help came, Charrael finally bowed his head and said, "LORD God, please help me to know what to do. I want to serve you, not Lucifer. Please show me the way out."

As he lifted his head, Charrael knew. *My sword! I can use my sword.* He let go of the hand crack to unsheathe. "Careful," he whispered. "Hold on tight. One careless move, and the sword could drop."

Charrael studied the rock surface. The tiny fissure directly in front of him would suffice. With as much might as he could muster in this cramped space, he jammed his sword into the crack. But when he did, his right foot let loose from the rock wall. His left foot followed suit and slipped off the ledge.

Dangling above the seemingly endless crater, clinging by fingertips and sword grip, Charrael wondered how this could be the answer to his prayer. "Help," he shrieked again, feeling his left fingers creeping off the knob. "Help!"

The extra weight of his armor pulled at his right grip, and it, too, loosened. *LORD God, did I misunderstand?* With sheer determination, Charrael willed his left foot to feel for the ledge again. And as he stretched, all his fingers gave out.

Feet first, Charrael felt himself drop into the endless chasm. But, in that very moment, strong arms grabbed him and hoisted him out of the crevice.

The walk back to the Armor Room led me alongside the River of Life. I lingered to allow the gentle rippling to calm me, yet it didn't. Disturbed by everything, I fretted most about Gabriel. I couldn't believe we'd quarreled again. *Why is this happening? It's so bizarre.*

My mind would not settle. And this thing with Gabriel? It had to be just a distraction because it kept me from my real focus, Lucifer. I still had to find him. *Should I check the Garden of Fiery Stones?* No, I'd be spotted flying in. And why would he go there anyway when he's leaving for Earth so soon?

If I were in charge of the mission, I'd be in my chambers, briefing my taskforce and going over final details. But since they left Lucifer's early...*oh...I have to figure this thing out...and quickly...before they enter the Throne Room.* Once God gave his last instructions and sent them off, I knew it would be too late.

Exhausted from his ordeal, Charrael closed his eyes and allowed himself to be dragged onto solid ground. Thinking it was Wyael, he said, "Thank you, Lieutenant."

"Lieutenant?"

Charrael gasped and jumped to his feet. "Chief Prince Lucifer, Sir. How did you find me?"

"I saw you from above as I was flying in." Lucifer handed Charrael his sword he had extracted from the crevice. "Would you like to explain why you were hanging in a possibly infinite crevice and not in the caverns with the taskforce?"

"My...my," he squeaked and cleared his throat. "My shin guard strap is broken, Sir. I need another one. First Lieutenant Wyael ordered me to get a replacement from the Armor Room, and on my way, I fell."

"Your strap is broken? Let me see."

Surprised it was still hanging on, Charrael fumbled at the other buckles. "Now, Private," Lucifer yelled, reaching for the piece.

Charrael's face turned ashen. *Will he be able to tell it was cut?* Feeling woozy, he bobbled and almost fell back into the crevice. Catching himself, he shuffled away from the edge.

Lucifer took a good while scrutinizing the shin guard and the strap, glancing now and then at Charrael. Stepping toward him, he slammed the piece into his chest. Charrael grabbed it with both hands and held his breath.

Maintaining a firm grip, Lucifer stared at Charrael. He squinted and narrowed his brows as though deep in thought, but never broke the stare. Finally, Lucifer let loose. And after what seemed an eternity, he spoke. "Charrael, I'm going to allow you to present to the Armor Room for a replacement."

Remembering the secret room incident, Charrael gulped. "Thank you, Sir," he said as he turned to leave.

"Not so fast, Charrael." Lucifer grabbed his arm and swung him around.

Oh no! Here it comes! "Yes? Sorry, Sir."

Stepping close, Lucifer whispered, "If you breathe a word to Michael about my room or the caverns, I will end your existence."

Wide-eyed, Charrael felt faint.

"Did you hear me, Private?"

"Y-Yes, Sir," Charrael said, realizing now his plan might not work, but it was all he had. And if it didn't work, would he be stuck serving Lucifer? *No, I can't.*

"Get moving, Private, and return quickly. You don't want to miss all of my address. This is the most important speech you will ever hear."

Charrael jolted. "Yes, Sir." He saluted and secured his shin guard.

Lucifer watched him round the bend and step into the clearing. When he tried to launch, his wings stuck. Charrael tried a second time and then, with all the muscle he could muster, a third, but they remained folded.

Lucifer flew toward Charrael and landed beside him. "Having trouble?"

"Ah…yes, Sir," he said. "Something must have caused my wings to malfunction when I fell. I couldn't use them in the crevice, and they won't open now."

"Let me have a look." Lucifer checked to see if his scabbard or the straps of his breastplate were blocking them. "Nothing seems out of order. Try again."

Charrael grunted and pushed his wing muscles harder this time, but still nothing.

"This is unacceptable, Private," Lucifer said, giving his back a solid whack. Suddenly, the wings sprang open, and Charrael launched toward Ivory Palace City.

One by one, Lucifer's hand-picked angels slipped into the cavern's opening. The stage, directly across the domed chamber, appeared tiny from their rear position, yet it was their only objective. With this assignment, the taskforce members had become instant celebrities. And since his initial visit, First Lieutenant Wyael knew it wouldn't be easy to make their way through Lucifer's adoring crowd. Every angel present would want to touch them, shake their hands, pat them on the back, or acknowledge them in some way. And because of this, Lucifer's devotees would innocently hinder their progress to the stage.

Wyael, being an astute leader, also saw this as a positive. Turning to his team, he said, "Angels, I understand recognition is undesirable most of the time, but right now, it's needed. To these followers, our presence in the caverns means Chief Prince Lucifer is nearby. I believe this will keep our leader's adoring but restless fans from erupting. Maintain a low profile, yet as we make our way to the stage, avail yourselves to any angel admirer. Stop to greet each one who asks. Shake their hands, or provide any other type of affirmation the devotees require. My goal is to pacify the fans until the Chief Prince makes his grand entrance."

However, Sergeant Major Gragael spotted the taskforce from the stage. He stepped up, pointed toward the back of the caverns, and said, "Please make way for Chief Prince Lucifer's taskforce. They're advancing to the stage right now."

He expected them to quietly create a corridor like before, but not this time. Cheers and applause exploded. Supporters crowded in to get a glimpse of the taskforce, embrace them, or even touch their garments. "Gragael's announcement is going to complicate things," Wyael yelled. "Be alert and on guard."

For most of Lucifer's followers, this might be the closest they would ever get to the Chief Prince himself, and his taskforce was the next best thing. The devotees crowded in tighter. Some even swooped down from the higher levels. Groping and mauling ensued. And because of the sheer number of enthusiasts, the taskforce needed a new directive.

"Angels," Wyael bellowed. "Sabers ready. Hind formation." The taskforce promptly split into three groups of four, back-to-back: Two members faced north-south and perpendicular to the two members facing east-west. Swords drawn, the synchronized groups moved with precision toward the stage area. Stunned, the angel admirers backed off and now observed in silent awe.

Charrael took to the air and breathed a sigh of relief. Lucifer never mentioned the cut strap. And it didn't seem like he suspected anything, even from his secret room. These are good things, Charrael thought, trying to run through his plan. But each scenario jumbled in his head, and as he flew, he wondered if he'd ever escape the taskforce.

When reaching the perimeter of Ivory Palace City, under-angels normally would land and walk as God had commanded. Nevertheless, the LORD always said that with urgent matters, angels could fly. If ever there were an urgent matter, surely this was one. Yet, flying through the city for the first time, Charrael felt disoriented. Decelerating to get a bearing on his location, he weaved in and out of the trees, keeping alert and cautious and making a mental note not to fly past the Armor Room.

Soon, Charrael topped a Tree of Life grove and spotted his refuge. *There it is!* Shooting down, he landed just beyond the orchard and slid the shin guard out from behind his breastplate. With eyes fixated on the Armor Room doors and the sentries stationed outside, Charrael found himself almost sprinting. "It's nearly over," he said to himself. "Safety in a few steps...."

"Private, Charrael!" someone shouted from behind.

CHAPTER 24

INTERCEPTIONS

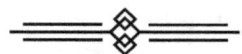

Charrael recognized the voice and skidded to a halt. He did an about-face, squared his shoulders, saluted, and said, "Sir, yes, Sir."

Focused on the Armor Room, Charrael hadn't noticed anyone on the walkway or in the trees. But there he was, and that feeling Charrael could not explain gripped him again. His legs wobbled like rubber. "Chief Prince Lucifer," he squeaked. "H-how may I serve you?"

"Well, Charrael," Lucifer said, gliding toward him. "I've been considering everything and have decided you may not serve me."

"Sir?"

"Yes, Charrael, you may not serve me because I know."

"I don't understand, Sir. Know what?"

"For starters," Lucifer said, grabbing the shin guard out of Charrael's hand and knocking him off balance, "your strap was cut. Did you cut it?"

Charrael steadied himself and held his breath while his mind searched for an answer. Any answer that would not give him away.

Lucifer glared, lowered his shoulders, and pushed past Charrael to block his path to the Armor Room. With a scowl, his fiery eyes pierced Charrael. "Answer the question, Private," he said, stifling his rage. "Did you cut the strap?"

Still holding his breath, Charrael didn't know what to say, but the moment he exhaled, words burst into his head and out of his mouth. "Chief Prince Lucifer, Sir, it could have happened when we were sparring to test our armor."

Lucifer took a step back as though he had been hit in the chest. He hesitated for a moment and finally said, "Perhaps." Locking eyes with Charrael, he moved forward to close the gap while the private instinctively took corresponding steps backward. Suddenly, Charrael saw they had relocated to the thick grove of trees. Hidden, trapped, and alone with Chief Prince Lucifer, Charrael hyperventilated, and his eyes darted back and forth. Could he get away?

Lucifer, quicker and more potent, blocked escape. Closer and closer he inched until he stood nose-to-nose with the private. Lucifer knew it might be his only chance to rid himself of this menace.

The heat of Lucifer's breath beat down on Charrael, and he shuddered. He wanted to run, but his feet felt fastened to the terrain. *Help! Please! Anyone!*

As Charrael tried to yell, Lucifer's arm shot out. He clenched the private's throat and lifted him while his feet dangled. "Private Charrael," he said, squeezing tighter and feeling for his sword with the other hand. "I saw you in my secret room. I know you didn't bow in worship. I told you there is no turning back. Confess your allegiance to me and accept my plans, or I'll annihilate you right here, right now."

I knew I needed to get back to the Armor Room, but I had not accomplished one thing I had set out to do. Rubbing my forehead, I remembered Gabriel's scolding. *Had I wasted my energy?* If I were an under-angel giving this type of report to my superior, I would expect a reprimand. Shaking my head, I sighed and quickened my steps.

Drawing closer to the Armor Room yet still a distance away, I saw two angels facing each other on the walkway. They slowly retreated near the grove of trees. One angel paced backward as the other, taller angel, surged forward. It was too far for me to see them clearly, yet the meeting seemed strange, like nothing I'd ever encountered. But I'd been having a lot of those lately. From what I could see, the taller angel looked very much like Lucifer, and he shaded the identity of the second.

Still, something didn't feel right with these two. If the one was Lucifer, then what was he doing? And, for that matter, what has he been doing? Was he inside the Armor Room while I minded his chamber?

I watched as the two angels entered the trees and then lost visual. Needing to see what was going on, I walked faster, but it was taking too long. In an instant, I was above them. Mystery solved. Swooping down, I saw Lucifer's hand clamped on Private Charrael's throat, and his feet were flopping above the walkway. "Lucifer!" I shouted, landing behind him. "What are you doing to that private?"

Lucifer released his grip and spun around. "Back off, Michael! Charrael is a member of my taskforce. His armor is faulty. I'm just confirming he did not sabotage it himself."

"Ridiculous. Why would you even think that?" I turned to Charrael and said, "If you're having trouble with your armor, I must see it in my workshop. Why don't you go on inside now, and Randiel will help you. I'll be in shortly."

Charrael picked himself up off the walkway as Lucifer glared—his steely eyes practically drilling holes into the private's back. "Remember our talk, Charrael," Lucifer said. "And your choices. Even though Archangel Michael is here, nothing has changed."

"Yes, Sir," Charrael whimpered. He hung his head and limped toward the Armor Room.

When Charrael was far enough away, I said, "Lucifer, why are you so cruel to your taskforce members?"

Lucifer's tone deepened. "Stay out of it, Michael. It's none of your business."

"Well, I'm making it my business. So, get used to it. I don't understand your altered personality."

Lucifer's hand went to his sword, but then fell away. "My personality is the same. It's your imagination."

I shook my finger at him. "No, it isn't. You're different. This new authority has gone to your head, and you can't handle it."

Lucifer closed his eyes, clutched his chest, and pivoted as though hiding something. "Think what you want, Michael," he yelled back over his shoulder. "It still doesn't change the fact that I have a taskforce with a mission to Earth, and you don't, so get over yourself. Take care of Charrael and send him back to me. I'll handle my angels the way I see fit."

Before I could respond, Lucifer was gone. He launched and flew toward the plains. Who knew where he was going or what he was doing? I couldn't follow him now. I needed to see what happened with that armor. Drawing in a deep breath and attempting to exhale my annoyance, I entered the Armor Room.

From above, Lucifer patted his chest, and his inner fire subsided. He surveyed Ivory Palace City, the expanse of Heaven's plains, his stones of fire, and the Mount of Holiness.

About a third of the way up the mountain rested the massive plateau, and scattered here and there across it, boulders jutted skyward. When the cherubim transported God's Throne to this base in a thunderous display of his holiness, these stones would illuminate and appear almost as hands lifted in praise.

Circling the quiet mountain, Lucifer said to the rocks, "If Charrael talks to Michael about my special room or the cavern meeting, my plan for Earth and all Heaven could be exposed. Did I put enough fear into him? Will he keep his mouth shut?" *He did seem frightened.* "Still, if Charrael talks, is there really anyone who would believe him? No—not even the Almighty." *Wait…Michael would believe him… but that's all. And ha…he's already on the outs with Gabriel and the Most High.* "So…I'll take care of Charrael before leaving for Earth. It'll be fine," he whispered to himself.

Landing on the site where God's Shekinah Glory rested when he received worship or instructed his angel armies, Lucifer threw his arms wide, spun around, and shouted, "How can I stay angry when all this will be mine!"

Exhilarated, he strolled the plateau's length sporting a malevolent smile. Lucifer knew what no one else knew. Beneath this plateau, neatly tucked into the mountain, lay an inconspicuous grotto he first spotted eons ago when he explored with Michael and Gabriel. Through this mountain opening, Lucifer had crafted a secret back entrance to the caverns. And…should he have a need…a way of escape.

No other angel had seen the cavity. This portion of the mountain was off-limits to all angels except the archangels, the cherubim, and the seraphim. Since the latter two were always in the presence of the LORD, that left them out. And neither Gabriel nor Michael had ever mentioned it.

A sinister smile crossed Lucifer's face as he rubbed his palms together and snickered. "Michael and Gabriel are clueless, just like the Almighty. All things are moving ahead as planned. Once on Earth, I will execute my takeover," he said, doubling over in laughter he could barely contain.

CHAPTER 25

A DISTURBING REVELATION

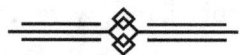

More dazzling than a sparkling gem was the magnificence of the Sovereign King upon his throne. Above him and surrounding hung a wispy ribbon of seven colors. Seven, meaning the LORD God was perfect and complete within himself.

Ruby red was the first. When red stretched to meet the third, yellow, a new color, orange, formed between them. Yellow comprised the primary shade of God's Shekinah and now also Earth's sun. But this blending of three colors represented God's three distinct personalities, yet being One in essence.

Emerald green held the ribbon's fourth and central position. Sometimes, this dominant color transcended the others. During those times, the bow encircling the Almighty appeared only as emerald. Still...blue, like Earth's daytime sky, indigo, as the night, and violet rounded out the seven.

Adjacent to the circular bow, the four cherubim—God's angel sentinels—who encompassed the throne and guarded his holiness, held their positions. The fiery, copper-hued seraphim stood overhead, saying, "Holy, holy, holy," in endless praise.

Seraphim were powerful but distinctive, six-winged angels. Using only two of their wings, they hovered and flew above the Holy God, spanning the breadth of his glory. Of their other four wings, two covered their faces, and two wrapped their bodies to hide their feet in great adoration and reverence.

Cherubim, on the other hand, were uniquely complex angelic creatures. The Almighty created them with hands under their wings, angel bodies, straight, knobby legs, hooves for feet, and a wheel-like extremity. Their bronze-colored forms sparkled and glistened with every move.

Of their six wings, two on each side lifted upward and touched the cherub beside them to create a square around God's throne. With their final two wings, cherubim covered their frame in humility, for they stood in the presence of absolute holiness.

In addition to their other choice characteristics, cherubim also possessed four faces, one for each direction. As such, their heads never turned. If the cherub moved forward, the normal face, the face of an angel, was used. To the right, the face of a lion became the guide. Traversing left, the ox face led the way, and if they needed to progress backward, the eagle face, with its piercing eyes, controlled the movement.

As melodic voices bounced from seraphim to cherubim, the Throne Room would fill with soothing, harmonious sounds. Although both were exceptional and unlike any other angelic being, the cherubim were exclusive in their function.

Once the Omniscient God, who dwelt between the cherubim, desired to move, these special angels would let down an appendage, appearing to be a wheel within a wheel, and position themselves beneath his throne. The rim of each wheel was full of eyes denoting the Most High's all-seeing nature. And when the cherubim ascended, their wheels and wings created sounds like rushing water or a thousand marching armies. In those moments, God's Holiness, as a diamond stricken by light, hovered high above while his Holy Spirit directed advancement.

Soon, God's Shekinah intensified, and the Throne Room's ethereal calm broke. Ablaze with white light, a band of vibrant hues streamed from his being, and the cherubim understood their Holy God would shortly desire to move.

Each cherub stirred and began their unique preparations for transport. When completed, these sentinels would wait, moving only as the Almighty gave his order.

After the clash with Lucifer, I plodded to the Armor Room. Disturbed by the events I had witnessed and the nagging thought I may have distributed pieces of faulty armor, I entered when the sentries opened the doors. Serenity washed over me as always, and I stood in the Grand Hall for a brief moment.

Gathering my thoughts, I crossed the room and called, "Randiel, have you fitted Private Charrael with a new pair of shin guards?"

"Yes, Chief Prince Michael."

"Good. I need to inspect the defective one."

"It's there on the cart, Sir." Randiel nodded and continued to check each piece of Charrael's armor.

I lifted the shin guard, turned it this way and that, scrutinized every inch, and ran my fingers over the straps. I could see it was not faulty. The strap had been cut, just as Lucifer suspected. *But why?* Did this happen while we tested the armor? *No, not possible.* Had it been cut all the way through, as this strap was, the shin guard would have fallen askew right there in the Arena. If it were only partially cut in the sparring and worked its way loose, I would see evidence of tearing, and I didn't. "Charrael," I said. "I'd like to see you in my office before you return to your taskforce."

He looked me in the eyes and nodded. "Yes, Sir."

"We're about finished, Chief Prince," Randiel said without looking up. I'm just rechecking to ensure he's battle-ready."

"Good. I'm heading to my office now."

"Sir, wait." Randiel handed me his report on the shin guard. "By the way, you have a visitor in your office."

"I do?"

Randiel shook his head. "It's Supervisor Jaysael from the Forge. He came in just before Charrael. If I understand correctly, he wants to discuss the armor alterations needed for Corporal."

"Of course," I said, nodding. "I'll talk to him. Complete your recheck, and send in Charrael when Jaysael leaves."

"I will, Sir."

———————⌄———————

The taskforce finally made it to the stage area, and First Lieutenant Wyael stepped up to the podium to speak. All angel devotees silenced, expecting information about Chief Prince Lucifer and when he would arrive.

"Salutations," Wyael said, holding out his arms to the audience in a grand gesture. "It's good to see you again. I am pleased you have endured the delay and waited to support our illustrious leader!" Applause erupted.

With raised arms, Wyael turned his hands forward and pulsed them downward to quiet the fans. "We, of his taskforce, consider ourselves honored to have been chosen by this celebrated, most high commander and chief." Applauding again broke out, hindering Wyael's speech. "In addition," he said, straining to quell the noise. "In addition," he repeated, then clamped his mouth shut until the angel devotees quieted.

"In addition," he said again, "we are excited about this new venture to Earth and the opportunity to serve under Archangel Lucifer's great leadership." Handclapping once more emerged but promptly quieted. "Chief Prince Lucifer is on his way and should be here shortly."

This time, cheers and accolades could not be hushed. The ovations morphed into another, more raucous round of chanting, "Lucifer; Lucifer; Lu-ci-fer! Lucifer; Lucifer; Lu-ci-fer!"

Wyael turned to Second Lieutenant Maysel. "We need to find out how close the Chief Prince is to arrival. This crowd is out of hand, and we are dangerously close to alerting the Almighty. Send Olivel and Dylael to the entrance so they can escort him to the stage. But when they get there, tell them to exit unnoticed and see if they can detect Lucifer flying in. He must be nearby. I can't believe he's taking so long."

"I know," Maysel said. "I'm concerned too." He turned to the privates. "New orders, Gentlemen. The two of you will have the honor of escorting Chief Prince Lucifer to the stage when he arrives. But we need to know where he is. An estimated time of arrival is crucial. When you reach the entrance, slip outside unobserved and try to spot him. If you do, signal us with an ETA. This is getting serious."

"Yes, Sir," they said in unison, saluting and doing an about-face.

Olivel and Dylael, little by little, made their way through the crowd to the cavern's entrance. With each step, they felt the stares, dodged the groping, and ignored the questions.

"Hey, is Chief Prince Lucifer close?" one angel devotee yelled.

Dylael scowled, slowed his pace, and watched as another follower grabbed the devotee's arm and said, "Why did you ask that?"

"See," the first said, pointing, "there goes some of the taskforce to the door."

"You're right. This is so exciting. I'm not taking my eyes off the entrance."

The highly trained privates positioned themselves on either side of the door, acting as though they were guarding it and awaiting Chief Prince Lucifer. When Wyael spoke again from the podium, and his voice boomed through the caverns, all angels quieted and gazed at him, even the angel who wouldn't take his eyes off the entrance. Dylael slipped out first, and then Olivel. Squeezing through the narrow cleft, they exited onto the backside of the Mount of Holiness. Lucifer was nowhere in sight.

Olivel paused to think. "Let's hike around to the front and see if we can spot the Chief Prince."

Dylael nodded. "Good idea. Maybe we'll see him flying in from Ivory Palace City."

"I hope so. But if not, I'm going to fly back to the city to find him. The Lieutenants are concerned."

Rounding the west corner of the mountain, both privates witnessed a blazing reddish-orange streak high above the plains, signaling Lucifer's imminent arrival. "Finally!" Olivel said.

"Yeah," Dylael agreed. "But…isn't he headed in the wrong direction?"

Olivel waved him off. "Who knows? He's the Chief Prince. He can do anything and go anywhere he wants. Maybe he needs an aerial view of the Shekinah Glory Base before he greets his fans. It's not our place to question him. Let's hurry back and give Wyael and Maysel the good signal."

"Okay, you lead. I'm not sure I could find the opening again."

Private First Class Olivel easily located the crag and secluded crack. The soldiers entered as covertly as they exited.

———⌄———

Wyael had been watching the door and saw them enter. His chest rose and he held his breath, hoping for a good sign. Olivel and Dylael began hand gestures, and together they gave the "Lucifer spotted" signal, along with what they estimated as his arrival. Relieved, Wyael exhaled, and his chest lowered. Stepping up to the podium, he smiled. "Chief Prince Lucifer is on the grounds of the Mount of Holiness. He should be here momentarily."

The crowd exploded with applause, cheers, howls, and screams. *Not again! What was I thinking?* It took Wyael, Maysel, the remaining taskforce, and the guards to quiet them to a low roar. Turning to Maysel, Wyael said, "Lucifer better get in here soon."

———⌄———

CHAPTER 26

CONFESSIONS

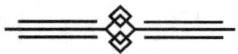

"**G**reetings, Jaysael," I said, strolling through my office door. "You wanted to speak to me?"

"Yes, Chief Prince Michael." He stood and lowered his head. "First, I wanted to apologize for the armor error and for those pieces needing adjustments."

"No need, Jaysael." I rounded the corner of my desk and gestured for him to have a seat. "We caught the error and corrected it. The armor has yet to be assigned, so no harm done."

"Still, Sir," Jaysael said as he sat, "I'd like you to know we are taking the necessary steps to see this doesn't happen again."

I squinted. "Do you know what caused the error?"

Jaysael sighed. "Yes, Sir. Water from the cooling vats splashed the clipboard containing the specs for the rank of Corporal. The numbers faded some. So, what my workers thought was an eight was, in reality, a three or a five in places. But please know, this has not happened before, and it was only the one batch."

"Good," I said, sitting straighter and folding my hands on my desk. "How do you plan to remedy it?"

He presented me with a clipboard-sized clear shield. "I've called for this to be placed on every clipboard," Jaysael said, "and I've cautioned all my workers to ask for clarification when unsure of the specifics."

I glanced at the ceiling and back at this Forge Supervisor. "Sounds very efficient."

"Yes, Sir." Jaysael gave a quick nod. "I'm confident we've found the perfect solution to resolve this error."

I stood and reached across my desk. "I believe you're right. Good work."

Shaking my hand, Jaysael said, "Thank you, Chief Prince. And thank you for speaking with me, hearing my explanation, and allowing me to settle this issue myself within the Forge."

"You're welcome. I'm pleased with your progress."

As we nodded our acknowledgments and Jaysael exited, I sat and leaned back in my chair to contemplate how I should handle things with Charrael. The whole scenario caused suspicion. I wondered if it was possible to pry information from him without raising distrust.

Before I even finished that thought, Charrael rapped his knuckles on my office door. "Please come in, Charrael," I said, pointing to the chair. "Have a seat."

He entered and sat across from me. "Thank you, Sir."

With Randiel's report in my hand, I perused its pages. I didn't speak, and the silence seemed to make Charrael fidget. He shifted, crossed his legs, uncrossed them, and shifted again. I peeked at him over the report, closed it, and studied this private. He didn't seem like an angel who would deliberately damage something. "Charrael,"

I said, sliding the report toward him. "Randiel has inspected your whole suit of armor. It's all there in his statement.

"In addition, I personally evaluated the shin guard. You know... I'm very picky about the armor in this room. Several different angels carefully analyze every item before it's hung or stored. Now, I suppose an inferior piece could get through our detailed examination. But, Private Charrael, your shin guard wasn't flawed. The strap was cut. Can you explain?"

He hunched over and hung his head. "I...I...I'm not sure, Sir."

"Alright. Let me see if I understand. You were just walking through Ivory Palace City, and the shin guard fell off. Am I correct so far?"

Charrael trembled. "Um, well, sort of."

"Sort of? You seem nervous, Charrael. Why?"

He looked me in the eye. "It's been a stressful period, Sir, and... and I've not been called to your office before."

I paused and stared at this soldier. "I'm just trying to make sure my workers are not turning out defective armor, Charrael. I need your input, and I want to understand your nervousness. To me, you look very guilty. Are you guilty? Or is your anxious demeanor because of the disciplinary action Chief Prince Lucifer put you through?"

No answer. Charrael's eyes grew big and darted around the room as though searching for a way of escape.

Trying to get him to open up, I leaned forward. "I know the encounter was rough, but I'm not Lucifer. I don't use his methods. However, I do want the truth. So, Charrael, if you cut the strap yourself, I need to know it, and I need to know why."

Charrael put his face in his hands and sobbed.

I jerked back. *What is this? Is he guilty or frightened?* "Private Charrael," I said. "Just because I'm the guardian archangel doesn't mean you should be afraid of me. I know I'm being hard on you, but at this moment, I don't have a choice."

He moaned and sobbed even louder, so I moved around the desk to where Charrael was sitting and patted his heaving shoulders. "Tell me what's going on, Charrael. We've not had this kind of thing happen before, and now I'm sensing there's more to the story. Is there? Keeping secrets won't help you. Talk to me. You can tell me anything."

Charrael wiped his eyes and inhaled deeply. "Sir, it's just hard to explain."

"Are you fearful of the mission on Earth?"

He shook his head. "No, Sir. I was looking forward to it."

"Then why are you here, Charrael? From what I've seen, I'm pretty sure you cut the strap yourself. Did you?"

After a long pause, Charrael squeaked out, "Yes. Yes, Sir, I did." His voice caught, and his eyes gushed with even more tears. Words interspersed with sobs followed. "I've never, [sob] ever, [sob] done anything [sob] like this before!" He howled and covered his face with his hands.

I listened, continuing to tap his spasming shoulders. "It'll be okay, Charrael. Just tell me."

Finally, the private regained composure, and I moved back to my chair. "Sir," he said. "Since my creation, I have gladly followed all the Almighty's rules. Never once did I question why. It has been my honor and delight to serve Him and you, for that matter."

"Very admirable, Charrael, and we are certainly pleased. But again, I have to ask. Why did you cut the strap? And why are you so distressed?"

Charrael inhaled, and as he exhaled, he blurted out, "Because of what I saw and heard!"

I jerked back again. "What did you see and hear?"

He stared at me, but his eyes did not engage. They appeared to see things a great distance away. Finally, Charrael took another deep breath. His chest and shoulders dropped as he let it out. Swallowing hard, he seemed to gather some resolve. "I'll tell you everything," he said. "And if I perish at the hands of Chief Prince Lucifer, then I perish."

"Perish? Where did you get that word? No one's going to perish, Charrael."

"Yes, Chief Prince Michael. Chief Prince Lucifer said once I saw what I saw, there was no turning back and no getting out. But I can't be a party to what he's doing. That's why I cut the strap."

I held up my hand. "Wait…you're going too fast. What do you mean you can't be a party to what Lucifer is doing? What is he doing?"

Charrael exhaled a sigh. "It's a long story, Sir."

"Well, we aren't leaving 'til I have all the information," I said, getting comfortable in my chair. "So, you might as well tell me."

After another long pause, Charrael narrowed his brows and spouted, "I think Chief Prince Lucifer may be planning to take over heaven. There, I've said it."

"What?" I said with half a chuckle. "You can't be serious?"

His head bobbed up and down. "Yes, Sir. I am."

"Look, Charrael." My hands went out as I shrugged. "That sounds far-fetched, even for Lucifer. And anyway, it would be futile on his part. No one can do what you say he's planning."

Charrael pounded the desk. "But I heard him, Sir. You have to believe me."

"I'm trying," I said, leaning toward him. "And even if I do believe you, it still does not explain why you cut the strap."

He pushed back from the desk. "Cutting the shin guard strap was the only way I could think of to get away from him and the taskforce so I could come here and tell you. But Chief Prince Lucifer intercepted me."

I stroked my chin. "Aw, yes. The encounter I interrupted."

"Sir, Lucifer made it very clear he would annihilate me before he would allow me to expose him. I'm not sure what annihilate means, but it can't be good."

"Expose him?" I said, glancing at the ceiling. "Hmm…interesting."

Charrael held out his hand to halt my thoughts. "Wait, Sir, those are my words, not his."

I stood, paced the room, and turned back to Charrael. "Your story does align with what I witnessed in the orchard, and Lucifer did seem threatening. I say he knows you cut the strap, but only suspects it was on purpose."

He cocked his head. "Why?"

I slid back into my chair. "If Lucifer knew for sure, you wouldn't be here. He would have stopped you before you entered the city."

Charrael swallowed, and his eyes blinked. "You're probably right. Chief Prince Lucifer did have the chance. Still, it's all true—everything."

"You do seem sincere. And, I have noticed some differences in Lucifer…so…it's not my imagination." I drifted off for a brief moment. "If what you say is true, it's much worse than I thought."

"Excuse me, Sir?"

"Never mind. Charrael. Annihilation means ceasing to exist. I don't know if annihilating an angel is possible. We are God's creations, after all, so please don't fret. I'm taking you under my protection. Lucifer will not harm you."

Charrael let out a huge breath, and his body relaxed. "Thank you, Sir."

Holding up my finger, I said, "But keep in mind the Almighty will decide your fate and his. You may think your thoughts and actions are hidden from him, but I assure you, they are not."

"Michael," boomed the voice of the Most High.

I raised my eyebrows. "Yes, Sire."

"Come to the Throne Room at once."

"On my way, Majesty." Turning to Charrael, I said, "See what I mean. We'll finish this when I get back. Until then, Randiel will take care of you."

I hurried out of my office. Randiel anticipated my departure and hustled alongside me. "Randiel, take Charrael to the inner chamber. Here's the key. Guard it with your life."

Strolling across the Shekinah Glory Base, Lucifer imagined how good he would feel possessing ultimate power and dominating the angel armies. "Earth and the universe are not enough," he said under his breath. "I want Heaven, too! So…where shall I position my glory base?"

Lucifer considered the sites of Heaven and inspected every inch of the plateau's flat terrain. "Ah," he said softly. "Right here! My base shall cover and crush the Almighty's. What a magnificent sight that will be. First, the Shekinah Glory Base, then on to the Throne Room." Lucifer snickered. "The cherubim shall worship me as I perch between them, and the seraphim…ha…they will sing my praises. It will be my cathedral—the place where my radiance shines. All shall serve my every beck and call. And, yes…declare my holiness!"

This scenario had become Lucifer's reality since his mind had replayed the recording so many times. Lucifer threw his arms up, narrowed his eyes, and his lips curled while his nostrils flared. He unfurled his wings, and a red, flaming glow ascended from his inner being. "Hear me!" he shouted to the boulders. "No one can stop my rise to absolute power!"

Quickly, he quieted. "No sense in alerting the Almighty just yet, or Michael, for that matter, at least not until I've amassed my army."

Tucking in his wings, Lucifer paced. "I've much to do before my takeover. The taskforce will ensure my angels in the caverns obey and swear allegiance. From these, I will choose the strongest and train them to be my guards—my law enforcers." Lucifer rubbed his hands together. "Then," he said, "they will gather even more to join me until I have them all. Ha…ha!"

Glimpsing God's creation, Lucifer pivoted. "But every angel must be devoted to me, or I will not allow them to exist. Once loyalty is confirmed, I'll move on to step two."

A slow takeover was the best approach. Lucifer planned for his faithful angels to undermine things in Heaven whilst he dominated and collapsed things on Earth. Slowly...but surely...he would conquer. "My coup," Lucifer said, cackling, "will be so subtle, no one will see it coming until it's too late. Then, not even the Almighty will be able to stop me."

Halting dead center, Lucifer announced, "I will rebuild Heaven as my abode, Earth as my footstool. And for my crowning achievement," he screamed as ecstasy enveloped him, "my word shall replace God's word."

Lucifer's inner fire prevailed as his wings unfurled. "I am Lucifer! Angel of Light. I am absolute supremacy...total authority, and...I am perfection!"

Gazing over the plains and out to creation, he wanted to shout again, but he whispered instead. "Citizens of Heaven and Earth! Watch out! Eternity is changing. Lucifer is your king!"

CHAPTER 27

THE STORY

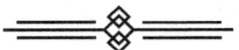

Bursting through the Throne Room doors, hoping this would be quick, I bowed before the Almighty. Upon rising, I said, "My King, how may I serve you?"

"Michael," the Most High said. "I brought you here to discuss your issues with Gabriel."

My hand slapped my chest. "You know?"

"Yes, Gabriel sought me after your second argument. I want to know what's going on with you. First, issues with Lucifer, and now Gabriel?"

I shook my head. "Gabriel just doesn't understand, LORD."

His Shekinah raged. "No, Michael, you don't understand. The two of you need to work together. Heaven depends on it. Lucifer is separate. But the two of you...I want this thing with Gabriel resolved now."

"But..."

"Ut..." he snapped as the resemblance of a hand flew up within his glory. "No buts! You are dismissed."

"Yes, Sire," I said, knee to the floor and head bowed. As I lingered, I felt a gentle breeze and a comforting hand on my shoulder. Rising, I caught a glimpse of God's Holy Spirit, absorbing back into the Shekinah.

He said nothing, but his touch saturated my being with a soothing calm. Before long, it transformed into a deep, unexplainable dread. I wanted to ask what that meant, but I had been dismissed. Withdrawing from the Throne Room, I remembered Charrael. And although my heaviness remained, somehow, I knew he held the answer.

———⌄———

"Randiel, what is this room?" Charrael said as he sat mesmerized in the inner chamber. "There's so much gold I don't know where to look first. I had no idea such a room existed."

"Prince Michael sometimes refers to it as the treasure room," Randiel replied.

Charrael wrapped himself with his arms. "I can see why."

"I don't know much," Randiel said, taking in a deep breath. "I think the golden objects and precious gems may be additional pieces for Ivory Palace, but mostly, it's outside of my understanding. However, I do know the room is huge, way beyond what we can see."

"Really?"

"Yes." Randiel waved his arm in a sweeping gesture toward the far reaches of the room. "Once, I walked to what I thought was the end, yet it wasn't. The room seemed to grow with my every step. It's ethereal."

Charrael's eyes widened. "What does that mean?"

"Spiritual—divine, sort of." Randiel took another deep breath and gazed upward. "I'm convinced this treasure room will never be full. I believe there's much more to it, more than either you or I can comprehend."

"Oh," Charrael said, exhaling.

"But I can tell you about the armor." Randiel pointed to the magnificent, glimmering breastplates and shields neatly suspended on the walls. "This is Chief Prince Gabriel's breastplate. See the enhanced scroll at the center?"

Charrael's mouth fell open. "It's beautiful."

Randiel nodded. "Quite. Chief Prince Michael designed the scroll insignia specifically for him. You see, when Chief Prince Gabriel is wearing his helmet, we under-angels would not need to see his face to know who's giving the order."

"Oh, right. Just like Chief Prince Lucifer's armor and his emblem."

"Correct." Randiel smiled. "Each archangel's armor is crafted to fit their frame and no one else's. Chief Prince Michael's is over on that wall."

Charrael pivoted to get a better look. "What is his symbol?"

Randiel strolled toward the armor displaying the sword and shield. "Chief Prince Michael is guardian and protector," he said, pointing. "See how the shield lies behind the diagonally placed sword. There is no better mark to identify him."

"I agree." Charrael's eyes lit up. "I saw Chief Prince Lucifer's armor in his chambers. Very impressive, and now that I think about it, much more appropriate than I realized." Charrael paused. "So, Randiel, may I ask a question?"

"Of course."

Charrael shuddered as he spoke. "What do you think will happen to me when I tell the rest of my story to Chief Prince Michael? I'd like to stay here in the Armor Room and serve him. Do you need help?"

Randiel held up his hand. "Whoa, Charrael. First, I didn't know you had a story to tell. Second, I can't say where you will be or what will happen. Everything is up to the Almighty. We'll have to wait and see."

Lucifer reeled in his wings and his radiant red glow. "I have been waiting for this moment ever since that stroll in the Garden of Fiery Stones and my first understanding of who I am." He took a deep breath and exhaled slowly. "Angel worship will empower me. I'll forge ahead and conquer. Nothing is beyond my grasp—for I am God."

He strolled forward to the edge of the Shekinah Glory Base, and his chest swelled. Gazing once more toward the city, Lucifer descended to enter his concealed passageway.

I blew past the Armor Room sentries and opened the doors myself. Hastening across the Grand Hall to the exit at the far end, I raced down the long corridor, around the corner, and skidded to a stop before the inner chamber. "Randiel," I said, pounding. "It's me."

Randiel yanked open the heavy door, and I rushed in. "Charrael, I need to hear the whole story."

Charrael jumped to his feet. "Yes, Sir," he said, lifting his hand to salute.

I waved it down. "Quickly, what else do you know?"

"Ah...well, I was with the taskforce in Chief Prince Lucifer's chambers when he exposed a door to a secret room."

My face scrunched. "A secret room?"

Charrael nodded. "Yes, Sir."

"I'm not sure I understand." I motioned for him to sit while I pulled up a chair. "What makes the room secret?"

His lips rattled as he exhaled. "The door to this room was not visible until Chief Prince Lucifer made it appear."

"What...?" I drifted off. *Does Lucifer have that kind of power?*

"I know the door wasn't there before," Charrael said, dragging me back.

"Oh? How?"

Charrael ran his hand through his hair. "I had laid my armor against that wall earlier, and there was no door. But once it appeared and we entered, when I yanked it shut, the door disappeared. I even felt the wall. It was gone. Chief Prince Lucifer said no one could enter or exit this room without his permission."

It disappeared? My hand cupped my mouth. "So, what was in this secret room?"

Charrael seemed to struggle to find the right words. "Ah...among other insignificant items, the room contained a large oval table on one side and a massive chair resembling a throne on the other."

My arm shot out. "Stop...I mean, wait. A throne?"

Charrael jerked and shrugged. "Well, it looked like a throne to me."

"Why am I surprised by this?" I said, scratching my head. "I know how strange Lucifer's been acting lately. But a throne? Really?"

The private cocked his head. "I beg your pardon, Sir?"

"Never mind, Charrael. Please go on. We need to stay on track."

"Yes, Sir." His finger tapped his lips, and I could almost see gears turning in his head. "So...after we entered, Chief Prince Lucifer had us stand around the table. Using a hand-drawn map of Earth..."

"A map?" I said, interrupting. "Where did he get that?"

"I don't know, Sir. It looked like something he might have sketched."

"Our visit. Even then!" My hand went to my forehead. "I knew he was up to something."

Charrael scrunched his brow. "Sir?"

"Just putting the pieces together. So, what did he do with the map?"

Charrael used his hands to demonstrate how Lucifer divided Earth's landmass, paired, and assigned the taskforce to the sections, and said, "All except for me."

"Why not you?"

"Chief Prince Lucifer said I was to join him as his assistant. I was scared but honored. Until his countenance changed..."

I stood. "His countenance changed?"

"Yes, Sir." Charrael jumped up and again became animated. "Lucifer's whole outward appearance changed, and he sort of floated to the center of the room, glowing from within."

"Glowing?" I said, shrugging. "Are you sure it wasn't the illumination we archangels achieve when worshiping the Almighty?"

Charrael nodded and set his jaw. "Very sure, Sir. I know floating isn't peculiar since we fly, but he wasn't using his wings, and his color was awfully strange. It appeared as a scaled-down version of God's Shekinah."

I tilted my head back, stared at the ceiling, and a thought speared my mind. "Wait. Perhaps you saw Lucifer's armor. I designed his breastplate with a flame insignia. Maybe the light hit at just the right spot to appear as though he was glowing."

The private dropped into his seat, and I did the same. "Chief Prince Michael," Charrael said in a low, subdued voice, "it wasn't his armor. This glow came from somewhere underneath his armor and shined out through it. But even that wasn't as disturbing as what happened next."

"Oh?"

Charrael bit his lip and then exploded with words he seemed unable to contain. "Chief Prince Lucifer went on a rampage, ranting about how he would crush the Most High and replace him. He raved he would exalt his throne above the angels of God and be like God, master of all."

I jerked and nearly fell off my chair. As I tried to compose myself, the LORD'S words from our last meeting speared my mind. Gabriel and I needed to work together. Heaven depended on it. *What?* I didn't know how Heaven could depend on us, but I knew God meant for me to fix this. *If Gabriel could hear Charrael, he might agree with me about Lucifer.* "All right, Charrael," I said at last. "Let me see if I've got this straight. You're saying Lucifer thinks he can depose the Sovereign LORD, usurp his throne, and become God himself. Is that correct?"

He shook his head. "But there's more."

"Stop," I said, holding up my hand. "Chief Prince Gabriel needs to hear this, too. Don't say another word until I return with him."

I turned to Randiel. He stood wide-eyed and trembling. I had forgotten Randiel knew nothing of my suspicions of Lucifer. He was unprepared for what he'd just heard, but I couldn't coddle him. "Randiel," I said. "Snap out of it. Same as before. I'll be back as quick as I can."

Lucifer strolled through the ample passageway, stopping at times to admire his handiwork. The closer he came to the cavern's rotunda, the better he could hear the wild and rowdy chanting. "Oh…I will make a glorious entrance!"

The steady voice modulation sucked him in, and he swayed side to side to the beat. "My loyal subjects have been waiting long, and they've not given up. What faithfulness to me, what dedication," he said. "Does the Most High have this? No. But I do! I can hardly wait for the applause, the adoration, exaltation, and…worship." *Ah… this…most definitely…is the way things should be.*

Lucifer inhaled. His chest rose, his head tilted back, and the euphoria of it all rekindled his fiery glow. He held it, enjoying the ecstasy and anticipation. Exhaling, the red hue receded. "Just a short distance now," he whispered.

CHAPTER 28

DEFECTION?

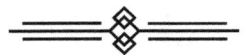

K nocking on the Scroll Room door, my mind raced. When the door creaked open, Gabriel scowled. "What is it, Michael?" I lowered my head at his sharp tone. "Listen," I said, raising. "I know you're frustrated with me, but I have a proposition for you."

Gabriel's lip curled. "What type of proposition?"

Trying to soften his displeasure, I smiled. "I'd like you to meet the private I have in the Armor Room."

He delayed his answer and squinted at me. "And why would I do that?"

Encouraged by his hesitation, I said, "Because it's important."

"Says you," Gabriel spat back. "Well, who is this angel, anyway? A new recruit to help with the armor?"

"No."

"Then, who? Besides, I know all the angels. I'm sure I've already met him."

I felt like giving up, but I remembered God's warning. "Okay," I said. "So I used the wrong word. I want you to hear what this private has to say."

"About what?"

My stomach knotted, yet I knew I had to answer. "Lucifer," I said.

"Lucifer! No!" Gabriel yelled and slammed the door shut.

This time, I would not allow him to dismiss me so easily. God said Heaven depended on us working together. I still didn't know how or why, but I pounded on the door. "Gabriel," I shouted. "Open the door! You need to hear what this angel has to say. Gabriel!" I pounded again, determined not to stop until he opened. "Gabriel!"

Finally, the latch clicked, and the door swung wide. Gabriel stood before me. "Go away, Michael. I have work to do. We're finished."

"No, Gabriel, we are not finished."

"Michael, go back to the Armor Room."

He started to close the door again, but I blocked it. "Please, just listen, and I'll make you a deal. Hear what Private Charrael has to say…and…"

"Private Charrael?" Gabriel said, interrupting. "Isn't he one of Lucifer's taskforce members?"

I nodded. "Yes, but that's what makes his information so vital."

Gabriel's nostrils flared, and he threw his arm out. "I can't believe it. You, of all angels…listening to a private. You know privates are naïve and imaginative."

My shoulders dropped with my sigh. "Look, I've heard enough of his story to trust it's true. I hope you will too. So, hear Charrael out. If you feel his report is a fabrication, I'll drop everything with Lucifer."

Gabriel crossed his arms. "No deal."

"Why?" I said, rubbing my forehead. "What do you have to lose?"

The silence was deafening as Gabriel stared at me. I could practically see him thinking and considering all the angles. After what felt like forever, he said, "Deal. I'll come. I'm not happy about it. But if this will cause you to let things go with Lucifer and focus on the important instead of the fringe, I'll hear Charrael."

I stifled a squeal and just said, "Great! We need to get to the Armor Room quickly."

"Fine. Let's go then."

Chaos continued in the caverns, and Wyael knew only a show of authority would quiet them. Organizing a row of power, he and Maysel stood at the front of the stage and placed a sentry guard at either side. Juael, Ennel, Alexael, and Huntiel followed the guard to the right. Willel, Stewel, Sebiel, and Carsiel trailed to the left. One additional sentry flanked each side of the taskforce. Their line stretched across the platform's entire length, and the lieutenants, with eyes fixated on the entry, held center, yet this did little to curb the noise.

Olivel and Dylael continued to guard the door. Hoping Chief Prince Lucifer would soon make his entrance, Wyael signaled for the privates to check outside again. They did and signaled—nothing.

Wyael shook his head as Maysel turned to him and yelled, "I can't believe Chief Prince Lucifer's followers are still here."

"I know," Wyael shouted back above the racket. "I'm not sure I would have stayed this long if I didn't have to."

"Why is he doing this?" Maysel hollered, scooching closer to Wyael. "He was ready to come and address his supporters when we left for the caverns."

"Yeah," Wyael bellowed, repositioning himself so he wouldn't have to yell. "I expected him to wait a short period to make a grand entrance, but never this long."

Maysel shrugged. "I don't get it."

"Me, either. And I'm done trying to contain this crowd." Wyael huffed. "If they grow so loud, they alert the Most High, then that's on the Chief Prince, not me."

Leaning in, Maysel said in hushed tones, "Have you thought about what could happen to us if the Almighty does find out?"

Wyael jerked, then lowered his voice. "No, not really. I guess I haven't wanted to go there."

"Well, maybe we should." Maysel took a deep breath. "I'm concerned."

Scrunching his brow, Wyael said, "Now that you mention it, I'm concerned too. We don't know what to expect. No one has ever challenged God before."

"I know. And I certainly didn't anticipate this when Chief Prince Lucifer chose me for the taskforce."

"Neither did I." Wyael shook his head. "I've been so caught up in obeying the Chief Prince I never considered the consequences."

Maysel shifted. "Me either. Why do you think that is?"

"Well…first off, we didn't know this was Lucifer's plan. I mean, how could we? It's not like he announced it and asked for volunteers."

"True."

"But once I knew and he seemed so sure he could do it, I didn't question him." Wyael lifted his shoulders and cocked his head. "I suppose I thought as long as we were being secretive and following orders, the Chief Prince would take over, and there wouldn't be consequences. Maybe I figured God wouldn't find out until it was too late. Then we, well, Lucifer, would be in charge."

Moving much closer, Maysel whispered, "But what if Lucifer isn't as strong as he thinks? What if he can't depose the King of Heaven and Earth? What will happen to us?"

Wyael jolted and whispered, "What are you saying?"

Maysel's lips puckered as he glanced up. "I don't know. But things have accelerated. They seem out of control."

Trying to maintain decorum, Wyael held steady. "What can we do about it?"

"Not sure. But if Lucifer can't pull this off, we'll be caught in the middle."

Wyael drew back. "You're right. I never thought of that. And if Lucifer goes down, we'll go down with him."

Maysel gasped. "I'm not ready to go down with Lucifer. Are you?"

"I don't know. You think we should get out while we can?"

"No. Maybe?" Maysel said, shrugging.

Wyael inched closer and spoke even softer. "It means we abandon Lucifer. Is that what you're suggesting?"

Gabriel and I launched in our synchronized style as though nothing had changed. "I have Charrael hidden in the Armor Room's inner chamber," I said.

"Seriously, Michael. All this covert stuff. Don't you think you are overdoing it a bit?"

"No, Gabriel. I'm not." We landed on the walkway, and I pointed. "You see that grove of trees over there?"

"Yes."

"I interrupted Lucifer threatening this private."

"Are you sure he wasn't just reprimanding him? You're probably blowing the whole encounter out of proportion."

I sighed. "Gabriel, please save your opinions until after you've heard Charrael."

"Fine," he said. When Gabriel and I stepped onto the porch, the sentry guards had already opened the doors. "So, where is this inner chamber?"

Waving, I said, "Follow me." We sprinted across the Grand Hall, down the long corridor, and into the inner chamber.

Charrael jumped to his feet and saluted. "Chief Prince Gabriel. It's an honor."

Archangel Gabriel returned the salute. "Thank you, Private Charrael, I'm just here for your story. Give me the abridged version."

Clearing his throat, Charrael said, "Okay…ah…well…Chief Prince Lucifer has a secret room in his chamber where he told the entire taskforce he plans to crush the Most High and take over Heaven and Earth. He claimed he was God."

Gabriel threw his arms out toward Charrael. "That's preposterous!" He spun around to face me. "Michael, you brought me here for this? I'm leaving."

I held up my hands to stop him. "Gabriel, calm down. Charrael, didn't you say you had more to tell?"

"Yes, Sir."

Stepping closer to Gabriel, I whispered, "Please, Gabriel, stay. Stay 'til the end. Then make your decision."

His eyes shot daggers. "Fine. I'll stay, but this better be worth it."

Letting out a huge breath, I said, "Good. Charrael, go on,"

"Um…Then Prince Lucifer changed, glowed fiery red, and caused us to worship him. The whole taskforce, except for me, fell on their knees, compelled to worship this thing he became."

"Worship Lucifer?" Gabriel yelled.

Charrael's lips trembled. "Yes, Sir."

Gabriel's arms flailed. "Blasphemous! No angel should ever be worshiped. Michael, this is crazy. I cannot believe it of Lucifer. He knows we worship only the LORD God Almighty. Charrael, why are you making all this up?"

Tears welled in Charrael's eyes. "I'm not, Chief Prince Gabriel. Please believe me. Everything is true. I'm telling it exactly as it happened."

Gabriel paced, halted, and scowled at Charrael. "How can I believe you? You have no evidence to back up these outlandish accusations."

Charrael hung his head. "I realize that, Sir. But if you stay and let me finish, I think I have an idea of how I can prove it."

Maysel glared at Wyael. "I'm not sure I should answer. But...I'm losing faith in Chief Prince Lucifer."

"Well..." Wyael paused. "Maybe I am too. This is not what I thought it would be. Lucifer seemed so strong when he chose us."

Maysel cocked his head. "Yeah. I believed you and I would stand on Lucifer's right and left when he seized control. I figured we would eventually rule Heaven together. Didn't you?"

"Yes, especially since we were the only taskforce members privy to Lucifer's initial plans."

"And Wyael, you know we deserved it. We worked hard to gain his attention and trust."

Visible to all Lucifer's rowdy followers, Wyael stood center stage. He pivoted, his eyes pierced Maysel's, and his hands flew out. "We did! And he rewarded us—elevated us to serve beside him. But Maysel, the longer and better I know Archangel Lucifer, the more I see flaws."

Wyael took a deep breath, rotated again toward front, and settled himself. Some devotees near the stage seemed confused by his earlier antics. With a strained half-smile, Wyael waved to acknowledge their stares. As he did, an angel involved in a brawl plowed into those followers, and Wyael was off the hook.

Maysel leaned in. "Do you think they heard?"

"I don't know." Wyael shrugged. "There's a scuffle now, so don't worry."

"Okay," Maysel whispered. "I see Lucifer's flaws, too."

Wyael drew back. "You do?" His brows raised, and then furrowed. "We need to be careful. He's still more powerful than we are. I'm just not sure I trust him anymore."

Maysel's eyes widened. "Even with what we witnessed in his secret room?"

"Yes." Wyael inhaled, held it for a moment, and exhaled. "Especially with that, and how compelled I was to worship him. I couldn't stop."

"I felt forced too. Did you ever imagine we would be worshiping Lucifer?"

"No, never." Wyael shook his head. "But I didn't think that far ahead. Maysel, do you think the rest of the taskforce saw what we saw?"

Pressing his lips together, Maysel said, "No one spoke to me about it if they did. Have you heard anything?"

"No, that's why I asked. It's strange, and I don't like it." Wyael's head tilted, and his face scrunched. "I guess I'm rethinking."

Maysel cleared his throat. "Good. But what should we do then?" Maysel whispered. "Defect?"

"Shh, shh! Someone might hear."

"Oh, right," Maysel mouthed.

Wyael leaned in. "If we do desert, how would we go about it?"

Maysel's eyes got big. "You got me, Wyael. You're the higher rank. What do you think we should do?"

"Not sure." Wyael wagged his head, and his foot scuffed the floor.

Studying the rotunda, Maysel said, "Well, whatever we do, we'd better do it fast."

"Right. Let me think."

CHAPTER 29

THE ARRIVAL

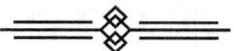

T he air in the inner chamber felt thick, like a weight on my chest. I shifted away from the tenseness and wandered the room while Gabriel decided. Would he stay or go?

"Charrael," Gabriel said, breaking the silence. "I don't believe you can prove it. But I will hear you out."

"Thanks, Gabriel," I said, rushing back to my chair. "Charrael, please continue."

Private Charrael took a deep breath and expelled it. "Somehow, through it all, I remained upright," he said. "Seems no one else in the room saw what I saw. It was as though I looked into Chief Prince Lucifer's inner being. And, Sirs, it's not good. I don't know how it happened or why I wasn't awestruck by his transformation like the rest, but I wasn't."

I straightened in my chair and glared at Charrael with a crumpled face. "So, was that the end?"

"No, Chief Prince Michael. When the sentry rang the door chime, I jolted, and it snapped everyone out of their trance. Since I was the only one standing, I started to kneel, hoping Chief Prince Lucifer wouldn't see me, but it was too late."

Gabriel shook his head. "And you know this how?"

"He told me when he intercepted me on the walkway outside the Armor Room. And before Chief Prince Michael arrived, he threatened me with annihilation if I divulged anything. I didn't even know what annihilation was, but I knew it couldn't be good." Charrael nodded in my direction. "Sir, I'm pretty sure you saved me."

"Not me, Charrael. it was the Almighty. He caused you to see with eyes open to truth, to think to cut your strap, and he's the One who knew to send me back to the Armor Room at the precise moment you and Lucifer arrived. That's our God. Perfect in every way."

"Yes, Sir. Thank you." Charrael gazed upward and said, "Thank you, LORD God."

Gabriel rubbed the back of his neck. "Listen, this all sounds sweet, and yes, our God is good with perfect timing. But none of this convinces me that what you're saying is true. Where's your evidence, Charrael? And where is Lucifer right now? Is he still in his secret room?"

"No, Chief Prince Gabriel."

I held out my hands. "Then, where is he?"

Charrael squirmed in his chair. "I don't know exactly, but Chief Prince Lucifer's followers have been gathering in the caverns of the Mount of Holiness."

Gabriel jerked. "Lucifer has followers? More than just the taskforce?"

Charrael's head bobbed up and down. "Yes, Sir. He is supposed to be addressing them right now."

Glancing at Gabriel, I said, "Hmm…Lucifer is giving an address."

Again, Charrael's head nodded profusely, and his eyes held great concern. "Yes, Sir. There are thousands and thousands of angels loyal to him. I thought I was, too, but only because I believed Lucifer was faithful to the Most High. Until his secret room, I would have gladly served him, just as I will now serve and honor you or Chief Prince Gabriel."

Gabriel jumped to his feet and flailed his arms. "Thousands and thousands of angels loyal to Lucifer? In the caverns? That's ridiculous!"

Charrael gasped and stood. "No, Sir. It's not. And it's my understanding every angel devoted to Lucifer is there."

I walked toward Charrael. "How did Lucifer amass such a following?"

He brushed his forehead. "I'm not sure, Sir. I heard he started small with just a few, and I think they increased by word of mouth."

Gabriel's eyes narrowed as he sighed. "Charrael, Michael and I would know if there were disgruntled angels or if this was true of Lucifer."

I spun around and looked him in the eye. "Are you serious, Gabriel? I've been trying to tell you something's off with Lucifer and that he's been volatile lately, but you wouldn't listen."

His hand flew up. "Even so, Michael, I'm still not convinced. Charrael is a private. Lucifer's an archangel. Charrael could be trying to interpret things he doesn't understand."

My shoulders dropped. "I get it. But this has been going on for quite a while. I hoped Lucifer would have settled down by now, yet he hasn't. I've had several disturbing encounters with him, and you are never around to see it. And twice now, I've seen red in his eyes."

"Red in his eyes?" Gabriel's nostrils flared. "Oh, that's it. I'm done. I'm going back to the Scroll Room, and Michael, don't bother me with this again. Not ever!" He pulled the heavy door so hard it slammed against the wall. Down the corridor, he sped as I dashed after him.

Mid-Armor Room, I finally caught him. Grabbing his arm, I swung him around. "You listen to me, Archangel Gabriel. Something is happening in Heaven, and we must discover the cause."

"Michael! Let me go!" he said, ripping his arm from my hand and turning to exit.

I reached out and yelled, "Gabriel, stop! I will not allow you to dismiss this as hearsay, at least not without doing everything possible to confirm or deny its validity. Besides, we must protect the Most High. If I'm wrong, prove me wrong. Don't just walk away."

Gabriel halted and stood motionless with his back toward me. "Fine," he said as he pivoted. "I will prove you wrong. But to do that, we need to find Lucifer. Charrael doesn't know where he is."

"True. But Charrael does know where he will be. And so do we if Lucifer is giving an address to his followers. I say we go to the caverns. If it's empty, we'll know. And that will be the end of it."

"Promise?"

"Yes, Gabriel. I promise. Just come with me."

Gabriel paused to consider my offer and then said, "Agreed. Lead the way."

After a brief pause, Wyael leaned toward Maysel. "I think I have a plan."

"Really?" Maysel's eyebrows raised. "What is it?"

Wyael took a deep breath and exhaled, "If we move to the back of the stage area little by little, perhaps we won't draw too much attention. Maybe then we can descend the staircase, sneak to the door, and get out of here before Lucifer enters."

Maysel pulled back. "Don't you think as soon as we step off this stage, the angel devotees will recognize us and make that impossible?"

"Probably." Wyael nodded. "But we wouldn't be any worse off than we are now."

"True." Maysel shrugged and cocked his head. "Maybe it'll work. And even if we get stopped, the fans couldn't possibly know what we were doing."

"So, either way, we'll be fine." Wyael shifted his stance and grabbed Maysel's arm. "We should go now."

Maysel twitched as his breath caught. "Wait. What about the rest of our team?"

"They're on their own. Think about it. If any of the others sense we are abandoning our allegiance to Lucifer, what would you expect them to do?"

"Ah…" Maysel's hand covered his mouth and slid down his neck. "I guess, if it were me, I'd detain the traitor until the Chief Prince could deal with him."

"Exactly."

"So, we're alone in this?"

Wyael tipped his head and whispered, "Yes. But we'll have each other's back."

Maysel stiffened. "Wyael, what if Chief Prince Lucifer catches us? What will he do?"

Eying the frenzied room, Wyael sighed. "I don't know. It could be bad. Still, if we want out, it's a chance we'll have to take."

"Bad? How bad?"

"Maysel! Having second thoughts?"

"No," he said as his head wagged. "I'm pretty sure I want out."

"Good." Wyael inhaled, held it, and exhaled. "Listen, I'm not doing this alone."

Lifting his head, Maysel made eye contact with the First Lieutenant. "Okay. Bad or not, I'm in. When should we go?"

"Now. Before Lucifer gets here. Slowly, one step at a time. You first, then me."

Returning to the inner chamber, I said, "Charrael, Chief Prince Gabriel, and I have agreed to visit the caverns to validate your story."

He lowered his head. "Thank you, Sir."

I held up my hand. "But Charrael, you must realize that if we find it empty and there is no evidence to support your story, we'll know it was fabricated. You will then fall into the hands of our Most High God."

Charrael set his jaw and looked at me with determined eyes. "I understand, Sir. And I would tell the LORD just what I told you because it's all true."

I nodded. "Good to know, Charrael. Sit tight; we'll be back."

"But wait," he called after us. "Let me help. Please!"

I spun around to face him. "Help? How?"

Charrael's fingers covered his lips, and then his eyes brightened. "I can lead you to the cavern's opening, Sir."

I turned to Gabriel. "What do you think?"

He shrugged. "I've not been to the caverns since we visited with Lucifer. The location of the entrance is a bit fuzzy. Charrael might expedite the process."

"I concur. And he did provide good intel."

Gabriel scowled. "That's your opinion, Michael."

I sighed and looked at the private. "All right, you're in. You, Gabriel, and I will do some reconnaissance first. We'll not engage Lucifer until we have all the facts, unless he resists. Randiel," I shouted. "Time to dress."

"Dress?" Gabriel said. "In what?"

"Our armor."

Gabriel rolled his eyes. "Really, Michael? Is armor needed?"

"Yes! Lucifer already has his, and so does his taskforce. We need to dress in battle gear if, for nothing else, to display our united authority and prove to him his rebellion is over. He may not come peacefully. And if he doesn't, we'll definitely need armor to engage him."

"Fine," he said as his eyebrows pinched together, "but I do this under protest."

"Noted." I pointed to the left wall. "Your armor is there."

Randiel lowered Gabriel's armor and helped him dress. I grabbed a hook, plucked mine from the pegs, and outfitted myself. Seeing the craftsmanship and quality, Gabriel's attitude softened. "Nice armor," he said, running his hands over the breastplate.

"Thanks. How's the fit?"

He smiled. "Perfect. I couldn't ask for better. Surprisingly, the breastplate melds right into my chest and feels like a second skin."

I inhaled, nodded with a half-smile, and exhaled. "I'm glad." Turning to Charrael, I said, "Are you ready?"

He hiked his shoulders. "Yes, Sir!"

My eyes connected with Randiel's. "Your duties concern the Armor Room. If we cannot stop this rebellion peaceably, you are to ensure enough armor is ready for all our troops."

"I understand, Sir. I won't let you down."

"Gabriel. Charrael. Let's move."

Maysel reached the rear of the stage and waited for Wyael's last step. Left foot back then, right, and the lieutenants stood side by side. Looking around the crammed rotunda, Maysel said, "Now, where?"

"We made this decision on impulse. I haven't developed a real plan." Wyael examined each staircase. "There are only two choices: exit the stage to the right or the left."

"Okay…which direction then?"

Peeking through the central hole their absent bodies created and out into the sea of angels, Wyael said, "Check out the crowd. Which way do you think provides the path of least resistance?"

Maysel shrugged. "It's so jammed with angels. Both? Neither?"

Wyael pointed to the right. "That way."

"Should we split up? Maybe I go left?" Maysel said. "Or should we stay together?"

"I think we have a better chance if we stay together."

"A better chance of what, Gentlemen?" came a slithery voice from behind.

CHAPTER 30

A RACE FOR TRUTH

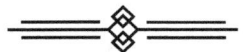

The four of us made our way back down the long corridor and out into the Grand Hall. Armor Room angels were unloading a shipment of armor when they saw us emerge. Halting their work, they saluted. Gabriel and I returned their salute, and I motioned for them to resume.

As we hastened through the gleaming battle armor, a thought speared my mind. I raised my hand to halt our progress. Setting my helmet on the nearest bench, I signaled, and they did the same. "Gabriel," I said, "I know combat is not your first station, however, I've trained you to fight when necessary, and your skills are good. I'm hoping they won't be needed, but if so, I'll keep you in my line of sight and help as much as possible."

Gabriel sighed. "I still think this is bogus, yet it's good to know you'll be there."

I gave him a nod and turned to Charrael. "I watched you spar in the Arena. You, too, are very skilled even for your rank, and I believe you've proven your allegiance to the Most High."

His head bowed. "Thank you, Sir."

"You're welcome. But I've been thinking. For this mission, we will need you to be of higher rank."

Charrael's eyes grew big. "You do?"

"Yes. Without your information, Gabriel and I would not know about Lucifer, his schemes, or where to find him."

"Michael!" Gabriel reprimanded.

My lips squeezed together. "Okay, fine. I would not know."

Charrael cocked his head. "But, Sir, I thought you said the LORD knew everything?"

I pondered my answer. "He does, Charrael. Still, he has designed things in Heaven and now on Earth to allow his whole creation to learn and participate in his plan. God will intervene as needed or when asked."

His face brightened. "You mean like he did earlier?"

"Yes," I said, smiling. "And although God already knows our need even before we ask, he wants us to ask."

Gabriel stepped toward us and said, "On the other hand, because of who he is, he expects our praise, worship, and exaltation no matter his answer."

Charrael drew back. "So, Sirs, why didn't you just ask him?"

Rubbing my chin, I took a deep breath and exhaled. "It's hard to explain, Charrael. God requires us to use the abilities he has given to make decisions and to govern our area according to his word. Before the shin guard incident, it was only speculation on my part. I felt Lucifer was up to something, but I didn't know for sure."

"Seems complicated, Sir."

"I know." I paused and pursed my lips. "Yet God's plan is always perfect, whether we understand it or not. And...besides...I did ask."

Gabriel's head snapped in my direction. "You did?"

Eying the floor, I said, "Yes. But he didn't answer."

"He didn't answer, Michael?" Gabriel shouted, throwing his hands up. "Don't you think that should tell you something?"

Setting my jaw, I glared at him. "No. I now understand God wanted me to wait until he directed Charrael to step forward with his information."

"Wait!" Charrael said with a huge grin. "The Almighty has used me?"

I nodded. "Without question."

Gabriel leaned in and whispered, "Michael, be careful. Don't sugarcoat Charrael's help. This still could be a fabrication."

My eyes squinted. Gabriel's cautions always made sense, so I weighed my words before I spoke. "You're right. But for now, I'm taking Charrael at his word. To me, what he has said thus far sounds true."

He cocked his head and shrugged while I looked over at the private. Golden armor surrounded Charrael. His eyes were closed, arms folded across his chest, and he rocked back and forth as though he was having a personal time of worship. "This is wonderful, Sir," he said when his eyes opened. "The Most High even allows lowly privates to serve him."

"Yes, Charrael," I said. "I'm grateful he uses all of us. For these reasons and the potential battle ahead, I am promoting you to Sergeant First Class."

Charrael gasped. "Sergeant First Class! Oh, Chief Prince Michael, thank you."

My hand went up to halt his exuberance. "Keep in mind, this is temporary. If we cannot authenticate your story, you will revert to private. And, the Almighty will have the final word."

He patted his chest. "I understand, Sir. That will not be a problem."

I turned toward Randiel. "Please show Charrael his new armor. Make sure the fit is perfect since we cannot test it."

"Yes, Chief Prince."

Randiel motioned for Charrael to follow. As they sped to the correct section, I called after them, "Charrael, once you don your armor, you will also possess the upgraded and enhanced skills of your new rank."

Charrael pivoted and saluted. "I'm here to serve."

"Dress quickly," I said, returning his salute.

———⌄———

Wyael and Maysel jolted as a chill ran through them. "J-just a b-better chance of containing the c-crowd, Sir," Wyael said, trembling.

Lucifer extended his arms around their shoulders and squeezed like they all were bosom buddies. "Surprised?"

"Ah…well…traumatized is more like it, Sir," Maysel said, recovering. "How did you get in here without us seeing you? We've had the entrance monitored."

Lucifer snickered. "I have my ways."

Wyael's brows narrowed. "Why did you wait so long? You have no idea how difficult it's been to contain this crowd. In fact, I just gave up. They may have alerted the Most High, but there was nothing we could do."

Clenching his jaw, Lucifer growled. "Wyael, if I were you, I would choose my words wisely, especially after the conversation I just overheard."

He stiffened. "What did you hear?"

Lucifer drew in a slow, steady breath and squeezed his arms tighter around the Lieutenants. "Enough to know I need to watch you and Maysel closely. And maybe I shouldn't trust you at all."

Maysel gasped. "Oh, Sir, y-you can trust us."

Cocking his head, Lucifer let go and glared. "Can I? First, Charrael, and now you two? Seems I don't have a choice. I have to concentrate on my mission." His eyes narrowed. "But take heed, one more misstep, and it's annihilation for all three of you."

"Charrael, Chief Prince?" Wyael said, deflecting the conversation. "Was it worse than his shin guard?"

Lucifer held his chin high and inhaled. "Yes, much worse. Long story...but I won't discuss it now."

Wyael lowered his head. "Apologies, Sir. You know, Maysel and I have been by your side since the onset. We are yours to command."

"Good. Keep it that way." Lucifer glared, crossed his arms, and huffed. "Now, about the Almighty. His days are limited. When I overthrow Him, you two will serve beside me in my kingdom as long as I can trust you. And if not, I'll pick others," Lucifer peered out through the small opening in the command line. "Observe my adoring fans. Any one of them would be thrilled to take your position. They're like a never-ending sea...and...all for me!" A smile spanned his face. "This is the moment I've dreamed of, and I will let nothing, not even insubordination, ruin it."

Wyael stifled a shudder. "No mutiny here, Chief Prince."

"Fine." Standing between the Lieutenants, Lucifer checked his armor and hiked his shoulders. "I'm ready for my introduction. Not that I need one, mind you, but I deserve it. I'll stay backstage until you and Maysel can quiet the crowd."

Walking together downstage, Maysel leaned in. "No escape now."

Wyael sighed and whispered, "Yeah, I know."

Dashing out of the Armor Room, I hollered, "Randiel, take care of things here. Gabriel, Charrael, helmets. Ready. Wings. Launch."

Our trio rocketed toward the Mount of Holiness. Drawing closer to the mountain, I shouted, "Sergeant, take the lead. Show us the entrance."

"Yes, Sir," Charrael yelled, moving to the point of the triangle. "It's around back."

"I remember. Gabriel, are you still with us?"

"Yes, Michael. Right behind you."

We landed silently at the backside of the mountain, and Charrael rifled his memory for a picture of the specific crag, but it was unclear. "Chief Prince Michael, Sir. I didn't realize there were so many crags back here. They all look the same, and now I can't recall which crag is the one we need."

"It's alright, Sergeant. You got us this far," I said, removing my helmet. "Gabriel, do you remember?"

Gabriel appeared to scrutinize the mountain and the surrounding greenery. "Well, I know we entered at an inconspicuous point."

"You're right." I turned toward him. "And wasn't it tucked back in?"

He nodded. "I believe so."

I pointed to the left. "Wait, I think I see it over there. Gabriel, what do you think?"

Squinting, he said, "It does look familiar."

"Charrael, your opinion?"

"That might be it, Sir."

"Good," I said, repositioning my helmet. "Let's move."

Maysel motioned for the taskforce and guards to clear the stage. As they retreated to the left and right, he signaled the trumpeters to herald Lucifer's arrival. Paaa—pa-pa-pa—paaa—pa-pa-pa—paaa-paaa-paaa, the golden trumpets blasted out in waves. Silence washed over the angels. Each turned toward the elevated stage as Wyael approached the podium. "Angels, your patience and loyalty have paid off. Without further delay, I give you the magnificent, the luminous, the wisest, and most benevolent leader any angel army could ever have. Please welcome our splendid Chief Prince, Archangel Lucifer."

Screams, applause, and whistles exploded from the floor and every nook and alcove. Lucifer moseyed downstage, absorbing the accolades. With a wave of his hand, the podium flew. Wyael had to duck when it whizzed by and crashed against the back wall. Lucifer unfurled his wings and placed himself center stage. Arms raised and head held high, he rotated so his followers could witness his full countenance.

Reveling in the adoration, Lucifer's true nature emerged. At once, ecstasy engulfed his essence, and red-hued fire mushroomed from the core of his being with a shrill, pulsing resonance. Reaching a fever pitch, it shot out like a flaming torch that stirred the nature of each devotee while a hypnotic stupor washed over the entire crowd. Every angel knelt in a wave of veneration.

Laser-fire from within encompassed Lucifer and kept all eyes riveted. An ear-piercing noise was the only sound. Nothing moved.

———∨———

Gabriel, Charrael, and I traipsed through the dense greenery, up and down small mounds, jumped some ravines, and arrived before an enormous vertical crag. Charrael scanned left and right but found no opening. "It's not the one, Sir. We need to keep looking."

I pointed to the right. "Sergeant, I think it is. Walk there and all the way to the end. I'm sure you'll find the crag is camouflaging an isolated gap. This, I believe, leads to the cavern's entrance. We'll wait here until you scope it out. Signal when you find it or if any of Lucifer's followers are lingering."

Charrael rushed to follow my orders, but standing before the sheer jagged rock, he couldn't see much else. *Chief Prince Michael told me to go right.*

Moving in that direction, the terrain seemed loose, and his foot teetered. As the edge began to crumble and give way under his weight, he wobbled, grabbed the rock face, and pulled himself back.

Surveying the surroundings with more diligent eyes, Charrael found the culprit. As the crag jutted upward, a deep crevice had formed. "This has to be where I fell," he said, shivering as though an icy breeze whipped around him. "Must be the right place, but I better make sure before calling the Chief Princes."

Tiptoeing around the gap and through tall grasses, Charrael found the path and spotted the narrow section edging the crevice. "Yep, this is it." With his back hugging the mountain, Charrael side-stepped the tapered trail and slipped in behind the crag. Around the next bend, he spied the entrance. "Now to get Michael and Gabriel."

I shifted from one foot to the next. "What's taking Charrael so long?"

Gabriel nodded. "It has been a while."

Searching our surroundings, I found the last place Charrael was visible. "I wonder if someone on Lucifer's team caught him."

"Seriously, Michael?"

Whipping around, I glared at Gabriel. "Look, I know you're skeptical, but we need to find Charrael. Something could have happened."

"I guess," he said. "I don't like you speaking of alleged suspicions as proven."

I shook my head and sighed. Advancing in the direction Charrael headed, I began to trace his route. But Gabriel didn't follow, so I stopped and motioned for him.

Gabriel pursed his lips. "Shouldn't we just yell for Charrael?"

I shook my hand. "No. Too much noise. I don't want to alert Lucifer."

"How will we find him then?" Gabriel retorted.

"Keep your eyes peeled."

Charrael shot out of the crag opening in time to see us in the distance. "It's here," he yelled and waved, but then quieted his tone. "Go around to the path. There's a crevice." Charrael paused. "Wait! I'll show you."

Gripping the mountain, he navigated the pass. With the crevice to his right and the slim trail before him, Charrael shifted his armor. He eased himself along the notched passage, grabbing the rock wall as needed to steady himself and secure his footing.

Gabriel and I used Charrael as a directional bearing to find the pathway, and worked our way toward him. "Be careful," Charrael said. "There's a crevice to your left."

I halted. "Good eye. You averted a calamity."

Charrael cocked his head. "Yeah. Wasn't too hard. This is where I fell, and Chief Prince Lucifer lifted me out."

"Right," I said, nodding. "Gabriel, are you okay?"

"Yes. Couldn't we just fly across this area?"

"No. It's better if we stay discreet and hidden by the tall grasses." I glanced at Charrael. "You lead, and we'll follow."

Inching down the narrow footpath, I recalled our first visit here with Lucifer and how different things were then. Locating the secluded crack, Charrael led us toward the door. The trail wound through a corridor that reminded me of an isosceles triangle. The vertical mountain rock wall to our right, attached to the apex, descended at a wide left angle and affixed itself to the path. It was roomy enough for us to maneuver, yet so constricted we walked single-file.

The lane widened as the door came into view, but Charrael motioned for us to stay back. He scouted the area again for Lucifer's devotees and waved us in once he was sure none were hanging around outside.

The cavern's entrance looked different from what I remembered, and the same apprehension I felt on my first visit crept in and rattled me a bit. "Gabriel, how do you think we should proceed?"

He shrugged. "I don't know, Michael. Military strategy is your thing."

I nodded. "Give me a moment." Standing in this remote pass, I knew whatever I decided had to be quick. Someone could exit and ruin our surprise. "Charrael," I whispered, "if your information is accurate, and there are thousands of angels inside, we can't just barge in. We must do this covertly."

"You're right, Sir," he said. "But how?"

I took a deep breath, collected my thoughts, relied on my creation as guardian, and exhaled. "Okay. Charrael, since you are a member of Lucifer's taskforce and already belong there, you enter first. That way, when the door opens, they'll see only you, and no one will be suspicious. Lucifer will think you are returning from the Armor Room. When that disruption calms, we'll slip in."

"Well, Michael," Gabriel said. "If all Charrael reported is true, and Lucifer is in the caverns with many angels, then I commend you. This plan is brilliant."

"Guess we'll know soon enough. But it only gets us in the door. The rest, I'll figure out as we go." I turned to Charrael. "Once inside, check everything and signal if acceptable to enter."

He hiked his shoulders. "Yes, Sir."

Nearing the cavern's entrance, Charrael pushed the door. As it inched open, an ear-piercing pulse streamed out.

"What is that?" Gabriel whispered.

"It's Lucifer," Charrael said, taking a deep breath like he was mustering courage to step through the entrance. Tiptoeing in, he turned back to us. "Dylael and Olivel are kneeling in worship. They seem completely unaware of my presence." His head moved left to right. "All the angels are either kneeling or lying prostrate before Lucifer." He quivered, calmed, and motioned for me and Gabriel. "Come on."

CHAPTER 31

THE ESCAPE

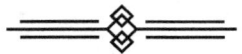

The rotunda pulsed red as we snuck in. And there we were, standing while the whole room knelt. "Charrael, unfurl your wings," I whispered.

Charrael faced forward, but he whispered back over his right shoulder, "Won't that make us more noticeable, Sir?"

"No, you're a taskforce member. Unfurl now! Gabriel and I will move in behind them."

"They might not open."

"Why?"

"I had trouble when I fell into the crevice and again when I tried to launch toward the city. Chief Prince Lucifer had to slam my back."

"You didn't have a problem when we launched for the Mount of Holiness. So, try. Quickly, we need the cover."

Charrael nodded and let out a muffled grunt. His wings unfolded as they always did. I stepped to the right wing, and Gabriel slipped in behind his left. We towered above the sergeant, but for the most part, his wings obscured our bodies, at least enough for the time being. As I looked over the colossal domed room, my chin dropped. Nothing in all my training had prepared me for what I saw, especially when my eyes reached the stage.

———⌄———

Lucifer stood on the platform, engulfed in some type of pulsing flame. His head tilted upward, his back arched, wings outstretched, and his eyes appeared closed. With each breath, his chest rose and fell, and his face held the expression of pure bliss. "This is bizarre," I whispered. "Gabriel, what do you make of it?"

He shook his head. "I have no words."

"Me either. It's much worse than I thought."

Gabriel shifted his stance and winced. "At least you recognized it. I'm so ashamed I didn't. But what's with the fire?"

Charrael looked back over his left shoulder. "Chief Prince Lucifer is doing the same thing he did in his secret room. The angels are frozen in place, compelled to worship."

As we maintained our cover, a sudden feeling of heaviness came over me. My heart ached. On the stage, Lucifer lowered his head and opened his eyes. He appeared to be hunting for something. I stiffened. *Did he hear our conversation?* "Ready yourselves," I said in hushed tones. "Lucifer may have heard us."

Gabriel, Charrael, and I primed our stances, but Lucifer didn't move from the stage. Instead, he began a panoramic scan of the rotunda and the cavern's alcoves. "Stay alert," I said. "He could still spot us, and we may need to engage." Lucifer's head turned in our direction. "Stand by. He's searching." When his eyes hit mine, they appeared glassy, vacant, and somehow, he overlooked me behind Charrael's unfurled wings.

"Lucifer didn't see us," I said, huddling up with Gabriel close enough for Charrael to hear. "He looked right at me, but it's like he's blinded to our presence."

I peeked up over Charrael's wings and watched Lucifer's gaze move further around the rotunda. Reaching the end, he started back the other way, smiling as he eyed the sea of angels. I again lowered to confer with Gabriel, and at the same time, Lucifer said in a grandiose voice, "I am your supreme leader. You may address me as God Almighty."

"What?" I said, jerking my head up. "This can't be real. He must be play-acting."

"Oh, it's real, Sir," Charrael whispered over his right shoulder.

Lucifer held out his arms to his adoring fans. "In my greatness," he said, "I will depose and annihilate the Most High."

I scooched down again behind Charrael. "Gabriel, your thoughts?"

Gabriel gulped. "I think he's lost his mind."

My head hung down. "I agree, but I don't understand why. Since the moment of our creation, Heaven and the Almighty's rules have been perfect. We've known no other."

"True," Gabriel whispered. "I've never once questioned the LORD, and I'm the one who pens his word."

"So, from where did Lucifer's insanity come?"

Gabriel shook his head. "I have no idea."

"Ah, Lucifer!" I wailed. "What have you done? Is your character flawed—damaged by your own doing?"

"Shhh, Michael." Gabriel tried to cover my mouth. "Quiet down, you'll blow our cover."

In my frustration, our location and mission eluded me. Maybe I wanted my voice to ring out through the caverns, yet I restrained myself and whispered, "LORD God, did you create him like this?"

"Michael!" Gabriel scolded. "You know better. No flaw ever came from the Almighty."

My shoulders sank. "I know. I'm just trying to make sense of it."

"You can't. You were right all along. Something is terribly wrong with Lucifer, and we have to figure out what."

"But, Gabriel, is it possible to damage your own character? And if so, can Lucifer's flaw be reversed?"

"I don't know," he said with a sigh.

In that moment, I saw the bigger picture. My chest tightened. "Gabriel." I gasped. "This is worse than just Lucifer being flawed."

His head jerked back. "How could anything be worse?"

"Think about it. Lucifer is one angel. But look." I extended my arm around to the angels in the caverns. "He's accumulated a following."

"He has…but how?"

My brows narrowed. "You can't gather devotees without first imposing your philosophies on them. Lucifer must have dumped his warped ideas on these under-angels and convinced them to follow him instead of the Almighty."

"Maybe that's the way it happened."

"All these angels, Gabriel!" My hand covered my mouth, and I slid it down to pat my chest. "Angels we've cared for and trained. Have they chosen Lucifer as their god?"

He wagged his head. "I can't answer that. But I see your point. Do you think the Almighty knows?"

I shrugged. "Not sure. I thought he knew everything, but now..."

Gabriel grabbed my arm. "Stop, Michael. Don't doubt! Let's just try to figure out how we can fix Lucifer."

My shoulders dropped. "Yeah. I'm not sure that's possible. Maybe God did create him this way."

"No!" he scolded. "God is perfect, and you know he only creates perfection. Something else must have happened."

I turned and held out my arms to Gabriel. "Then, you explain why the LORD refused to hear anything I had to say about Lucifer and his questionable activities."

He shook his head. "I can't."

I held up my finger. "I know! But as guardian, it's up to me to stop Lucifer and protect the Almighty. I need a plan to round up these angels and restrain this rebel."

"Yes, a plan," Gabriel said, nodding. "I think we've collected enough information. Let's go back to the Armor Room and strategize. Maybe then we can approach the LORD together."

"Gabriel! Be serious! You know we can't leave or allow Lucifer out of our sight. Look at him now."

Lucifer pranced around the stage and shouted, "Soon, I will be Lord and Master of Heaven and Earth, the sovereign king of the universe. You, my obedient angels, will follow and serve me well, privileged to do all my bidding."

"Yes, Master," droned a myriad of voices, and a shiver ran through me.

"Sirs," Charrael whispered over his shoulder. "These are some of the same things I heard in the secret room."

Lucifer cried out again, compelling us to watch. "The Almighty is an evil dictator. He controls you and is not fit to reign. I am benevolent," he bellowed. "A ruler who listens. You will have freedom like never before. My plans for heaven, the universe, and you, my loyal subjects, are great, and…"

"This is nonsense!" I said, throwing my hands up. "Lucifer must know how futile it is even to try to overthrow our Sovereign LORD."

Gabriel shook his head. "I don't think he does. Seems he actually believes he can…and…will."

"Well, he can't! I've seen enough, and it ends now. Are you with me?"

"All the way."

"Good. Charrael, lower your wings and bar the doors. No one gets out."

"Yes, Sir," he said as his wings swooshed down.

"Gabriel, Charrael, swords!"

Light hit our armor, and the blinding reflection bounced with our every step. We drew closer to the stage, and one beam caught Lucifer's eyes, disrupting his tirade. When he reached for his sword, his followers jolted from their trance-like state. Dylael and Olivel jumped to their feet. They raised their sabers to fight, but Charrael intercepted.

Private Charrael was now Sergeant Charrael. Outranked, the privates retreated. Others close by tried to escape and found the exit blocked. "We're trapped!" yelled one.

"Run!" shouted another.

Panicked, angels darted this way and that. They crashed into each other. Some fell to the floor. Confusion and chaos overflowed the caverns.

Charrael stood his ground, and I was pleased. Not one angel was able to access the door. Gabriel and I attempted to make our way to the stage while Lucifer's followers scrambled and hindered our forward movement. "Gabriel," I shouted. "These angels are defying our authority."

"I see," he yelled back. "Lucifer must have them so deceived they disregard protocol."

We pushed through the angels and inched toward the stage area, closing in on Lucifer. However, his lieutenants saw the danger and sounded an alarm. At once, the devotees stilled and rotated to face the stage. At that exact moment, Lucifer flung out his arms, and this stationary sea of angels stood shoulder-to-shoulder, staunch and rigid. In their frenzied state, we were able to squeeze through. But now, forward progress had become impossible.

There, in the center of the rotunda, Gabriel and I stood back-to-back, hedged in and confined by hordes of mesmerized angels. The tight space made our wings unusable, and we needed a new plan. I shoved at the fixed angels. Not one budged.

"Gabriel, suggestions?"

"None, Michael."

"Maybe we can snap them out of their stupor," I said, grabbing the shoulders of the angel to my right. I shook him, and his head bobbed back and forth, yet his eyes remained vacant. "Wake up, soldier," I yelled, but nothing. I removed my hands, and the angel returned to his former position.

"Michael, look. The taskforce remains free-thinking."

Olivel and Dylael zoomed to Lucifer's side and joined the other ten on stage. "Follow me!" Lucifer shouted, releasing his followers and disappearing through a backstage opening. At once, the taskforce and every devoted angel unfurled. Their wingtips whipped our faces and caused us to duck.

Appearing like a raging flood slicing through topography, torrents of angels streamed out behind Lucifer. "Gabriel," I yelled. "Did you know there was another entrance?"

"No!"

Charrael came running toward us as the caverns emptied. "Charrael, did you know about the second door?"

"No, Sir."

I pointed. "From the direction of the exit, I'm guessing it opens up somewhere near the Shekinah Glory Base. We need to follow."

CHAPTER 32

THE PLUNDERING

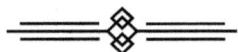

Lucifer led his followers through his secret passage and out the opening beneath the Shekinah Glory Base. Once the last devotee exited, Lucifer yelled, "Ennel, Stewel, Alexael, Sebiel, cave in the opening and follow when you are finished. Wyael. Maysel. Lead the troops to raid the Armor Room. Empty it. I want all the armor—every rank. Do not leave one piece. All my angels must be fully outfitted and ready to fight." Turning to his remaining taskforce, Lucifer bellowed, "Juael, Willel, Huntiel, Carsiel, disburse yourselves throughout the soldiers. Olivel, Dylael, bring up the rear. We are taking over Heaven and deposing the Most High."

"Yes, Sir," they said in unison.

"Angels, once fitted," Lucifer shouted to his vast army, "meet me back in the caverns for combat orders. Now get going."

Maysel joined Wyael, and he motioned for the devotees to follow. "Angels, this way."

While the troops moved to the launch spot, Lucifer pivoted and yelled, "Wait! Wyael, come here."

Turning to Maysel, Wyael said, "Stay with the soldiers. I'll be back."
Wyael sped to Lucifer. "Sir?"

"Listen, there's an inner chamber off the back hall of the Armor Room. Michael keeps the door locked with a key tethered to his belt. When I picked up my armor in this room, Michael mentioned the other items present, but I saw nothing. Something valuable must be there, or else he wouldn't keep it locked. I want that key."

"But Chief Prince, if Michael has it on him, how can I get the key?"

Lucifer huffed. "It's possible there's a second. Randiel might carry it, or it could be somewhere in his cubicle. Find that key and bring it to me."

"Yes, Sir. Wyael pivoted to return to the troops.

"No, Wyael," Lucifer said. "On second thought, don't take the key. If Michael thinks I have it, he'll remove whatever's in there. Trace the key. I'll make a copy. And Wyael, keep this between us."

"I'll do my best, Sir." He rushed back to Maysel.

"What was that about?"

Wyael shrugged and shook his head. "Nothing really, only a few more instructions for raiding the Armor Room. Let's get going. Soldiers!" he yelled. "Ready. Wings. Launch."

Taking flight, Lucifer's angels resembled a million silver blades propelling through the sky. But beneath the plateau, at the mouth of the grotto, stood four sergeants, swords raised. They struck the boulders, and the giant rocks tumbled, rendering the opening impassable. Shooting upward, they easily caught up to Olivel and Dylael. Together, Lucifer's army raced to ravage the Armor Room.

Satisfied with his soldiers' activity, Lucifer climbed to a concealed place on the mountain. *Would Michael and Gabriel be able to exit the passageway?* He removed his helmet and rubbed his head. "Did we do enough to thwart Michael? Maybe. Still, this is happening too fast. My plan isn't complete. But now I have no choice, I must be ready."

Lucifer zeroed in on the blocked opening. "At least I'm a step ahead of Michael. How did he find out about the caverns and my followers anyway? There's got to be a snitch. If he and Gabriel know about these, what else do they know?"

———————⌄———————

Gabriel, Charrael, and I chased after Lucifer and his angels, but we decelerated after entering the backstage opening. Although we still moved at great speed, Lucifer and his followers were too far ahead. "Slow down," I yelled. "We won't overtake them. This tunnel is unfamiliar, and I need to survey our surroundings."

As my pace tapered off, the others followed suit. "I've not seen anything like this passageway," I said, coming to a complete halt. "Have either of you?"

"No," Gabriel and Charrael answered back.

With mouths agape, we scrutinized the massive tunnel lit with Heaven's light. "This is very odd," I said.

Gabriel removed his helmet. "How so?"

I lifted mine off, fastened it to my belt, and said, "Well, all Heaven was here when we came on the scene. Anyone could tell that the mountain and the caverns formed as God created, yet this corridor is different." I stepped closer and touched the facade. "Gabriel, these walls don't appear natural. They look chiseled."

Gabriel ran his hand over the veneer. "They feel chiseled too. Are you thinking this is a hand-crafted tunnel, that it wasn't here originally?"

I shrugged. "That's what I see."

He spun around to face me. "Who would have carved it? Lucifer?"

I didn't answer. Instead, I turned to Charrael. "I'm going to ask you again. Did you know anything about this passageway?"

Charrael puckered his brow. "No, Sir. I did not. And I'm pretty sure none of the taskforce knew about it either."

My head jerked back. "Why do you say that?"

"I saw their faces when Chief Prince Lucifer yelled, 'Follow me,' and disappeared through the backstage opening. They were surprised."

I stroked my chin. "This was all Lucifer then."

"Really?" Gabriel gasped. "How long do you think it took?"

"It's large, wide enough for several angels to fly side by side. I'd say Lucifer's been working on this for quite a while. Which means he's been planning a revolt for at least that long."

Gabriel crossed his arms. "I don't get it, Michael. Why didn't we know?"

"I'm not sure." I looked around to calculate our directional bearing. "Lucifer is all about secrets. Gabriel, do you remember exploring the mountain with Lucifer?"

"Yes, why?"

I inhaled and pursed my lips. Exhaling, I said, "I'm positive this passage will open up just under the plateau. I think it's the indentation Lucifer found when we were with him."

Gabriel's hand slapped his forehead and pushed back his hair. "He said it was nothing special! How could we have been so blind?"

"Seems Lucifer has learned to be a master of deceit. I knew something wasn't quite right, but when I'd start to zero in, he would cover and throw me off. Then I'd think it was just my imagination." I sighed. "But in all my thoughts, I never imagined this."

"No one could," Gabriel said, patting my shoulder.

"Ah," I moaned. "Maybe I just didn't want to see it."

"Hey," Gabriel said, throwing out his hands. "I thought you were jealous. Explain that."

I wagged my head. "It doesn't matter now. You're a good friend, Gabriel. Let's just go and stop Lucifer."

"Agreed." Gabriel detached his helmet from his belt and slid it on. "I'm with you."

"Me too, Sir," Charrael said.

I grabbed my helmet and acknowledged their encouragement. "Okay, then. Stay alert."

Lucifer's corridor was not a straight shot. The curves and twists caused us to use less than full speed, which turned out to be a good thing. When we reached what I presumed should have been the end with an opening onto the mountain, we encountered a wall of boulders. "Of course!" I huffed. "Lucifer blocked our way."

Charrael gasped. "Are we trapped?"

"Calm down, Charrael," Gabriel said. "Michael always has a plan."

Shaking his hands, Charrael paced. "Sorry. Flashbacks."

Gabriel nodded to Charrael and turned to me. "So, Michael, what's the plan?"

I stood before the barrier, examined the rocks, and how they fell. "I'm pretty sure we can blow through these boulders in one swift move, especially if we combine our power." My companions took their places beside me. "Gabriel, Charrael," I said. "Swords unsheathed and strike on my command. Ready? For the LORD God Almighty. Strike!"

———⌄———

Lucifer's lieutenants pounced onto the front stoop of the Armor Room, startling the sentry guards. Wyael took out the sentry on the right as Maysel handled the one to the left. They blew open the doors, and the force of the blast hurled Randiel against the far wall. Picking himself up, Randiel cried, "Stop!" Wyael and Maysel ignored his command.

"Randiel," Wyael yelled, his wings carrying him forward at a swift pace. "You know we outrank you."

"Yeah," Maysel interjected while the Armor Room flooded with Lucifer's followers. "It's useless for you to try to stop us."

"I don't care," Randiel shouted, running toward them. "It's my job to protect the Armor Room."

———⌄———

At a time when every other Armor Room angel had duties elsewhere, Lucifer's army invaded. Alone, Randiel pushed through the lieutenants and struggled to stop the invasion. Wyael whacked him from behind, and he fell flat, face down. Maysel attempted to jump on top of him, yet Randiel rolled to the left. Maysel crashed to the floor, and Randiel scrambled to his feet.

Grabbing the only weapon within reach, a brass rod used to lift armor pieces to their hanging pegs, Randiel stood his ground. Wyael laughed. The long and slender rod with a rounded hook at the end was certainly no match for a sword. "What do you think you're going to do with that?" the Lieutenant said, moving closer.

Randiel pointed the hooked end at Wyael and Maysel and yelled, "You must leave! You cannot be in this Armor Room without Chief Prince Michael's authorization."

"We don't need Michael's authorization," Wyael shouted back as he noticed Command Sergeant Major Ennel sneaking up behind Randiel. "We have Chief Prince Lucifer's authorization," he said, keeping Randiel's focus forward. "And we have his orders to raid this Armor Room."

"Lucifer has no authority here," Randiel bellowed. "This is not his station."

Ennel inched closer. "It doesn't matter," Maysel hollered. "Soon, all Heaven will be Chief Prince Lucifer's station. He will reign as Sovereign. If you cooperate, you could serve him as we do."

"What?" Randiel screamed. "Never!" He lunged forward and jabbed the brass rod into Maysel's chest.

Under the Shekinah Glory Base, a flash exploded. The boulder obstruction barricading the opening crumbled, sprinkling the ground like fine dust. Michael, Gabriel, and Charrael emerged.

"Charrael!" Lucifer screeched under his breath. "I knew it! I should have silenced him once I caught him outside the Armor Room. Ahhhh! And how did Michael convince Gabriel to believe Charrael? When I get my hands on Charrael, I'll squash him like the repulsive peon he is."

While Michael conversed with Gabriel and Charrael, Lucifer listened from his hiding place. He couldn't make out everything, but he was sure he heard Michael say, "Head to the Throne Room."

As the Archangels and Charrael took urgent flight, Lucifer cackled. "Ha, ha! Michael has no clue my angels are ransacking his precious Armor Room. Poor Michael. It's hard to believe he's so naïve. I thought he was smarter than that. And he thinks he's as powerful as I am. Ridiculous!"

Beginning his short jaunt back to the caverns, Lucifer said, "You magnificent archangel. No doubt about it, takeover's a cinch. Heaven and all creation are yours!"

Randiel, Michael's supervisor and loyal under-angel, was not as skilled in fighting as Lucifer's angels—combat not being his primary duty. Randiel had mostly trained in service like the chamber angels, so when he lunged forward with the brass rod striking Maysel, he lost his balance. Ennel quickly pounced, forced him to the floor, and his fist connected with Randiel's face. Although Randiel did get in a few licks, he was outranked and overpowered.

"Enough," Wyael said, halting the beating. Grabbing Randiel by the scruff of the neck, he hoisted him to a standing position. On the way up, Wyael saw a glimmer in Randiel's garments. Was it the key? "Ennel, secure his arms and feet. Maysel, gag him. I'll throw him into Michael's office and bar the door."

Wyael shoved so hard Randiel sprawled onto the office floor and skidded against the far wall. His head cracked, and he lay there comatose. "Perfect," Wyael whispered, patting Randiel's garments. It was the key! He searched Michael's desk for tracing material and a utensil. As Wyael completed the tracing, Randiel stirred. Stuffing his pocket, Wyael exited.

Randiel's dazed mind finally cleared. He maneuvered himself around and pushed to a sit. Somehow, even with his wrists tied behind him and his ankles bound, he managed to stand and hop over to the window. Woozy from the beating, Randiel leaned against the casement and peered through the glass.

Catching sight of the devastation, Randiel slumped into the chair. He had tried his best, fought as valiantly as he knew how, yet he could not stop the invasion. Randiel peeked up over the sill and out into the room. "I've failed to protect the armor," he wailed, "and I've let Chief Prince Michael down." Helpless and hopeless, he watched Lucifer's angels consume all in their path like a ravenous swarm of locusts.

When the last evil soldier departed, Randiel's strength evaporated. His head bobbed once and then a second time. On the third bob, it hit the desk, and his body slid to the floor, unconscious.

CHAPTER 33

GREAT DESPAIR

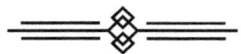

The three of us arrived at Ivory Palace, and Lucifer was nowhere in sight. I stationed Charrael as a lookout at the Throne Room door, and an extra arm to aid the sentries while Gabriel and I rushed to speak with the Almighty. We bowed and knelt in his presence.

"You may rise," the Most High said in a firm yet subdued voice.

I stepped forward. "Sire, Lucifer has amassed legions of followers. He's planned a revolt…and…"

"We thought he and his army were headed here," Gabriel said, finishing my sentence. "Has he shown himself?"

God's Shekinah rumbled and brightened. "No, Lucifer has not been here."

I turned to Gabriel and back to the Almighty. "I don't understand. Where else would he go?"

"Michael, I'm glad to see you and Gabriel have worked things out."

I bowed my head quickly. "Yes, Sire, we have mended our disagreements. But this thing with Lucifer is serious."

Gabriel stepped closer and interjected. "It's very serious, LORD. We tried to intercept him in the caverns, but he and his army escaped through his hand-crafted tunnel."

Shifting my stance, I jumped back into the conversation. "When we emerged from the caverns, Lucifer's troops were streaking toward Ivory Palace City. We were sure they were on their way to attack you. They haven't been here?"

God's Shekinah blazed. "Michael. Gabriel. No, they have not."

I clutched my head and closed my eyes for a moment. "I don't know where they went then. But I do know they will eventually come here. Majesty, we must get you to safety."

Within his glory, a vague resemblance of a hand waved in an arc, and his voice became stern and low. "Archangels, find Lucifer. You are dismissed."

Gabriel's shoulders raised and lowered as his arms shot out. "Sire, how can we when we don't know where he is?"

Stepping closer to the throne and ready to beg, if necessary, I said, "Most High, if Lucifer and his army aren't here, then where are they?"

Gabriel shouted, "Wait! What about the Forge? Do you think Lucifer and his angels went there?"

I spun around to face him. "I don't think so. The Forge has mostly unfinished armor." Suddenly, like a spear impaling a bullseye, a thought pierced my head and shook me to my very core. *An army needs finished and ready armor.* "No!" I yelled. "They're plundering the Armor Room! Gabriel, let's go."

We bowed quickly and rushed out. Reaching the Throne Room doors, I hollered, "Charrael! Come on."

Below the Shekinah Glory Base, Lucifer snaked his way through the now not-so-secret passage and again entered the stage area. Once crammed with angels, the caverns stood deserted.

Lucifer hurdled the crashed podium, descended the stairs, and hustled to the rotunda center. He surveyed the space framed by the colossal dome and announced to the rocks and alcoves, "My army will soon arrive. War strategies need to be in place for a swift attack. Michael and Gabriel may be aware of my plan, and while they could amass an army…ha…they have no armor. We will defeat them with minimal effort."

Lucifer brooded as he roamed. "This wasn't supposed to happen until after I conquered Earth. My army is not prepared." He raised his foot and pounded the rotunda floor, but stomping didn't satisfy. He searched the cavern, found a small boulder, and slung it against the wall. As it smashed into pieces, he screamed, "Ah! Charrael betrayed me! Michael is forcing my hand! And my angels don't know my attack strategy. I need to sketch battle tactics, but how can I when my tools are in my chamber?"

Lucifer clomped around a few more times to calm himself. "If I am going to depose the Most High, there's no room for error. My troops cannot fight blind. One mistake could thwart the whole thing. Exact procedures must be visible when my soldiers return. I'll have to improvise," he said, kicking the scattered pieces of boulder. As they skidded across the surface, marks appeared. "Aha…" he said, as his face brightened. "Maybe I could use the boulder pieces to sketch combat directives. But I'll need a flat surface." Strolling around the rotunda, he examined the walls, the floors, and the stage area. Nothing accommodated. "Come on, Lucifer, think!"

After a short period, his lips curled into a menacing grin. "If I can craft an invisible room in my chamber…and…I am like the Almighty. No!" he shouted. "I am the Almighty! I don't just have the power; I am the power!"

Moving back to the heart of the domed room, Lucifer extended his arms upward in a mirrored arc. He inhaled deeply. His chest rose, and his head lifted. Again, the red hue streamed from his being and enveloped him.

Oblivious to armor-clad angels trickling into the caverns, Lucifer strategized. As thoughts came to mind, drawings appeared on the rotunda floor and then projected up for all to see. His troops would storm Ivory Palace and invade the Throne Room while he slipped in behind the throne to incapacitate each seraph and cherub and, of course, annihilate the Most High.

As the scene displayed midair, more strength and power surged through Lucifer. Unsheathing his saber, he shouted, acted out the demise of the LORD, and those in attendance kneeled. "I will lift my sword and strike down this feeble, pathetic God. I will obliterate him, and my conquest of heaven will be complete. Brilliant! Brilliant, I say! I will not fail. I alone shall be worshiped! And at the sound of my name, every knee in Heaven and on Earth will bow…to me!"

Reminiscent of a shaft of white light, our trio streaked from the Throne Room. Using the shortest route to the Armor Room, we shot into the Tree of Life grove, wove our way through, and arrived just as the last of Lucifer's angels whizzed toward the Mount of Holiness. Maybe I should have followed, but the Armor Room doors were blown out—ripped off their hinges. The sentries sat dazed, with gashes on their heads. "Charrael," I yelled. "Tend to the sentries, then join us inside."

"Yes, Sir." Charrael saluted and rushed to help the wounded.

Gabriel and I dashed into the Grand Hall. It appeared as though a cyclone had whipped through. Papers, articles of clothing, footwear, and other debris were strewn about, yet not one piece of armor remained, not even a single belt. And where was Randiel? Had they captured him? Randiel would never willingly join Lucifer…of that, I was sure. So, what did they do with him?

Instantly, the weight of everything, all I heard and saw, came crashing down. My shoulders bent with heaviness, and my head hung. Great despair, like never before, engulfed me, and another unknown emotion surfaced—one that made me want to beat something. The thought of ripping off Lucifer's head gripped my being. *Ahhh!* Was I losing control? No! I was always in control.

Somehow, I had to quiet myself, yet the thoughts wouldn't leave. They badgered. And I sensed they would consume if I didn't conquer and take them captive. I paced, dodging the rubble, and stomped a few times, but nothing soothed. "LORD God," I said. "What's happening? Help me. Please!"

The gentle, calming voice of God's Holy Spirit flooded my essence. "Michael," he said. "This emotion is anger. You must not give in to it—it's very destructive. Even if the emotion is righteous, like reacting to wrongdoing, it easily becomes anger, and here, it needs to stop. When left unchecked, anger quickly escalates to rage. If that happens, you will lose control. And Michael, anger, and rage are never our will. Things will become clear soon, but for now, rule over your emotions, control your actions, and you will overcome."

"Yes, Majesty," I whispered.

"Michael?" Gabriel said, waving his hands in front of my face. "Are you okay?"

"I will be," I said, marching back to Randiel's cubicle and forcing myself to regain composure. I filled my lungs and exhaled tension. Calmed, I detected what sounded like pounding fists and muffled cries. The noise came from the direction of my office. "Gabriel…my office! I think someone's in there. It might be Randiel." We both ran and found the door bolted from the outside. I couldn't see anyone through the window, so I beat on the door and shouted. "Randiel, are you there?"

"Uh-huh," came his muted voice.

Gabriel unbarred, and I rushed in. Lying on the floor, Randiel had been kicking the door with shackled feet. His face…battered and swelled with slits for eyes, his mouth gagged, and his arms… twisted and bound.

Until this thing with Lucifer, there had not even been an argument. Matters had been tense lately, yet never could I have anticipated this. When I saw Randiel lying there, my heart screamed. *What's happening in Heaven?*

We sat Randiel up, removed the gag, and freed his arms and feet. When he tried to stand, he wobbled and fell into my arms. I eased him onto the floor. He looked up and tears gushed from Randiel's swollen eyes. "Sir, I've failed you. The armor is gone. What are we going to do?"

I sighed. "I don't know yet, Randiel. I'm working on it."

———————⌄———————

Lucifer's last warrior angel arrived in the caverns, and the door slammed behind him. The soldier jolted and peered at the Chief Prince. Their eyes locked. "What took you so long?" Lucifer said, causing a shivering chill to grip the angel.

"I...I had some trouble with the Armor Room sentry guards, Sir. They tried to restrain me, but I got loose and flattened them for the second time."

"Good. Take your place."

He slipped in amongst the troops, and some commented or patted his back in approval, which Wyael noticed caused too much commotion. "Angels!" he shouted. "Give full attention to our illustrious leader." Silence swept over them.

"I am dividing you into field armies," Lucifer said, pacing back and forth before the frontline of the soldiers, "and as such, I need generals. Ten members of my taskforce will now hold the rank of lieutenant general. Wyael and Maysel answer only to me. They are elevated to general, numbers one and two, respectively. Of course, as your sovereign leader, I will hold our army's top rank, General of the Army—Commander-in-Chief."

Dylael and Olivel stared at each other, mouths wide with shock and excitement. They wanted to do a happy dance, but thought it best to contain themselves. Lucifer would not approve. And while this display of joy might be appropriate for privates, it certainly did not befit the rank of Lieutenant General. Still, Dylael leaned in and whispered to Olivel, "I can't wait to get my hands on Charrael now."

Olivel's eyes brightened. "Yes. Won't the brand-new Sergeant be shocked?"

They both snickered. "Taskforce!" Lucifer shouted, causing the privates to jump. "The extra armor you collected from the raid is stacked against the stage. Gather your new armor and dress."

Lucifer's elite soldiers hastened to obey. Dressing in the new armor, they could feel their upgraded height, skills, strength, and attitude transforming them into generals. Finally, they came to attention, held a straight line, and awaited inspection.

The taskforce appeared as perfect as the armor they wore. Lucifer studied each chosen warrior, scrutinizing every detail. When satisfied, he nodded his approval and moved on to the next. Wyael was last. After a quick inspection, Lucifer leaned in and whispered, "Did you find the key?"

"Yes, Sir." Wyael dug the tracing out of his pocket. Lucifer grabbed it and ascended the stage to continue his orders.

"A member of my taskforce will lead each of the first twelve armies," he shouted. "These, in turn, will choose leaders for the few remaining field armies and all corps. Troops, divide now and do it quickly."

As the field armies took shape, companies, battalions, brigades, and divisions formed within them, and the taskforce observed every move. "Taskforce," Lucifer ordered. "Pick your army. Wyael first, Maysel second, and so on."

The taskforce complied, and each stood as the vanguard. "Now," he said, "choose soldiers from your command, the best you can find, to direct the divisions and leftover armies. Do not dally. We must be swift to strike. Michael cannot be allowed to forge more armor and amass his army."

Every soldier followed orders and moved into position while Lucifer continued. "Although Michael grasps what I intend to do, he has no distinct understanding of my plan. This is the way it must stay. By now, he knows we've raided his beloved Armor Room, but believe me," he said, sporting a sinister grin, "he cannot even fathom what's coming." Laughter erupted and echoed through the caverns, yet Lucifer raised his hand and choked it back.

With the field armies divided, one taskforce member after another called theirs to attention before Chief Prince Lucifer. From above, he gazed at the sea of soldiers, and his chest swelled with the pride that filled him. *I am God! I have the best and most powerful army ever! Nothing can stop me.*

Agitated, I paced. From my office door to the far wall, left a few steps, about-face, and more steps to the right. Back and forth until I was so deep in thought and off course, I ran into my desk. Yet, this interruption did not deter me. In fact, the jolt helped. "I'm going to the Forge," I said. "I need to see what type of armor is available and how many soldiers we can outfit. Gabriel, stay with Randiel. Charrael is still helping the sentries."

He looked up at me. "Alright, Michael. Just hurry. Who knows what Lucifer is doing now that he has armor for his warriors. I'm concerned about the Scroll Room."

From my office doorway, I looked down at Gabriel and Randiel. "I know. I'm concerned, too, but I'm most concerned about the Almighty. You saw how vague and indifferent he was when we informed him about Lucifer."

Gabriel nodded. "I remember."

"It's like he didn't believe us, Gabriel." I held up my hands. "Since Lucifer plans to rule Heaven, he will, at some point, rush the Throne Room. I'm not sure the cherubim can handle such an attack. They're strong but not really equipped for battle."

He winced in distress, and for a moment, we connected the way we used to. "Do you think Lucifer's army flew back to the caverns?"

I pushed my hair back. "That's the only place big enough to hold them other than the plains, and I don't think he wants his soldiers out in the open."

"Good point." Gabriel stood and faced me. "We should be able to see them coming from any direction, right?"

Inhaling deeply, I held it for a moment and nodded as I exhaled. "Yes, and Lucifer knows it. Since he didn't immediately attack Ivory Palace, I think we surprised him. If that's the case, he probably wasn't ready to execute his plan. So, I expect him to delay his attack just a bit."

He sighed and bent down again to tend Randiel's wounds. "Good to know, Michael."

I gazed around at the Armor Room disaster and looked back at Gabriel. "Still, without armor for our troops, I don't know how we'll stop Lucifer. If worse comes to worst, and it's just the three of us with armor, you and Charrael go to the Scroll Room. Randiel, you, and the under-angels retreat to the inner chamber. I'll station myself in the Throne Room to perform my duties as guardian. I refuse to let the LORD down. I must protect Him whether he wants me to or not."

Gabriel glanced at Randiel, acknowledged his nod, and then peered up at me. "We understand, Michael, and we're with you."

"Alright, then. If you're good here, I better get going. Stay calm but alert; I'll be quick."

CHAPTER 34

EVIL PREPARED

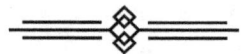

Exiting the Armor Room, I launched and called to Charrael, "Lucifer stole all the armor. I'm heading to the Forge. I'll return soon." His jaw dropped, but still, he rose and saluted.

The Forge was quite a distance, and my matter, urgent. But as I flew, I reflected on the Forge's beauty compared to Heaven's current chaos.

Beyond Ivory Palace City to the south, and directly opposite the Mount of Holiness, stood the Forge. Like the Arena, it, too, was an immense structure much larger than the Armor Room.

Resembling a curved hand cresting a table, its domed top sloped downward, extending into eleven columns with ten arched openings. Each entryway led to the finishing room above the central hearth zone. From there, ramps for transport and worker walkways spiraled down and emptied into the main furnace area. Several lanes then branched off into Heaven's strata, and where they led, I did not know. I hadn't had a reason to explore.

The central hearth was the hub of the Forge. This enormous stone-lined firepit housed the flame used for extracting and purifying metal. Suspended above its glowing embers hung a great bucket from which the molten metal poured. Molds were filled. Sheets were formed, rolled, and cut to desired lengths.

Tools for sculpting the hot metal lined the walls of this fabrication room: hammers, chisels, punches, drifts, and every type of tong imaginable. To the right were the anvil workstations, complete with their own cooling vat to expedite production. Here, Forge angels hand-shaped the rough armor and swords.

Cart racks awaiting the crude product stood off to the left. Once fully loaded, the carts were transported up the ramps to the finishing room. The armor was inspected, sorted, smoothed or sharpened, buffed and polished, and dispatched for a final inspection.

Work at the Forge never ceased except for worship, and before all this, I often wondered why it even existed. Of course, I didn't fully understand its necessity or ultimate function until now.

But with all that has happened, I was learning. Not how I wanted to learn, but…well…. A wave of apprehension washed over me. *What if I fail? What if Lucifer succeeds? What then?*

I shook myself out of it. "No," I whispered. "Can't think like that. I cannot fail. I won't fail! There has to be ready armor at the Forge. There just has to be."

I swooped onto the threshold of one arched opening, and heat blasted my face. As I entered, the sentries nodded their greeting, and the cadence of pounding hammers with sizzles of cooling metal filled my ears. This was a sound I loved.

Here, angels worked tirelessly to fashion suits of armor for every soldier in God's army. Occasionally, I would take off my Chief Prince garments and don the garments of a Forge angel. I'd hammer pieces of hot metal, and once I achieved the correct shape, I'd dip them into the cooling vat. It was, to me, tranquil work, yet through it, I gained such a sense of satisfaction and accomplishment. Exhilaration often filled me.

Still, forging armor was a lengthy process. I saw none finished on the first level. And as I descended the walkway toward the central hearth, I hoped beyond hope to at least find carts of rough armor.

With the division of troops complete, Lucifer continued his orders. "Each combat unit will hit Ivory Palace like a wave, field army after field army as needed. Most commands will remain on the front lawn, and if yours does, I insist every soldier stay alert. Watch for the enemy and prevent Michael or his soldiers from entering the palace. Report their whereabouts and any peculiar activity. Use whatever force is necessary.

"Now, for those field armies who do make it inside, I prefer to take no prisoners. If the palace angels choose to join us, they will live. If they oppose, you can restrain them or end their existence.

"Taskforce, when Ivory Palace Great Room is captured and locked, slip down the long hall. Quietly, and I stress quietly, eliminate the door sentries, break through, and charge the Throne Room. Engage the Most High while I slink in behind the throne. I'll strike the cherubim and seraphim first and then finish the job by crushing the one who thinks he's almighty. Does every angel understand?"

Cold yet exuberant voices shouted, "Yes, Sir." And the caverns rumbled with the echo.

A flurry of activity filled the fabrication room. As I entered, each angel halted, acknowledged their allegiance, and returned to their duties. These hard-working angels were oblivious to the crisis brewing outside, and right now, they didn't need to know.

Angel Supervisor Jaysael strolled toward me. "Chief Prince Michael, how may I help you?"

"I'm here to collect the finished armor."

Jaysael's face scrunched. "Sir? I don't understand. Your angels came in a while ago, and we transferred all the completed armor. My workers are just now crafting a new batch, but nothing is ready. Look there." He pointed to the row of carts. "The racks are empty."

My heart sank. Lucifer's army had every last piece of armor. We had nothing. How could I possibly defend the LORD God and all Heaven against such an enemy? *There are only three of us with weapons and armor against thousands upon thousands!* Could we hope Lucifer wouldn't attack until we fabricated more? We could, but that was unlikely. Lucifer wanted to win. And, if it were the other way around, I would attack before the enemy could suit up.

Jaysael peered at me with concerned eyes, and even though I tried to hide it, I knew he detected my anguish and deep disappointment.

I couldn't tell him what troubled me, nor would I. Lucifer's army was already outfitted in armor. For now, the Forge angels were safe—no need to cause alarm. "Thank you, Jaysael," I said. "Keep working, and as quickly as possible, get us the armor."

"We will, Sir."

I nodded to him and departed the Forge. Arriving back at the Armor Room, I circled above to clear my head and strategize. Below, Charrael helped the sentries. Lucifer's army was nowhere in sight, and that relieved me. Still, even with all my training, battle tactics garbled and drifted around in my thoughts, but none would come together.

Out of options and no clear plan, I descended and flew through the blown-out doors, not stopping until I reached my office. Gabriel had Randiel up, sitting in a chair, and neither angel needed to ask. The expression on my face said it all—Heaven's Forge was as empty as the Armor Room.

In the belly of the Mount of Holiness, Lucifer's soldiers stood in formation. With meticulous lines of gleaming armor, brigades, divisions, and corps stretched out from the center in every direction. Perfectly configured units awaited orders.

Lucifer took great care inspecting each, and when he was satisfied, he said, "Warriors, prepare yourselves. Before we leave this cavern, I will infuse you with a touch of my all-mighty power."

"Attention," Wyael said.

Promptly, hiked shoulders and erect postures of stern-faced soldiers moved to surround Lucifer and await an individual tap. What they received was not what they expected. No personal touch came.

Standing midpoint on the rotunda floor, Lucifer inhaled deeply, and his inner flame emerged. Exhaling, he spun around, and like a laser, his fiery red hue shot out and settled upon each angel warrior. Their once beautiful, serene faces distorted to express viciousness, hatred, and pride, yet the armor remained untouched. "Finally, my army is ready," he said, expelling a sinister laugh.

"I'll take the lead," Lucifer shouted. "Each taskforce member, along with their field army, will follow." He turned to the remaining armies. "Exit in the order you were chosen, and reconvene at the Shekinah Glory Base for final instructions. We'll launch from there. Remember, fight hard and win. After this battle, I will be the sovereign ruler. And, it will be my glory you see emanating from this mountain."

Lucifer moved to the stage area to observe his ominous army once more. "You are my work of art, and you will serve me well. Taskforce, are you ready?

"Yes, Sir," they said.

"Good. Troops, let's fly!"

Lucifer shot out of the rotunda through the backstage passageway, followed by hordes of soldiers. The caverns emptied, and the Mount of Holiness illuminated as this fiery army emerged and whipped up onto the plateau just below the Shekinah Glory Base. "Warriors," Lucifer shouted. "Breach the city and target Ivory Palace. The front lawn will be your assembly point. Taskforce! Remember, once the Great Room is seized, advance quickly on the Throne Room."

"Yes, Sir," they said in unison.

"Fighters!" Lucifer shouted. "Ready. Wings. Launch."

Red bands of soldiers set Heaven's firmament ablaze as evil raced to end holiness.

CHAPTER 35

HOPE REVIVED

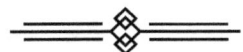

"Chief Prince Michael! Chief Prince Gabriel!" Charrael yelled, running in from the Armor Room's front stoop. "Where are you?"

"In my office," I hollered. "What's wrong?"

Charrael grabbed the doorjamb and swung around into the room. "Wow! I thought the Armor Room would be bare after I saw the blown-out doors and spoke to the sentries, but especially when I heard you say Lucifer stole the armor."

I scrunched my face. "What do you mean, Sergeant?"

Charrael's arms emphasized his words. "Just after you returned from the Forge, Sir, it seems something happened. I was bent over caring for the sentries. When I finished wrapping their wounds, I stood, turned to join you, and then I saw it."

"Saw what?"

"The Armor Room doors, Sir. They were fixed."

I shook my head. "No, Charrael."

Nodding wildly, Charrael's eyes sparkled. "Yes, Chief Prince Michael! The doors are good as new, as though they were never blown out in the first place. And…and, when I rotated to ask the sentries if they saw it too, the sentries were back at their posts, standing guard. No bumps, no bruises, and no sign they had ever been in a struggle. I couldn't believe it. So, I came to find you. And when I entered the Armor Room, it too was like nothing had ever happened."

Gabriel sighed while he held a compress to Randiel's eye and looked up at Charrael. "Sergeant, I think you're hallucinating. Sometimes we don't want to believe what's actually there. You've been through a lot. Still, we all saw it. The Armor Room is empty."

"And Charrael," I said, situating myself in my chair. "I just flew through it. There's nothing left."

Charrael moaned and hung his head. "But, Sirs, that's what I'm trying to tell you. The doors are fixed, and the Armor Room is full."

I stood and slid by Gabriel and Randiel. "Okay, Charrael. Show me."

Gabriel pulled Randiel to his feet. "Wait for us."

Charrael, Randiel, Gabriel, and I stood in the Armor Room's Grand Hall, wide-eyed and dumbfounded. The room was as pristine as before. Every piece of armor was there, and it was just as Charrael said…like nothing had ever happened.

"This can only be the hand of the Almighty," I said, breaking the silence.

Gabriel's fist went to his chest. "So, he must have believed us."

"Yes. He did!" I cried, gazing upward. "LORD, I'm sorry I doubted. It's more than I could have imagined." With that, a flash of wisdom speared my being. "Gabriel, I know what to do now. Randiel, are you up for duty?"

Randiel patted his body. "Actually, Sir, I'm back to normal too, and you know I'll do my best."

"Yes, Randiel, I do. Sound the Call to Arms! And…make sure the angels know this is not a drill."

For the first time in all eternity, Randiel sounded a genuine Call to Arms. While the signal blared through each barrack and throughout Ivory Palace City, he summoned the Armor Room under-angels to help. Every angel warrior who had not followed Lucifer headed for the Armor Room. Randiel and his helpers directed each rank to their assigned section. Gabriel and Charrael stood by my side to assist when needed.

"Charrael," I said. "Station yourself at the door. As the soldiers depart, do a quick inspection. Make sure each warrior is dressed in a full set of armor, and then meet me outside."

"Yes, Chief Prince," he said, doing an about-face and sprinting to the Armor Room doors.

"Gabriel, I need you to supervise and assist Randiel and the under-angels."

"On my way, Michael."

I ascended the platform near my office and announced, "Soldiers! We've been called to duty. This is not a drill." Every fighter came to attention and peered in my direction. "We will forego armor testing. Grab your gear quickly. Once Sergeant Charrael conducts your final inspection at the Armor Room door, then report to your platoon leader. Platoons, group with your company, companies with battalions, battalions to brigades, and so on. Warriors fall out."

"Yes, Sir," the troops answered in unison.

"Generals, make sure your field armies are complete and lined up on Glory Street. I will brief you there." Each General saluted and shouted to affirm. Returning their salutes, I moved to a better position to observe my army's compliance.

With Randiel's help, Gabriel had gathered the Armor Room angels at the back wall near the exit to the Arena. He halted his instruction and yelled, "Michael, what's the plan?"

I held up a finger. "Not sure yet." I pivoted to watch Charrael complete his preliminary inspection of the first soldier. He had followed my orders well, so I turned my attention to designing a scheme to outsmart Lucifer.

Gabriel disbursed the angels to different sections to aid the soldiers and rushed toward the platform. "Michael, remember, whatever plan you come up with has to include protection for the Scroll Room. Lucifer knows how valuable it is. He'll surely target God's written word."

My hand stroked my chin as I looked down. "Right. We must shield it from any attack." Descending the steps, I said, "Listen, General Bradiel's Platoon 10 is the best we have. I'll send them with you to guard the Scroll Room."

He cocked his head. "Are you sure that'll be enough soldiers?"

"Actually, if all goes according to plan, I hope to contain the battle on the Mount of Holiness plains. That way, Lucifer's army won't even come near the Scroll Room."

Gabriel's eyes widened. "That far already in your planning?"

I shrugged. "Yeah. Once we started talking, the strategies just poured in."

"I'm thankful, Michael."

"Me too." I nodded and turned my attention back to the Armor Room interior. "The soldiers are dressing too slowly. I'm going to walk the aisles to hurry them along."

Gabriel pointed to the other end. "I'll start over there, and we'll meet in the middle."

"Great. Thanks."

⎯⎯⎯⎯⎯⎯⎯⌄⎯⎯⎯⎯⎯⎯⎯

As each rank dressed, I strolled the aisles, overhearing many conversations but mainly with the same content. Nearing the sergeant section, one sergeant asked another, "Do you know what this is about?"

The second lowered his breastplate and said, "No. It's probably another drill."

"I'm not so sure," said the first. "This seems different. We've never actually dressed in full battle armor before." He buckled his belt. "And, Chief Prince Michael did say it wasn't a drill. Hey. do you see Chief Prince Lucifer?"

The second sergeant's head jerked. "He's not here?"

"No," the first said, attaching a shin guard. "Well, at least I don't see him. Prince Gabriel is over there. Look around; maybe you'll see him."

"I can't. I'm still dressing."

I knew every angel had questions, and they were missing Lucifer. But I needed them to hurry. And since my presence did not produce the desired effect, I sprinted back to the platform.

Randiel saw my frustration. "Angels!" he yelled. "This is not a drill. Our situation is critical. Immediate action is required, and Chief Prince Michael expects every angel warrior to be dressed and ready within the designated timeframe or sooner."

"I guess we better move," the first sergeant said, heading to the door.

Impressed with Randiel's new wave of confidence, I smiled. "Way to take charge, Randiel."

He nodded. "Thank you, Sir."

Together, we watched the last warrior sprint out following final inspection. Charrael saluted and turned to head for Glory Street. "Wait, Charrael," I said, motioning for him to come.

While Charrael jogged toward me, I looked at Randiel. "Gather the Armor Room angels. Escort them to the inner chamber and bolt the door behind you. Stay there until I return or unless I call you into service. I have no idea how widespread the battle will be, and I want you and the others safe."

"Yes, Chief Prince." Randiel clapped his hands, and every Armor Room worker halted their activity. "Angels, attention. Meet me at the back wall at once."

When Charrael arrived, I pointed to the platform. "I'll need this moved to Glory Street so I can address the soldiers."

"Right away, Sir."

As my warriors grouped into their field armies and Charrael and I lugged the platform outside, a whirring sound came from high above. In the distance, the fiery red streaks of Lucifer's army zoomed closer. We watched through the trees as they reached the gate, invaded the city, and hovered over Ivory Palace like a swirling microburst.

With wide eyes and mouths agape, every angel in my army appeared shaken. None had an inkling of Lucifer's plans or what they were about to face. I knew these soldiers were unprepared, and although it was not what I wanted, we had no other choice.

───────⌄───────

Assembled on Glory Street, my angels waited for me to convey explanations and orders. I ascended the platform and announced, "Chief Prince Lucifer has rebelled against the Most High God." Gasps escaped angel lips. My warriors needed a moment to process, but we had to rush. "What you are witnessing is the army Lucifer has amassed. They are preparing to attack Ivory Palace. Lucifer desires to depose the Sovereign LORD, and it is our duty to stop him. We must protect the Almighty at all costs."

I saw horror in their faces and the toll this news took on them. "Soldiers," I said, trying to ease their alarm. "Trees of Life shroud Glory Street. Even though we could see this enemy arrive, they could not see us. Be calm, and do not fear. We alone hold the element of surprise. Lucifer is not expecting opposition. His army emptied the Armor Room earlier, but the Most High had other plans."

"Chief Prince Michael," General Bradiel called from below. "How may I serve?"

Bradiel was a great asset, and there was no under-angel I trusted more. "General," I said, climbing down from the platform. "When your army is assembled, I'd like you to fight alongside me."

Bradiel saluted. "It'll be an honor, Sir. My field army is mustered and prepared for combat. We're ready to fight and defend the LORD on your order."

"Thank you, General." As he turned to leave the platform area, I said, "Hold up. I do have one addition to your army."

"Sir?"

Charrael stood off to my left, and I motioned for him to come. "General Bradiel, this is Sergeant First Class Charrael. I want him to join you, but keep him close. Charrael defected from Lucifer's taskforce, and his insight is valuable. Lucifer has already threatened him."

Bradiel straightened his stance. "Understood, Sir."

"You, Charrael, and your soldiers will follow me," I said, holding up my hand to halt their movement. "Not until I've dispatched each field army to their specific region."

"Message received, Chief Prince. But how will we communicate with the field armies without Chief Prince Lucifer intercepting our directives?"

I pursed my lips and inhaled. "Fair question, General. The only solution is to develop a communications frequency Lucifer cannot detect."

His head tilted, and his eyes appeared concerned. "Is that doable?"

"I'm working on it. I should have the communication completed when we need it."

Bradiel nodded. "Good to know, Sir," he said as the sound of Lucifer's army overtook our conversation. We both gazed skyward.

The churning, red fusion hovering over Ivory Palace began its descent.

CHAPTER 36

THE INVASION

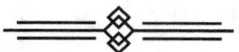

Resembling a torrential downpour, Lucifer's soldiers landed and fell into attack formation. While the Chief Prince charted his entry point, Wyael and Maysel organized a special operations team comprised of one angel from each taskforce member's field army. Wyael then pulled the best brigade from his army, and Maysel chose one from his.

"Soldiers," Wyael shouted. "We will begin with two brigades, this special ops unit, and each taskforce member. All others are to remain here on the grounds of Ivory Palace, ready to advance on my command."

"Affirmative, Sir," the leaders responded.

"Front line," Wyael shouted. "Let's move."

Beneath the trees of Glory Street, my angels stood as a vast sea of gold. Their armor glimmered in the light of God's holiness as their numbers spread south past the Scroll Room and beyond. Just observing, no one would guess we were preparing for the most crucial battle of our existence. But how we would fare was the question uppermost in my mind, and I guessed, in the mind of each soldier.

With eyes fixated on me, I walked to the edge of the platform, and the field armies held firm. "Soldiers," I said. "Since Lucifer's army has landed, we must move quickly but quietly. Stay out of sight as you march. The trees here provide good cover, and the Ivory Palace lawn is far enough away that Lucifer will not see us or pick up on our conversations. However, once you reach the gate, the cover is sparse. Take care in exiting."

They nodded to express understanding, but the many puckered brows revealed anxiety. "Host of Heaven," I said. "We are the Almighty's only line of defense. Do not take that lightly. March through the city gate and into the perimeter trees. Fill the west border first and then the east. The city's wall should conceal you as you assemble. But bear in mind, no angel can be spotted by Lucifer's warriors. If any are seen, the enemy will scatter, and our plan to protect the Most High and Heaven will fail. We cannot fail. Follow my orders, and victory is ours."

"Yes, Chief Prince," the soldiers shouted.

Back down on Glory Street walkway, I had planned to receive each general's account of their field army's readiness, and as they reported, I would assign battle regions. "General Justel," I said. "I'm placing you as prime for the west. Lead your army to the plains and occupy the western boundary of Heaven. Stay in the trees and undercover, yet, prepared for battle at all times."

Justel saluted. "Yes, Chief Prince. But, Sir, won't Lucifer's angels be able to see us in the perimeter trees?"

"You would think so, but no. Just after creation, I had an opportunity to examine Heaven's border. I believe the LORD allowed me to see something I never saw before. The perimeter trees were dense, yet spacious enough to hide many field armies."

"I've not noticed that, Chief Prince, but I'll take your word for it." Turning to his angels, Justel shouted, "Field Army Two, ready yourselves to march!"

Pivoting, I slid to the next army. "General Paynael, your army will follow Justel's, and orders are the same. In fact," I said, realizing I needed to expedite this process. Ascending the platform so all could hear, I said, "Orders for all field armies are the same. Some will occupy the west perimeter, following General Justel, and some will fill the east, led by General Nichoel."

My commands seemed to cause a disturbance, and discussions arose among the soldiers. "Listen up!" I yelled. "We must hurry. The following field armies will control the east border: Generals Nichoel, Lewel, Bowmanel, Steelel, Byrdael, Jodiael, Rusiel, Landonel, Thomiel, and Patrikael. General Nichoel is prime for the east. Are we clear?"

"Yes, Chief Prince."

"These armies will hold the west perimeter. Generals Justel, Paynael, Shawniel, Reedael, Coliel, Logael, Scottel, Alaniel, Kellel, and Edvardiel. Justel is prime for the west."

"Yes, Sir," came their unified response.

"Remember, each army will remain secluded until I give the signal."

"Understood, Chief Prince," both lead Generals said.

"Lieutenant Generals Brownel, Victoriel, Brookael, and Waleriel will direct the last of the field armies to fill in the perimeters as needed. Once the east-west borders are sufficiently covered, the balance will return here to the Armor Room and wait undercover. I plan to lure Lucifer and his army out onto the plains before he has a chance to break through to Ivory Palace.

"Armies remaining inside the city, pay close attention. When you see Lucifer's soldiers vacate the city, advance to the gate, and hold the southern border. Stay alert and out of sight until I give the order. On my command, close in behind Lucifer."

"Yes, Sir," the leaders said, responding as one.

Wyael's chosen brigade led the siege on Ivory Palace, followed by taskforce members and special ops. Maysel's brigade, under the leadership of Colonel Fraciel, trailed.

Standing before the palace door, all angels felt puny. Wyael considered demolishing it, but stopped. The noise would not only alert palace guards and quell a surprise attack but also signal the Most High. Maysel jogged to his side. "Do you want me to call for the battering ram?"

He shook his head. "Think about it. The palace angels aren't expecting an assault. I say we just ring the gong and see what happens?"

"Sounds good to me. Shall I?"

Wyael nodded. "Yes. Do it."

Reaching up, Maysel pulled the golden cord, and the gong sounded. When the angel servant opened, Wyael flicked the tip of his sword to the servant's throat. The angel squealed, and Wyael pushed a little harder. The slight piercing forced him backward, and the brigades invaded the palace. One after the other, soldiers poured through the door.

"Stop," cried another angel, but it was too late. Lucifer's army, like an insect infestation, overran the Ivory Palace Great Room.

"General Bradiel," I said. "If all goes according to plan, you, your army, and I will do the luring. Once Lucifer's warriors see us depart the city, you must be prepared to hold the northern border near the mountain."

Bradiel nodded his understanding. "Very good, Chief Prince."

I turned back to the field armies and yelled, "Soldiers! One last command. My location will be the Shekinah Glory Base. From there, I will direct operations with a new communications frequency undetectable to Lucifer. When his army advances far enough into the center of the plains, I will order the ambush. As I call out, be swift to emerge from all perimeters and surround them. Cut off his soldiers completely. Leave no gaps, and do not allow them to escape. This trap will force Lucifer to concede.

"Be brave, my gallant soldiers. We outnumber Lucifer's warriors two to one. I expect a peaceful surrender. However, should he decide to fight, I will handle Lucifer myself. By no means are you to engage him. He is much too powerful for anyone but me. Understood?"

"Yes, Sir," came the corps' response.

I held my arms in the air, "Excellent. Prepare for the trek."

Gabriel rushed to the platform. "Michael. The Scroll Room? Platoon 10?"

Raising my finger, I said, "Right. Angels, listen up. Chief Prince Gabriel needs General Bradiel's Platoon 10 to accompany him to the Scroll Room. We must protect it from any enemy who would seek to ravage the Word of God."

Platoon 10's Second Lieutenant Meecael stepped forward with his small contingent of soldiers and saluted. I returned his salute and observed until Gabriel led them toward the Scroll Room. Turning to the troops, I yelled, "Fall in and advance."

Wyael, Maysel, and the other taskforce members gathered the palace angels by sword point and drove them into the Dining Hall.

"You have two choices," Maysel announced. "Join us or perish."

"Never," shouted Senior Angel Gordel.

"Oh yeah?" Maysel said, positioning himself to pierce Gordel through.

"Maysel," Wyael whispered. "Just lock the door. We'll deal with these angels later. Right now, we need to charge the Throne Room. Chief Prince Lucifer is waiting."

"I thought we weren't taking prisoners."

Wyael scowled. "Just do it, and don't question me."

"Fine. Willel. Juael," Maysel shouted. "Lock up the Dining Hall."

"Yes, General," they said, racing to accomplish their orders. As the lock clicked, they signaled Maysel.

He nodded to them and turned to Wyael. "Dining Hall is bolted, and the outer rooms are secure."

Wyael tipped his head to the side and snorted. "Good. This was easier than I thought. Seems we won't be needing additional soldiers after all."

Maysel delivered a thumbs-up.

"Lieutenant General Stewel," Wyael called.

Stewel hastened from his spot and saluted. "Yes, General?"

Wyael waved it down. "Inform the front lawn field armies they are to stay put, but alert and battle-ready. Keep the palace door open so if I call for more troops, they can join the fight quickly."

"Understood, General." Stewel gave a crisp nod and pivoted to carry out orders.

"Wait!" Wyael held up his hand. "One more thing. Remind the soldiers to be on the lookout for Chief Prince Michael. We need to know his whereabouts and what he's up to."

"Yes, Sir."

Spinning around, Wyael shouted, "Maysel, muster the teams. I'm changing the marching order. Your brigade will remain here."

Maysel clapped, and the room quieted. "Taskforce. Special Ops, assemble. General Wyael has new directives for his brigade and us. Colonel Fraciel, hold the Great Room."

Fraciel saluted. "Yes, General."

"Warriors!" Wyael's stern voice caused the soldiers to stiffen. "I want the taskforce first, special ops unit next, and my brigade will follow. Advance to the Throne Room silently. A surprise attack is our goal."

I motioned for General Bradiel and his field army. "Let's go. Our destination is Ivory Palace."

He hiked his shoulders and saluted. "Yes, Sir." Turning to the soldiers, he shouted his command, "Angels, fall in behind Chief Prince Michael."

Approaching Ivory Palace, yet keeping our distance and cover, we observed Lucifer's soldiers congregating close to the palace door and crammed in on the north and east lawns. "Halt," I whispered and pointed. "The main entrance is blocked. Lucifer is there, near the door, but I don't see his taskforce. They must have penetrated the palace already."

Bradiel's eyes widened. "Now what, Sir?"

I inhaled, and my cheeks puffed as I blew it out. "Chances are, Wyael won't charge the Throne Room without Lucifer. As long as Lucifer remains on the front lawn, I have an opportunity to get inside and prevent advancement. If I can keep the taskforce from securing the Great Room, they won't be able to attack the Most High. Lucifer knows the only other place battle-worthy is the Mount of Holiness plains. And, that's exactly where we want him."

"Right, Sir," Bradiel said, nodding. "But how will you get in? Won't you need backup?"

I shook my head. "Not yet. The battle with Lucifer cannot happen here…too many places to hide and too many obstacles. Whatever we do now must be low-key. I'll sneak in, collect the sentry guards, and force the taskforce out. Once they vacate the premises, I'll return, and together we will lure Lucifer and his army to the plains. For now, we'll march through the trees and flank the southwest side of Ivory Palace. There is another entry."

Bradiel jerked and stared at me. "Another?"

I nodded. "It's rarely used. Lucifer must have forgotten, or else he would've had it covered too."

Continuing our trek, Bradiel said, "What kind of entrance are we searching for, Sir?"

"It's small and masked, hard to see, but it's on this side of the palace, so our army can remain hidden. Hurry, keep moving until I can spot it."

Bradiel gave a quick nod. "We're following you, Chief Prince."

Stepping up our pace, we hiked up Glory Street until I found the entrance. "General, there's the door," I said, pointing. "It appears unguarded."

He shrugged. "I'm not seeing it, Sir."

I held up my hand. "Watch where I enter and you'll see the door."

Just past the mouth of the long hall, Wyael halted Lucifer's troops and motioned for Maysel to join him at the front. "Soldiers," he said in hushed tones. "The sentries must not see our army until General

Maysel and I are upon them. Remain here while we sneak up and take them out. Once the sentries are down, advance on my order, and we'll charge the Throne Room."

Elegant alcoves and benches, perfect for masking a top-secret operation, sprinkled the long hall to the Throne Room. Wyael and Maysel moved in flawless precision, using the cover to time their assault. Concealed in the final recess, Wyael nodded to Maysel. With swords raised, they rushed the door. A diagonal slash across the sentries' chests and the angels dissolved. "Whoa, that was a surprise," Wyael said in hushed tones.

"Yeah," Maysel whispered. "Are they really gone?"

"Better confirm," Wyael said, pointing to Olivel and Dylael to come forward.

The former privates ran to help Maysel certify disintegration, and as they did, Wyael gestured to the rest of Lucifer's elite soldiers. The taskforce and special ops approached, along with Wyael's brigade. "Huntiel, Carsiel," Wyael mouthed. "Get the door."

CHAPTER 37

SURPRISES

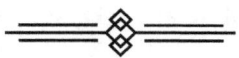

While countless numbers of Heaven's warriors marched toward the perimeters of the Mount of Holiness plains, I slipped into the palace. This obscured entry opened into the southwest vestibule, a small but regal room with one door leading to the interior. I rotated the knob, tugged gently, and eased my head through the opening. None of Lucifer's soldiers were in sight, so I hastened down the long hall from the direction opposite the main entrance.

Nooks, settees, and ornate features provided cover while I snuck closer to the Throne Room to alert the sentries. Passing the throne's rear door, ready to round the bend, I heard voices and skidded to a stop. Their words were muffled. *Was it Lucifer's army or palace angels?* One more move should get me to a place where I could see. I tiptoed quickly to the alcove at the bend so I could observe in either direction. As I hurried in, I bumped the bench situated at its mouth. It screeched, but hoping no one heard, I crept into the opening and peeked out.

Wyael, Maysel, and the taskforce, minus Lucifer, stood outside the Throne Room. "They're here already?" I whispered. *Has Lucifer entered the palace, or is he still on the front lawn?* The Throne Room doors remained shut. *At least, that's something. But wait! The sentries... where are they?*

Wyael's head snapped in my direction. "What was that?"

Oh no! I ducked back in. *Was it the screech?*

"What was what?" I heard Maysel say. Flattening my chest against the wall to the right, I cocked my head and peeked out with my left eye.

"A sound or something up the hall. That way," Wyael said, pointing toward me.

That's not good!

"I didn't hear anything." Maysel turned to the others. "Did any of you?" Their heads wagged no.

Wyael scowled. "I'm sure I heard something, and I want it checked out. Olivel. Dylael."

"Yes, General," they said, rushing forward.

"Run up the hall and see what or who caused that noise."

No! They can't find me. I pushed back from the wall and scanned the alcove. On one of the shelves sat an ornate golden vessel. *Perfect!* I grabbed it, rolled it out into the hall as far from my hiding place as possible, and dove down behind the bench just as Olivel looked my way.

"Hey, Dylael, I do see something."

Was it me?

"Yeah?" said Dylael. "What?"

Olivel cocked his head. "Not sure, but I'll go. You run back and inform Wyael I'll be bringing in the culprit momentarily."

"Okay. Hurry. You know how he is."

Nodding, Olivel said, "Yep, but he'll be happy to wait for this."

How could I have been so clumsy?

Through the slats on the bench, I watched as Olivel neared my hideaway. His eyes scanned left to right and back again, yet he didn't seem to notice me. *Strange. I wasn't hidden that well.* Olivel saw only the golden vessel. I hoped he would pick it up and sprint down the hall to Wyael. But no, he just stood there examining the vessel and the place where it lay.

With his back toward me, Olivel gazed up and down the long hall and even stepped closer to peek around the bend. Rotating slowly, he spied my alcove. I held my breath. And as he advanced, I prepared.

"Olivel," Maysel called. "Did you find anything?"

Olivel halted and jerked his head toward Maysel. "Yes…no… never mind," he said. "I'm coming."

When Olivel rejoined his pack, he held out the vessel, and I eased myself from behind the bench to the recesses of the alcove. *Whew!* I relaxed, then stiffened. *Where are the sentries?*

With the guards gone and Wyael this close, nothing would stop them from storming the Throne Room but me. *Can't lure Lucifer now.* Why was I so convinced the battle would take place on the plains? And why didn't I at least have Bradiel's army escort me into the palace?

Gabriel and Platoon 10 reached the Scroll Room. Once the perimeter was secured, Gabriel said, "Soldiers, come inside. I want you to view the room's layout and understand the value of what you are protecting. Lieutenant Meecael, I'll lead. You bring up the rear."

"Yes, Chief Prince." Meecael saluted.

Narrow and unassuming with its rounded apex, small window, and plain doorknob, the Scroll Room door veiled an immaculate white room. Single-file, Platoon 10 entered. The quiet of holiness hung heavy in the air and filled their beings. Meecael's breath caught under its weight.

It was an immense room, much larger than it appeared from the outside. A simple desk and chair occupied the very center, and like the spokes of a wheel, rows upon rows of golden shelves stretched from this hub to the outer walls.

Miles of white papyrus-like material wound around solid gold rods lined each shelf. Two rods containing one length of material, rolled in from opposite directions, met in the middle to create one scroll. A finely braided, golden cord bound the two spindles together. "These," Gabriel said, "hold the written and eternal Word of God. He speaks. I write. And his word is settled here in Heaven. Once spoken, it never changes because God does not change. He is perfect, and his words are holy."

Every Platoon 10 soldier sighed in awe. "Sometimes," Gabriel continued, "on special occasions, I have the privilege to declare God's word, like I did when we observed creation. I, alone, am responsible for this room and its contents. And for this moment, you have been enlisted to help."

As he walked to his desk, Gabriel said, "I have one more item to show you. Please follow me." He led them around the desk, down the aisle opposite the entrance, and had them stop before a solid gold door adorned with rich moldings.

Gabriel took the key tethered to his belt and unlocked it. He pushed the door open, and a small but spotless room came into view. It contained one article—a golden rectangular-shaped box with two cherubim figures atop its lid. From opposite ends, each cherub had two of its wings extended toward and touching the outspread wings of the other.

The angels crowded the doorway to observe the beautiful box, but soon parted for Gabriel to enter. When he passed, they squeezed back in through the door.

Gabriel approached the treasure, removed the lid, and carefully lifted its contents: a scroll with seven seals. "This," he said, "is the LORD'S last completed work, and it is the most precious item the Scroll Room contains."

Outside of God's Shekinah, Platoon 10 had never seen any item so exquisite. Their glazed-over stares and gaping lips said it all. The sealed scroll, the golden ark, and the beauty of the Scroll Room overwhelmed, and each angel bowed their head, captivated by God's holiness flooding every inch.

Beneath this sacred load, Platoon 10 understood their privilege. No other under-angels had ever seen these sights. They were the first, and if Lucifer succeeded, maybe, the only.

Gabriel motioned for the angels to return to the center of the Scroll Room. While they did, he re-locked the door. "Soldiers," he said, arriving at his desk. "I can't say whether this room will come under attack or not. What I can say, though, is I, well, we, must be prepared for battle. I'm counting on you. Stand ready to protect and defend the Word of God against any and all odds. Do you understand?"

"Yes, Sir," they responded.

"Good. Station yourselves around the building's perimeter. I will guard the door."

Behind Ivory Palace's southwest corner, across the Glory Street walkway, and hidden by the towering Trees of Life, Charrael gasped. Scooting out from among the soldiers, he approached General Bradiel, saluted, and said, "Sir, I just saw Lucifer enter the same door as Chief Prince Michael."

Bradiel's head snapped toward Charrael. "You did?"

"Yes, Sir." Charrael pointed. "He emerged from the greenery near the door and quickly entered."

"Do you think he saw Michael enter?"

Charrael shrugged. "I don't know, Sir."

"Well, that won't do." Bradiel's brows narrowed. "Major General Hectael!"

Hectael dashed to the front. "Yes, General."

"Lucifer has entered the palace. Sergeant Charrael and I are going in to assist Chief Prince Michael. If Lucifer encounters Michael, the war will commence. If we don't return in a short period, alert the Field Army Generals that the battle has begun at Ivory Palace instead of the plains. As soon as they're notified, lead this field army into the palace through the hidden door. Michael will need all of us."

Major General Hectael hiked his shoulders. "You can count on me, Sir."

———————⌄———————

With ambush foiled and the battle site changed, I needed to alert my whole army, so we could advance on the palace before Lucifer entered. As I hastened to vacate my shelter and collect my soldiers, I glimpsed Lucifer strolling up the long hall from the same direction I had entered. I hopped back in. *No! He remembered the southwest door. I'm stuck.*

Still a ways back, Lucifer eyed the throne's rear entrance and moved left. Would he strike the Almighty from behind while his army attacked from the front? It appeared that way. I must intercept. *But I'm only one angel.* How can I handle both Lucifer in the rear and his army from the front? *I need my army!*

The communiqué frequency wasn't quite ready, but maybe it would work for short distances. I tiptoed to the back of the alcove and whispered, "General Bradiel. Can you hear me? General, come in. Bradiel? Anyone?" Nothing. Did I dare abandon my position to fetch them? The cherubim might be able to fend off Lucifer and his army long enough for me to call mine into action. But could I take that chance?

Regardless, I didn't want to fight in the Throne Room. The area was too small. My ability to protect the Almighty would be hindered, and this would place him smack-dab in the center of the battle. I can't have that. Besides, the enemy could scatter, hide, or escape, and then where would we be?

The plains provided a much better opportunity for ambush and for containing Lucifer's entire army in one fell swoop. Yes, they could try to fly away, but my angels would catch and confine them, and clip their wings if necessary.

On the other hand, with Lucifer here, I had no choice. Could I stop him before he reached the throne? Would his army fight the Almighty without their leader? I didn't know, but I had to protect the Most High. If Lucifer entered, I would follow, army or no army. And if he made a move against the LORD God, I'd strike.

I tiptoed to the mouth of my alcove and peeked toward the taskforce. As I watched, they pulled open the heavy doors, and an onslaught of red-hued soldiers, swords in hand, stormed the Throne Room. In the same moment, I heard the shrill scrape of Lucifer unsheathing his saber. He pulled open the throne's rear door and slipped inside. "Oh no you don't, Lucifer."

I leaped from my hiding place, bolted to the door, yanked, and jumped in. The force of my tug sucked the draping tapestries that filled the area beside and behind the throne. Their movement entangled me and obstructed my view.

As I fought to get loose, I did my best to search for Lucifer. I couldn't see him, but I could hear his steps. I threw off the last snag and slid from one tapestry to the next. Finally, I spotted him. He stood in a small open section near the throne area, swinging his saber. *What's happening with Lucifer's army?* Would they engage the Almighty while Lucifer crushes the two rear cherubim and slices the seraphim?

I moved closer, hoping the cherubim could defend themselves while I protected the seraphim and the Most High. I started to raise my sword, but my hand was empty. In my haste to stop Lucifer, I had neglected to ready my weapon. I reached behind my head and grabbed my sword's grip, intending to unsheathe, but stopped. The noise could alert Lucifer and his army. Did I have a choice? No. I slipped back into the tapestries, hoping they would muffle any sound. Holding my scabbard steady, I extracted the blade and heard Lucifer shift. I froze.

When he moved again, I carefully parted the tapestries, but even more drapes blocked my view. Lucifer sounded dangerously close to God's throne. I advanced, staying hidden from his sight, yet ready to emerge and strike. Still, if I was going to intercept his attack, I must see him.

"Ahhh!" Lucifer screeched.

I stiffened and clenched my weapon. *Was he attacking?* I couldn't tell, but I didn't hear clashing swords. In fact, I didn't hear anything, not even the seraphim or cherubim. *Why?* I needed to see. I raised my saber, parted the last few tapestries, and silently sprang through the opening, ready to fight.

Empty? *What?* The Most Holy Place, where God's throne rested, lay deserted. The Almighty, his throne, the cherubim, and the seraphim were gone. Lucifer stood dead center. With his back toward me, he stared out into the Throne Room. His soldiers lined the far wall and eyed the floor. Not one noticed me. I hopped back into the maze of tapestries, thankful for the reprieve but puzzled too.

"Where is he?" Lucifer screamed.

⸻

I asked the same question as the shrill grate of metal confirmed Lucifer had sheathed his sword. The answer didn't matter. If Lucifer didn't know where God was, the Most High would remain safe. And here was my cue to exit.

With the Almighty gone, I knew Lucifer wouldn't linger. Sprinting out the rear access and down the Long Hall, my mind raced, and I nearly crashed into General Bradiel and Charrael.

They both held up their hands to halt a collision. I skidded to a stop.

"Chief Prince Michael, Sir," Charrael whispered. "I saw Lucifer enter the side door. General Bradiel thought you might need help."

I quickly resheathed and motioned for them to follow. "Come on, we need to keep moving. I would have needed assistance if the LORD had been in the Throne Room, but thankfully, he wasn't. And this is our chance to lure Lucifer. We'll make sure his soldiers see us as we fly to the Mount of Holiness. Let's go."

We raced down the hall, tore out the side door, across the street, and into the trees where my army awaited. "Troops!" I yelled. "Ready. Wings. Launch." We lifted off in full sight of Lucifer's warriors but decelerated as we flew over them. I recognized Sergeant Major Gragael, and my heart sank. Gragael, I thought, was one of my valiant soldiers, wholly dedicated to the Almighty. How could he have been swayed? All we could do now was set the trap and hope it worked.

CHAPTER 38

THE TRAP

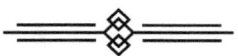

Lucifer ripped off his helmet and flung it at Wyael. "God must have gone to Earth to meet with those worthless humans again," he said, pausing to rub his head.

Every taskforce member knew from experience not to respond or interrupt the Chief Prince when he was in this frame of mind. Back and forth, Lucifer paced, covering the full length of the Throne Room, inhaling deep and exhaling hard. On his third pass, he slowed and touched each piece of furniture. His hand brushed the gleaming table of showbread to the right of the throne area. Continuing around, he gazed at the golden altar of incense and lingered for a moment, taking in the aroma. To the far left stood the solid gold lampstand. Lucifer glided seamlessly to it, and as he caressed its ornate spindles, the flickering light reflected in his armor.

Rolling left again, Lucifer traveled from the Holy Place toward the outer court furniture and his taskforce. While encircling the golden laver, he squinted and scowled as though deep in thought. Moving forward, he wandered past his soldiers and headed for the brazen altar. Halfway around, Lucifer raised both fists. "Yes!" he shouted. "The Almighty always returns to Heaven and Ivory Palace City by way of the plains."

Lucifer charged toward his unique army. "We cannot allow the Most High to reenter this city," he said. "Before he reaches the gate, we'll attack. We must be prompt in our assault. That way, the Almighty cannot summon assistance. And if he's been on Earth this whole time, he has no idea the rest of his angels are helpless. Ha! They have no armor! God only has the cherubim and seraphim, and they're no match for me or my army. Soldiers, to the plains. Follow me."

The taskforce and armor-clad devotees streamed down the long hall behind Lucifer and out into the Ivory Palace Great Room. "Chief Prince Lucifer, Sir," Wyael said as they ran. "Do you think Chief Prince Michael is waiting for us somewhere outside?"

"No," Lucifer spat. "Why would he? Michael has no armor or weapons for an army. He has himself, Gabriel, and that sniveling, Charrael. They were the only angels with armor before I ordered the Armor Room raid. It's three against all of us. Michael isn't stupid. He's probably hiding in his office, sulking because all is lost. Don't worry about him. He's powerless to stop me."

"Good to know, Sir."

Arriving at our destination before Lucifer's army reached the city gate, I divided Bradiel's field army. Half I placed on the west perimeter under his leadership, and half I sent to the east with Major General

Hectael. I locked eyes with Charrael. "Serve General Bradiel as you would me. I'll see you in the Armor Room when the war is won."

"Very well, Sir," he said, saluting.

I returned his salute and watched them march to their designated spots. With the division complete, this army of the LORD stood rightly positioned to execute the ambush. Satisfied, I soared to my point of observation, the plateau of the Mount of Holiness.

While Lucifer was nowhere in sight, I walked from one edge of the Shekinah Glory Base to the other and chose the boulders I'd use for cover. The plains and perimeters appeared deserted, yet forces of my soldiers, arrayed in perfect armor, hid amongst the trees bordering these spacious plains. When Lucifer arrived, he would see nothing out of the ordinary, just as intended. And now, one way or another, his rebellion had come to an end.

Exiting Ivory Palace, each taskforce member and elite soldier hastened to rejoin their field army. As Lucifer took his place and prepared for lift-off, Sergeant Major Gragael approached. "Chief Prince Lucifer, Sir."

"What is it, Gragael?"

He hiked his shoulders. "Sir, we saw Chief Prince Michael and a complete field army in full battle gear soar over us toward the Mount of Holiness."

Lucifer jerked. "What?" His eyes narrowed. "That can't be. They have no armor."

Gragael swallowed the lump in his throat. "I beg your pardon, Sir, they do."

Lucifer groaned and shook his head. "There must have been finished armor at the Forge. I knew I should have raided it too." His fist tapped his lips. "It's fine. We still outnumber them—twelve field armies to one. Gragael, you're dismissed."

"Yes, Sir." He saluted and hurried back to his position.

"Wyael," Lucifer said. "Did you hear Gragael?"

"I did, Chief Prince."

Lucifer edged closer. "This information changes things. I want to wipe out Michael and his puny army before the Most High returns from Earth. That way, we'll crush the Almighty with little opposition. Afterward, we'll strike the Scroll Room, destroy God's Word, and replace it with mine."

Wyael nodded. "Understood, Sir. Shall we fly directly to the Mount of Holiness?"

"No," Lucifer said. His eyebrows furrowed and released. "Our armies must stay near the city to intercept the LORD just in case he returns before we can rid ourselves of Michael."

"But, Chief Prince, how can we defeat Michael if we stick to the plains?"

Lucifer exhaled a sigh. "Wyael. Gragael said Michael was on the mountain, right? The Shekinah Glory Base might hide a few angels, but it cannot hide a field army. We should be able to see them as we fly and land on the plains. Once positioned to attack the Almighty, I'll take your field army and Maysel's and obliterate Michael's. It's that simple."

341

Wyael shrugged and pursed his lips. "What if the Chief Prince attacks while we're landing or setting up, Sir?"

Lucifer held up his hand. "He won't attack when he knows he's outnumbered. He'll wait for us to make the first move. Hmm...." He rubbed his chin. "Maybe it's not necessary to take Michael out before. Ahh...I'll assess the situation when we get there and decide then."

"Right," Wyael said. "Will you lead, or shall I?"

"I will. Let's take the River of Life all the way to the gate. It's the shortest route—no obstacles or interference."

"Affirmative, Sir." Wyael saluted and pivoted. "Troops. Follow Chief Prince Lucifer to the plains. Angels. Ready. Wings. Launch."

The River of Life glowed crimson as Lucifer and his army jetted above the water toward the city gate. The Trees of Life on either side of the river swooshed and rocked in their wake. While he cruised, Lucifer reveled. "Here we go." He whispered to himself, "Michael's annihilation, the Almighty's demise...and...my victory!"

Standing front and center on the Shekinah Glory Base, I beheld the entire plain. Reviewing our trap, I moved to a boulder near the west edge, and peering east, I observed the trees, God's creation, the universe, and Earth. Continuing south, I noted Ivory Palace, Heaven's Forge in the distance, and the city wall and gate. Spanning around to the west perimeter trees and back to my boulder, countless thoughts filled my head. *Where is the Almighty? Why is this happening? What will occur when the battle commences?*

If I had questions, my soldiers did as well. But I shook it off—a watchman keeps his lookout. I must stay alert and not allow uncertainties to divert my focus. Still, one conversation from the west perimeter did capture my attention. I looked on and listened in as Private Andrel spoke his concerns to Specialist Joeal.

"I know we've sparred in training," Andrel said. "But then we had a different type of sword, and it was more play-acting than real. I never imagined we'd be fighting some of our own. Did you?"

Engrossed in his question, I found myself answering. *No, this was completely beyond anything I ever envisioned.*

Specialist Joeal answered the same, but added, "I have questions I'd like to ask my superiors, yet in reality, I'd love the chance to ask Chief Prince Michael himself."

Private Daviel chimed in. "Hey, I have questions too. What will happen when we strike with our sword, and it connects with another angel? Do you think the angel will feel it?"

Joeal shook his head. "I'm not sure. But if they do, how does a sword strike feel? And what does it accomplish?"

Andrel nodded. "So far, we've only struck shields and swords. Wait! We should ask Staff Sergeant Dannel. He might know."

"Good idea," Daviel said, "but Joeal, you do it. You're the Specialist."

Joeal looked around. "Ah... Okay...he's right over there. Follow me."

Andrel waved. "Come on, Daviel."

I was high enough to see soldier action on the west perimeter near the mountain. As this trio approached, Staff Sergeant Dannel's brows furrowed. "What can I do for you?"

Specialist Joeal saluted. "The three of us have questions, Sir."

Dannel squinted. "Like what?"

Joeal took a deep breath. "What specifically will happen when we strike Lucifer's angels with our swords? Will they feel it?"

"I don't know," Dannel said, shaking his head. "All of this is an enigma to me."

Joeal peered at the others and back to Dannel, "Why do you think the Most High would allow such a battle?"

Dannel exhaled a heavy sigh. "Specialist Joeal, I don't know. I'm sure it serves some purpose, but this is not the time for discussion. You three, like all of us, have been well trained. Do what you were taught and trust the Almighty. Now get back to your positions. The battle is imminent."

The soldiers jerked and saluted. "Yes, Sir."

I thought Dannel answered well. He had wisdom beyond his rank. I watched while the three returned to their posts and readied themselves. Every field army I had dispatched seemed to do the same. They quieted and prepared to advance as though they heard Dannel's orders.

Once more, I gazed over the vast, open plains. But this time, when my eyes reached the gate of Ivory Palace City, I was the first to witness Lucifer and his army soaring high above. Like a flock of red sheep cascading down a mountainside, they descended upon the plains. "Here they come."

CHAPTER 39

THE WAIT

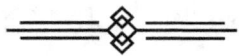

Lucifer and his army swooped onto the plains and inched their way toward center, halting not even a quarter of the way out. "I don't see Michael and his angels anywhere," Lucifer screamed. "Wyael! Get Gragael."

"General Maysel," Wyael shouted. "Help me find Sergeant Major Gragael for the Chief Prince."

"Yes, General." As Lucifer watched, Maysel hurried to check his field army while Wyael checked his. Gragael was not among those soldiers. Maysel next searched Ennel's, and here, he found him. "Sergeant Major Gragael."

Gragael rushed to Maysel and saluted. "How may I be of service?"

"Chief Prince Lucifer needs to speak with you immediately. Follow me."

"Right behind you, Sir."

The two sprinted to the front line, and Wyael intercepted. "Gragael, come with me."

Approaching Lucifer, his scowl revealed rage.

"Chief Prince," Wyael said. "Sergeant Major Gragael."

Lucifer squinted and looked Gragael up and down. "I need you to recount every detail of Michael's army."

Gragael jerked. "Yes, Sir. Um, ah, well…"

"Out with it, Gragael!"

"Okay, um… When we were waiting on the front lawn of Ivory Palace."

"Gragael!" Lucifer shouted. "I know where you were. Just the details."

Trembling, Gragael rehashed all he'd seen.

With eyes that pierced Gragael like a dagger, Lucifer asked, "Michael's army flew where?"

Gragael pointed. "Toward the Mount of Holiness, Sir. I didn't see their final destination. The trees obstructed my view. I assumed the mountain…it was the direction they flew."

Lucifer's fists clenched and unclenched. "Look around, Gragael. Do you see Michael or his army on the Shekinah Glory Base, the plain, or anywhere? I don't. These are details someone of your rank should know to observe, especially since I ordered my soldiers to do so." Lucifer edged closer until he and the sergeant major were nose to nose. "Gragael, I refuse to tolerate this type of insubordination," he said in a low guttural growl, while unsheathing his sword.

Gragael shook and tried to back away, but Lucifer grabbed his throat and raised his saber. "Please forgive me, Sovereign Prince," Gragael squeaked. "I'll never let you down again."

Lucifer halted mid-strike. His scowl softened, and his eyes glazed. He cocked his head, lowered his sword, and whispered, "Sovereign

Prince? Sovereign Prince. Ah…yes…Sovereign Prince…" Inhaling, Lucifer's chest swelled. His eyes closed, and his grip released.

Gragael collapsed to the ground, gasping, and quickly crawled away.

Lucifer didn't even notice. "Sovereign Prince," he mumbled over and over. "What a perfect title for me. Yesss…" Once more, floating off into his thoughts… *Sovereign Prince…Absolutely perfect…*

From my vantage point, I couldn't quite tell what was happening in Lucifer's army, but it seemed like turmoil. "Angels," I said, using my newly completed covert wave frequency. "Can you hear me?" I saw their nods and continued. "Hold your positions. Remain camouflaged and deploy on my order. We'll wait until Lucifer's army moves closer to the Shekinah Glory Base. When they have advanced far enough for ambush, I'll give the order."

Each angel commander stepped forward to a place where I could see and saluted in compliance. I knew my troops were eager for their first battle but apprehensive. I was, too, mostly because I still had no idea how all this would play out. What would we do with Lucifer and these rebellious angels once we had them surrounded?

The Almighty's been vague in his orders for battle preparation. He's even left me to design my own war strategies when I had no full understanding. I believe I've met God's challenge, but now what?

If all went according to plan, we would ambush Lucifer's army, yet what if it didn't? What if full-scale war broke out, and I was forced to strike Lucifer with my sword? Would he cease to exist? I gasped. *Was that what happened to the Throne Room sentries? They would never desert their post.*

Did Wyael, Maysel, or both use their swords to strike the sentries, and when the blade connected, poof, they vanished? *Possibly.* Would the same happen to Lucifer? I shuddered at the thought. "Still," I whispered, "if this is the only way I can preserve Heaven and protect the Most High, then so be it."

As those words left my lips, a more distressing notion sliced through. If a sword strike would disintegrate Lucifer and his angels, would it not do the same to my angels and me? *Ahh! I can't think about this right now.* "Concentrate on the battle, Michael," I said under my breath. "And prepare to fight Lucifer."

"Chief Prince Lucifer," Wyael said, tapping him on the shoulder. Wyael tapped again. "Sir? Chief Prince, Sir?"

Lucifer's eyes rolled open, and he turned his head slowly in Wyael's direction, seeming groggy as though roused from sleep. "Sir," Wyael said once more, dragging him back to reality. "The troops are practically on top of one another, and a few skirmishes have broken out."

It took Lucifer a moment to reconnect, remember what was at stake, and return to his old abrasive self. "So, take care of it, Wyael," he said, irritated at the intrusion.

Wyael lowered his eyes. "I'd like to, Sir, and I could if we had more room."

Lucifer raised and scrutinized their position. "I'm happy with where the troops are situated. I prefer to stay near the gate since this is where the Most High arrives."

"No disrespect, Sir," Wyael said, shaking his head. "But wouldn't it be wiser to advance to the center of the plains? This would give the soldiers room to maneuver and cover more of the plain. We'd be set up to attack the Most High from all directions and cut off any avenue for escape."

"Wyael!" Lucifer screamed, nostrils flaring. "How dare you question my plan!"

He gasped. "Forgive me, Sire. I was only thinking of keeping our troops engaged in battle with the Almighty and not with each other."

Lucifer jerked back, squinted, and stared at Wyael. "You see the troops unfocused and problematic because they are crowded, correct?"

"Yes, Sir."

"By all means, move them forward. And, Wyael, the soldiers concentrating on the battle before us is top priority. The Almighty should be returning momentarily."

"Thank you, Chief Prince," Wyael said, turning to leave, but stopped and pivoted back toward Lucifer. "May I ask, Sir, what have you decided about Michael?"

"I've decided if Michael wants a fight, he'll have to come to us. I'm not concerned about him anymore. I'm intent on defeating God. Michael and one field army make it a bit more difficult, but believe me, they aren't a real threat."

Wyael nodded. "Good to know, Sir. Will you muster the troops, or shall I?"

"I will."

"As you wish, Chief Prince."

"Field Armies, prepare to advance," Lucifer shouted as each warrior sheathed his saber and shouldered his shield for marching. "Soldiers! Move out."

I slipped from boulder to boulder across the Shekinah Glory Base. The good elevation and cover allowed me to view every angle of the plains. Still, with Lucifer's angels hugging the city gate, I knew it would be a struggle for my soldiers to sneak up behind them.

A stirring in Lucifer's army below caught my attention. I sprinted to the rock formation on the east side and watched as his soldiers shifted their stance. It appeared as though they were preparing to march. *Are they? Yes! Where? Further into the plains? Oh, please...* But would it be far enough for my plan to work?

Anyone observing from this height would agree Lucifer's army looked impressive, even with the red hue. Sections of squared regiments, straight lines, and angels moving as one. Buffed and polished armor that now protected such malicious characters glimmered with every step. Boots pounded the plains in fine precision and a soothing cadence.

I wanted to feel satisfied since I trained them, but how could I? Lucifer and all these angels had chosen to rebel against the Most High God. Battle was forthcoming. Everything had changed.

Reaching midpoint, I heard Lucifer shout, Halt. Wyael then yelled for them to spread out so they had enough space to maneuver in combat.

Lucifer's massive army had marched north and expanded southward across the plain. But when they did, the last field army hadn't moved very far. Little room separated Dylael's detachment from the gate. I knew their position was not ideal for the trap I had planned. My soldiers might be spotted moving out to block the rear escape. If discovered too early, fighting could commence before my east and west armies got into position. Ambush would be spoiled. "South perimeter field armies," I said.

"Yes, Chief Prince Michael," my Lieutenant Generals said.

"We may have a problem with the way Lucifer has positioned his army. If you stay where you are, intending to exit through the city gate, it will be slow going. Some of Lucifer's angels could escape. So, here's a new plan. Fan out behind the wall, but leave several brigades by the gate to block their exit. When I give the order, the hidden armies should fly up and over the wall.

"Be prepared to launch swiftly and close in fast on Lucifer's soldiers. Lieutenant Generals, there is no margin for error. I'm counting on you to execute my orders precisely. Do you understand?"

"Yes, Chief Prince. We will follow your orders to the letter."

"Excellent. Stay alert and wait for my command."

"Wyael. Maysel," Lucifer yelled.

Maysel sprinted to join Wyael, and together the generals presented themselves before the Chief Prince. As they saluted, Lucifer said, "I'm positive Michael is not here. I think he only flew in this direction to throw us off. I bet they circled around and entered the city from the south. They're probably hiding somewhere inside, like the Arena or maybe even the Forge."

"What would you like us to do, Sir?" Wyael said. "Should we lead a small unit to search for them?"

Lucifer shook his head. "No. Trying to locate Michael and his angels would be a waste. The Almighty should return from Earth soon, and our conflict is with Him. Our chance will never come again. I don't want you or any of my angels concerned about Michael. Just be prepared to fight the greatest battle ever. Michael, with his piddly army, will try to protect the Most High, but there's no way he can win. I'll deal with him once I am ruler."

"In the meantime, Sir?" Maysel said. "What are your orders?"

"Prepare for our eastward turn. The perimeter trees provide enough concealment, and the cherubim are clueless about our trap. They'll transport the Most High right into our hands. His doom is sure. So, back to your posts and confirm your soldiers are ready."

"Yes, Sir," the generals said, saluting. Lucifer returned their salute, and they each stepped back, pivoted, clicked their heels together, and off they went.

As Wyael and Maysel reached their armies, Lucifer moved to a front and central position. He unfurled his wings and elevated himself high enough for the whole army to see. His red glow filtered through his armor and encompassed him. With his back to the Shekinah Glory Base, Lucifer faced his soldiers. "Angels!" he commanded in a blaring voice. "Shields up. Blades ready. Right face. Battle positions. Hold tight, and attack on my command."

CHAPTER 40

THE DIVERSION

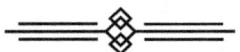

"Soldiers," I said, moving to a better observation spot. "Lucifer has his army facing east, and at the moment, I don't know why. East perimeter armies stay vigilant."

I knew the eyes of every rank were upon me, and each leader would be nodding their understanding. Thankful for their obedience, I turned my thoughts to Lucifer. Why is he facing east and hugging that perimeter? Why not north? Did he think I was on the east with my army? His soldiers must have seen where we landed. *Is it possible they didn't?* Either way, Lucifer had to know I was here somewhere, but why would he assume east?

I knew my plan would work well only if everyone thought the battle was north. What was it about the east perimeter that had drawn Lucifer's attention? "Think, Michael," I whispered. *Okay. It had trees. It was the boundary of Heaven.* "Wait! Was Lucifer interested in the east because he believed I was there? Or was he interested in what lay beyond…God's creation, the universe, and Earth?"

I reviewed Lucifer's rant in the rotunda, his goal to conquer the Most High and occupy God's throne. But then I remembered the empty Throne Room. I gasped. "Lucifer doesn't think I'm on the east. Lucifer thinks the Almighty is on Earth!" *Is he?*

"If God is on Earth, Lucifer knows he returns by way of the east." I could barely breathe. The cherubim would deliver the Almighty right into Lucifer's grip, and he would be defeated. I could not allow Lucifer to intercept. "We must set the trap now."

Moving to a spot where I could better alert my soldiers, I realized it would be foolhardy to execute an ambush if the enemy saw you coming. "I need to divert Lucifer's attention north without exposing my army. But how?" I muttered, pacing behind the boulders.

My soldiers held east, west, and south. I occupied north. *Of course!* It had to be me. Only I could cause enough commotion to distract Lucifer and turn his army north. That way, my troops could set the ambush. Would it work? *Yes? No? Maybe?* And if I disintegrated in the process, then so be it. My army would still protect the Most High, preserve Heaven's holiness, and win this battle without me. Lucifer's evil would be wiped out by whatever means necessary. I didn't matter…only the Almighty did.

"Soldiers," I said. "The LORD God may be on earth. If he is, Lucifer's army is positioned to seize him as he returns. We cannot allow this plan to succeed. However, before we move out, his whole army must turn and face north toward the Mount of Holiness. But Lucifer will not abandon his east-facing position easily. Therefore, I will generate a diversion. This will be our means of ambush. Soldiers, as soon as I become visible, advance. Don't wait. Just swoop in and surround them."

My Generals again nodded their understanding as I moved east. "General Bradiel," I said. "Lead the halves of your army to unite quickly and cover Lucifer's northernmost warriors."

Bradiel came to attention. "Yes, Chief Prince?"

"Troops, if there's going to be a battle, let Lucifer's soldiers engage you. They must strike first. If they don't attack, good, but keep them surrounded, trapped, and contained. Should any attempt to escape, do whatever you deem essential to stop them. Neutralize the threat. The LORD will decide their fate."

"Sir," Senior Angel Captain Greysiel said from the west perimeter. "I don't like the idea of you creating the diversion alone. Some of us should be with you. Or maybe we wait out Lucifer's army. When they tire of holding battle positions, then set the ambush. All your soldiers should be fighting with you."

"Captain, your concern is appreciated, but this is not up for discussion. I've made my decision. We cannot wait. The Almighty could return at any moment. We must strike now."

"Understood," he said. "We'll do our best."

Standing at the head of his field army, Maysel heard much commotion behind him—arguments, shoving, and general unrest among his soldiers. Wondering if it was only his warriors, he moved to a place where he could observe all of Lucifer's armies and found the same. *This won't do.* He jogged to Wyael's side. "I think we still have a problem. Our soldiers are distracted again. They're annoyed and don't seem to care about remaining combat-ready. What should we do?"

"I see it, too," Wyael said. "I thought the battle would commence way before this, and I don't understand why the Most High has not yet returned."

Removing his helmet, Maysel rubbed his neck. "Has he ever stayed on Earth this long?"

Wyael shrugged. "I don't know. But his delay is causing us problems. Our only option is to alert Chief Prince Lucifer."

Maysel's eyes widened. "You know he'll be furious."

"I know." Wyael shook his head. "But it can't be helped."

"I guess I agree," Maysel said with a sigh.

Wyael inhaled deeply and exhaled. "We'd better get this over with."

Taking steps toward the Chief Prince, Maysel and Wyael approached. "Sir," Wyael said, "it's been quite a while. The troops are restless again."

"Even with the extra room, Sir," Maysel chimed in, "skirmishes are breaking out. The soldiers are unruly, losing motivation and purpose. What would you like us to do?"

"Keep them in order!" Lucifer said through gritted teeth. "This is why I chose the two of you to lead my taskforce. Among all ranks, you were the best at giving orders and having them obeyed. Did I make a mistake? Can you do your job? Or should I replace you right now?"

"No, Sir," Maysel said, gasping. "I – I mean, yes, Sir, we can do our job. No need for replacements."

"Wyael. Maysel. I require every angel with me without question. And if you are having second thoughts…"

"No second thoughts, Sir," Wyael said, interrupting and motioning to Maysel to be quiet. "We're behind you one hundred percent."

"Good. Get back to your posts. Control the troops. I do not want to see this weakness again. You hear?"

Wyael saluted. "Yes, Sir."

The Generals did an about-face and hastened toward their field armies. Once they were out of Lucifer's earshot, Maysel leaned in and said, "Wyael, we should've run when we had the chance."

He nodded. "I know. But it's too late to defect. We're stuck in this role, and we have to see it through to the end."

Maysel sighed. "Yeah."

"See you on the other side, General," Wyael said as he reached his field army.

"Until then, General." Maysel saluted and continued on.

The commotion below in Lucifer's army intrigued me. His soldiers appeared distracted and fidgety. This was the perfect time to strike. Without delay, I unsheathed my saber, stepped out from behind the boulder, and allowed my radiance to glow. Instantly, my wings flared. With sword raised, I launched high into the air, and as I did, I shouted, "For the Glory of the LORD and His Righteousness!"

Lucifer and his whole army did precisely what I was hoping. They turned north to see what was happening. My army read their cue well. Each unit advanced from the perimeters and the city as ordered. They swooped in and encircled the enemy. Shocked by the ambush, Lucifer's soldiers did not move, yet they stood their ground, ready to strike if engaged, as did mine.

I landed directly before Lucifer, and our eyes locked as our swords clashed. Sparks flew. Lucifer swung around and struck a second time. I ducked, pivoted, and raised my sword just in time to deflect his third strike. Lucifer lunged. I parried. Again and again, and not one of our soldiers interfered.

With equal ability, neither of us dominated. I wondered how I would win, yet I knew right must triumph. Lucifer struck once more. I wavered but delivered an off-balance counter. He snickered and taunted me while he set up for his next hit, "What's the matter, Michael? Can't get the best of me?"

"You will fall, Lucifer!" I shouted as a fierce sense of righteousness welled. "I am protecting the Most High and all Heaven. You are trying to destroy both!" With my sword high, I struck with greater force. When Lucifer jammed my blow, he lost his footing and fell. But even on his back, he was able to parry. I sliced down with a right diagonal hit to keep him from getting to his feet. And although he deflected, this strike came much closer to his body. *Ha, he's weakening. I will defeat him.* More strength surged, and I attacked again. My blade clashed against Lucifer's. His sword vibrated in his hand, and the jolt caused him to lose his grip.

Lucifer's saber went flying out of reach. He lay on the floor of the plains, defenseless. With one slice, I could end this battle right here and now. I could stop Lucifer's evil forever, but I hesitated.

In my split-second pause, Lucifer jumped to his feet, grabbed his blade, and ran full force toward me. He leaped. Airborne and sword raised, Lucifer struck downward with the burst of power his descent provided.

Distracted by my earlier hesitation, he caught me off guard. Somehow, I managed to deflect, but I stumbled backward with the weight of his hit. Lucifer lunged, and I retreated just out of reach. He again took a stance. Sword in hand, he charged straight forward with a grand thrust. I dodged to the right to avoid being skewered. Pivoting, I slammed my saber down upon Lucifer's. He tottered but regained his balance.

Spinning around, Lucifer slashed upward. I parried, and with renewed vigor, I promptly swung around with a riposte, nicking his helmet. He staggered under my force. Disoriented, he dropped to one knee. This time, I'll not hesitate. *I will end his evil once and for all.* With both hands gripping my sword, I raised it to strike the final blow.

"Enough!" boomed the voice of the Almighty. "Michael, stand down."

CHAPTER 41

ANSWERS

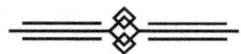

Like an opulent unveiling, God's Shekinah Glory blazed from the Mount of Holiness. Shock permeated my being. I stood frozen in battle position. Sword still raised, ready to strike, yet eyes fixed on the pristine white light washing over the plains, illumining the already lighted sky above Ivory Palace City, brighter than it had ever been.

As I began to thaw and lower my arms, Lucifer scooted out from under my saber. In a surge of humility, every angel present, no matter whose army or whom they served, removed their helmets and bowed the knee to the majestic, all-powerful King. Gabriel and Platoon 10, Randiel and the Armor Room angels, Jaysael and those at the Forge, the palace and chamber angels, and all sentries, even the missing ones, heard God's voice, saw his glory, and hastened to join us.

The battle was over.

"Michael and Gabriel, well done," the Almighty said. "Take your places before me. Lucifer, as Commander-in-Chief of your army, remain there on the plains."

When Gabriel and I hurried to obey, both armies stood, sheathed their swords, and waited. Bradiel's army split again to either side as Lucifer strutted back to his command with a haughty, arrogant smirk. Reaching front and center, he rotated and sneered at God.

Facing the LORD in all his glory was an awesome and formidable task at any time. But with willful disobedience involved, we had no idea what to expect. Yet, Lucifer stood before the Most High without an ounce of fear.

I bowed. "Majesty, you're here?"

"Yes, Michael," he said from between the cherubim. "I've been here all along."

My head popped up. "You have?"

Peering at our magnificent Creator, his Shekinah persisted in hiding distinct features. Still, within the glowing haze and shifting waves of fire, I thought I saw his head nod. "Remember, Michael, I am everywhere present?"

"I remember." My head bowed again as I realized I hadn't understood the everywhere present concept, and maybe, I never would. But when I lifted, I asked, "May I have a moment to speak?"

"You may."

Taking a deep breath to calm myself, I failed to hide my frustration. My face pinched as I said, "Sire, why did you stop me? I need to finish this with Lucifer. We cannot allow his evil to remain."

The Almighty's flaming hand went up, and his voice deepened. "I acknowledge your concern, Michael. Nevertheless, you must stand down."

My head involuntarily wagged. "I don't understand."

"I know," he said. "Your chance to battle Lucifer and his angels will come again, just not now." The Most High shifted, and his glory rippled as he called, "Gabriel!"

Gabriel straightened his stance. "Yes, LORD?"

"Prepare to write."

Reaching into his garment, Gabriel pulled out the tablet and quill he had grabbed when he and Platoon 10 departed the Scroll Room. "I'm equipped, my King."

God's Word flowed from his Presence as smoothly as the ink from Gabriel's quill. As he wrote, I saw an expression of seeming recognition on Gabriel's face. Were the words the LORD spoke familiar? Uneasiness gripped me, and my eyelids squeezed shut. *Had I missed something?*

"Michael," the Most High rumbled, "Fear not. Nothing was missed, and Lucifer cannot remain here."

My eyes sprang open. "I'm relieved, Master."

He shifted and bellowed, and his Shekinah flashed. "Angels! Look toward My creation. There in the distance, what do you see?"

No one dared speak, some out of fear, but mostly because we didn't know what we were witnessing. The thing appeared to be a giant, blazing circular disk spinning, weaving, slicing through the infinite blackness, and whizzing toward us at a high rate of speed. Ever closer, it whirled as though it would saw right through Heaven.

I squirmed. My body felt electrified, and even though the fiery disk was still afar off, its intense heat, hotter than the Forge, blasted my face. The closer it spun, the more I had to suppress the feeling I wanted to escape.

This fire-filled ring careened toward us without a hint of slowing. Nearer now, I could see sputters and splashes flying off, lighting up the darkness and then extinguishing. I started to quiver. *Would it strike us? Would the LORD allow it to damage Heaven all because of Lucifer?* I gasped and held my breath, but I couldn't stop shaking.

Finally, the circle braked, and I started to breathe. This thing stood stationary in the second heaven—the vast expanse outside Earth's atmosphere, yet very close to Heaven. In an instant, our view magnified, akin to the way we observed God's creation. The saucer-shaped object had a flaming brilliance, much like the Shekinah, but even though God's glory appeared to burn, it did not radiate the heat I felt from whatever this was.

The horizontal fiery disk had a deep red center that spat and swooshed, causing the contents surrounding it to oscillate, stir, elevate, and wane. It materialized as liquid, displaying waves and obvious depth similar to the great sea of Earth, yet it seemed to possess unexplainable strength, a power to envelop, suck downward, and forbid escape. I shuddered. *What is this?*

"Michael," the Almighty thundered, causing me to jolt. "Since no one has answered my question, I'm asking you. What do you see?"

I gulped, keeping my eye on the alarming spectacle. "I'm not sure, Sire. It appears to be some sort of sea or lake, like what we saw on Earth, but it's very different. It's hot and seems to be made of a molten substance that burns with no sign of extinguishing or even diminishing in intensity."

Within his Shekinah, I saw his head nod. "Very good, Michael, you have described it well. Angels, I call this the *Lake of Fire*. It is fire burning with brimstone that I have now created alongside the planets, stars, Earth, and Heaven."

Gabriel gasped. "Most High, I remember this name from the seven-sealed scroll. But why did you create it?"

My head whipped in Gabriel's direction and then to the Almighty. "And, Sire, what purpose does it serve?"

The LORD's glory radiated and settled again. "The answers to your questions are complicated. Not one will fully understand. Yet, I will answer.

"Since I alone know the end from the beginning, I knew Lucifer's thoughts and the intents of his heart, just as I know all of you and my humans. When I created Lucifer, I understood he would surrender to the lure of his beauty, give birth to pride, and choose to do all he has done. Despite that, I fashioned him as flawless as you, for I AM perfect. I cannot and do not make mistakes or imperfections."

Gabriel elbowed me and nodded toward the Most High. I returned his nod, remembering my tirade. But still, this truth didn't answer the questions swirling in my head. "Majesty, if you knew all this about Lucifer, why then did you create him?"

"The answer is simple," said the LORD, "yet again, hard to grasp. I AM Love. And as such, I desire a love relationship with the whole of my creation. However, true love cannot exist without free will."

I jerked back. "Free will, Sire?"

His Shekinah brightened, and I'm not sure how, but I detected a smile. "Yes," he said. "Free will is the ability to choose—right from wrong, good from evil. All angels and humans possess it."

My breath caught. "Wrong and evil? Like what Lucifer is doing?"

"Watch it, Michael," Lucifer spat, tapping his foot. "That's your opinion."

"No, Lucifer," the Almighty resounded. "Not opinion! Fact! Truth! I AM Truth. My word is truth—forever settled—and unchanging because I change not. All actions and thoughts, whether in Heaven or on Earth, are weighed against my divine standard of absolute truth. And Lucifer, Michael's opinion, like Gabriel's, is always based on my truth."

As the LORD finished his rebuke, I peered down at Lucifer. He smiled, chuckled a bit, and stroked his chin. "You don't say." Lucifer laughed outright, causing gasps from God's under-angels. His brows narrowed, and his eyes caught mine. If possible, the hate in them would have burned a hole right through me.

Breaking from his stare, I said, "Sire, if free will allows for evil, it seems destructive, not loving. Look what Lucifer was able to do to Heaven."

He nodded, and I felt a wave of comfort wrap around me. "Yes, Michael, but look what you were able to do. When I gave you nothing to go on, your free will kicked in, and you stopped Lucifer anyway. What you did, you did because you love me."

My head lowered. "I do love you, Majesty. You will always have my love, honor, and respect."

Turning toward the host of Heaven, the Sovereign LORD said, "Angels, those who are not free to choose cannot love. It may appear as love, but it's merely devotion and obedience—doing, in essence, what I programmed them to do. On Earth, it is called instinct.

All land, air, and sea creatures have it. But Angels and humans are different. I granted them the ability to choose."

Finally, things started to make sense, and I took a deep breath. I still had questions, but scanning the sea of angels assembled on the Mount of Holiness plains, I saw signs of understanding, or maybe, just agreement with the Almighty's words. I couldn't tell.

The LORD God interrupted my thoughts when he continued. "My desire for my creation, which includes Lucifer," he said, "is for all to choose to love me…because…love is a choice. Lucifer, however, chose to reject me. His free will enabled him to exalt himself above me and love himself instead of me. This mindset is pride. It's worshiping self rather than me, the One True and Living God."

Although I knew we wouldn't fully comprehend God's answers, I had to ask one more question. Inching my hand up, I said, "Pride, LORD? Did you create pride?"

"No, Michael. Pride is imperfection. Granting free will allows the possibility for pride to develop. Lucifer's self-love caused pride to spawn from within his being. His nature altered, and now he believes he is like me."

I gasped. "Is he like you?"

"Fear not. Lucifer remains a created being. He will never be more than he is at this moment. No one is like me. I AM God, and there is no other."

Lucifer threw out his arms and screamed, "Says you! Not only am I like you, I'm better! And I will have the last word."

"Enough," the Almighty said in a voice so deafening Lucifer's mouth clamped shut. "Once identical to Michael and Gabriel—my faithful archangels, Lucifer, you are now opposite. Your self-love caused in you a desire to be worshiped. This compelled you to deceive, to persuade others to deny me and follow you. My Spirit is grieved.

"Angels!" The LORD shouted. "Lucifer's disciples came from your numbers!" Gasps again rose from the plains as God continued. "Lucifer swayed one-third of you. But no more! In heaven, his evil is finished!"

"Praise the Almighty," I said, joining wings with Gabriel. And although I hurt for the deceived angels, we illumined for the first time without Lucifer.

"Glory to our Excellent King!" Gabriel said with me as the host of heaven joined our worship. I bowed my head and resolved to adore and serve the Sovereign God for as long as he allowed me to exist.

Lifting, I observed God, within his Shekinah, extend his hand toward the Lake of Fire. "I AM Holy," he said, and I bowed again. "My eyes are too pure to behold evil, and I will not look on wickedness forever. For this reason, I have prepared my Lake of Fire—the place of eternal punishment for Lucifer and his angels."

My head snapped up. Gabriel's chin dropped. Our wings ripped apart, shattering illumination. No one moved.

I squeezed my eyes shut and muttered, "Never-ending burning? Ceaseless torment and agony? Eternal punishment sinking in the deep, sucking bog that forbade escape?" I couldn't imagine.

My heart hurt for them, that is, until I saw Lucifer's smug, self-satisfied demeanor. The earlier blast of God's voice didn't humble him at all. My pity quickly evaporated. Lucifer and his angels deserved this, deceived or not, and our Holy LORD knew it all along.

CHAPTER 42

THE ETERNAL DECREE

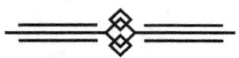

"**L**ucifer," roared God Most High. "Step forward with your angels for judgment."

Head high, nostrils flaring, chest lifted and swelled, Lucifer sauntered toward the Almighty. His angels followed, but at least they cowered and trembled. "LORD God," Lucifer said in his arrogant tone. "Your word stands as true throughout all eternity. Correct?"

"Yes, you know that."

"And," Lucifer snorted, "you said your word cannot be altered or changed unless, of course, you change it, which you will not do because you do not change. Am I also correct in this?"

Waves of fire within his Shekinah oscillated. "Yes, you are correct."

Lucifer nodded with a patronizing sneer. "Good answer."

I jerked and took a step back. Why wasn't Lucifer humbled in God's presence? Why wasn't he begging for his life, especially facing such unbearable punishment? My hand covered my mouth, while my head wagged. Lucifer had planned to depose the Almighty. Why was I surprised?

The Sovereign LORD shifted, and surges of his glory stretched out from the base. "Get on with your point, Lucifer."

Thrusting out his arm, Lucifer shouted, "I will! So, when you said, 'Earth, Eden, and all its inhabitants are mine to rule and guard,' were you not stating truth? Oh, oh, and when you said, 'You will have as many angels to help you as you desire,' was this also an untruth? No, no." Lucifer shook his finger and mocked. "It couldn't be. For you," he said, pointing at God, "cannot lie. You know what you spoke is truth. You know you will not change what you said... or...what you gave me."

I gasped, expecting Lucifer to be terminated or to dissipate like a vapor right on the spot. But no, he remained. Why was the Almighty tolerating his arrogance? I'd wipe Lucifer out if I were God, or at least I'd throw him into the Lake of Fire right now. It was the only way I could see to stop pride from infecting everything. *But...I'm not God.* For the first time, that thought really hit me. I clearly understood my inferiority and the Almighty's superiority. *How could Lucifer ever think he is like God?*

"Lucifer," the LORD's voice exploded and shook me from my thoughts. "You are correct to a point."

My head drew back. *What? Correct?*

"I AM Eternal," God said. "I AM the Sovereign, Three-in-One King. I AM complete within myself, all-knowing, and everywhere present. We have always existed and always will. We have need of nothing, but we chose to create. Thus, life, in any dimension, does not and cannot exist apart from me.

"You, Lucifer, are not God. You are just one of our creations. We alone hold your life in our hands, and we can snuff it out in an instant. You have no say in any of this. And because of pride, you will always underestimate me.

"I said what I said for a reason. Therefore, what we spoke will stand, but only because it will help fulfill my purposes."

My shoulders fell at the exact moment my mouth dropped open. *What?* The word God spoke to Lucifer will stand? *No! That can't be!*

With a wave of his hand, the Almighty's Lake of Fire catapulted out to the edge of the black expanse and now appeared as a tiny red dot. "Lucifer," the Most High said, "Earth, Eden, and its inhabitants are yours to rule and guard, together with the angels who have chosen to follow you instead of me."

"Nooooo, Sovereign LORD," Gabriel and I screamed.

Lucifer slapped his thigh. "Ha! I knew it!" He glared and pointed his finger. "Michael. Gabriel. You two are pitiful. You have never understood the way God works. And you have always misjudged my power. No one will stop me—not even Him! I will be worshiped. I am God, and I will have the ultimate victory."

"Silence, Lucifer!" the Almighty blared, and his voice echoed throughout Heaven.

Lucifer tried to defy God again, but the LORD's finger sealed his lips.

"Please, Most High," I begged. "Do not allow Lucifer to have Earth. He will destroy it."

"I agree, Majesty," Gabriel said. "Michael told me how Lucifer tormented the humans. And with all we learned, I'm sure he'll continue to do so if he is not stopped."

A gentle breeze wrapped around me, and I felt the comforting hand of God's Holy Spirit. I looked over at Gabriel, and I could tell he, too, was comforted. We both bowed our heads as the LORD spoke. "We know you are perplexed. But trust me, I AM in control. In time, you will understand everything."

Turning to Lucifer, the Holy LORD of Hosts said, "All angels who chose to follow you will be your servants on Earth. You and they are restricted to this planet and its atmosphere. They cannot leave, but you may depart Earth—limited by a tether. Your chain will stretch from Earth to Heaven, and no farther, and nowhere in between. I will grant a short audience and permit you to enter our presence briefly. Then, in a timely manner, you must return to Earth."

The Almighty moved his glorious hand and pointed eastward. "Access to Heaven will be through this gate."

Instantly, in spectacular fashion, a grand wall materialized on the edge of Heaven's east perimeter. Streaming north, it appeared to attach to the south-facing rocky cliff of the Mount of Holiness. Extending south, the wall stretched behind the trees on the east and past Ivory Palace's main entrance to the southernmost point of Heaven. An ornately crafted gate, similar in shape to the Scroll Room's door, emerged at the central point of the wall. Two identical gates, equally spaced, materialized on either side of the first. All three gates contained the soft silvery gleam of a giant pearl.

With the completion of the east perimeter's grand wall, we watched as the LORD extended the wall to attach seamlessly at the four corners of Heaven. These wall segments also contained three gates matching the east's. The wall itself was almost as magnificent as its Creator, yet nothing in all creation can truly compare to him.

Without delay, twelve angels flew, one to a gate, to act as guards. Then, gazing at this grand wall, I noticed twelve foundations supported it, and different precious gems comprised the individual layers. The first level appeared to be the brick-red of jasper, the second deep blue sapphire, and the variegated light blue of chalcedony followed. The fourth, emerald, reminded me of the central color in the bow surrounding God's throne. However, the twelfth tier, amethyst, the sparkling lavender, took my breath away. Soon, inscriptions, with words I didn't recognize, appeared on each of the twelve foundations and upon each of the twelve gates.

But this beautiful grand wall, towering above the plains and perimeter trees, enclosed Heaven. For the first time, I felt cut off from everything beyond. Once boundless, spacious, and open, Heaven was now fenced in and constricted. Yet God alone was wise. He knew the reason for the wall and its mission.

At the same time, the gated wall separating the plains and Ivory Palace City changed. The wall disappeared along with the swinging metal enclosures. Only the arched framework of the gate remained, hovering mid-air. As we looked on, God caused this arch to lengthen and attach to the new east and west walls. The name of the city I had read many times upon entering became unfamiliar text within the metal scrollwork. Without a gate, the city seemed to sprawl out onto the plains.

Standing on the mountain's plateau before God's Shekinah Glory, I could see it all—the whole remarkable sight. Awe gripped my being, and I fell to my knees.

"Lucifer," the Almighty bellowed, causing me to jump to my feet. "Keep in mind, I have made it impossible for you to fly over Heaven's perimeter wall and gates. You must remain outside and request entrance. When you are approved, my guards will escort you into my presence. On the other hand, because I see and know all, I will hear when you speak from the earth. There will never be a need for you to enter Heaven again, even though I know you will.

"One last warning. If you attempt to roam elsewhere in our creation, you will forfeit this intermediate prison and be promptly transferred to the Lake of Fire. As I said at first, all these privileges are yours for a season. At a time we deem fit, your freedoms will be revoked, and you, together with your angels, will enter into final confinement and everlasting judgment. Do you understand?" the LORD said, unsealing Lucifer's lips.

"Ha!" he spat. Lucifer held his head high and growled, "We'll see about that."

"Lucifer!" the Almighty roared as the blast of his voice rattled Heaven and every angel present except for Lucifer. "Do you understand?"

"Yes," he said in an icy discharge. "I understand."

God's Shekinah flamed brighter than we had ever seen it, and the cherubim lifted his throne even higher. "Lucifer, hear my Eternal

Decree: You are the embodiment of evil. Pride has filled your heart, and wickedness has prevailed. Henceforth, you shall be called the *Devil* and *Satan*. Your angels shall be known as *demons*. For you and your followers, there is no forgiveness, no recompense, no vindication, and no change to My Word.

"You, along with your cohorts, are hereby expelled from Heaven. While you await permanent incarceration, Earth is your temporary abode, and deep within its fiery belly, you shall place your throne."

Lucifer started to counter, but the Most High struck him mute. He grabbed at his throat, touched his lips, thrashed his arms, and shook his fists as though cursing the Almighty. In the next instant, Lucifer, now Satan, and every angel under his command began to levitate, but not by their own power. This was God's doing. Their feet appeared frozen in place, and their bodies wavered as if they were losing their balance and would most likely fall, yet none did.

Fear seemed to wash over Lucifer's army, and their vicious countenances darkened and transformed even further into ugly, gnarled, loathsome faces. Their bodies contorted, and bony appendages with claws became visible. The golden armor they wore transmuted and now appeared dingy and corroded. The taskforce also altered. Although vile-looking, their bright armor only dulled and, for the most part, remained unblemished.

Lucifer, however, didn't change. His appearance stayed as beautiful as he had ever been, and his armor as perfect as the day it was forged. Why, though, I had no idea.

Ever so slowly, Lucifer and his fiendish army continued to rise and move eastward. But the LORD halted the hideous angels while their rebellious leader continued on. He floated above the Garden of Fiery Stones, over the east perimeter trees, and across Heaven's now gated boundary. Lucifer emerged as a fragment on the black canvas of God's newly created universe, and he hung suspended, awaiting his soldiers.

Once the entire army hovered out past Heaven's edge, the Almighty began to let go. As head of his army and instigator, Lucifer was first to fall. His body hurled toward Earth in a streak of fiery light.

EPILOGUE

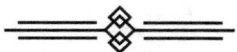

E arth, as God created it, contained the goodness of the Almighty. It was pure, innocent, and without evil, the antithesis of Lucifer. He, the once luminous seal of perfection, now oozed wickedness.

Ordered out of Heaven, Lucifer, renamed Satan, fell, streaking closer and closer to the blue orb. As he entered Earth's atmosphere, the planet wrenched, detonating a crystalline charge that rocketed to meet him. A deafening clap exploded when these two polar opposites collided. Earth's deep azure sky broke, etched with a colossal, jagged vein of white light, brighter than the sun it revolved around.

What would happen next, I did not know. My heart ached for the humans and this small planet. Only the LORD God Almighty knew how long he would allow Satan to rule. And I, for one, planned to leave that decision in his hands.

AUTHOR'S NOTE

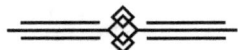

Thank you for choosing to read *Archangels – Beginnings*. I pray you enjoyed it and are left wanting more. The sequel is in the works, and it picks up with Satan on Earth. What will he do to the humans? For a hint, read Genesis 3.

However, while you wait, I would encourage you to read the Bible, the True Word of God. In it, you will find your purpose in life and your final destination.

Where will you go when you die? There are only two choices:
Heaven <u>or</u> Hell and the Lake of Fire.

God's desire is for you to live with Him for eternity, not to perish, not to go to Hell, or suffer the second death in the Lake of Fire. God's will is for you to receive eternal life through Jesus Christ, the Lord. But if you never did that, you're probably wondering how. I can help:

1. Repent or acknowledge you have sinned and fallen very short of God's glory.

2. Believe Jesus Christ was crucified to pay your sin penalty, and arose the third day.
3. Receive His gift of eternal life and love Him.
4. Allow Jesus to fill you with His Holy Spirit and change you from the inside out.
5. Walk in God's Spirit.
6. Read His Word, the Bible, and pray by talking to God every day.
7. Go to a Bible-believing church and fellowship with other believers.

If you have done these things, or at least the first four, then welcome to the family of God. Yet keep striving to finish the other three. Trust God. He is holding you because He LOVES you, and now, <u>you</u> <u>are</u> <u>His</u>!

"And I am sure of this, that He who began a good work in you will bring it to completion at the day of Jesus Christ."
(Philippians 1:6 ESV)

I know for some, this is all new, and you are unsure of what you've read. The scenes and scenarios I've imagined cannot truly compare to the glory of God or Heaven, because I am, like you, a sinful human. However, I have been saved by the grace of God, and when I die, I will be present with the Lord as Scripture says. If this assurance is something you desire, believe on the Lord Jesus Christ and pray this prayer or one like it:

Heavenly Father, I know I have sinned and fallen short of Your glory. I believe Jesus, God the Son, died on the cross to pay the penalty for my sin and arose from the dead the third day. I repent, turn from my sin, and ask for forgiveness. I open the door and invite You into my heart and life. Fill me with Your Holy Spirit and make me a brand-new person. Help me to walk in Your Spirit and know I will be with You when I die. I love you, Lord. In the name of Jesus Christ, I pray. Amen.

Now, go out and tell someone you prayed to receive Jesus Christ as your Savior and Lord. Then email me at: Anita@anitagwilliams.com. I want to celebrate with you.

Love you much in Christ,
Anita

AUTHOR BIO

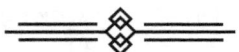

A former National Editor and writer for the Women's Missionary Fellowship Programs and Devotionals for Evangelical Friends Church – North America, Anita continues to write Bible Study curricula for teens and adults. She has been an active member of Alliance Evangelical Friends Church since the early 1990s. Singing with the first service Praise Team and teaching almost every Sunday has given her great joy. Anita has led Biblical Workshops at women's retreats and has spoken at smaller gatherings.

After raising her children, Anita worked as a medical office manager for twenty years. She's a wife, mother of two, and grandmother of six who loves Jesus and has been writing children's stories and women's devotions since 2007. She has blogged since 2012 (www.meatforthehungry.com), and for 18 years, her devotional Newsletter, *News From His Feet*, has gone out monthly to about 200 women. The Newsletter is also posted on her blog, Facebook, Truth Social, X, and now her website, www.anitagwilliams.com.

As a former student of The Institute of Children's Literature, and a lover of the "Left Behind" series, Anita joined the Jerry Jenkins Writers Guild and later Serious Writer. She has attended several writers' conferences, including The Write to Publish Conferences in Wheaton, Illinois, and the Serious Writer Conferences in North Carolina.

Anita's publishing accomplishments include a devotion chosen for publication in the book <u>Anchor In The Storm Volume 1</u>, published by EABooks, Living Parables, and a non-fiction article, *"Spine-tingling Care"* for boys 9-14. *"Spine-tingling Care"* was published in the November 2022 issue of <u>Cadet Quest Magazine</u>, and this issue went on to receive a magazine publication award.